On the Road to Bagdad

F. S. Brereton

ON THE ROAD TO BAGDAD

CHAPTER I

A Frontier Station

A gun, a small brass piece, an interesting relic of other days, boomed forth the hour of noon from the lowest embrasure of a hill fort overlooking the cantonment of the − − Sikhs, and warned all and sundry that it was time for tiffin. The cloud of grey smoke which blew upward from the muzzle, and which was wafted ever so gently by the breeze floating toward the hill-top from the depths of the giant valley below, spread out into a thin white sheet, and, ascending slowly, first wrapped the time-scarred walls of the old fort in its embrace, and then, getting whiter as it ascended, reached the battlements above, and, percolating through the many gun embrasures, floated over the roof of the fortress, till the misty haze hung about the portals of the veranda of the Officers' Mess bungalow.

There were a dozen or more figures, dressed in khaki or in pure white, and stretched in every sort of attitude, and in every variety of chair, beneath that veranda. There were young subalterns, joined but a month or two since, and other subalterns whose hair at the temples was already showing some suspicion of grey while still they failed to get promotion. There was a rather stout old field officer who had seen more years of service in India than many of the subalterns could boast of in their lives. A rubicund, jolly officer he was, upon whom the detestable climate of the many stations in which he had been forced to serve had made not the slightest effect whatever. There was another officer, too, short, slim, and active as a cat, whose hair and moustache were as white as the snows capping the distant mountains. A glance told one intuitively that here, too, was an old soldier, an old Indian soldier, that is, who had spent the better part of a long life out in the "shiney".

"Hallo! What's the time? Anywhere near time for tiffin?" asked one of the "subs", whose cap had fallen over his face, and who now awakened from the reverie into which he had fallen, and suddenly started upward.

"What! So fast asleep that you didn't hear the gun?" cried a brother officer, smacking him heartily on the back. "Man alive! The fort's still shaking."

"And yet," smiled the rubicund Major who had seen so many years' service in India, "and yet, my boys, I'll vouch for the fact that I've slept the hot hours of the morning away on the roof of this fortress a hundred times and more and failed to be awakened by the gun. What is more, that report at twelve o'clock has become a sort of habit with me, so that I've lain here smoking and perspiring in the heat, and though the gun's gone off as usual, and, indeed, as it's never failed to do this last twenty years or more, I've been startled when the mess waiter has come out to announce tiffin. Ha! Listen! That should be proof enough that the gun has gone; the burra Mem-sahib's butler is ringing for the Colonel. Between you and me, my boys, the Colonel isn't half as punctual a man in his own house as he is in the orderly-room, and, what's more, he expects a great deal more of that commodity from us poor fellows than he exhibits himself. But, tut-tut! That's heresy. That's preaching revolution. Don't any of you fellows mention it."

He stretched his arms, and waddled, rather than strode, from the veranda, across the roof of the fortress, and through those wisps of smoke which still curled upward, till he was leaning upon the low wall which protected the edge of the fortress; and there for a while he stood, looking out upon a scene which enchanted him more on every occasion when he went to view it. It was habit, indeed, with the old Major to take stock of that view every day before tiffin, just as a bon viveur takes his apéritif before luncheon.

"Braces a fellow up, don't you know," the jovial Major was wont to tell his brother officers. "It's glorious; it's elevating; it's positively exhilarating; and gives a fellow a right down sharp hunger! That's what you boys want to cultivate out in this country. Look at me! Never sick or sorry, and have

3

always taken my meals like a good 'un. That's because I've a cheerful heart, a sound digestion and constitution, and take a delight in my surroundings and in all that's doing. No grousing for me, my boys. Take everything as it comes and don't bother."

Everyone knew the Major, and not one of the Subs but listened to what he said with respect and amusement.

"Decent old fellow," he was always voted.

"And teaches a fine lesson, too," the Colonel had told his officers on more than one occasion. "Grousing's the curse of the British army in some stations. I don't say that British officers are in the habit of grumbling always; far from it. But when there's nothing doing, and a fellow is tied by the leg in some frontier station, and must stay there and groan under a roasting sun, why! if he doesn't keep himself fit and in first-class condition he gets out of sorts, and then there's grumbling."

Let us look over the wall of the fortress, where a number of officers had by now joined the stout Major, and take stock of that view which he had proclaimed to be "exhilarating". True enough, it was one of those marvellous views only to be obtained on the frontier of India. The fort stood perched on a projecting eminence, around which nature, guided by the active hands of many a succeeding garrison of soldiers, had grafted a most enchanting garden. A stream trickled from above and behind the fort, and descending the gentle slopes of the mountain, and broadening as it came, splashed through the very heart of the cantonment gardens, and sent off a broad canal of shimmering water down beside the main street. From that point it splashed over the edge of the precipice just beneath the fortress, and, tinkling musically as it went, splashed its way to the bottom. You could hear it from the roof of the fort. Often enough the sun's rays, glancing through the mists and spray thrown up by the fall, formed a most gorgeous rainbow; while in the height of summer, when the sun, then almost overhead, poured down such furious heat that the roof of the fortress glowed and almost simmered, then that same misty spray would be wafted up by a cooling draught from the valley below, and would fall upon the blistering skins of the officers who gasped beneath the veranda.

Yes, even in those hill forts it can be hot enough, and where the − − Sikhs were quartered there were seasons when, not long after the sun had risen, no sane white man dared to venture abroad.

And what a valley it was below! Rugged and winding, narrowing here and there, till from the height above it looked as though a wagon could not be driven along it, and then widening most unexpectedly and suddenly till there came a huge saucer, as it were, in which a whole city could have been safely deposited. Trees clad the side of the mountain as it descended into the valley, trees which, scattered at first, grew later in thick clumps till they became almost a forest, and which, severed by the river which wound its way through the valley, had taken root again on its farther bank, and went straggling up the opposite heights till almost the snow-line was reached. Those heights perhaps provided the summit of grandeur to this magnificent scene. Wooded below, as we have seen, they became rugged and broken and rocky as they ascended, till there was presented a row of broken irregular pinnacles, which cut along the sky-line right opposite the fortress, and which presented day in and day out, even on those days when the sun's rays bore down so relentlessly upon the roof of the fortress, a continuous line of snow, hollowed here and there into deep crevasses and gullies, presenting most gorgeous blue shades in the depths of a hundred dimples, and showing elsewhere a smooth, unbroken surface of light, which altered only when north-eastern gales were blowing.

"A sight for the gods! yes," the jovial Major told his comrades, snuffing at the breeze as if he were a dog, "and who could be down-hearted, or dull, or miserable, or even discontented, with such a view to look upon?"

"More particularly when one knows so well that tiffin's ready, and that the words of wisdom of our dear old friend the Major always precede the announcement of that meal."

It was the white-haired senior officer who had spoken banteringly, and who stood at that moment beside the Major, one hand affectionately on his shoulder, the other on the parapet of the fortress.

"There, Charlie! Didn't I say so! Listen! There's the gong going."

The silvery notes of a gong reached their ears at that very moment, and, turning, all saw a most magnificent personage — to wit, the mess butler — standing at the door of the mess bungalow, sounding the call for luncheon. Then all turned and trooped across the roof of the fortress, across the veranda, and disappeared within the door of the bungalow.

It was perhaps three minutes later when a tall and immaculately dressed officer sauntered on to the roof of the fortress, and having taken stock of the view — as if he too must needs partake of some fillip before venturing upon luncheon — then strode off into the mess bungalow. There he found his brother officers already seated, and, striding down behind them, sat himself down at his accustomed place.

"Hallo! Back again, Joe?" ventured the jovial Major, who occupied the neighbouring chair. "Hardly expected you."

Major Joe Douglas dropped his eyeglass as he helped himself to curry, and turned smilingly upon his brother officer.

"Oh! Really!" he said, in those very quiet tones for which he was noted.

"Never saw such a chap," laughed the jovial Major, as he attacked the food which lay before him. "You come and go like a wizard. In fact, you're here one day, and gone to-morrow, and goodness only knows where you spirit yourself to. My dear old boy, you can't deny the accusation. Mind you, I'm not trying to be inquisitive, very far from it, for I know that inquisitiveness in the case of 'politicals', such as you are, is a deadly sin; but let's call it simple curiosity, harmless curiosity — the curiosity one's allowed to display with regard to one's brother officers. You see, you come and go."

"Yes. Quite so," smiled Major Douglas.

"And sometimes you're here, kicking your heels about, and dawdling for a month and more at a time. Then you disappear, where to, goodness alone knows. If you were going on leave to England the whole station would be aware of it. But you don't. You haven't been home for ten years at least. Then where do you get to?"

Till that moment a babel of sounds had been proceeding from the members of the mess, for a dozen subalterns can create quite a considerable amount of noise between them. Yet, as they ate their meal and bantered with one another, not one had failed to notice the arrival of Major Joseph Douglas. They liked the man. Not that they saw very much of him, nor could he be accused of ever being garrulous. He was just a smart, tall, immaculately dressed officer, who had a great reputation for smartness and soldierly qualities. At first sight his eyeglass rather awed young subalterns, till they grew to know that the Major was like Charlie, his fat brother officer, a most excellent and unaffected fellow. Beyond their liking for him there was, however, a depth of curiosity to which their senior officer had only just given expression. Such a cross-questioning of Major Douglas not one of the subalterns would ever have ventured upon. For somehow it had come to be generally known in the mess that the Major's movements were essentially secret. He was a political officer, they all knew, though what "political" meant in his case few of them had but the faintest idea. Yet one and all were very naturally consumed with a desire to know something of this quiet, reserved, yet exceedingly pleasant brother officer. Thus it happened that even in the midst of their banter they heard the old field officer cross-examine the Major, and promptly became silent.

"Well, now," they heard him say, "I've cornered you, Joe; you're here, next door to me, and can't get away; and remember it's just friendly curiosity. Do, for goodness' sake, tell us something about yourself: where you've been of late, what you've done, and what's the meaning of it."

All eyes were turned promptly upon Major Joseph Douglas. He groped for his fallen eyeglass, and fixed it very deliberately in his eye, then he

7

signalled to one of the mess waiters and just as deliberately helped himself to another share of curried chicken.

"I — Oh — Why, Charlie!" he began. "Have you — er — that is, did you try this curried chicken? I declare it to be the best that I've tasted for a year or so. What's happened? Have you fellows been indulging in a new cook since I last went away, or — — Do try some, Charlie, there's a good fellow."

Those who did not know the officers of the — — Sikhs, and didn't know either Major Charles Evans or Major Joseph Douglas, might have expected at this moment quite an explosion on the part of Major Evans. The jovial fellow had had the audacity to show curiosity. Taking advantage of his age and of his seniority, he had ventured at the mess table to cross-examine a "political", and now, just as he was listening with bated breath for the answer, he received — merely a "put-off", and heard his brother officer asking him, in that suave, quiet voice he knew so well, whether he would not indulge in a helping of curried chicken. Yet those unacquainted with the officers of the — — Sikhs would have found themselves signally in error when expecting an explosion. Those two bright eyes, of which Major Evans boasted, twinkled as he listened to his brother officer. Then the corners of his mouth dimpled, and a moment later he was roaring with laughter.

"Beaten, hopelessly beaten!" he cried jovially; "and I might have expected it. For an oyster, my dear boy, you really are exceptional. Now any other fellow, any other "political", that is to say, would have indulged in some sort of hint to relieve our curiosity, would have pitched some sort of yarn, even though it were not an exactly true one. But you — well, you're hopeless, incorrigible, and most utterly disappointing. Boy! Bring me some iced water, I must cool myself down after such a rebuff, and I'll — — Hallo! Hallo! Here's a message."

A native soldier stood saluting at the door of the ante-room, and presented an official envelope to the mess butler.

"The Major Sahib," he said.

"The Major Douglas Sahib," the mess butler corrected him severely. "The Major Douglas Sahib. Quick! Important!"

He placed the envelope on a silver salver, and, holding it there with the tip of his thumb, came swiftly and silently round to the seat occupied by that officer.

"From the Colonel, Sahib," he said as he leant over Joe Douglas's shoulder.

Very slowly and deliberately, as if unconscious of the fact that every eye in the mess was surreptitiously fixed upon him, Joe Douglas tore open the envelope and read the contents of the missive.

"Proceed at once to Bombay. There call for orders at Governor's office. Mesopotamia—urgent," he read, and those who watched him saw not so much as a flicker of an eyelash or the smallest change of expression. He folded the letter up again and very deliberately placed it back in the envelope and very leisurely deposited it in a pocket. Then he finished his curried chicken, called for a cup of coffee, and sat smoking a cigarette and chatting with his brother officers.

"Well?" asked Major Evans, as Joe Douglas rose to leave. "I'm serious, my boy, this time. Everyone knows that things are moving over in Europe and elsewhere, and everyone can guess that you are off again on some expedition. Here's good luck! If I can do anything for you in your absence don't fail to write, for you know that Charlie Evans will stand by you."

Joe Douglas nodded to the dozen subalterns seated about the table, and puffed a cloud of tobacco smoke above their heads.

"Come out for a moment, Charlie," he said. "Good-bye, you fellows, I'm just off on a little trip. Keep things going till I come back again to the mess."

He was on his feet by now, and strode clanking out on to the roof of the fortress, followed by Major Evans. Then the two men walked to the parapet of the fortress and stood side by side looking out over that gorgeous scene, neither of them venturing to speak for a few minutes. At length Joe Douglas turned to his companion.

9

"Listen to this, Charlie," he said. "I'm off on something bigger than I've had to tackle before, though I'm to cover much of the ground that I'm used to. It's Mesopotamia again."

"Ah! Mesopotamia—a nasty place, up North of the Persian Gulf—heat—mosquitoes—Arabs," muttered Major Evans.

"Not to mention Turks and Germans and ruffians," said his brother officer quietly; "but I'm used to them all, Charlie, and am not thinking of myself. I'm thinking of Geoff. You know I've been his guardian ever since my old friend, his father, was lost in that Frontier expedition. He's joining the Mahrattas almost at once, and I badly wanted to keep an eye on him. You'll do that for me, eh?"

"Willingly."

"And will take charge of his father's papers?"

"Everything."

"Then good-bye."

The two men gripped hands most cordially and firmly, and then Major Joseph Douglas turned on his heel and strode from the roof of the fortress, just as quietly and unostentatiously as he had strolled into the mess bungalow. This going away at a moment's notice was nothing new to him. An hour was sufficient in which to see that his servant had packed all his belongings. Half an hour later, in fact, saw him riding down the rough track which led from the mountain, and three days later he was in Bombay itself. The journey before him was something a little out of the ordinary. There was war in the air. There was already talk of a giant European conflagration, and of an outbreak of hostilities between Germany and Austria on the one hand, and France and Russia on the other. We all know now that that war quickly drew into its toils other combatants. That Great Britain came into the struggle to uphold her honour, and with the object of retrieving the downfall of Belgium and of wrecking the power of the German Kaiser. Yet this tale has little to do with the main theatre of that gigantic conflict. It deals with a part of the world hardly known in Europe, a part consisting of wide wastes of sand and gravel, and peopled by Arab and Turk and Armenian and Jew, not to mention Persians and peoples of other Asiatic races.

What Major Joseph Douglas did not know of Mesopotamia and of the valleys of the Euphrates and of the Tigris may be said to have been hardly worth knowing. As a "political" he had made perhaps a dozen trips to this out-of-the-way part of the world, and being by nature attracted by the desert, and being vastly interested in the peoples living therein, those trips had become a source of huge enjoyment to him, so that return to his regiment in India had, after a while, become a sort of penance. His heart leapt at the thought of a further trip, yet, when he had read the papers, and when he had had an interview with the Governor at Bombay, even he — even light-hearted, cheerful, confident Joe Douglas — could not fail to see that danger, perhaps death, lay before him in those deserts. Yet he took ship for the Persian Gulf without hesitation, and, having landed at the township of Basra, disappeared entirely.

The desert had swallowed him up, and thereafter, within a short while of his coming to this outlandish post, that Armageddon, that gigantic conflict, which now tears Europe to shreds, and which has already seen so many of her people slaughtered, began along the frontiers of France and Belgium and of Russia, and, proceeding in violence as the months went by, slowly immersed the Balkans in its turmoil. Turkey, too, was dragged into its trail, so that the venturesome Joe Douglas, the "political", sent on a secret mission from India, found himself in the heart of a country in the occupation of Britain's enemies. Indeed, when this gallant officer reached the neighbourhood of historic Bagdad, those elements of the city other than Turkish were in a turmoil. Soldiers were elbowing their way through the bazaars, and the Turks alone, those people the placidity of whom nothing can destroy, seemed to be the only inhabitants of the city who had not escaped from Bedlam. It was in Bagdad, then, that Major Douglas found himself surrounded by enemies, and in danger of instant capture.

11

CHAPTER II

Geoffrey Keith and Another

What a thing it is to be young and enthusiastic! The very news which, cabled far and wide, set the world almost trembling; which gave information of vast armies hurriedly mobilizing and rushing to meet one another in deadly combat; and which saw families divided, husbands and fathers and brothers torn from those they cared for, found Geoffrey Keith in the very highest of spirits.

Not, let us explain, that this young man did not, and could not, realize the gravity of the position—of the terrible conflict which, at that moment, was bursting forth in Europe. He was not such a dunce that he had not learned of the might of Germany, of the military spirit which, for forty years or more, had swept from end to end of that country, and of the dark Hohenzollern cloud which had hung over the fair lands of Europe for many years past. Nor had the gossip of brother officers in clubs and in messes failed to reach his ears. He knew well enough that the outbreak of war between Germany and Austria, and France and Russia, meant terrible fighting. He knew, better still, that if Great Britain came into the struggle that fighting would become even more strenuous still; for was not that the character of all Britons—slow to take up a quarrel, patient and forbearing, they had yet proved themselves in many a tussle to be stern and stanch fighters. They had shown indeed that pluck, that grit and determination, which long years since has won for our nation a wonderful reputation. Bulldogs we are known as, and bulldogs the British were to prove themselves in the course of this tremendous upheaval.

Yet, war meant excitement! It meant active service! It meant perhaps journeying to another country; seeing strange sights and hearing unfamiliar sounds, and taking part, for all one knew, in deeds which would become historical.

"Bad luck for some people, no doubt," said Geoffrey as he sat in the corner of a railway carriage and panted, for the heat was great. "Just think of it,

Philip, my boy! You and I have only recently completed a special course in England and have not yet joined our regiment, and here we are, only just arrived in India, and already under orders for active service. What will they do with us, do you think?"

His companion, a tall, slightly built young fellow of some nineteen years of age—a few months older than Geoffrey in fact—answered him with energy. To be sure, he too was lolling listlessly in the opposite corner of the carriage, and was fanning himself with The Times of India. It was desperately hot outside, and now that the train had come to a halt at a wayside junction, what current of air there had been passing through the compartment was stilled entirely, so that the interior was like an oven. Outside the sun poured down upon the broad platform of the junction till one's eyes ached if one looked out through the gloom of the carriage at its bright reflection; and there, crowded upon it, careless and unmindful of the sun, chattering and gesticulating and shrieking at one another as only a native mob can do, were hundreds of natives, waiting for a train to take them in the opposite direction.

"Where shall we go, eh?" answered Philip. "Where will the Mahrattas be ordered to? Well now, Geoff, that's rather a large order. To begin with, you don't suppose, do you, that every regiment—native and British—now in India will be taken out of the country?"

"Why not?" ejaculated Geoff, peering hard at him through the gloom which filled the interior of the carriage.

"Why not! Well, of course, there are reasons. For instance: supposing you were to remove every soldier in the country and leave only civilian white people behind, those agitators—those native agitators, that is—always to be found in such a huge population as we have in India, might stir up trouble, knowing that they had only the police to deal with. That's a reason, and a very good reason, for keeping troops in India; and I have got another. Great Britain has already got an Expeditionary Force fully organized and planned for fighting with our French ally. But she'll be hard

13

put to it to get that force fully mobilized and equipped. Not until then will our country have time to turn round in other directions. So you can take it from me, my boy, we are likely to stay in our station for some time before we get marching orders."

As a matter of fact the declaration of war between Germany and Great Britain produced a great deal more than excitement in far-off India. There was a great coming and going of trains, a great concentration of certain of the troops—both native and British—in parts of the Empire, and, when a few weeks had gone by, transports set out across the Indian Ocean carrying those two native divisions to France which were to do such signal service. And, in the interval, those troops not yet under orders were being busily prepared for fighting. Indeed, Geoff and his friend Philip had hardly reached their station—within a few miles of that so recently quitted by Major Joe Douglas—when they found themselves hard at work training.

"Of course, you young officers have only just joined us," their Colonel told them a couple of days after their arrival. "But we are fortunate in one thing, you were both of you born in India—in cantonments—and may be said to have been brought up in the Indian army. Then you have done work with the O.T.C. in England, and gone through a special course before leaving that country. But you will have to nail in at your work as hard as possible, for it is more than likely—more than likely," he repeated with emphasis, "that the Mahrattas will be wanted very soon for foreign service."

"Foreign service! Hurrah!" cried Geoff enthusiastically, when he and his chum were alone together. "That's what I've always thought and wished for. But where? France, eh?"

"Hardly likely," came the answer. "Everyone knows that the Meerut and Lahore Divisions are bound for that quarter. Isn't there any other spot where there's likely to be fighting?"

Months later, had their question been answered, it would have caused the one questioned to smile ironically. For indeed this gigantic conflict has spread across the globe, till there are few places in which fighting has not occurred; but Mesopotamia! Who would have thought that the Mahrattas were to undertake service in the neighbourhood of the Persian Gulf. Why, Philip hardly knew of the existence of such a place, though Geoff was well acquainted with the country. Let us explain the circumstances of this young fellow a little more fully before he becomes immersed in the excitement and adventures of a campaign in the valley of the Tigris.

Geoff Keith was the only son, the only child in fact, of Captain Robert Keith, once of the − − Sikh Regiment, in which Major Joe Douglas was an officer. Subalterns together, they had grown up side by side, and had become inseparables. Often enough, when Joe Douglas happened to have been with his regiment − which was seldom in later years − these two had spent their leave together, and many a hunting trip had they taken together in the neighbourhood of the Himalayas. But circumstances in the end tended rather to separate these two old friends, for, as we have explained already, Joe Douglas became a "political" − a very well-thought-of and frequently employed "political", we should add − while Robert married, and therefore was seen less often in the mess of his regiment. Yet the old friendship never died away, and when Robert, who in the meanwhile had had the misfortune to lose his wife, went on an expedition to the frontier, and there sustained a wound from which he died, it followed as a natural course that his old friend Joe Douglas was left as guardian of the boy.

No one could say that this gallant officer had not carried out his duties with every sympathy. Indeed, Geoffrey had become like a son to the Major, and during the years that he was in India − for Geoff was sent to a school for English boys in the hills − the two saw a great deal of one another. With an eye to the future, the Major went so far as to give long and painstaking instruction to his charge; so that, when at length, at the age of sixteen only, Geoff accompanied his guardian on one of those expeditions of his into Mesopotamia, he found himself by no means a stranger.

"It will be your own fault, Geoff," said the Major, as they took a river boat up the Tigris towards Bagdad − "it will be your own fault, my lad, if you don't, one of these days, follow in my footsteps as a 'political'. I have taught you Turkish, and the Arabic the natives in and around Bagdad speak, and though I dare say at times you have found it an awful bore, yet you've stuck to your work like a good 'un. Now you'll see the advantage of that work. You'll be able to understand what people are saying round you, and will be able to make your way amongst the Turks and amongst the Arabs with comparative ease. The few months we are here during this trip will familiarize you with the country and the people, and one of these days this trip will prove of immense advantage to you."

That sojourn in Mesopotamia had indeed been one long delight to Geoff Keith. The open-air life; their residence, often enough with some wild Arab tribe; their tent dwellings; those long rides on horseback which they took across the desert, fascinated him, so that when the time came for the Major to turn his face towards India, Geoff was by far the most disappointed of the couple. In the Persian Gulf they bade farewell to one another, Geoff trans-shipping on to a boat on its way to Suez. From there he went to England, where he spent a couple of years at one of the finest of our public schools. A short course at Aldershot followed; and then, on the eve of this tremendous conflict which had just broken out between the Kaiser and his hosts, and the free nations of Europe, and in which Great Britain had just commenced to take her part, Geoff Keith had taken ship for India once more, where a commission already awaited him in the Indian army.

To look at the young fellow you would not have imagined for a moment that he was in any particular way accomplished. Moderately tall and straight, he was as jolly as a sand-boy, and as careless as a boy of fifteen. Yet there was a deep look about the eyes which, to those who took the trouble to notice it, gave signs of something better, of serious thought in fact, of accomplishments hidden by his joyous manner. To be precise, you would not for a moment have imagined that Geoff could speak Hindustani just as well as he could speak English; that he could gabble Turkish in the markets of Bagdad with such ease and such precision that even a native

16

would not have suspected him — that is, provided he were dressed as a subject of the Sultan. In addition, there was his knowledge of those Arabic tongues, knowledge imparted at first by his guardian, and since then improved and perfected by residence in the country.

"Great accomplishments!" you will say. And yet so easily and so gradually acquired — for youth makes light of such matters — that Geoff was not conscious of his accomplishments. He was, in fact, just the careless, happy-go-lucky fellow we have endeavoured to describe him. Not conceited in the least, but merely a very ordinary specimen of British youthful humanity.

"Mesopotamia!" he shouted, when the news of their proposed expedition reached him. "George! That's splendid!"

"Ripping!" echoed Philip, extracting a cigarette from his pocket and lighting it with a most elaborate show of unconcern, and yet with fingers which trembled as they held a lighted match to the end of it. "Ripping! How awfully lucky for the whole lot of us that you've been to that country! You have, haven't you? But — where on earth is it? I'll confess at once that geography isn't a strong subject with me, and even now I haven't done much more than conquer the bare outline of India. Of course a fellow knows that Mesopotamia is somewhere adjacent to Persia, and Persia, if I remember rightly, isn't so frightfully far away from Turkey and Afghanistan. How far'll we be away from our Russian allies there? And, I say! I suppose it'll be a 'walk-over'!"

Geoff grinned back at his companion.

"Don't you think it!" he told him, his face now serious. "The average fellow seems to have got hold of the idea that the Turk is a lazy, idle, good-for-nothing, easy-going beggar, who'll hold up his hands and go under immediately war is declared on him. Why, I was reading a paragraph in the paper last evening which told us that Turkey was committing suicide by joining forces with Germany, and that Russia and England between them would mop her up and sweep her out of Europe."

17

Philip looked puzzled. When he said he had no great affection for geography, and had no particularly good bump of locality, he told his chum only the bare truth. To be quite candid, and yet essentially friendly with reference to Geoff's friend, we have to say that not even Geoff could have described this young officer as brilliant. He was just a gay, light-hearted, and, when he liked, an energetic and useful officer. When he liked to apply himself to his profession, or indeed to any other work of not too exacting a character, Philip could do as well as any other, though, to be sure, he did not shine as a rule. As a soldier, he was no better and no worse than his fellows, only his gayness of heart and his natural dash and courage might easily, under circumstances of exceptional stress, bring him to the fore and make him conspicuous. But, to speak bluntly, Philip was a bit of a dunce, and had lived his short life so far without taking extraordinary notice of his immediate surroundings, and of the world in general.

"Half a mo'!" he said, blowing a cloud of smoke in Geoff's direction. "What's that? Turkey in Europe! But Mesopotamia's Asia, isn't it? Here's a pencil, my boy, and here's a copy of to-day's 'orders'. Just you sketch out on the back of it the outline of Mesopotamia. I'm not such a fool that I can't follow a sketch when it's made for me."

A brother "sub" joined them at that moment, and as Geoff sketched diligently and drew in the outline of the Persian Gulf, of the Afghan frontier, and of Persia, another and yet another subaltern strolled up, till, quite unknown to him, a little group of officers were looking on over his shoulder. Then he suddenly became aware of their presence, and, colouring furiously, for the young fellow was essentially modest, he crumpled the paper up and threw it into a corner.

"No you don't, my boy! No you don't!" said a well-known voice from behind his shoulder. "We are all of us keen on knowing something more about the place we are bound for, and you are the only one amongst us who has ever been there. Take it as an order, Geoff. I'll guarantee that there shall be no larking, and I'm sure that every one of your brother officers wishes you to give us just a short lecture on the country called Mesopotamia."

Under the circumstances it was not to be expected that a junior officer, so junior indeed as Geoff, could refuse the request—the order if you like to call it, though it was given so pleasantly—of one of his seniors. It was the senior captain, in fact, who was leaning over his shoulder, and who patted his arm encouragingly.

"Fire ahead, Geoff," he told him. "It's not showing off! There's no swank about it! I'd like awfully to know all about this Mesopotamia. I'll admit the fact, before you young officers, that I'm just about as ignorant as I can be. Up to now I never imagined that there were any Turks to speak of in the neighbourhood of the Persian Gulf, so why on earth they should send an Expeditionary Force there from India is more than I can guess at. The Colonel says it's so that we shall protect the oil-supply which comes down from Persian territory to somewhere near the Gulf. Know it, Geoff?"

"Yes, sir! And if you really won't think it's swank — — "

"Of course not. Now, here's a piece of paper, and get on with it."

To one who had visited the country, and, more than all, to one who had accompanied the studious Major Joseph Douglas, there was no difficulty in drawing a map which showed all the essential points in Mesopotamia. It was not exactly Geoff's fault that he knew a great deal about the country. Thanks to the tuition of his kindly guardian, and the long discussions which that officer had so frequently indulged in, Geoff had contrived to visit Mesopotamia and live there, not as an ordinary tourist might have done, but as an explorer. Brought into the closest contact with the Turk, the Persian, the Armenian, and the Jew, it was only natural that, with his guardian's help, he should have learnt something of the international situation as it concerned Turkey. A visit to Constantinople had shown him the more civilized side of the country, while the outbreak of the war between the Balkan Powers and Turkey, and the dissertations of Major Joe

Douglas, had familiarized him more or less with the situation of Turkey in Europe.

"Of course, there is the 'pipe' line," he told his listeners, "and, going by what Major Douglas has always told me, it cannot fail to be of great importance to Britain. You see, numbers of our battleships now use oil fuel almost exclusively."

"Quite so! That's got it!" chimed in the senior officer. "You've hit the nail on the head, Geoff. Go ahead!"

"So an expedition to the head of the Persian Gulf may very well be for the sole purpose of protecting the oil-supply of the British Navy. As to why the Expedition should come from India rather than from England, I can say that anyone—any white man that is—who has been to Mesopotamia will know that it's a beast of a climate. As hot as India in the plains in the hot weather, and often enough, when the cold season comes along, bitterly cold and wet. But for the most part it is hot, and damp, and trying, so that native troops are far more suitable. There's the 'pipe' line," he told his listeners, sketching in a line from the southern border of Persia. "It strikes across the desert to the east of the River Karun, and joins up with the Shatt-el-Arab, close to a place called Mohammera. I ought to explain that the Rivers Tigris and Euphrates join up somewhere in the region of Kurnah and Basra, and then flow on, picking up the River Karun and opening into the Persian Gulf some twenty miles farther down. As to Turks, of course the bulk of them are up country, particularly in the neighbourhood of Bagdad. But there are fortified posts along both rivers and right down to the mouth of the Shatt-el-Arab. At Basra there are quite a considerable number of Europeans and Indians, and they tell me that an increasing trade is done from that port. If we land somewhere about there we are sure to be opposed, and if there weren't any Turks there are any number of Arabs, some of whom, at least, are likely to be unfriendly."

"So that there'll be fighting, eh?" asked the senior officer.

"Plenty of it, I imagine," Geoff told him. "Those Arabs are wily beggars to deal with."

"And where's Bagdad?" he was asked. "And how does it lie compared with Constantinople?"

"And what about Persia, and Russia, and Turkestan, and Turkey in Europe?" demanded Philip, anxious to improve the occasion.

Thus pressed, Geoff could not do other than sketch in the various positions, showing Persia to the east, and Russia where she abutted on Turkey in Asia, along the line of the Caucasus Mountains. Then, having shaded in the Black Sea, thus showing the southern shore of Russia and the Crimea, he sketched the Sea of Marmora and the Narrows, where, at the Dardanelles, the British fleet was so soon to be hammering.

A glance at the map will show better than any description the chief features of the situation, and only a few words are needed to explain the intrusion of Turkey into the gigantic war which had so recently arisen. If one looks for the cause of Turkey's joining with Germany and Austria against the Powers of the Entente, one is bound to confess that no adequate reason can be discovered. Turkey had nothing to fear from Great Britain or from her allies; yet, for years Germany had been secretly scheming to expand her sway over Turkey. It may be conceded that, whereas, exclusive of Russia, the whole of Europe was highly industrialized, and the greater part of the "middle East" that was easy to come at was already being busily developed by France or Great Britain, or others of the European nations, there yet remained the whole of Turkey in Asia and of Persia—a gigantic sweep of country—the natural riches of which were, still, not even tapped, and which, thanks to the listless idleness of the Turk, were likely to remain untapped until some European Power, with need for extending her commerce, swept upon the scene and took advantage of such golden opportunities.

Already Russia had brought a portion of Persia under her sway, while Great Britain had secured the other portion. No doubt, too, Russia had her eyes on the northern portion of Turkey in Asia, while Britain was not entirely ignorant of the riches lying undeveloped in Mesopotamia. What had once been, according to legend, the Garden of Eden, and, since the Turk had come upon the scene, had been utterly neglected, and had woefully depreciated till it had become hardly better than a barren desert, was capable of being coaxed back into its old condition. Riches, now hidden, might be won from the country by Western energy and resource, while the country, once firmly occupied by Germany or by any other nation, would open a way to the subjection of Persia and to an approach upon India by way of Afghanistan.

Let us say at once that Turkey had no adequate reason for joining in this vast struggle against Great Britain and her allies; but she was cajoled into that action. Perhaps her leaders were heavily bribed by the Germans, who themselves had reason enough in all conscience. The coming of Turkey into the conflict would of itself detain large forces both of Russia and of Great Britain; and then again, supposing France and Britain and Russia to have been defeated in Europe, Germany would have a clear field in the "middle East", with a prospect one day of even approaching India, and so of coming nearer to the consummation of that vastly ambitious scheme the Kaiser had set before him, of becoming the Ruler of the World.

But Geoff and his brother officers cared not a rap for such thoughts. That little lesson in geography proved of vast assistance to them all, and the thought of fighting in the near future, of Turks and of Arabs, roused their excitement to the highest. A couple of weeks later they took train down-country, where the bustle about the port, the presence of other troops who were to take part in the expedition, and the sight of the transports they were to board brought their spirits to fever pitch. Two days later they set sail, and within a very short period found themselves steaming to the head of the Persian Gulf. Before the dusk fell that evening they were within sight of land, and had the huge felicity of seeing the gunboat which escorted them exchange shots with the Turkish forts at the mouth of the Shatt-el-

Arab. It was the opening of their campaign. It was the first shot that many of them had heard discharged in actual warfare.

"Hurrah!" shouted Philip as he watched a shell bursting in the distance. "To-morrow, my boy, we'll be in the thick of it."

CHAPTER III

The Persian Gulf

What a scene of movement it was as the transport bearing the Expeditionary Force from India, destined to operate in Mesopotamia, steamed slowly up the Shatt-el-Arab, its naval escort proceeding ahead and gingerly feeling its way forward. Now and again excited Arabs were to be seen near the bank of the river, some of whom brandished their rifles, and then, as if fearing retaliation, disappeared amongst the palms. Women and children gazed in amazement at the armada which had come so unexpectedly to visit them, while the few Turks present looked on placidly—for your Turk is the most placid of all individuals.

It was some way up the river that a site had been chosen for disembarkation, and, almost before Geoff and his chum Philip could have thought it possible, the troops were disembarking.

"Of course they'll get off some of the cavalry at once," said Geoff, as he watched the horses being slung over the side. "They'll go off on a reconnaissance, and we ought soon to hear whether the enemy are in the neighbourhood."

"That's just what beats me," Philip rejoined, as he sucked at the inevitable cigarette. "Now you'd have thought that a chap like you would be sent with them, Geoff; for what do the officers with our Indian cavalry know of Mesopotamia, of the Turks, of the Arabs, and of all the different sorts of people you've told me of? They ought to be able to speak the native lingo, so as to cross-examine people. No one doubts that they are splendid horse-soldiers, but then, don't you know, there's a limit to a fellow's usefulness. 'Pon my word," he went on, getting quite indignant, "I really can't imagine what the G.O.C. can be doing! I've a jolly good mind to somehow drop him a hint that there's a chap called Geoff Keith along with the expedition. Eh! Oh!"

He gave a start as he turned round, for there was a movement on the deck immediately behind him. Geoff, too, who had been lounging on the rail of the ship, swung his form round to see what was happening. There was a dusky soldier behind them—one of their own Mahrattas—standing, tall and thin and erect and motionless, as is the case with native soldiers.

"The Officer Sahib," he said, as he held out a tiny "chit" (note). "From the Colonel Sahib."

It was perhaps characteristic of Philip that he seized the missive and glanced at the name written upon it.

"What! Not me! It's you, Geoff!" he exclaimed almost indignantly, and certainly with disappointment. "My word! Wonder what it's about. Supposing the Colonel has done just as I suggested a moment ago, and has dropped a hint to the G.O.C. Open it, there's a good fellow, for I'm full of curiosity."

Geoff obliged his friend in such leisurely style that Philip was almost stamping with impatience before the missive was opened, and then stretched out his long neck so as to be able to read the contents of the letter.

"You will please report at my orderly room at once," was written in pencil, while below there was his Commanding Officer's signature.

Philip whistled.

"Oh!" he exclaimed, and then looked sideways somewhat quizzically at his friend. "Ructions, eh? Adjutant reported badly on you! Something wrong with your parade this morning, I shouldn't wonder. Anyway, 'bang goes' all hope of your getting special employment."

To speak the truth, a feeling of dismay oppressed our hero as he glanced at those few words, while his brain got busily to work to discover the reason for the message. So far as he was aware, there had been no dereliction of duty for which he could be reprimanded. Indeed, Geoff's keenness was well known to the Adjutant and to his Commanding Officer. That the special knowledge he had of Mesopotamia should have anything to do with this sudden and unexpected summons never crossed his mind for a moment, in spite of Philip; for, after all, as we have said, Geoff was an extremely modest fellow, and made light of those unusual attainments which he had developed by a visit to this ancient Garden of Eden. Colouring to the roots of his hair, he coughed loudly to clear his voice, and, pulling down his khaki twill jumper, set off for the orderly room at once. A knock on the open door was followed by a peremptory command to enter, when he found himself face to face with his Commanding Officer.

"Ha! That you, young Keith? Sit down. Now look at that; it's a message from the Head-quarters of this expedition."

Geoff took the paper with fingers which almost trembled, for surely, surely a message from the Commander-in-Chief concerning himself must have reference to something far transcending in importance the question of a trifling dereliction of duty on his part.

"My dear — —," he read, "I am told by one of my Staff Officers that Douglas's young ward is with the force, and that the young officer knows Mesopotamia and the native tongues. Please send him along to me at once."

"At once, you see," said the Colonel, smiling kindly at our hero; "that means a feather in your cap, my lad. But perhaps you'd rather stay with the Mahrattas, eh?" he asked quizzically, now laughing loudly as he saw the puzzled expression which spread across Geoff's features. "There! There! Don't try to be polite," he told him. "I know exactly what you want to say; you're keen on your own regiment, and you'd like to work alongside the brother officers with whom you've been trained. You know well enough that, if there's any fighting to be done, the Mahrattas will be right in the midst of it; and, if they're not, it will be a piece of atrociously bad luck. But there's this other billet. Though you like your own regiment well enough, this order means special service. Now, Geoff, off you go without delay. You'll find the General ashore, and please give my compliments to him, and hand him this 'chit'."

A little more than ten minutes later, with his sword buckled on, his revolver in place, and with his full kit in evidence, Geoff clattered down the gangway and swung along the strand, and halted in front of the native house where the General had taken up his quarters. He was ushered in at once by one of the Staff Officers, and found himself face to face with the brilliant soldier who had sent for him. We admit only the bare truth when we state that it was a trying moment for our hero, for, after all, subalterns — junior subalterns in particular — are very small fry as compared with General Officers, and, unless cram-full of assurance, are apt to feel extremely insignificant, almost humble, in fact, when brought face to face with an officer of lifelong experience. Yet Geoff had been born and brought up with the Indian army. Standing stiffly at attention, he returned the General's gaze with a gaze which was as frank, as unflinching, and almost as politely inquisitive as that which had been turned on him.

"Mr. Keith, sir," one of the Staff Officers told the General. "You sent a note to the Officer Commanding the Mahrattas, asking him to send this young officer to you. You will remember, sir, that he is the son of Major Robert Keith, killed in that Frontier Expedition in which you served, and that Major Douglas has acted as his guardian."

That brought another penetrating glance in Geoff's direction — a glance which seemed to take in every characteristic of the young fellow standing so stiffly at attention: his tall, stout, active figure, his clean-cut person, his undoubtedly refined and gentleman-like face, and the intelligence which gleamed from behind the dark eyes which were turned still politely, yet unflinchingly, upon the General.

The latter cleared his throat, and brushed away the flies which were hovering in myriads about him.

"Of course," he said brusquely, "I remember perfectly. Mr. Keith, I understand that you have been in Mesopotamia with Major Douglas; please let me have some further information. I imagine that you must have gone up country. What more?"

27

Thus encouraged, Geoff promptly stated how he and his old friend had ventured to Bagdad and beyond, and had spent months in the country, sometimes in a native city or village, sometimes amongst the Armenians or Arabs, and often enough in the heart of some purely Turkish city.

"And you speak Turkish?" came the sharp question.

"Yes, sir."

"Well? Quite fluently, I mean."

"Like a native, I believe, sir," said Geoff modestly.

"Um! And Arabic? and other tongues?"

"Almost as well, sir."

"You can ride, of course?"

"Certainly," said Geoff.

There was a long pause, whilst the General once more inflicted upon Geoff that cold, stern, penetrating, yet kindly glance of his. Evidently he was thinking deeply, and just as evidently he was summing up the character of the young fellow standing at attention before him.

"Remember his father well," he was saying to himself; "he was a nice, clean-cut fellow, like the boy here; and, of course, everyone knows Joe Douglas, one of the best officers, one of the best 'politicals', India has ever possessed. This youngster looks as though he would go through fire and water to carry out his duties. I like his modesty, both of speech and of appearance, and, by Jove! he ought to be a very valuable addition to us.

"Attached to the Head-quarters Staff," he suddenly blurted out, turning to his Staff Officer. "Mr. Keith, I should be glad to avail myself of your services, but please understand that they may very well bring you into circumstances of very considerable danger. Recollect that we are now at war with Turkey, while your previous visit was made at a time when there was peace between us. That may very well have brought about a drastic change in the usually gentle Turk; and to be captured by them might result

28

in serious consequences. I mention this question of unusual danger, seeing that you are such a young officer, and, of course, should you prefer to go back to your regiment, there is nothing to prevent you."

Would he prefer to go back to the Mahrattas? Why, Geoff's two legs were simply twitching and shaking so violently with excitement that he could hardly keep his knees from hammering together. It wasn't fright. The officer facing him knew that well enough. It was merely keenness — keenness for the work to be entrusted to him. It wasn't necessary even for Geoff to give a verbal answer; his decision was written all over his face. Why, he was simply dying for some form of active employment. It was a relief, then, to receive a kindly nod of dismissal from the General, and to retire precipitately from his presence. Outside the native hut a hand was laid firmly on his shoulder, and once more he found himself addressed by the Staff Officer.

"We want you at once," he said. "You'd better go on board and get rid of all this kit as soon as possible."

"Yes, sir."

"And — — of course you've got your own saddlery and gear of that sort."

Geoff promptly assured the officer that he was fully equipped, and as a matter of fact had brought his own stout little Arab with him.

"Then bustle, my lad. We've a couple of troops of cavalry ready disembarked, and are anxious to find out what the Turks are doing. You'll go with them, and I needn't tell you that you'll do your utmost to help the officer who goes in command. You'll be under his orders, of course, and I feel sure that you'll be able to render very great assistance. Don't forget to take your water-bottle with you, and some food too; but there, I was forgetting that I'm talking to a young officer who knows the ground and has been in Mesopotamia before. Still, there are no hotels in these days, I imagine, though it is to be hoped that we shall come across friendly inhabitants, ready to feed us if need be, and prepared to give us a welcome."

Geoff went along that strand as if he were possessed of wings, and raced up the gangway.

"Half a mo'! Why in such a hurry? Look here, Geoff, what's all the ruction about? You've been to Head-quarters, haven't you? My word! That means something—either a frightful ruction and summary dismissal, if not a general court-martial, and shooting in the cold, early morning, or—or— what does it mean?" demanded Philip, gripping the unwilling Geoff by the arm and firmly retaining him.

It was no use attempting to shake off his friend, or to plead that he was in a hurry and that there was no time for delay. The utmost that Geoff could do was to bid Philip follow him down to his cabin, where he at once began to throw off certain of his kit and rummage for other items amongst his half-packed baggage. A shout brought his native servant, and another shout was echoed along the ship and soon sent his syce racing towards him.

"You'll get Sultan disembarked at once, with all his blankets and clothing," commanded Geoff. "Just run him up and down a little once you get him ashore, for he'll be stiff after the voyage. Now, my beauty," he went on, addressing his native servant, "just look lively with it, for I'm due back at Head-quarters in a few minutes."

"And what's the game?" demanded Philip insistently, impatiently in fact, already envying his chum immensely. Not that he was jealous of Geoff at all, for, if Philip were himself eager for some form of special service, he knew at least that Geoff had special attainments, special knowledge which fitted him for a post of that description. How Philip bewailed the fact that in his younger days—though to be sure he was still only a youngster—he had made such ill use of his opportunities. For, like his friend, Philip had been born in a cantonment, had lived the better part of his young life in one or other of the hill stations in India, and had grown up in the atmosphere which surrounds the army in British India. Hindustani and native dialects had come naturally to him, had been acquired without effort when he was a mere slip of a lad, but Turkish, that was an altogether different question.

"Well," he demanded eagerly, "you've got a job, have you? A special job, Geoff? Congratulations!"

He smacked his friend heartily on the back when he had heard the whole story, and emitted a shrill whistle of amazement, perhaps even of envy, when Geoff told him that he was to be attached to Head-quarters.

"Well, that's going it!" he exclaimed. "Attached to Head-quarters, eh! And just off on a reconnaissance. Mind you ain't captured, Geoff, for I've a very particular reason, and I'll tell you what it is. What's the good of my being chums with a fellow whose attached to Head-quarters for special service if that chap can't somehow or other squeeze me in one of these days and take me along with him? That would be fine, wouldn't it, Geoff? One of these days you'll probably want to sneak off, dressed as an Arab or something of that sort. How'd I do to come with you, even if only as a humble servant? But then − −Oh, hang it! There's the language! But never mind, somehow or other you'll manage to take me with you."

Not for one moment did the eager Philip cease to chatter and cross-examine Geoff, as the latter and his servant plunged into the midst of the half-packed baggage and extracted sundry articles likely to be of use to him. As to agreeing to take Philip with him on some expedition, of course Geoff could not even give so much as a thought to the matter at that moment, though, to be sure, as he told himself, having Philip with him would be tremendous fun, and would add to his enjoyment. However, there was little time for thought, and none for discussion. In the course of half an hour he had selected all the kit he required, and had dispatched his servant ashore with the remainder. Then he dived down to the orderly room to formally report his impending departure, while he received the congratulations of his Commanding Officer and the Adjutant.

"Don't forget, Keith, you're one of the Mahrattas," he was told, "and the regiment looks to you to maintain its high reputation wherever you may

go. But you'll do that, Geoff. I knew your father, and if I know you at all —
and I ought to seeing that you've been trained under my eye — you'll follow
in his footsteps, and will do well in the post for which you've been
selected."

A firm grip of Philip's hand as he stepped upon the gangway, a cheery
good-bye, and a nod to others of his brother-officers, and Geoff was ashore,
where the first object that his eyes lit upon was Sultan being walked up
and down the strand, tossing his handsome head and shaking his mane,
caracolling, and looking as if such a thing as a voyage from India were of
no consequence. Patting his animal and talking to him for a few moments,
Geoff then went on briskly to the native hut selected as Head-quarters,
near which the two troops of Indian Horse he had been told were about to
move away on a reconnaissance were already drawn up, the men at their
horses' heads, standing expectant and immovable, and the officers strolling
to and fro, smoking cigarettes and showing as much impatience as any of
the soldiers. Striding up to the senior of the officers, Geoff at once reported
himself.

"I've been ordered to accompany you, sir," he said.

"Lieutenant Keith, Mahrattas."

"And glad to meet you, Keith," came the hearty answer, whilst his hand
was gripped. "I understand you've been in Mesopotamia, and know
something of the country and the languages. Ward of my old friend, Joe
Douglas, aren't you?"

It made Geoff glow with pride to hear so many eulogistic remarks made
concerning the old friend who had cared for him now for so many years,
and who indeed had filled the place of his father. That Major Joe Douglas
was appreciated wherever he was known in the Indian army — and to be
sure this "political" was known in very many stations, and to a host of
officers — was a fact that Geoff could not fail to know, for in India all that
concerns the army is known by its officers. Yet to hear him spoken of so
very highly now by senior officers, to hear him eulogized, and to realize

that the welcome extended to himself, Geoff Keith, was due, in part at least, to the old friendships made by his guardian, could not fail to make every impression on our hero. It made him then and there register a silent vow that, come what might, he would do nothing that would not reflect favourably upon the Major.

"He stood by me all these years," he thought, "he taught me all I know, though I fear I am still very young and an ignoramus. But he's tried hard I know to impart all his own special knowledge to me, and he's given me chances that many a young officer would give his ears for. Right! I've got to remember that always; and if I don't carry out this job to the satisfaction of my seniors, well I'll just deserve kicking."

The voice of the officer commanding the Indian Horse awakened him from the short reverie into which he had fallen.

"We'll be off in five minutes," he told Geoff; "we're just waiting for maps of the country to be issued, and for special instructions from Head-quarters. Now, Keith, since you've reported, I presume that you're quite ready to move off with us."

"Quite, sir!" Geoff told him with energy.

"Then what about a mount? Of course you will have brought one, seeing that all Indian officers are mounted, but if by chance your horse has not yet been disembarked, we'll leave one of our men behind and you can make use of his mount for the time being."

Geoff turned at once, and, looking towards the strand where Sultan was being exercised, signalled to his syce to bring him along immediately. A minute later Sultan was prancing and circling close at hand — the admired of all admirers.

"'Pon my word, Keith, I admire your choice of horse-flesh," the officer told Geoff with enthusiasm as he walked slowly round the fretful Sultan, noting every handsome point. "No need to ask you whether you can ride or whether you've only recently gone through a school of instruction, for no fellow would dare to put his leg over that beast who hadn't had any amount of experience. Easy to handle, eh?" he asked, bending down, the better to take a look at Sultan's feet and legs. "My word! but there's pace there, and there's strength in those shoulders, while, if I know a horse at all, this fellow will be a stayer."

If you had wanted to give Geoff Keith some particularly great pleasure, or desired to pay him some extraordinary compliment, you could not have done it better or more easily than by admiring Sultan. Let us explain at once that Sultan had once upon a time belonged to Major Douglas — indeed, he had been bred by the Major, and came of a famous stable. He had, one might almost say, grown up with our hero; though to be sure he was yet only a six-year-old, full of life and youth and strength. Nor had Geoff's temporary absence from India in Mesopotamia, and during those months he had spent in England, been sufficient to allow Sultan to forget his young master. It was with a whinny of pleasure that he had greeted his return to the "Shiney", and though there were many who would not have dared to mount the animal, and, indeed, few whom Sultan would allow to ride him, yet in the hands of Geoff Keith this fiery beast became as gentle as a lamb, as docile and as easily handled as any horse. To be short and explicit, Sultan was a most splendid Arab, one in a thousand, and a steed of which even a General would have been proud, and the possession of which might easily have turned the head of any junior subaltern.

"A nice little horse. Yes, as nice a little horse as ever I set eyes on," declared the officer in command of the two troops of Indian cavalry, as he paced round Sultan, patting him now and again, talking to him, and admiring his handsome points and his general appearance. "A grey was always my fancy, Keith, but they want a heap of handling. Let's see what he looks like with a man on his back. I'll wager that his paces are as good as his looks; trot him along, lad, and open him out a little. Our horses have already had a gallop, and they needed it after their confinement on board ship."

It was with a keen discerning eye that the officer watched Geoff pick up his reins and swing himself into the saddle. It was all done in an instant, though, indeed, the fretful Sultan made it difficult for anyone to mount him. But a word from Geoff quieted him for just a few seconds, and in that brief space of time the lad had gripped his mane, had thrust one foot into the stirrup, and was well home in his saddle.

"Let go!" Geoff told the syce, and there for a moment he sat motionless, Sultan standing as still as any statue—his head thrown back, his muzzle raised, and his eyes gleaming wickedly. Then with a bound he leapt to one side—a leap which would have thrown the average rider—and a second later, shaking his head free, he went off towards the desert like the wind, as if determined to have his freedom.

"Steady! Steady, boy, steady!" said Geoff, holding him firmly with the reins. "You're here to do what I want and not what you want; and, besides, a burst of speed so soon after coming ashore might be bad for you; you're coming back to let those officers take a good look at you."

The mad impulse of the Arab to be off, to be galloping wildly across the loose sand and gravel thereabouts, to be hurtling amongst the palms which covered the country-side, was controlled in an instant, and with such little effort that those officers who watched could not discern it. Geoff brought his mount back towards the troops of horse at a steady trot, a trot in which Sultan showed magnificent action, so much so that riding him gracefully was a matter of difficulty. Then a gentle pressure of the reins again brought him to a standstill, his feet well spread, his head held high, those eyes of his gleaming and shining. Indeed, all could see the spirit of the horse, and none were surprised when, a moment later, as the Officer in Command approached, Sultan rose on his hind legs and thrashed the air, Geoff sitting him and talking to him gently.

"A very handsome piece of goods, Keith," he heard, "'pon my word! I'm as envious as I can be; but in fairness to all of us you ought to take him out a little bit and give him a breather. Gently at first, and then some quick pace, so as to let him get rid of a little of that spirit. Otherwise he'll be kicking other horses in the ranks or disabling one of the officers."

A gentle word from Geoff, the merest relaxation of the reins, and Sultan was off again, but curbed this time ever so gently; off at a trot again, showing that magnificent action with his fore legs, his quarters gleaming in the sunshine. And, slowly as they went, the pace increased till it became a canter, which Geoff allowed his mount to keep up until they had covered a good mile of desert—until, in fact, he was well out in the open and away from the palms which spread themselves some distance from the bank of the river. Then he pulled up his mount and patted him on the shoulder.

"That's your first breather, old chap!" he said; "now I'll allow you to have a burst of speed till we are near the trees again, just to get rid of the devil in you. After that you'll behave yourself, and go along quietly like the rest of them. Now off!"

"Handles the beast as if born to it," declared the Commanding Officer, as he watched the figures of man and horse racing towards him, while his brother officers crowded about him. "That lad has hands and a seat to be proud of, and the beast he rides is the best bit of horse-flesh I've seen—and that's saying something."

There was no doubt, in fact, that Geoff's arrival on the scene, his unexpected attachment to these horse-soldiers, his unconscious exhibition of horsemanship, and his possession of that fine Arab, had created quite an enviable impression upon the officers who were to be his companions.

"A young chap, such as he was, who could ride so well, who had the pluck to manage such a horse, must be a good fellow," they told themselves; and, thinking that, the information which was now given them—that Geoff was no new-comer to Mesopotamia, but had spent some months there with a famous Indian "political", and even knew the languages—prepossessed them still more in his favour.

36

"You'll do, my lad," the Commanding Officer whispered in his ear some few minutes later, when Geoff had dismounted, and had handed over Sultan to the syce. "It wants judgment to ride a beast like that, and judgment's the virtue required for the job to which you have been appointed. Now, Keith, our orders have come, and here are the maps; pop this one into your map-case. I shall take the troops up beside the river towards Basra, and if it seems necessary I shall send one troop off to my right to see what's happening farther out in the desert."

There were sharp words of command, and then a whistle blew, at which those stalwart Indian soldiers mounted their horses as one man, and sat there like so many dusky statues; then the whistle sounded again, and the cavalcade moved off, Geoff, at the invitation of the Commanding Officer, riding beside him.

It was as well, perhaps, for our hero that he was all unconscious of the fact that those Indian cavalry officers were not the only witnesses of that exhibition he had given with Sultan, and that other eyes than the curious ones of the natives of those parts followed the troops of horse, and his own upright figure, as they swung away from the site of disembarkation. It might have turned his head, and robbed him of his natural modesty, had he known that numbers of the Head-quarters Staff were outside their hut, looking on at this first movement of the expedition in Mesopotamia; and it would most certainly have caused a flush to rise to his cheeks, and possibly, had he not been a steady, sensible fellow, might have induced a degree of swollen-headedness, had he been able to hear the remarks of some of those senior officers. For, like those with the Indian horse, they, too, had fixed their eyes on Sultan, had seen the masterly way in which he was managed, and had admired the horsemanship of this new-comer amongst junior officers.

"He's a find," declared one of the Staff Officers, "and I'll eat my hat if young Keith doesn't prove a most promising officer!"

But that was a question for the future. To make good resolutions, to register silent vows, is, after all, a very easy matter, and one to which we all of us are prone. Promises are, we know, very much like pie-crust, so easily are they broken, and good intentions and vows, made ever so solemnly and so secretly, are difficult to keep. Would Geoff, with all his youthful enthusiasm, with all his keenness, with his undoubted steadiness of character, do well? Or would he prove only an egregious failure?

"Trot!" The command rang out loudly, and in a moment the troops of horse were swinging away across the now fast-opening desert, their horses' feet kicking up clouds of sandy dust and gravel debris. Those palms were left behind in a trice it seemed, and within half an hour the landing-place was little more than a memory. It was perhaps two hours later when an officers' patrol, which had been riding well in advance, signalled the troops to halt, and one of their number came back at a gallop.

"A strong force of horsemen away on our left front, sir," he reported. "Turks, I think, but I am by no means certain."

"Halt! Mr. Keith, you will ride forward to the patrol, and if necessary beyond them. Let me have your report at the first possible moment," came the sharp order.

A second later Sultan was bounding forward, and in a little while Geoff had joined the officers' patrol at the point where they had now halted. Yes, there was a force of horsemen away in front, and to all appearances the campaign in Mesopotamia was about to open.

CHAPTER IV

The First Encounter

"There! Over there you can see a mass of horsemen, and I think there are infantry just behind them," said Daglish, one of the officers forming the patrol which had gone out in front of the two troops of Indian Horse sent out to reconnoitre. When Geoff pulled up his Arab, Sultan, he found close beside him the young officer who had just spoken, standing with his reins hooked over one arm, his feet wide apart and sunk almost to the ankles in the soft sand of the desert, and his glasses glued to his eyes, as he surveyed the ground to his left front, adjacent to the River Shatt-el-Arab.

"Hang it!" Geoff heard him say as he too dropped from his saddle and let his reins fall on Sultan's neck—for Sultan had been trained by the knowing and experienced Joe Douglas to stand as still and as steady as a rock without a rider, so long as his reins were left in that position.

"Hang it, Keith! there's a sort of a mist out there, and while just a second ago I could have sworn that there were several hundred horsemen, either Turkish or Arab, there is now nothing but shimmering water and palm-trees and houses, and a devil of a big village."

Daglish, a young, spirited, and handsome cavalry officer, dropped his glasses and let them dangle about his neck, while he turned impatiently towards Geoff.

"See!" he cried, stretching his hand out. "Look for yourself, Keith; there's the village yonder and hundreds of palm-trees round it; but it can't have sprung up in a moment, and can't have taken the place of those horsemen. What's it mean?"

The line the officers' patrol had taken had brought them to a low elevation—for though the estuary of the Tigris and the Euphrates is more or less flat, and the greater part of it but desert country, the ground rises here and there almost imperceptibly into hard gravel patches, and it was on the summit of one of these that the patrol had halted, and from which they had first sighted what was taken to be enemy horsemen, and which now, to the amazement of the officer, had developed into merely a native village. Pulling out his glasses, Geoff first of all surveyed the scene without their aid, and noticed that from the slight elevation to which they had attained he was able to look down upon the course of the river as it ran through a broad belt of green palm-trees. He could see stretches of the water flashing here and there under the brilliant rays of the sun. Elsewhere peeps of it only were obtainable, while in other parts the brilliant reflection from its surface shot through a thousand apertures between the trunks of the palms, the light almost dazzling him as it reached him. It was to a point, perhaps more than a mile away, and just outside the closest belt of palm-trees, that Daglish was pointing, and as Geoff looked in that direction he too saw a native village embowered in palms, its white houses gleaming faintly across the yellow stretches of desert.

"Well?" Daglish asked him impatiently.

Geoff smiled.

"Just a mirage," he told his companion. "They are funny things till you get used to them, and you have to come and live in this country for quite a while often before you get a chance. Before now I've seen a whole Turkish city rise up before me out of the desert, looking wonderfully realistic, with people moving about, and horses, and asses, and dogs in all directions. Then I've gone on a little way, or gone back, and the whole scene has vanished. That's a mirage. Some trick of the sun's rays playing upon the atmosphere spread out over the desert. How it's brought about beats me altogether; but it's real enough when one sees it, and equally elusive when one's moved from one's position. Let's walk our horses across here to the left; we needn't trouble to go downhill at all, for if you have seen the enemy horsemen out there in the open, they will most distinctly have seen you up here on this little bit of an eminence."

Leading their horses, they strode off some distance to their left, sinking ankle-deep into the sand at almost every stride. There were three of them by now, for Harmer, another of the Indian cavalry officers—the one who had come back to make his report—had joined them; and as they went, each one cast glances over his left shoulder, till of a sudden Daglish gave a cry of delight.

"I was beginning to doubt you, Keith," he said with energy; "but now, by James! you are right. That must have been a mirage, though I have never seen one before in all my life. The native village has gone completely; and look at those horsemen!"

They came to an abrupt halt, the three wheeling round at once and raising their glasses.

"Eh! What do you make of 'em?" Daglish said, when a minute had passed during which Geoff focused the distant horsemen carefully and watched them critically. "Turks, eh? Or Arabs?"

"A mixed force," Geoff told him promptly. "Arab horsemen, perhaps two or three hundred strong, and Turkish infantry behind them; there are no guns with them, so I take it that it's simply a reconnoitring force, or maybe it's a garrison, from some point lower down the river, retiring before us."

"Then the sooner we send back to our fellows the better," cried Daglish. "There's open ground before us, and the two troops could operate so as to drive in a blow at those fellows."

Pulling his notebook from his pocket he wrote a few hurried lines, and, having folded the "chit" up, he addressed it to his commanding officer.

"Take it back, Harmer," he ordered. "You can tell them that Keith and I will go on a little and make out those fellows a trifle more clearly."

A minute later the third of the officers was in his saddle and galloping back towards their comrades, whom they had left some distance away, halting at the bottom of this long sloping eminence. Then Geoff and Daglish climbed into their saddles and urged their horses forward, Geoff looking critically at the mount upon which his companion was riding.

"Better go easily, Daglish," he told him, "for that little horse of yours doesn't look as though he was fast, and I can tell you many of those Arab horsemen are superbly mounted. We can go on a little way, of course, and then, if it's the same to you, I'll push on still closer, for there's not a horse yonder that can even look at Sultan."

It was perhaps five minutes later when the two drew rein, for even though Daglish was full of energy and enthusiasm, and indeed was a brilliant cavalry officer, yet he was not devoid entirely of discretion. Though he was itching with eagerness to get to grips with the enemy, and to come to close quarters, he could not fail to realize the weight of the warning which Geoff had given him; nor, having seen that little exhibition which Sultan and his master had given them so close to the place of disembarkation, could he doubt that there were few who could come up to the magnificent Arab Geoff was riding.

"All right!" he told Geoff, a little reluctantly, as he pulled in his horse. "I'll stay here and keep my glasses on them, while you go on a little. Now, don't be reckless; for recollect you are of some value to the expedition, seeing that you speak the lingo."

Shaking his reins, Geoff set Sultan in motion, while Daglish watched him for a while as he cantered towards the enemy; then he threw up his glasses, and, fixing them upon the Arab horsemen, watched their waving lines, the chiefs who sat their horses in front of them, and one man in particular, who cantered slowly along their front—his white cloak thrown back, his dusky arm bare, the weapons he was carrying distinctly visible. It was fascinating to watch that gallant horseman, for a fine sight this Arab made. He pulled in his horse after a while in front of his men, and from the movements of his head it seemed as if he must be haranguing them; then of a sudden he stood in his stirrups and flung the pistol he was carrying high in the air, while an instant later there rolled musically across the desert the sound of shouting—a sound unfamiliar to Daglish's ears.

"Allah!" he heard; "Allah!" That weird, majestic, inspiring call of the Arab. It made the young officer almost twitch; made him admire those horsemen even more, and made him start violently when a second later he saw through his glasses that self-same chief swing his horse round, shield his eyes with one hand as he stared in Geoff's direction, and then set his horse going at a mad pace which promised to bring him rapidly up to him. Almost at the same instant the Turkish infantry — a mere handful of men — who had been hidden behind the horsemen almost completely, debouched into the open at their left, and at once the sharp rattle of rifle-fire came echoing across the desert. As for Geoff, he heard the sounds and saw that horseman. Little puffs of sand began to rise up all round him, while now and again something buzzed past his head, humming its way on into the distance.

"Near enough," he told himself coolly, pulling Sultan up, while he felt for his glasses; then, dropping his reins, he focused the enemy again, and took very careful stock of them. "Doubt if there are three hundred horsemen there," he thought; "two hundred is more like their number, and a mere handful of Turkish infantry I should say, though having infantry with them points to the fact that they are a garrison retiring up river. And what's that chief mean by riding out like that in front of all his people? Anyway, he's now between the infantry and me, and that will put a stop to those bullets."

If he could, Daglish would have shouted to his companion so far ahead, and for a while he was consumed with the fear that Geoff had failed to notice that single horseman, that magnificently mounted chief, who came galloping across the desert. Then he swung himself into the saddle, and, gripping his reins, sat motionless, watching the figure of his comrade.

Ah! Geoff was beginning to move a little. He had dropped his glasses, and, peering at him through his own, Daglish saw that he had opened the pouch containing his revolver.

"Confound the chap!" he exclaimed. "Does he mean to stay out there and have a single-handed encounter with that beggar? If I'd have thought that possible I'd have sent the idiot back long ago."

Then he dropped his glasses again and sat spellbound, peering across the desert, longing for Geoff's return, and yet hoping, in spite of himself, that the young officer who had so recently joined them would stand his ground, would face this Arab enemy, and would show right at the commencement of this coming campaign that an Englishman was not to be frightened easily.

"Steady does it!" Geoff was saying to himself as he watched the furious approach of the Arab. "By the time he gets up to me his horse will be winded, and he'll be considerably shaken; that will be my chance, and, by George! I'll take it. A captive at this stage would be a tremendous thing for the General; for once an Arab sees that the game is up, and once he realizes that rewards are given for information, he will speak, will speak the truth, indeed. That's one of the curious parts about these Arabs—they've no fondness for the Turks, though many of them will fight for them, seeing that we are heathen and the Turks are of the 'Faithful'; but, on the other hand, they are just as likely to turn against the Sultan and help an invader. Ah! That's just a gentle reminder to let me know that the beggar is armed, and quite eager to kill me."

The horseman galloping furiously towards our hero was now within some sixty yards of him: a picturesque figure, his turban and his flowing robes blowing out in the breeze he made, his Arab horse and the gaudy harness with which it was decorated making quite a remarkable appearance. It was just then, when Geoff was able to clearly distinguish the man's face, that the Arab's right arm was suddenly raised, a puff of white smoke swept away from above the head of his galloping horse, and something sang past Sultan's tail and kicked up a splash of sand beyond him. Then a dull, deep report reached Geoff's ears, and caused Sultan to bound sideways. Speaking to him, and pressing his knees into his flanks, Geoff then set him in motion, and instead of galloping away towards Daglish—who still watched the proceedings with bated breath—he set him flying off at a tangent, a movement which caused the Arab to swing his own horse round and come hurtling after him. Nor was he on the new course more than a few seconds when, pulling another pistol from his belt, he sent a second bullet in Geoff's direction.

"A little too close to be pleasant," thought our hero as he heard the missile hum past his head, and saw the splash of sand it made beyond him. "I'll let Sultan out a little, and increase the distance, so that, if one of his bullets happens to strike us, no great damage will be inflicted. That's doing it! That's making him writhe with anger! He's grandly mounted, and I shouldn't wonder if he had the idea that there was nothing he couldn't come up with; but Sultan knows better. Don't we?"

He leaned forward in his saddle and patted his horse's neck, while he glanced backward again at the pursuing Arab. That sudden spurt had taken him some hundred yards in front of his enemy, and even at that distance Geoff could see the chief brandishing his smoking weapon, and could hear as he shouted curses at him. Then slowly, almost imperceptibly, he circled from his course, till in a while he was heading almost direct for the point where Daglish was waiting.

"Give him another two or three shots at the most," thought Geoff, casting many glances over his shoulder. "That Arab fellow may have two or three pistols with him—double-barrelled fellows—and if he's rich and lucky it may be that he's got a revolver. But I'll wager my hat that he ain't, or he'd have used it already."

Ping! There came another shot, very wide of the mark, for the rage into which the Arab chief had worked himself, and the disappointment he was suffering, had unsteadied him—that and his frantic gallop across the desert. By now, too, his horse was blowing hard, and was slackening its pace, a fact which Geoff noted clearly, and made allowance for by holding Sultan in and curbing his paces. It was perhaps a minute later when he swung Sultan round on his haunches and pulled him in abruptly, the sudden halt causing the Arab to decrease the distance between them rapidly and to come rushing towards them.

"Now shall Allah reward me!" the chief bellowed, his eyes gleaming, his teeth set, and his lips parted in a snarl of triumph and anger.

Thrusting his empty pistol back into his belt, he dived for his curved scimitar, which was dangling beside him, and, getting his horse well in hand at the same moment, sped onwards without halting. It was then that Geoff revealed his own weapon, and, taking careful aim, pressed the trigger. An instant later the horse which the chief was riding reared up on its hind legs, whinnying loudly, and there for a moment it stood, pawing the air and snorting; then it collapsed of a sudden, as if the strength which had permitted it to fly so rapidly across the desert had been suddenly torn from it, and, crumpling up, fell back, bearing its rider with it.

"Drop your scimitar," shouted Geoff, covering the fallen chief as he staggered from his saddle and got to his feet. "Now throw your pistols on one side. Good! You'll run in front of me as fast as you can, without looking to either side or behind you; if you fail in this, I have still another bullet to spare for you."

Amazement was written on the face of the chief — amazement which was far greater for the moment than his wrath and his disappointment at being made a prisoner. For wrath does not last for long when a man has met with a fair opponent and has been fairly worsted. Moreover, whatever your Arab may be — fierce revengeful, treacherous, a false friend, if you will have it — he is yet a philosopher, a child of the desert, one who takes things as they come, and makes the best of them.

"By Allah," he grunted, "but this is a strange thing that has happened. A while ago and I thought that you — a white man, one of the race of unbelievers — were surely in my hands, were surely killed or captive; but a while ago, had a man dared to tell me that I, Suliman, should fall before one of the invaders, and this at the very first encounter, I would have slain him; while, had one dared to say that this fine Arab I ride could meet his match anywhere in the desert, I would have had him stripped and beaten. But now, surely this is fate. Allah is great! and if this is his reward, then why should I be wroth with it? My master, I obey."

Quite cheerfully he cast his empty weapons aside and threw his scimitar to a distance; then, with long active strides he set off in the direction that Geoff had indicated, casting not a single glance back at his comrades, content as it were with his fate, and careless of what was before him — a true philosopher indeed, a true child of the desert.

Perhaps ten minutes later they came up with Daglish, finding that young officer amazed, delighted beyond words, hugging himself with enjoyment.

"My word!" he exclaimed as Geoff rode up beside him; "of all the cheek, of all the dare-devils I ever saw. But what the devil do you mean by it?"

He quite exploded as he recollected the fears which had assailed him; indeed, as he sat there, a witness of the moving scene which was taking place before him, he had had many and many a twinge of conscience, and had recollected that Keith was an officer whose loss would reflect on the head of any of his brothers responsible for it. "Why hadn't he told him to halt some hundred yards ahead? Why had he allowed him to go off on such a fool's errand? What the devil was the fellow doing? He'd be killed if he didn't look out, for look at all those splashes of sand about him, and listen to the rifles of those Turkish infantry, and — and — — Good Heavens! He was going to wait for that Arab chap! He was going to — — Bravo! Bravo, Keith! — took his fire without flinching — and now he is giving him a run for his money. There goes another shot, and can't have missed Keith by more than a trifle. Dash the fellow! He'll get killed yet, and here am I unable to help him."

Imagine the shout of delight the enthusiastic Daglish indulged in when he saw that last manœuvre of Geoff's, and watched as the Arab's horse reared and then crumpled up beneath him. Why, he had never been so excited in all his life, and now watched with staring eyes as the Arab clambered to his feet and then set off at a fast trot towards the eminence whereon he was standing. But that was a few minutes ago—minutes of huge relief to Daglish, minutes during which he could congratulate himself on a fortunate escape from something approaching a disaster, and upon a tale which would make excellent telling; and then, as a sharp order from Geoff brought the Arab to a standstill, and that young officer halted like a culprit before him, the anger of this other officer—who was senior to Geoff—burst out as he recollected the qualms which had assailed him.

"My word," he bellowed, "what the dickens do you mean by it? Isn't it enough to draw fire from those Turkish infantry, and to stand quite still, like an idiot, to make their shooting more perfect? Isn't it enough to make a fellow swear to see an officer chucking his life away out there in the desert? And, by James, Keith," he cried, as he stretched out a hand and gripped Geoff's, "but it was fine! I wish to goodness I'd been in it; and to think you've got a captive at this early stage. Here, what's your name? Who are you? And where do you come from?"

The Arab, tall, calm, almost austere, handsome and active, stood erect before the two young officers, not a shadow on his face, not a look of animosity about him; he even smiled, and then addressed himself to our hero.

"Doubtless it is one of your chiefs, my master," he said, looking across at Daglish; "doubtless, too, he is both angry and overjoyed at something. Maybe you are his brother, and in that case, seeing that Allah has spared you, and it is I who am a captive, why, I joy with him in his delight and pleasure. My master, if it is ill to be taken by an enemy, it is still an honour and a fine thing to be taken by one who is doubtless of value to his own people—a man respected and looked up to."

"Can't make a word out," exclaimed Daglish, impatiently casting anxious glances over his shoulder and then away towards the enemy. "But, as I said, Keith, you've got a captive, and if you handle him rightly you may make him jolly useful. Now, I'll stay here and keep my eye on those beggars, while you trot this fellow back towards our comrades."

A sharp order from Geoff set the Arab in motion again, and presently, steering a course towards the two troops of horse which could now be seen advancing towards them, they halted a few yards before them—nor is it to be wondered at that a torrent of questions was immediately poured out in Geoff's direction.

"What's this? Who's this fellow?—a fine-looking beggar, a chief I should say. How did you get hold of him? Where's he come from? And what's the latest about this enemy force that Harmer has reported?"

As quickly as possible Geoff told his tale; merely mentioning that he and Daglish had advanced towards the enemy, and that by a fortunate chance they had managed to capture this chief, who had ventured out to meet them.

"I think, if you'll allow me, sir, I may be able to get some important information from him," he told the Officer in Command. "Of course he was very angry, in fact furious, at being captured, but, like a true follower of the Prophet, he is a born philosopher, and is already quite reconciled to his fate. I have told him already that no harm will come to him; and if you will allow me to make promises of good treatment and of reward, I think he'll tell us as much as he knows of the Turks and their movements."

"Then fire ahead! The horses have come along at a smartish pace and will do with a breather. I have already sent off strong advance- and flanking-parties, so that we are not likely to be surprised, particularly as Daglish is still out there in front watching the enemy and can signal back to us. Now, Keith, get on with the cross-examination. I think I may say that you may promise your captive a handsome present of money if he will give us every scrap of information."

Saluting with precision, Geoff dropped out of his saddle, and, leaving Sultan to take care of himself, faced his captive. Then, handling him with that care and tact which residence amongst the Arabs had taught him, and in fact winning his confidence at once—for it was impossible for the Arab chief to have suspicion of this British officer's good intentions—Geoff very quickly gained from him information as to the positions taken up by the Turks and Arabs in the immediate neighbourhood, together with such news as the chief had of forces in other directions.

"But, my master, it is mere rumour—this latter information that I have given you," the chief told him. "I and my men have been posted down beside the river, and know little of what is occurring elsewhere. Doubtless there are Turkish troops here and there, and it may be that in parts there are large forces of them, but between this and Basra they are few. That is true, as Allah hears me!"

As a matter of precaution the chief was handed over to one of the sowars (Indian troopers) as soon as Geoff had repeated to his Commanding Officer what had been stated.

"Then I think we will make short work of those beggars in front of us," said the latter abruptly, as he swung himself into his saddle. "A brush at this stage of the proceedings will liven the men up wonderfully, and will raise the spirits of the Expeditionary Force from India—not that their spirits can be called exactly low, or the men in any way down-hearted."

Setting off at a trot, one of the troops rode to the left of the eminence from which Geoff and his comrades had watched the enemy, while the other took a course to the right and galloped off into the desert. But an officer and a couple of sowars were left on the eminence itself, from which point of vantage they could keep a close watch on the Arab horsemen.

It was perhaps half an hour later that the two troops, separated till then by quite a wide stretch of desert, and hidden entirely from one another and from the enemy by that long, low eminence, converged upon one another and rode out into the open. A careful advance near the bank of the river, where the palms hid them, and the fact that the attention of the Arab horsemen was fixed for the most part on the signallers and their officer left on the eminence, had allowed one troop to get within striking distance of the enemy. Then they suddenly debouched from the trees, and, trotting out into the desert, formed up for a charge; almost at the same moment a cloud of dust far away in the open showed them the position of the second troop, which, riding faster, had got almost beyond the position held by the Arabs. In fact, a rapid movement might enclose the enemy between the two troops, and in any case this menace from two points at once threw them into confusion; shouts were heard from the Arabs, while at once loud reports burst from their ranks, all manner of weapons being discharged at the Indian horsemen. To these was added the sharp, clear-cut snap of modern rifles, with which the Turkish infantry were armed. Then a trumpet blared in the distance, and that cloud of dust suddenly grew bigger, grew bigger and wider, and stretched out till it covered quite a large area. The troop close down by the river, which had just emerged from the trees, cantered out now till six feet of space separated the horsemen.

Then the pennons at the tips of the lances waved, a sharp order snapped down the ranks, and in a trice the lances were lowered. That trumpet blaring in the distance had set every horse in this other troop curveting and prancing, and now, as a note came from their own trumpeter, the horses were off, the men leaning low down in their saddles, their eyes glued on the enemy, their knees gripping their horses, and their lances pointed well out before them.

What a shout those Indian sowars gave! Their comrades coming from the opposite direction answered with a shrill yell of triumph, and then, like a flash, the two troops were launched against the enemy.

Converging as they came, till there were perhaps only some four or five hundred yards between the flanks of each of the troops, the horsemen plunged into the midst of the Arabs. Here and there they had left a horse rolling on the sand behind them, and there was more than one animal without a rider as they got close to the enemy; but nothing stopped the Indians, neither the shouts nor the bullets of the Arabs. With a crash they were in at them, thrusting right and left, riding them down, riding over them, and then it was over. What was left of those Arab horsemen scattered and fled in every direction, leaving the Indian Horse conquerors.

As for Geoff, his fingers trembled as he pulled Sultan in and dropped from his saddle.

"My word," exclaimed Daglish, offering him his cigarette case with a hand which jerked and wobbled badly, "but that was something! If that's war — the sort of war we're likely to have in Mesopotamia — then the more of it we have the merrier. Come here, Keith! I want to know what yarn you've been pitching to our Commander? You've been fibbing, eh? I asked him as we were trotting along through the palm-trees what report you had given. You said nothing about that flare-up with the Arab chief, about the bullets you were idiot enough to wait for, and about the way you captured him. My boy, there's a lively time coming!"

CHAPTER V

News of the Enemy

When the youthful and enthusiastic, and, let us add, immaculately and smartly dressed Daglish of the Indian Horse declared with such gusto to Geoff Keith that there was a lively time coming, and that that young fellow was likely to hear more of the adventure that had befallen him so soon after his landing in Mesopotamia, he attained to only a portion of the truth, and hinted only in some small degree at what our hero was to put up with. Like a flash the tale of his meeting with the Arab chief went round the camp after the return of the Indian Horse, and not even that exhilarating and most dashing charge could swamp the details.

"Wanted at Head-quarters, sir! Colonel – – gave me horders to find you at once. Pressing, sir! Ve-e-ery pressing, sir!" said a British "Tommy", as he discovered Geoff in the act of leaving the horse lines, where Sultan had been picketed.

It was always a habit of Geoff's—as it is of every good horseman who possesses a fine animal, and is fond of it—to make it a custom and rule to see to the comforts of his mount before sitting down to eat and drink. Thus, as Geoff came striding away from beneath the palms where the Indian cavalry had picketed their horses, and where the officers' mounts were made fast to a long picketing-rope close beside them, he came face to face with this British "Tommy"; in fact, the man barred his way to the ship still unloading at the river bank, and arrested his further progress. A big, brawny chap, he was sweltering in the moist heat of Mesopotamia, with the perspiration pouring from his forehead and down both cheeks. His thin khaki-twill jacket was sticking to his manly chest in many parts, and showed a number of moist patches. From under his sun-helmet a pair of shrewd, sharp eyes peered at this young officer—the tale of whose adventures had reached the orderly's ears—while a fierce and somewhat grizzled moustache—for the man was an old soldier, who had seen many days' service in India—projected on either side of the chin-strap which secured the helmet. In the smartest possible manner he came to attention, and, shouldering his rifle, saluted briskly.

"Horders, very speshul, sir," he said, his eyes twinkling; and then to himself, and almost aloud — for this gallant fellow had a way of addressing his remarks to no one in particular, and his thoughts to the open: "Lor'! Bless me 'art! If he ain't no more'n a baby, just a mere shaver; and they tells me he speaks this 'ere lingo like a good 'un. Lingo, do they call it? Just a norrible mess o' words, that's what I says, and yer can't make not one of 'em understand. Why, bless me soul! I sees an old chap with coal-black eyes, an' a beard as white as snow, a-sittin' in a doorway o' one of the things round 'ere they calls 'uts — 'uts, is they? My word! My uncle! — as some of these 'ere orficer men calls it — just 'oles I call 'em. 'Uts! And there was that there man — more like a monkey he looked — and though I shouted at 'im, not a word could he understand, nor me the lingo he flung back at me. I should say — — "

Geoff's rather short and abrupt "Well?" brought the good fellow's ruminating to a sudden ending; he coughed loudly to clear his voice, and those sharp eyes of his again twinkled.

"Bless my 'art! I was a-wanderin'," he told himself; and then aloud: "Horders, speshul, sir. Colonel — —, sir, said I was to find you at once, and you was to report at Head-quarters immediately. Shall I dismiss, sir?"

"Please," Geoff told him, and stood watching the man and pondering — pondering not so much as to the reason for this order and the nature of the interview before him as to the reason which had produced what he was sure was a twinkling in the eyes of the man who had brought the message.

"Confound the fellow!" he was saying. "I'm sure he had a little joke on of his own, and was almost laughing; and I've seen him before somewhere. Now where?"

In his turn, he too was cut short abruptly, and enjoined to remember his orders, and not to allow himself to indulge in a species of "brown study".

For if that gallant soldier had been duly and correctly dismissed, he was still and always a soldier, a punctilious fellow, who throughout long years had never failed to carry out the orders of a superior, and who, now that he had conveyed such an order to an officer, considered it only his mere duty to see that that young officer acted on the order promptly. He was standing near at hand, his rifle still at his shoulder, his head thrown back, those eyes of his watching Geoff shrewdly.

"Horders, speshul, sir," he muttered in guttural tones, which just managed to reach our hero. "Beg pardon, sir — — "

But Geoff had already come to his senses again, and went striding off to the Head-quarters hut, with the orderly following closely. There he found himself confronted just outside the hut, and beneath a tope of palms which threw its grateful shade above some chairs placed there for the Staff of the expedition, by one of the senior Staff Officers.

"Ha, Keith!" he said genially enough. "Sit down, my boy, and have a cigarette. Now tell me all about it. By the way, that has been a very pretty little affair, that rounding up of those Arab horsemen and the charge of the troops we sent out, a very gallant little bit of business, and I shouldn't wonder if it brought credit to the officer in command. But, as I am chiefly concerned with the Intelligence Service, I'll leave that alone for the moment and get you to tell me of the news you obtained from your prisoner. That reminds me. Young Daglish has been telling us a fine tale. Very well done, Keith! Very well done indeed! Though I doubt the wisdom of an officer on special service — as you happen to be just now — making himself the open, unabashed target for Turkish bullets. Take the enemy fire like a soldier when you have to, but don't seek it out; don't look for points or for places where you can expose yourself. In other words, don't be reckless, or, to quote our friend Daglish again, don't 'behave like a careless idiot!' Now then, having said my say, let us get on with our particular business."

Very quickly Geoff gave him all the information he had been able to extract from the captured chief, and then, at a suggestion from the officer, the Arab was sent for, and presently appeared with an escort of sowars about him.

"If I may say so, sir," said Geoff, "I think we shall do far better by showing our trust in this prisoner and dismissing his escort. I do not assert that an Arab is to be trusted. As a general rule, speaking of those in Mesopotamia, he is certainly not; he will join the cause of the highest bidder, or he will leave any sinking ship if only he can discover the danger in which he is standing soon enough. But by making this man realize that we are not a sinking ship, and that his interests are best served by serving us, we shall be able to get from him not only information which he already has, but might even employ him to obtain further facts of importance. For that a liberal reward, to be paid some months hence, should be promised."

For a little while the Staff Officer regarded the chief sternly, and yet with interest. No Englishman could look at such man and fail to find in him much to attract attention. For, as we have said before, this Arab chief was an exceedingly fine specimen of Arab humanity. Tall and straight and austere-looking in his native costume, his features were refined and handsome. There was nothing of the negroid type about him; and indeed this man, dressed in European costume, might have made his appearance in the most exclusive parts of London, and one could guess that his features, his delicately shaped hands, his well-kept nails, his manners, indeed, would have rendered him by no means inferior to his fellows. The chief returned the officer's frank gaze with one just as frank, with one distinctly haughty, with a glance which told of courage, and pride, and also determination.

"Dismiss the escort," commanded the officer sharply, addressing the Indian officer in charge of them; "let them rest in the shade at the back of the Head-quarters hut. Now, Chief," he said, smiling at the captive, "sit down. Keith, ask him to make himself comfortable."

"The officer here wishes you to feel that you are a friend and not a captive," said Geoff at once, taking upon himself the liberty of somewhat enlarging upon his senior's pronouncement. "He invites you to sit down with us, and, as a chief of honour, he knows that by doing so you give your word that you will not attempt to escape, and that what shall be spoken between us will be the truth, and the truth only."

A beaming smile broke over the face of the chief instantly, and he nodded in friendly fashion to both officers; then, pulling a chair nearer, he sat down with an easy grace which proved beyond fear of refutation that if indeed he were a child of the desert, yet he had some knowledge of Western customs, and unlike his fellows was accustomed to a chair, and appreciated the comfort to be obtained by the use of it.

"My master," he told Geoff, "doubtless His Highness who sits there with us is a great chief in your country, and is one whose words should be honourably listened to. If he says that he desires Suliman as a friend rather than as a captive, and that at a time when he discovers this same Suliman a mere harmless and helpless prisoner, then, indeed, is he a man of great honour and liberality. And what should I say? I, who am a helpless, harmless captive, who am bid to sit as friend before him, and who thereby assents to join your forces. My master, from this day forward I am your man, sworn to your service, sworn to do my utmost for the British. If I depart from this saying, if it should happen that in later days I break my oath, then, indeed, may I be proclaimed to be a faithless scoundrel, one deserving of instant execution. My master, as a friend I sit before you, and I thank you for this great concession."

For more than an hour the three sat there in the shadow of the palms, Geoff acting as interpreter; and slowly, and little by little, as the Intelligence Officer asked questions which would never have occurred to Geoff, information of considerable value was extracted from the chief. Indeed, the latter was undoubtedly greatly delighted at the treatment afforded him — for to be kept a close captive had seemed to him inevitable. And partly by the judicious offer of a handsome reward—a small portion of which was to be paid within a month's time, so soon as he had produced results, and the remainder when the war was finished—together with the promise of certain allowances whilst he was with the British Expeditionary Force in Mesopotamia, the chief was led to give a most willing assent to aid his captors further.

"More than that, my master," he said eagerly enough, addressing Geoff while he looked across at the Staff Officer, "I can make even greater promises; for have you not honoured me much by thus making a friend of me rather than a captive? Listen, then! And as Allah hears us, treat this not as a promise, but as a plan to be carried out without doubt and of a certainty. You have treated me handsomely, and have made promises which will give me wealth if I but live to earn it. See, these men about me, these Indian horsemen, these British soldiers, these native troops whom you have brought across the water to fight the Turk and the Sultan and those white men—those unbelievers—who have joined your enemy! You pay those soldiers of yours, doubtless, my master; your British king has gold wherewith to fill their pockets?"

"Certainly, Chief," Geoff told him promptly. "Each man draws his regular pay and allowances. Every one of the soldiers you see here is a free man— free to join the army or not, just as he likes. But, once he has joined, he is paid just as a man who may work as a servant in one of your camps is paid, for the British king forces service upon no man."

"Then listen further, my master. There are in my tribe perhaps a thousand men, all well found with horses, all with great knowledge of this country, and not one of whom would fail to fight if the opportunity came to him. Give them money, pay them the same amount that you pay these Indian soldiers, and find them in certain necessaries and in ammunition. Promise this, and trust your slave still further. For then he will ride out to them, and if they be not willing to return with him and join forces with these soldiers, he himself will return—whether they wish it or not—and will render himself up again to you. My master, I am a man of honour, and this thing I will do, as Allah hears me."

The suggestion made by the captured chief was one which, naturally enough, needed much consideration, and, also, the consent of higher authority; yet, so excellent did the plan seem, and so clearly was Geoff able to put it before the Intelligence Officer, that by the following morning it was adopted, and, a good horse having been handed to the chief, and weapons also, he was allowed to ride out of the camp in search of his followers.

"Of course we may, or we may not, see him back," said the Staff Officer somewhat sceptically. "You tell me, Keith, that Arabs are not to be trusted, and that is a tale I have heard often enough before. Yet I have little doubt that many of them are just as trustworthy as people in our country."

"Just!" Geoff agreed with him promptly, if not warmly, for during his short residence in Mesopotamia, when he had been with Major Joe Douglas, he had met with, and lived with, more than one tribe of Arabs, with whom he had become more than usually friendly. Moreover, he had known them to be absolutely trustworthy; and though, during this coming conflict, some might already have sided with the Turks—who were their nominal rulers—and though, as the campaign went on, it might happen that they would leave that service and join the British—for such is a habit of nomadic Arab tribes—yet that did not prove them to be utterly devoid of trust or of honour.

"If I know a man at all, sir," he said respectfully, "I know this chief, whom I was instrumental in capturing. He has given us his word of honour, and he has called upon Allah to witness the words which he has spoken. That will compel him to carry out his promises whether he wills it or not; and should it happen that his followers arrest him, and do their utmost to prevent his return, yet I feel sure that he will make every effort to come back to us."

As a matter of fact, some three days later, when the embarkation of the British Expeditionary Force was completed, and the troops had settled down in their camps beside the river, the outposts—placed well beyond the encampment—reported a large column of horsemen approaching. The information was brought to Head-quarters, and within five minutes of its arrival that same Intelligence Officer had sent a hurried message to our hero.

"Get on your horse at once, Keith," he told him, "and come along with me. This force approaching may be our friend the chief bringing in his followers or it may be an enemy force come to try conclusions with us. If I happened to be an officer in the Indian Horse I rather think I should hope for the latter, for those boys are dying for more fighting. As it is, I trust that it will be the chief, and that he'll bring with him a lot of useful fellows. Horsemen used to the country and to the tricks of the Turks will be a valuable acquisition, and we shall be able to make the most of them."

Quickly mounting the fretful Sultan, Geoff was ready within a few minutes, and, together with the Intelligence Officer, made rapid progress to the outposts. Then, fixing his glasses to his eyes, he carefully scrutinized the force approaching across the desert. A tall figure in flowing robes, riding at their head, was without doubt the chief who had given them his promise, and, having reported this fact to the Intelligence Officer, the two of them rode out to meet the cavalcade approaching. Then they led them back into the camp, and within an hour the Arabs had settled down as if they had never been anything else but a portion of the British Expeditionary Force destined to advance so far up the River Tigris.

Two days later the camp broke up, and, with a naval flotilla steaming beside them up the river, they marched on Basra, which town they occupied, after meeting with only small resistance. They were now approaching the confluence of the Rivers Tigris and Euphrates, and were, indeed, within striking distance of that portion of the desert which, in days long gone by, was known as the Garden of Eden, where the toil of the inhabitants then living in those parts had converted what may have been a desert in their earlier days into a smiling garden the fame of which has descended through the ages. Yet now it was a desert, a sandy, gravelly stretch of dried-up, waterless, and inhospitable desert, peopled but sparsely, and for the most part only along the actual banks of the river, where the moisture, finding its way into the soil on either side, kept it fertile, and where grew a thick belt of palms, descending past Basra to the open sea. There were marshes, too, for the River Euphrates in particular, which traverses a flat country, has changed its course through the ages on numerous occasions. Some particular course may remain open for a considerable period, and have the appearance of being the main channel, yet always there are overflows, and often enough such a main channel is silted up with the dirt and debris coming from higher parts of the desert; then the water, bursting over the low banks, and particularly the southern bank, has gouged some other channel for itself, or has widened out into broad stretches of marsh—perhaps only two feet in depth—leaving no semblance of the river channel.

"It's there, amongst the marshes, that the Turks lie hidden," the chief told Geoff that evening. "Of their numbers and of their exact positions I know nothing, yet the rumour has reached me that they are there, and that soon they will attempt to come in behind the British and attack them. It were well, my master, if some of those ships that I see floating upon the water, and in particular some of the smaller ones, were sent into the marshes. There are channels deep enough to take them, and if careful search were made it may be that the Turkish enemy would be discovered."

Geoff was not such a young soldier that he could not at once perceive the importance of the information just conveyed to him. With the knowledge he already had of Mesopotamia, he had been able to inform his friend on the Staff that, above the town of Basra, wide stretches of marsh would be discovered, which at certain seasons of the year were greatly extended by the heavy rains which fell in that part of the world. But if residence in Mesopotamia had given him some idea of the course of the rivers, of the towns and villages dotted here and there, and of the numerous peoples who inhabited that region, he could not, naturally enough, be expected to know where the Turks had disposed their forces on the outbreak of this gigantic war. Some had undoubtedly been posted towards the mouth of the Shatt-el-Arab, for had not the Indian horse already had a lively brush with them? But where were the others? Higher up the river, preparing their defences and waiting for the onward march of the British forces, or sneaking in those marshes to the west of them, which spread themselves along the broken and irregular course of the River Euphrates, from a point perhaps fifty miles away to the spot where the river joined with the main channel of the Tigris? And if they were there, hidden in the swamps, perhaps camping on some piece of ground elevated sufficiently to give them a dry footing, then indeed they would be a menace to the safety of the forces invading the country. They might march down along the edge of the swampy ground, or if provided with native boats, known as bellums, might steal over the shallow waters and cut off the retreat of Geoff and his comrades.

"Chief," he said suddenly, "you know this marsh land, perhaps, and you would help us to discover these enemies?"

"My master, an Arab is a man of the desert, a man who is happiest when far away in the open, or when mounted upon his horse, with leagues of sandy soil before him. We are not given to venturing upon the water, and thus it follows that I am ignorant of these marshes, and could be of little service. But listen, my master! There is one within this town of Basra who could assist you. A man known to me – a native of these parts, of uncertain nationality. He is but a poor fisherman; and if His Highness, whom I have met, cares to arrest him, he has then but to command and the man will carry out his bidding."

"And suppose – for I must tell you, Chief, that we of Great Britain do not force our orders upon helpless and poor people – supposing a reward is offered to this man. What then?" asked Geoff.

"Then, indeed, you may count upon his assistance, his ready assistance," said the chief, "and for all I know he might be willing enough to carry out the work because of his hatred of the Turks. Yes, my master, they are hated in this part of the world. Though they molest the Arabs but little, and indeed fear us greatly, for we are swift to move from spot to spot, and can strike a blow and be gone in an instant, yet to those who live their lives on the bank of the river, where the Turks can reach them easily because of their boats, to these they are often harsh and cruel, taxing them heavily, and treating them as slaves, or little better."

Geoff gave himself a few moments in which to deliberate, and then, asking the chief to accompany him to Head-quarters, he sent in a message to the Intelligence Officer who has already been introduced to our readers. To him he promptly gave full information of the marshes, and of the rumoured Turkish forces lying hidden in them. It was apparent at once that this Staff Officer considered the news of the utmost importance; for, bidding Geoff stay outside the house taken over by the General, he disappeared inside, and remained there for quite a considerable period. When he came out again, it was clear from the expression on his face that he had come to some decision.

"Those Turks must be found, and routed," he told Geoff. "And of course we shall be glad to take advantage of the services of the native whom the chief has mentioned to you. That means that you must go along too, Keith, for otherwise there will be the language difficulty. Orders will be given to the naval contingent. There are some motor launches with them, and I imagine that one of them should be able to make its way through the marshes. In fact, the expedition will have to be a naval one almost entirely, with you and this native guide accompanying."

Geoff coughed discreetly to attract the Staff Officer's attention, for of a sudden a brilliant thought had struck him. He was thinking of his chum Philip, who had almost "lived in his pocket" these last few days, and who eagerly waited a summons to accompany our hero.

"You are the luckiest beggar I ever came across!" he had told Geoff when he had heartily congratulated him upon his capture of the Arab chief. "Any other fellow would have been shot down by those Turkish bullets, which Daglish says you were idiot enough to stand up and face—but I'll be honest, though, and add that Daglish, though he said at first you were an idiot, said afterwards that he admired your pluck, and wondered whether he'd have been as cool if he'd been in your place. But we're not talking about Daglish, we're talking about you and myself, and don't forget that I come into the discussion. What I want to impress upon you is the decided need you have of assistance. You can't go off on jaunts like that without having another fellow to look after you. Supposing one of those Turkish bullets had hit you after all, what then?"

He stood in front of Geoff and watched him expectantly.

"What then!" repeated Geoff, smiling at the impulsiveness of his chum.

"What then!" cried Philip indignantly. "Why! Well, supposing I'd been there I could have carried you off and could have stood my ground, and captured that chief when he got out to us. But there you are, the thing's over now, and what you've got to do is to look out for trouble in the future. Geoff, you want a fellow alongside of you, a friend, one you can confide in, one ready to assist you at any moment. I'm that friend; and don't you forget it, my boy, or else there'll be ructions."

Geoff did not forget it, for nothing in the world would have pleased him better than to have his old friend along with him. It was nice, and exciting, indeed, to find himself in the company of other officers—such as Daglish and those of the Indian troops who had attacked the Arab horsemen—but, after all, a friend is a friend all the world over; and if Philip had been there, he told himself, Why! He would certainly have enjoyed the whole adventure more thoroughly. And here was a new adventure proposed by this Staff Officer. He, Geoff, was to go off with some of the naval contingent, and was to penetrate into that huge stretch of marshland lying along the course of the Euphrates. Anything might happen! Turks were rumoured to be there, and if they were it was more than likely that there would be a sort of guerrilla fighting. What chances the thing presented! And how jolly to have Philip along with him. He coughed again discreetly, yet in such a way that the Staff Officer glanced at him swiftly and inquisitively.

"Eh?" he asked, smiling. "You— —"

"I rather thought, sir," said Geoff diffidently, "that if I could have another officer—an infantry officer, I mean, sir—along with me, it might be some assistance. I— —"

"In fact," laughed the Staff Officer, "you have one particular friend, and would be glad to have him ordered to join you with this expedition. Well, I don't know that there is any particular objection," he continued, to Geoff's huge relief and enjoyment. "A smart young officer might be of great assistance, and in any case he'd be very good company. What's the name, Keith?"

Geoff gave it with suspicious promptness, and the Staff Officer jotted it down in his notebook.

"Then you'd better both of you get ready," he told Geoff. "It'll take the navy a little time to make their preparations, but they are not the boys to sit still and think too long, particularly when an expedition is on foot which promises excitement. I imagine they will work most of the night, and by to-morrow morning early they will be ready to steam off into the marshes. In the meanwhile you had better hunt up this native that the chief has mentioned, and interview him. Offer him a reasonable reward, to be paid after the successful termination of the business."

By nightfall Geoff had fully carried out the instructions given him, and, having visited the naval contingent, learned that a small motor-launch would be fully armed and provisioned, and ready to set off at the first streak of dawn on the following morning. Also, he had interviewed his chum Philip, whose delight and enthusiasm were almost overwhelming.

They were up shortly after two o'clock in the morning, and, having eaten a hearty breakfast, and armed themselves with rifles and revolvers, they stole down to the landing-place, where the motor-boat was to wait them.

"Aboard there!" Geoff hailed, for it was still quite dark, and it was impossible to make out even the outline of the boat.

"Ahoy!" a voice came back. "Who's that?"

"Two officers waiting to come aboard. Have you got that native there yet?" asked Geoff, as an oar splashed in the water and the boat was rowed in close to the bank of the river.

"Aboard this hour or more," came the hearty answer. "Easy does it, now, or you'll be capsizing us! There we are, two officers aboard, and all ready!"

"Push her off, Cox; let her go!"

There was a sound of machinery and the clack of valves as the engine was set going; then the tiny motor-boat trembled as the propeller rotated. A moment later she was stealing out across the river, still hidden in the darkness, and, having traversed a long stretch of water, approached the opposite bank, where the marshes empty themselves into the river. The daylight was just coming, and for a while they lay to, so that the native guide could be sure of their position. Then a sharp order was given, the propeller thrashed the water again, and in a little while they were threading their way amidst a mass of reeds and islands of oozing mud, which formed the eastern boundary of the marshes. In less than five minutes they were entirely lost to view, and were launched on an expedition which was to prove as interesting as it was exciting.

CHAPTER VI

An Exploring-party

"And now, supposing we lay to a little and think about some breakfast? Not a bad idea that, eh?" exclaimed a cheery individual, upon whose brawny figure Geoff's eyes had many a time been fixed during the half-hour or more which had elapsed since the motor-boat had stolen so silently and secretly from the main channel of the Shatt-el-Arab into the wastes bordering the River Euphrates, and who seemed to be in command of the expedition.

He was a moderately tall, broad-shouldered, heavily-built, red-faced, and exceedingly—not to say delightfully—healthy-looking specimen of sailor humanity. His thin khaki-twill garments hung loosely about him—for if young subalterns, like Philip and Geoff, must needs have their clothes for active service cut almost as smartly as for residence in London, there were others, older than they—wiser, let us dare to venture—who, with much experience behind them, preferred comfort to elegance, and ease to any degree of smartness. Underneath the helmet which clothed the head of this naval officer was a broad and very rubicund face—as we have already mentioned—a strong, open, and peculiarly prepossessing figure-head, which was seamed and lined, partly by the action of the sun, but more by the almost constant smiles of the owner.

"Just shut down that throttle, Marsden," he called cheerily to the man operating the engine; and then to one of the sailors right for'ard: "You can let go that anchor, Clark. Now, boys, we'll pipe down to a meal and a smoke of tobacco, for there's no violent hurry. Glad to meet you two young officers. I'm Commander Houston, lately of H.M.S. — —, the ship the Admiralty authorities in Whitehall insisted on keeping in the Persian Gulf—a nasty sort of a place that Persian Gulf, I can tell you. Aboard-ship life in those parts is worse than any 'hole in Calcutta', and when the hot weather comes, phew! it's a wonder that a white man survives, and to me it's a miracle that I remain so robust and stout, when you'd expect me to get as thin as a lath, and waste away rapidly."

Waste away indeed! No one who cared to look at the jovial Commander Houston would ever imagine that to be possible, to have been probable even at any stage in his career. For the man was heavily built, as we have said, his bones well covered with muscle, and the latter clad with an amount of fat which made his figure rather rounder than was desirable. Geoff smiled back at him, while Philip unbent and let himself go in a moment. They couldn't help themselves, for the Commander made them feel at ease almost immediately. His smiling crew, the oil-stained individual who worked his engine, the Cox who sat right aft with the tiller, every one of them smiled, as if happy to be in his company.

"Looks jolly promising," Philip told his chum sotto voce, "It never occurred to me before that in joining this expedition we might have found ourselves under a high and mighty sort of fellow, who would order us about like dirt, just because we're junior subalterns. Ahem! Breakfast? Rather!"

"And to think that we had a meal just before we left our side of the river," said Geoff; "but I'm hungry enough, and ready for anything."

By now the Cox had gone for'ard, where the tall, raw-boned, grey-bearded native—whom Geoff had interviewed on the previous day, and who was said to have an intimate knowledge of the marshes—had now joined them. The Commander himself came aft from the central cabin, in which he had been stationed, and sat himself down near the two young infantry officers, and, opening a locker, pulled out a basket of provisions.

"The man who wants to get on in the world, and carry out a job successfully, must look after his health whatever happens," he smiled at them. "So, having started this expedition successfully, and slipped into the marshes with, I feel sure, no one being the wiser, we can look after the inner man before proceeding farther. Which one of you young officers happens to be known as Geoffrey Keith?"

"Guilty, sir!" Geoff told him, with a laugh. "I am the individual."

"Oh!"

At once our hero felt himself being surveyed with that same sort of polite, yet searching scrutiny which the General and his Staff Officers had directed upon him. Perhaps it is a habit of the Services; more likely it is a habit engendered in men placed in a position of command, who wish, in the space of a few seconds—seeing that often enough there is no longer for the purpose—to sum up those who are to serve with them, those upon whom they may have to call for action, and to assure themselves at the very commencement that they are to be fully relied upon.

"Oh!" he said at last, as he dived into his basket and produced a Thermos bottle, some cups, and a paper parcel. "Young enough, at any rate, Keith, but they tell me not too young to stand fire. Ah! Ah! Tales do spread, don't they? Never saw such people as the army for gossiping! I give you my word that, long before this expedition was mooted, I knew all about a fellow with a thundering fine Arab who had gone out and captured an Arab chief. That's you, eh, Keith?"

It was hopeless for Geoff to attempt to hide his modesty, for the very flush which rose to his cheeks seemed to raise the mirth of this naval officer. He glanced sideways at Geoff as he chuckled loudly, and then handed him a ponderous sandwich and a cup of steaming coffee.

"And the other young officer?" he asked between his own mouthfuls.

"Philip Denman, at your service," laughed the owner of that name, entering into the fun of the moment. "You don't happen to have heard any sort of report about that officer, do you, sir? That is to say, anything against his character, I hope."

"Well, not at present," the Commander laughed back at him, enjoying the joke immensely. "Nothing at present. But you never know! For before we are out of this business there may be lots of opportunities for reports, good and bad and indifferent. But just listen to this: I feel like a schoolboy, for

I'm off on a jaunt, after being tied up aboard ship for two months and more. This expedition ought to be like a holiday; and, of course, if we happen to run into the Turks and have a little affair of our own, why, who knows? a poor chap who has been condemned for more than a year past to steam up and down the Persian Gulf may be promoted to something better. Now, Keith, another sandwich. No? Well, well, save it up till later. A pipe then? Oh, you don't smoke pipes! Then turn on your own particular brand of cigarettes while I light my pipe. And now let's have a sort of council of war. I ought to explain that I know precious little about this business. I have been told that these marshes extend for perhaps fifty miles, and even more, due west from the Shatt-el-Arab, and running a little north as they go westward; in fact, following and embracing the course of the River Euphrates. Turks are said to be hiding somewhere about in the marshes, and our job is to find 'em and rout 'em out if we can, and, if not, to bring back information."

He looked at Geoff inquisitively, and the latter nodded with energy.

"Quite so, sir!" he said. "We have brought a native along with us who knows the marshes."

"And a precious-looking old scoundrel he is too," laughed the Commander, turning his eyes towards the bows of the boat, where the native sat on his haunches amongst the sailors, consuming their rations with such energy that there was little doubt that they met entirely with his approval. "A precious-looking old scoundrel too," the Commander repeated; "but no doubt under that dusky skin of his there lies hidden something admirable. It seems to me, Keith, that the first thing for us to do, now that we have looked to the inner man, and have commenced to soothe our nerves with tobacco, is to cross-examine that old scarecrow, and find out something of what he knows about the marshes. I understand that that is your particular job, seeing that you are something of a linguist."

Geoff flushed. It made him quite nervous when people referred to his linguistic accomplishments, and more particularly so when the one who spoke was a merry naval officer who smiled quizzically at him as he asked his question. But a moment later Commander Houston was as serious as he could be, and, stretching out a friendly hand, gripped Geoff's shoulder.

"Only my fun!" he said. "Look here, Keith, there's nothing for you to be ashamed of in the fact that you can talk these Eastern languages. My word! I wish I could! For it would be worth quite a handsome little addition to my daily pay—and that to a Commander in the Royal Navy is something always worth considering. Besides, think of the added interest it gives you in a campaign such as this is! How free it makes you! And what possibility it presents of splendid adventure! Now I wouldn't mind guessing that if you were surrounded by the enemy, and were, as it were, blockaded in one of their towns, you would be quite capable of turning out as a Turk, provided you could get the disguise, and of giving them the slip. How's that, eh?"

Geoff admitted the possibility with a cheery laugh, for no one could be serious when Commander Houston was addressing him.

"I've done it already, sir," he told him, with a grin. "You see, Major Douglas—who's an Indian 'political', and who happens to be my guardian—brought me to Mesopotamia some while ago, and we went right into the heart of the country. The Major knows all sorts of Arabs and other people, and it's part of his job—or was, at any rate, in peace times—to find out everything that was going on; what the Turks were doing, what the Arabs thought of them, and how the various nationalities lived."

"Half a minute!" smiled the Commander. "What about the Germans?"

"Germans! Of course," admitted Geoff, "they were to be met with in all sorts of odd corners, and conducting every sort of extraordinary business. My suspicion is that their businesses, on many occasions, were absolutely fictitious; in fact, they had no real business in many cases, and were simply agents of the German Government sent into the country to worm out the secrets of the Turks, and more particularly to find out precisely what opportunities there were for trade, and what portion of it the British had secured."

"Hear! Hear!" echoed the Commander. "You can quite understand that being ordered to the Persian Gulf, and having to steam up and down that extremely uninteresting, not to say unhealthy part, left a man plenty of time for ruminating, for discussing matters in general, and for learning in particular something of what was happening in this portion of Turkey and in Persia. A fellow couldn't steam up to Basra — as we did now and again in one of our pinnaces — without knocking up against Germans — fat Germans, thin Germans, ugly Germans (lots of ugly ones, my boy) — Germans who were conducting some sort of trade, and who appeared at first sight to be the most harmless and almost the most helpless people under the sun. But that's your wily German all over!

"I remember one particular individual — a big, fat, jovial fellow — Von something or other, I've forgotten his name, except that it was a regular 'jaw-cracker'. Von Schmidt let's call him for the moment. A nicer chap to meet you couldn't wish for, that is, just at the beginning. I remember that he was trying to get together a business in dates. His sole object in life seemed to be that of bribing Arabs to bring in camel-loads of dates, and to deposit them in an old hut which he had hired just on the outskirts of Basra; and now and again he sent off a barge full of these same dates, consigning them to some place in Europe. But it was not his real business, my boy! And I found that out quite by accident. For, happening to get stranded one evening when darkness had fallen, and in the midst of a violent rain-storm, I claimed shelter from him — for there was a light in the window of his house. It was blowing big guns just then, and I suppose he didn't hear the rap I gave on the door. As a matter of fact, he was in his bedroom, which was at the back of the building. It wasn't the sort of time when one waits for a summons, for the rain was pouring down in torrents, as I told you, so I just pushed the door open and went into the main room of the building, and, shutting the door, shouted for him. Even then he didn't hear, so that I had time to take a good look round, and couldn't help seeing that the table in the centre of the room was piled with papers, and that maps—maps of Mesopotamia, maps of the Persian Gulf—diagrams showing the 'pipe-line', which brings our oil from Persia, and lists of Arab tribes, against which was placed a note in German, which showed that they were to be considered friendly, were spread out over the remaining portion of the table. You see," he added, with a chuckle, "I know a little German. Not much, you know, but just sufficient to read it. I can't tell you now all about those papers, and of course it isn't quite the thing for a man to enter the house of an acquaintance and read his private correspondence. It isn't 'cricket', of course, you know, and no Britisher does it; but accidents will happen, and that night it so fell out that my eyes were unwittingly opened: the fat, pleasant, jovial Von what's-his-name was undoubtedly a German Government agent."

Geoff nodded briskly, for he and Major Douglas had had many an experience with German agents in Mesopotamia.

"I don't profess to know all about it, sir," he told the Commander, "but the Major was very chary of the Germans he met, and often told me that Germany undoubtedly had her eyes on Asiatic Turkey, and was preparing the ground for some future occasion. But you were saying that I could dress up as a Turk and move about amongst them. I've done it, sir! You must understand that the Germans in Mesopotamia were very jealous of the Major, they not only suspected him to be a British agent, but knew what his mission was in the country, and for that reason set a watch on him. They bribed men to follow us, and put the Turks on our tracks, so that had we not been very quick and very wide awake we should have learned nothing—that is to say, the Major would have learned nothing—for the British Government. We had to give the Germans and the Turks the slip, and we did it, time and again, by adopting a disguise and moving off amongst the people. But about this native, sir; you suggested that he should be cross-examined."

"That's it!" cried the Commander, filling his pipe again. "Call the old boy up! 'Pon my word, now that one looks at him, he's quite a handsome scoundrel!"

By then the men for'ard, and the native whom they had been entertaining, had finished their meal, and, like their officer, were enjoying a quiet smoke before pushing onward. Sailor-like, too, they were endeavouring to their utmost to make themselves pleasant to their passenger. It was quite amusing to watch a big, burly sailor discoursing eloquently to the native and listening intently; Geoff and Philip and their Commanding Officer overheard some of this conversation.

"Look 'ere, old soul," they heard the A.B. exclaim in the most friendly fashion, while he tapped the native on his bare chest, "what's the use of this 'ere place at all? This 'ere Mesopotamia? What's the good of a country that's all sand and grit, with no good and decent water about it? Now, I could tell you of a country that's worth seeing! Know England, my lad?"

You would have thought the native was perfectly acquainted with every portion of Great Britain, for he positively shook with merriment, and grinned a ghastly grin at the sailor. Then, as if to make the point quite certain, he gave vent to a volume of guttural sounds, snapping his fingers, grinning and grimacing, till the sailor brought him to a sudden stop by tapping his chest again with one of his ponderous fingers.

"Just so, mate," he said as he puffed a cloud of smoke above the native's head. "Just so, old soul. But 'arf-a-mo'!"

The burly sailor extracted from his mouth a short black "clay" with a hand which was so big and horny that it instantly attracted attention, and having puffed another huge cloud of smoke just past the ear of the giggling native, he tapped him on the chest again, with a peremptory and extremely firm finger, while he wagged his head sideways.

"'Arf — a — mo', my beauty!" he said, while his comrades grinned their appreciation of him. "What's this 'ere you're a-sayin'? Sounds to me like so much gibberish, as if you was just a-cussin', and a-cussin' 'ard too. What's it all about, old soul? Why not speak good, decent, honest English?"

No doubt the native had as little idea of what the sailor was saying to him as that latter had of the dusky native's own remarks, yet the smiling faces round him, the friendly attitude of all, and that particularly friendly tap he was still receiving on his chest seemed to fill him with the utmost merriment. He positively bubbled over and gurgled with amusement, and grimaced till the honest sailor turned a face of good-humoured disgust towards his comrades.

"Lor'," he exclaimed, "if one had to live alongside a chap like this all one's born days! But he can't help it! He means well, you can see that, can't you? 'Ere, Jim, flick out that packet of fakes you had this mornin' and let the chap try a whiff. Perhaps he ain't used to cigarettes, but we'll soon larn 'im!"

And "larn" him they did! For in a very little while the native was purring away in the most contented manner possible, grimacing and gesticulating towards the group of sailors who clustered about him in the bows of the tiny motor-driven vessel.

Meanwhile the Commander, and Geoff, and Philip were interested, if not highly amused, spectators; and it was only when the native had his cigarette fairly well going that the Commander coughed loudly so as to attract the attention of his men, and called to them.

"Now, my lads!" he said cheerily, for that was his habit with the men, and they loved him for it. "Now, my lads, pass along that old scarecrow!"

You should have seen the grin on the faces of his men as they heard him, and hastened to obey his orders; and it seemed natural enough that their spokesman of a few moments earlier should be the one to pass the request on to the native.

"'Ere, old soul!" he said to him, pleasantly enough, and yet with a ring of authority which the native noticed instantly, and with perhaps a rather firmer tap of the finger upon his naked chest. "'Ere, old soul, you're under orders! And just you pass yoursel aft, and no 'ankin' mind you, with the Commander! You'll just answer all his questions straight out, and tell him the truth, and nothing but the truth, s'welp me!"

If it had been left to the native to gather the meaning of these words he might have been still in the for'ard part of that motor-vessel, for, as the reader will have gathered already, not one single letter of the British alphabet, and not one single word of good, honest English did he understand. But sundry significant nods of the head, and winks, and pointings in the direction of the Commander told him what was wanted, and presently he came climbing over, passing round the edge of the cabin, his long, lanky legs bare, his feet unshod, the scantiest of native wrappings around him. Yet for all his semi-nakedness the man was one to look at twice; one rather to admire than to despise; a child, and a handsome child withal, of this curious desert country. Like the Arab chief whom Geoff had captured, he was a fine specimen of humanity, fully grown, big and expansive, yet with refined features, and possessed of small hands and feet which gave him rather an air of breeding. A closely-cropped beard, getting a little grey at the point of the chin, set off a face which was honest, firm and intelligent. Yet he was only a humble fisherman, this man, and although possessed of fine physique, and of handsome appearance, yet had reserved the utmost respect for his superiors. He bowed low as he reached the aft part of the tiny vessel, and, at a word from Geoff, crouched native-fashion at the feet of the three officers.

"Not such a scarecrow as I thought, after all," said the Commander. "Keith, tell him he can go on smoking, and let us cross-examine him. Ask him where he thinks the Turks are hiding?"

"Who knows, Excellency?" came the answer in a voice which was even and musical; "who can speak of anything for certain in these parts, where the waste of waters changes its outline every day and constantly. But there is a rumour that there are many of these proud and stiff-necked Turks hidden somewhere away in these marshes, and, if that be so—as indeed it may be, for though rumour was ever a lying jade, yet often enough there is some truth in her—then the Turks will not be in these parts, but farther up the river, where the waste of waters breaks away from patches of rising ground, and where camps may be located."

"Ask him how many days' journey from here?" asked the Commander, when Geoff had interpreted what the native had said. "We've enough fuel on board to take us, say, 200 miles, and if the marsh throughout is as it is here, with beds of reeds and mud sticking up in many places, and no doubt shoals where you least expect them, then progress will not be rapid, and we may be able to cover only ten miles a day. How many days, travelling at that rate, does he think it will require to bring us into the neighbourhood of the Turkish camp?"

The native wagged his head sagely when Geoff had asked him the question, and sat for a while staring out across the water at the nearest bank of reeds, now lit up and glistening in the glancing rays of the rising sun.

"Excellency," he said at last, "that is a question to ask a wizard; it is of a truth a riddle, a riddle which none but this waste of waters can answer at the moment. But it may be that the journey will not be such a long one, for though these marshes change so constantly there is yet a line, down which the River Euphrates pours its waters, which may be followed at speed without fear of drowning, and without meeting with these islands of mud and reeds which fill the marshes in other directions. If the Excellency desires, I will direct the boat to that line and convoy it westward. But there will come a time when we must depart from the course, for to adhere to it would mean the danger of running into the centre of the enemy, and so of becoming prisoners."

For a little while the Commander and his two young officers discussed the situation, and then the former signalled to the man in charge of the engine to start it up.

"We'll get ahead at once," he said; "but let us try to be cautious. We have plenty of time before us, for the boat is well victualled, and there is ample water all round us; of course it is not fit to drink, and no one but a fool, or one utterly unused to these tropical climates, would dare to drink it. A mouthful, even, would mean a fever, perhaps a good deal worse. But some of those reeds cut from the islands and laid on the deck would make excellent fuel, and we have a stove right for'ard, and a boiler in which we can easily purify the water. You young fellows will already have learned the importance of a pure drinking-supply to troops on an expedition; the same applies to sailors, of course. Give either of them absolutely pure water whenever you possibly can, and prevent 'em both from drinking from the first pool they come across; supply them with good rations in addition, and don't march them about in a grilling sun unless it cannot be avoided, and you will keep your men in good health and strength, and fit to meet the enemy. It's the secret of campaigning—the great secret I ought to add—for, after all, when you send troops into the field, or into a place like Mesopotamia, you send 'em for one purpose only, and that to meet the enemy. The men who fall sick weaken your forces, and encumber your hospitals and your transport; and sick men are men who go under, often enough, because of lack of pure water. Now, Keith, tell the old boy to give us the line for the river. Denman, I am going to post you right aft, to keep a watch in that direction. Keith, you'd best go forward with the native right into the bows, so as to be able to interpret anything he tells you. Now, lads, pick up your rifles, and let one of you come right aft with this officer, two others will station themselves for'ard, and two more will be on either side of me in the cabin. We have got to remember that we may very well find ourselves not the only inhabitants of this waste of waters. We have taken the precaution to make a very early start, and got in amongst these reeds during the darkness, so that I think I am right in feeling that no one is aware of this expedition. But there may be natives about. Ask your fellow, Keith."

For answer the native shook his head vigorously.

"Excellency," he told Geoff, as they stood up in the bows of the vessel, "it may be, for all I know, but it is hardly probable; for in these wastes there is nothing to be gathered—no fish and no game—and why should a poor man come in this direction? Yet, listen a moment. There may be scouts of the enemy. No doubt the Turks are provided with bellums—the native boat we use in these parts—and it may well be that they have sent off scouts to pass down the waters and spy upon your brothers."

"Then we have got to keep our eyes open," the Commander sang out to his men, when Geoff had interpreted. "If you see a boat, pass the word along at once, but don't fire, for we shall be wise to make a capture, and so learn something of the enemy."

By now the propeller of the little boat was thrashing the shallow waters of the marshes, with a vigour which made itself felt throughout the timbers of the tiny vessel. She throbbed from end to end, and vibrated under the feet of those who manned her. Steered by the Cox, and directed by Geoff—who took his line from the native—the vessel shot off at an angle, and, pushing her way rapidly through a maze of reed-clad islands, and hummocks of oozy mud, which cropped up in many parts, she finally reached a spot where the waste of waters stretched uninterruptedly to the west and north of them. Here, too, there was a distinct change in the appearance of the water, for, while amongst the reedy islands of mud the marshes consisted of stagnant and dark-coloured water, there was a stream where they now were—a stream flowing gently past them—of lightish-yellow colour, in which particles of sand and debris swirled as one peered over the side of the motor vessel. The way of the boat, too, was retarded just a little as she headed up against the stream, a proof—if further proof was necessary—that they had now gained the channel of the Euphrates River. For three hours they motored their way steadily up this stream, seeing nothing to attract their attention, and finding on either hand the same water waste, with its margin of muddy islands, extending into the far distance. A haze hung over these islands, as the heat of the sun drew the water upwards, while a faint, sickly odour was wafted from them.

"Fever!" said the Commander, as he smoked another pipe. "A night spent in amongst those islands of mud would be bad for a white man, let us hope that we shall find some pleasanter place as the darkness draws in upon us."

That night, as a matter of fact, they tied up beside a sandy shelf which bordered the stream they had been following, and which ran upwards towards the desert. It was a species of sandy hillock, perhaps a mile across, which, being elevated, divided the waters. But who could say? Perhaps some years ago it had formed actually the bed of the Euphrates River, which had then flowed over and through it. But in the course of time the debris and sand borne along in the water had silted up, and formed a bank at this precise position; and succeeding layers of sand deposited by the water had finally raised the bank, till, gathering firmness and dimensions as the days passed, it finally defied and defeated the river which had been the source of its existence. Then the channel of the Euphrates had been changed, and what had once been its bed, swept by the ever-descending flood of water coming from the centre of Mesopotamia, from Asiatic Turkey, had become now a glistening heap of firm, dry sand, which gave the expedition a splendid bivouac.

"An excellent place!" the Commander told Geoff, as the anchor was dropped, and the boat was paddled in close to the bank. "We'll make our boat fast by driving pegs into the sand itself, and then we'll get ashore. A couple of men in the boat will be all that will be required, and the rest can accompany us."

In half an hour they had their fire going, and that evening Philip and Geoff enjoyed the experience of an open-air camp under the starlight. Yet it was not always to be so pleasant, as they were to find, for, on the morrow, having set off soon after the first streak of dawn, and having pushed their way rapidly up the winding and almost invisible channel of the river, they suddenly came upon a sight which caused them to halt instantly.

"Stop that engine!" ordered the Commander suddenly, "'Bout ship! If that's not a Turkish flat-bottomed vessel I'm a Dutchman."

A long, low-built steamer had suddenly hove into sight far up the winding river, and, looking at her swiftly, Geoff realized in a moment that her decks were crowded with men dressed in khaki-coloured clothing. Swinging his glasses to his eyes, he fixed them on the vessel, and then called back at the Commander.

"Turks, without a doubt, sir," he said, "I can recognize them easily. There's a man standing on a low bridge just above their heads who is wearing a fez, while opposite him there is an officer whom I should take to be German. There are fifty or more on the boat, and it is likely enough that they are an exploring-party."

An instant later a shrill shriek was heard from the approaching vessel, as her steam whistle was put into operation; then there was a flash from her side, and perhaps a quarter of a minute later a shot hit the water just behind the motor-boat, and, throwing up a huge cascade, almost drenched Geoff and his comrades. When they had shaken the water out of their eyes, and looked again at the approaching vessel, they saw a string of boats which were towing after her being pulled for'ard. Then men tumbled over the low sides of the vessel into the boats, while others ran into her bows, and, seizing their rifles, opened fire upon the occupants of the tiny vessel lying down below them.

"Go ahead!" said the Commander, as bullets spluttered into the water all round the vessel. "Keith, come along aft here, so that we can talk the matter over. What do you think, lad?" he asked, as Geoff joined him. "I don't like to put my helm about, and show my stern to that Turkish fellow."

"Nor I!" Geoff agreed with him; "and besides, we shan't have accomplished that for which we came into the marshes. It's bad luck, of course, sir, running into an exploring-party of the enemy so soon after coming this way, but there are sure to be more coming behind them, and those are the fellows whose positions we have to make out. Why not try to dodge them?

By running right off to our left into the marshes we should soon be hidden by the islands of mud and reeds, and then we could steal westwards till we were above those fellows!"

"Wait! What's that? Another vessel, eh?" exclaimed the Commander, pointing to a spot higher up the river than that occupied by the Turkish vessel. "Ah!"

Geoff looked, and took in the situation in an instant, for, beyond the low-built Turkish steamer which they had so unexpectedly sighted round a sharp bend of the river, he saw another steamer—a small pinnace—low, like themselves, and speedy, and making towards them now on the stream, at a pace which heaped a mass of water up in front of her. Once more his glasses went to his eyes, and for a while he remained silent. Then he slowly dropped them into their case, lit a cigarette, and turned to his Commanding Officer.

"A fast steam-launch, sir," he said; "twenty men aboard her. It looks as though we should have quite a brisk little action."

For perhaps a minute the Commander turned his gaze upon the pursuing vessel, whilst his own craft sped down the river; then he smiled grimly, and Geoff heard him chuckle.

"Right!" he said. "A pretty little action! I believe you, Keith. Starboard your helm, Cox, and edge the boat off gradually towards the marshes. We'll induce that fellow to follow us till we are well away from the other vessel, so that she cannot support the launch with her gun; then we'll see what sailors can do at carrying out an ambush. Lie down, men, it's only fools who won't take cover; keep as low as you can, and don't give 'em anything to fire at."

Bullets, meanwhile, had been sweeping above the boat, and streaming their way past the ears of its occupants. Spurts of water rose on every hand, while now and again a cascade—a mere child to that thrown up by the shell which had been fired at them at the commencement of this encounter—would splash over the sides of the motor-vessel. Obedient to the order given them, yet grudgingly, for your sailor is a gallant fellow, the crew crouched low behind the sides of the vessel, leaving the Cox fully exposed, and the Commander still standing to his full height in the open cabin, and beside him Geoff, holding his ground—not wincing, not even dodging or bobbing his head, as bullets flicked past him.

"Nervous?" asked the Commander, as he stuffed tobacco into his pipe and calmly set the weed alight. "Not you, Keith! Nor Denman either! That's good to see, though it is only what I expected. Now set her going at full speed, and we'll see what we can do to dodge those fellows."

A long island of mud, clad with reeds, stood up before the motor-vessel, and it looked for a while as though the Commander had every intention of running her upon it; but at a signal from him—a signal made with a jerk of the hand which gripped his pipe—the Cox pushed his helm over, and the motor-boat shot past the end of the island, and, turning again, sped up behind it. A further jerk, and she turned off at a tangent, and, speeding across a waste of stagnant water, thrust her nose in between two reedy islands, following a channel which hardly seemed wide enough to accommodate her. Turning and twisting, and dodging to right and left, and once grounding with a dull and gentle thud upon the tail of an island, and breaking loose again because of her momentum, the vessel shot across another waste, and, rounding the end of a second stretch of oozy mud, was rapidly brought to a halt.

"Ask your old gentleman whether the mud would bear a man," the Commander told Geoff abruptly.

"Truly, Excellency," came the immediate answer. "These banks, though they quiver as one walks upon them, are yet solid, for the roots of the reeds have bound the mud together. Excellency, if I may ask a favour, let me land here, so that I may convey a warning to you."

A moment later the man was ashore, and, at a nod from the Commander, Geoff accompanied him. Then, pushing their way through the reeds, they gained the farther side, and, cautiously making an opening through which they could watch, waited for the coming of their pursuers. It was perhaps five minutes later when the rattle of machinery came to their ears, and within a few seconds the Turkish vessel hove into sight as she thrashed her way through the waste of waters. That she had lost the direction of the motor-boat seemed certain, though the Turks aboard her must have known that they were not far behind their quarry. A loud order reached Geoff's ears, while the clank of machinery died down of a sudden; then he saw the launch drift on towards the end of the island behind which the motor-vessel was hiding. Creeping back towards the Commander, he waved to him to attract his attention, and then called softly to him.

"In five minutes they will be crossing the far end of this island, sir," he said; "it ought to give us an opportunity."

"Come aboard, and bring the old gentleman with you," the Commander cried on the instant. "Now, boys, line the gun'l there, and hold your fire till I give the order. I've a little scheme on foot, and I'll be particularly grateful to you if you don't sink her. Shoot some of the crew, and capture the rest of them if need be. Now, my man, set her going!"

The engine revolved again, and in a trice the propeller was thrashing the water; then, ever so gently and quietly, they stole up beside the island, while on the far side the Turkish launch drifted ever closer to them.

CHAPTER VII

Major Joseph Douglas

While Geoff and his friends are aboard that motor-vessel, on the point of attacking the Turks aboard the steam-launch which had so unexpectedly opposed their progress up the River Euphrates, let us for a moment turn aside to follow the fortunes of another individual who has already been introduced to our readers.

We have already recounted how Major Joseph Douglas, a "political" officer, said farewell to his friends in that frontier fortress far up amongst the hills of India, and how he disappeared, as indeed was his wont, on another of those long expeditions on which the Government of India employed him. We have said that he reached the Persian Gulf and made his way to Basra, and thence up country on a river steamer till the walls of Bagdad enclosed him. Then, having disappeared from the ken of his fellows entirely, and having contrived almost to reach the heart of Asiatic Turkey, the war — which was to drag so many nations into its toils — broke out, and saw the Kaiser's legions overwhelming Belgium, and invading France and Poland.

That Turkey should have been drawn into this conflict was perhaps as much a matter for astonishment to the Turks themselves as to other peoples, for they had, in fact, no grievance against Great Britain or her allies. Indeed, Britain has always befriended the Turk, and done what she could for him; yet late years — those years just prior to the outbreak of this vast war which now tears Europe into pieces — saw what may be termed a revolution in the country of the Sultan. The "Young Turk Party" arose, a party which grew in power — thanks, no doubt, to the scheming help of Germany — till it was able to dethrone the Sultan himself and capture the reins of Government. In the hands of German schemers — the agents of the Kaiser and his war lords — these ambitious young Turks were easily deluded, and, carried away by the successes they had already met with, listened eagerly to the words of the tempters. There was gold to be had in abundance, gold, if the Young Turk Party would but carry out the behests of the German War Lord, if they would but follow a plan which, they were told, would lead not only to their own wealth—for rewards and presents would be poured upon them—but to the greatness of Turkey. War was imminent, they no doubt were informed, and Germany had designs upon the conquest of all nations. Why should Turkey be unfriendly to the Germans? Why should the subjects of the new Sultan fight with the subjects of the Kaiser? There was no desire on the part of the War Lord of Berlin to conquer the dwellers by the Bosphorus, the Turks living in Europe or in Asia, but only the fervent wish to be friendly with them. Then here was the opportunity! Let Turkey side with Germany against France and Russia, and, if need be, against Great Britain; let her close the Dardanelles utterly, and so shut off the Russian enemy from the Mediterranean; and then let her but wait till Germany had broken the fighting forces of France and of the Tsar of Russia; then would come the turn of those Powers in the Balkans—once the subjects of Turkey. Serbia would be overridden, would be decimated, would be stamped out of existence; if need be, Bulgaria, the ancient enemy of Turkey, would be destroyed completely. And then see what would happen! The forces of Germany and of Austria would be linked up with those of the Sultan, and who could stay their progress? With millions of men under arms, with engineers to construct railways throughout Asiatic Turkey, Egypt would be wrested for the Turks from Great Britain—Egypt the heritage of Turkey; Persia could be gained; Afghanistan itself, and even India conquered. Look at the prospect! The eyes of the Young Turk Party were blinded by the brilliance of such a proposition; and for those who were more sagacious, who knew the German to be a schemer, there was gold—gold in abundance—with which to bribe them, gold with which to gild their doubt, and to make them unwilling friends of Germany.

Little wonder, perhaps, that the guileless and inexperienced, if unscrupulous, "Young Turk Party" listened to the crafty words of the Kaiser's agents, and decided to throw in their lot with them. Little wonder that, following upon the outbreak of the war, they welcomed the coming of the Goeben and the Breslau—two of Germany's most powerful vessels—and, having admitted them to the Bosphorus, closed the Dardanelles entirely. Now, see the result of such a movement! In the Black Sea itself the Turks were hopelessly outnumbered and outgunned by the vessels of the Russians—that is, prior to the coming of the Goeben and the Breslau; but now that those two vessels had reached the scene, there was not a vessel in the Tsar's navy capable of easily standing up to them. Those two, with the help of what Turkey could send from her dockyards, might very well clear the Black Sea of all Russian vessels, and make the transport of Turkish troops to Trebizond, and to the frontier lying between Turkey and Russia, along the Caucasus Mountains, a matter of ease and safety. Then the coming of those two powerful vessels would enable the Young Turk Party to reinforce their army in the Caucasus, and, perhaps, to strike a blow there which would cause heavy Russian losses. In any case, a force so disposed would necessitate the placing of Russian armies to oppose them, and Russian armies so withdrawn from the forces of the Tsar would weaken the troops needed to stem the tide of Germans and Austrians then pouring into Poland.

Looked at from every point of view, the coming of Turkey into the conflict was likely to be of enormous advantage to the Kaiser, and of signal disadvantage to Britain and her allies. That it was likely to improve the fortunes of the Turks was problematical only. Indeed, there is little doubt that if Germany had carried out to the full the first portion of her programme, and had shattered the forces of France and of Russia, Turkey would have become merely a puppet in the hands of the Hohenzollerns. Germans would—and may even yet—sweep into Asiatic Turkey, and, had they broken the power of their enemies elsewhere—as fortunately they have not done—the Turks would undoubtedly have become vassals of the Kaiser. As it is, they have thrown in their lot with the Germans, and it would appear as if they were to gain nothing but losses and privations.

But, in any case, they had become enemies of Britain and her allies, and, seeing that Major Joseph Douglas was most decidedly a Briton, they were enemies of his, and he was an alien in the midst of them. Such a well-known person as the Major—for let us say at once that if Major Joseph Douglas was known far and wide in India, a welcome guest in many an officers' mess and in a host of cantonments, he was, in a rather different way, just as well known in the heart of Mesopotamia—was now an alien, an enemy, and must needs look to his own safety.

Douglas Pasha had, in fact, a most uncanny way of eluding the Turkish governors of the various provinces he visited. He came openly to them, and often enough called upon them in the most friendly manner possible, receiving from them the warmest welcome. Yet, under the silken cloak of friendship, and beneath the welcome which every well-bred man extends to another—and your Turk is a gentleman, whatever else you may say of him—there existed always, when Douglas Pasha turned up upon the scene, a feeling of doubt, of hesitancy, almost of danger, in the minds of those Turkish governors. Crafty themselves, they knew well enough that he had come to investigate every feature of the country, to ascertain what Turkish forces were maintained, to map the roads, no doubt, to investigate the progress of such railways as Turkey possessed, and to unearth a hundred different matters. It followed, therefore, often enough, that Douglas Pasha's exit from the palace of a governor was followed, almost automatically, by the dogging of his footsteps. Spies followed him from place to place, spies who watched his every movement like a company of cats; spies whom the cheerful and cunning Douglas Pasha on every occasion managed to elude.

Thus, he was within a few days of the outbreak of war at Bagdad, where news of European matters had not yet reached the populace. Yet the governor knew that war was impending—that Turkish governor upon whom the Major had called that very afternoon, and who had bowed the gallant officer out of his palace, had smiled in such friendly fashion upon him, and who, once his back was turned, had snapped his fingers, had clapped his hands, and had set machinery in motion to have Douglas Pasha followed and watched. Yet, strange as it may seem, Geoff Keith's most excellent guardian was by no means the simpleton he seemed, and by no means ignorant of events then impending.

He strolled down the centre of the Bazaar, a likeable figure in his dust-coloured travelling-suit, a tall, active man, with the face and the bearing of a soldier. He stopped to converse with an Arab dealer in brass-ware, seated cross-legged upon his little stall, and chatted with him as if he were himself a native. Then he passed on to another stall, leaving the Arab, usually so uninterested in the affairs of this world, keenly curious as to the nationality of the stranger who had addressed him. A dozen yards higher up, there was an Armenian Jew selling jewellery, and with him, too, Douglas Pasha chatted in the most pleasant manner and in the Armenian tongue; and then he strolled on for a while, till, noticing the angular figure of a big-boned Jew seated upon another stall, with a mass of embroidery laid out before him, he turned back and strolled towards him.

"Many fine wares to sell, my friend?" he said, addressing him in the Armenian tongue. "Our brother yonder has jewellery beyond compare; but, in truth, these wares that you have to offer would delight the heart of a houri."

Bending down, he picked up one of the gaudily-embroidered pieces of cloth and admired it openly; while the Jew, after answering him in a monosyllable, and casting his eyes up at the Major's face for just one moment, bent them down again upon his goods, as if fearful that someone might filch them from him.

"Fine gold, friend, and stuff woven in the heart of Persia," the Major told him. "And what may be the price of this, my friend?"

As might be expected, the price which this hook-nosed and somewhat ancient Jew set upon the article selected was simply immense, more than treble its actual value. But, then, it is a habit of the East, where a purchase more or less is not a matter of importance, where there is time for everything, and hurry is a thing not to be dreamed of. Shopping in London or in some busy provincial city and shopping at Constantinople or in the Bazaar at Bagdad are two utterly different affairs altogether; the one all haste, intermingled with the most business-like methods, and the other all dilatoriness, with a strong flavour of friendly haggling, when hours must be passed before the price of the simplest object is settled.

"And low in price," the Jew told the Major, glancing cunningly up at him. "Low in price, Excellency, as truly as I sit before you. But wait, there are other goods for sale within this store; be seated, take a post of honour on this bench, and let the youth bring coffee to us."

His bent figure became upright for a moment, and he clapped his hands loudly. At the same instant he swung his eyes round that portion of the Bazaar visible from the stall where he was wont to sit the livelong day, and dropped them instantly. Yet that one glance seemed to have sufficed, for a smile seamed his face for just one second. Then he rapped out a sharp order to the Turkish boy who appeared at his summons, and sat on motionless, without a word, without even venturing to offer more of his wares, till the coffee had been produced and laid before himself and the Major. It was then, as the English officer tipped the tiny egg-shaped cup to his lips, that the eyes of the two met.

"Well!" demanded the Major.

"Excellency, beware! There is news from the outside world," the Jew told him, and then again swept a swift glance round the confines of the Bazaar. "Listen, Excellency!" he said, snatching another piece of embroidered ware and holding it up before the Major, while he made pretence to point to the gilded work upon it; "listen, Excellency! There is war!"

"Ah!" came from the Major.

"War between France and Russia on the one hand and the German enemy on the other."

"And Britain?" asked the Major breathlessly, though to an observer, even more than casual, he seemed to be engaged in most carefully scrutinizing the embroidery. "And Britain?" he asked again. "She — — "

"There are things that seem strange to one of us people in this land of Turkey," said the Jew quietly, stretching out a hand to pick up more of his wares. "There is a place, a country, perhaps peopled by a great nation for aught I know, a country known as Belgium. Listen, Excellency! The Germans have invaded that country, have burst their way into it, have fired upon the people, and have killed many of them."

"That means war, war for Great Britain," said the Major, tossing the pieces of cloth down and shaking his head as though he could not agree to purchase them. Then he picked up another piece, and while he scrutinized it told the Jew to go on with the story.

"Proceed!" he said. "Belgium is a country of much importance. Germany had sworn, with Britain and France and other nations, to preserve that country inviolate. Then she has broken her word!"

"As Germans ever break their word," the Armenian Jew told him. "Yes, Excellency, in the years that have gone by, and increasingly so in these last few years, I have met with German after German. In public life I know them not, but in trade, I say, beware of them! They steal behind the scenes, they are mean, and thrifty, and energetic, and possessed of many virtues and many failings. I like them not, and trust them not at all! So, Excellency, they swore to defend this country! And yet tore up that treaty, and poured soldiers upon her? Truly that is an act of baseness seldom heard of."

"And means war for my country," the Major told him. "And then, my friend?" he asked swiftly.

"And then, from the same source, I gather that there is a stir in Constantinople, that there is a great movement of troops and of vessels, and that in a little while, even as we speak, perhaps, Turkey may have joined in with Germany."

If Major Joe Douglas felt inclined to give vent to a shrill whistle of astonishment, for, after all, he was astonished — though this was a happening which he had expected now for many years past — he managed to suppress the wish very promptly. He contrived to go on bargaining and haggling with the old Jew for perhaps half an hour, and then, throwing down another piece of embroidered cloth and shaking his head, he passed from the stall and again along the Bazaar.

Some twenty yards higher up, when near the Turkish portion, he cannoned into a man of moderate height, dressed like himself in European clothing, a fat, very stoutly-built man, possessed of a head so closely cropped that it was hideous, and of a face from which sprouted a greyish-brown moustache, the centre of which was stained a darker colour by much cigarette-smoking. This individual wore a broad-brimmed panama upon his head, as a general rule, but at that moment carried it in one hand, and was fanning himself with energy.

"Pardon!" said the Major. "Sorry!"

"Ach! It vas you!"

Undoubtedly German, the stout individual into whom the Major had cannoned turned at first an angry face upon him, a face which a moment later was lit up by smiles and divided almost asunder by a capacious grin, stretching a most enormous mouth from ear to ear and disclosing two rows of stained and yellow teeth within it. Of a truth, the appearance of this individual was not altogether prepossessing; and yet, putting his yellow teeth aside, forgetting for one moment his huge and unwieldy proportions, and his smooth-cropped head and other undesirable features, the frank expression of his face, the broadness of his grin, even, were at once captivating.

"My tear Major!" he exclaimed, holding one fat hand up, palm foremost, while he still continued to fan himself with his panama. "My tear Major, and who would have thought to meet you here, you of all people!"

"Why, von Hildemaller!"

"Jah! Von Hildemaller! Dis is der greadest bleasure in mein life. Mein tear Major!"

The big, fat German stood back from the tall, sprucely-dressed, and brisk-looking English soldier, and surveyed him with a smile which would have melted the heart of the most implacable of enemies. Von Hildemaller was geniality itself, brimful of smiles and of friendliness; and, having mopped his streaming face and fanned himself again with his panama, he stretched out his broad palm and gripped the one which Major Douglas presented to him.

"My tear Major!" he exclaimed again, puffing heavily, for, to be sure, what with his own stoutness of figure, and the close and confined atmosphere within the Bazaar, the German was none too comfortable. "And to think dat you vas here of all der places in der world!" He held up his two hands now, the better to express his astonishment, while his twinkling and extremely merry eyes shot a swift, if not cunning, glance at the soldier.

"And you vas here long?" he demanded, mopping his face again with energy, and using for that purpose a huge handkerchief of Turkish red silk, which would have done duty at a pinch for a table-cloth. "Nein? Nod long, you say? Perhabs four, five, six days?"

The Major extracted his cigarette case from his pocket and offered it politely to the German, as if hinting at the same moment that questions were hardly to his fancy.

"And you?" he asked when von Hildemaller had helped himself and lighted up. "But there, what is the good of asking you, my friend, von Hildemaller? You are here to-day and gone to-morrow. One finds you in Bagdad perhaps, and then, within a week, in Constantinople; in Kut, or even in Basra. And, ah! you are such a busy man, von Hildemaller. Men, such as you, who purchase in such large quantities the dates grown in this country must be up and about, to make your businesses thrive."

Was there a cunning glint in those rather deep-sunk, small, yet merry eyes of the German? Did those two uneven rows of yellow teeth come together of a sudden with a snap indicative of annoyance? No, no! such a suggestion was entirely out of the question, for see, von Hildemaller was smiling most genially at this tall Briton.

"Ah! der you vas!" he told the Major, laughing uproariously. "It vas you who always liked to make der fun! 'Here do-day and gone do-morrow.' Ha! ha! you make me laugh! And you? And you, my tear Major, id is you who go here do-day and dere do-morrow, and you do nod even buy dades or oder produce of dis country."

Behind the cloud of smoke which he shot from between his thick lips, and sent bubbling out through his discoloured and drooping moustache, there was a cunning leer on the face of the German—a leer hidden a moment later by a smile transcending in its friendliness any that had gone before it. Fanning himself with his panama, and smoking violently the cigarette with which the Major had presented him, he stood in the centre of the Bazaar, careless of the obstruction he formed and of the difficulties he made for the passers-by, while he chatted with Teutonic eagerness with Douglas Pasha. And all the while, as he smiled and smirked, and sometimes leered, behind clouds of smoke, he was summing up the appearance, the height, the broad shoulders, the shapely figure, and the active limbs of the Englishman.

"Mein Gott! But if all my brothers were like him!" he told himself. "If all the subjects of the Kaiser were as tall, and as straight, and as slim, and as active! Then the thing would be done! There would be no doubt about it; the World would be surely conquered! But, pshaw! It will be done! The war-dogs are unleashed already, and though there is not much news as yet, though it is only Belgium which is already almost conquered, to-morrow, the next day perhaps, surely within a few hours of this, there will be news of the undoing of France and the capture of Paris. Himmel! And then?"

This breezy, stout, perspiring, and extremely genial fellow quite lost himself in a brown study as he reflected on the greatness of his own country and on the news of triumph which he anticipated.

Let us explain the case in regard to the jovial von Hildemaller — a man who knew the inside of Mesopotamia almost as well as Douglas Pasha did. After all, though he might be a trader in dates, as indeed he professed, he was still before all a German. A German in heart and in thought; a German, above all, in ambition. Was it likely that he had come to Mesopotamia for the single purpose of trading in dates alone? Bearing in mind the fact that practically no German has left the Fatherland for some foreign country for the single purpose of following his own fortune alone, one may take it for certain that, like all the others, von Hildemaller also went on a mission for his Government. He was one of that enormous band which practised peaceful penetration for the Kaiser, who went armed with Government funds to some desirable spot in some still more desirable country, and who there made for himself a business which gave ample excuse for his remaining in the country. Yet all the while he was engaged, with Teutonic energy, in looking well about him, in discovering the secrets of the country, in ascertaining its defences, and in sending sheaves of notes to his Home Government. Let us say at once that this von Hildemaller was none other than the stout and genial German whom Commander Houston had come upon in Basra — the one whom he had indicated as von Schmidt — and from the gallant Commander we have already learned that, genial, and smiling, and friendly though this German trader might be, and very charming to those with whom he came in contact — whether they were Britons or not — yet behind his guise of merchant he was indeed a Government Agent — an energetic, far-seeing, and most likely an unscrupulous agent — placed in Asiatic Turkey for the one purpose of informing the Kaiser and his war lords of the doings of the Turks, of the British, and of the Russians; and kept there, ostensibly as a merchant, but really as a spy, to foster the ambitious designs of his countrymen.

Did Douglas Pasha suspect this German? Did he realize that behind those smiling eyes and those wide curving lips there was a cunning brain and a lying tongue, ready to deceive and thwart him? If he did, he gave no indication of that fact. For he chatted easily, smiling back at the German in as friendly a manner as possible, apparently watching more closely the people passing to and fro in the Bazaar than the face and the figure of the man who had accosted him. It was with a hearty handshake and a friendly nod that he parted with the German, and went striding up through the Bazaar, past the hook-nosed Jew with whom he had appeared to bargain, and so on to the rooms he was occupying.

As for von Hildemaller, he tossed away the stump of the cigarette he had been smoking, and watched the departing figure of the British officer through half-closed lids, while he still panted and mopped his forehead. Then, thrusting his panama upon his shaven head, he looked craftily about him for a moment, and, having assured himself that no one in particular was watching him, lifted his right hand to his shoulder and made a sudden signal. A moment later a tall, sleek Turk slid up from an adjacent stall, and halted beside him:

"My master?" he asked, in the Turkish tongue.

"You saw him," demanded the German curtly, with that brutal abruptness common to the German. "That man—that Douglas Pasha—you saw the man?"

"I did. I watched and waited yonder. And then?" asked the Turk.

"Go and kill him, that's all! Go and slay the man!" von Hildemaller told him, turning upon his emissary just as friendly a smile as ever he had turned upon Joe Douglas. "There is no need to discuss the matter further, for you know the man and you have the method. Go then! When it is done come back to me and you shall be rewarded."

Who would have thought the worthy von Hildemaller capable of such words, or of giving such a dastardly order? Indeed, at the very moment when he was condemning the gallant Major to death by the hand of this Turkish assassin, the stout German looked so utterly genial, so entirely friendly and harmless, that none could possibly have suspected the real gist of his orders. Yet, as we have inferred already, behind those smiling, merry eyes, which looked so frankly and so honestly at people, there was a clever scheming brain, and behind those lips which were never stern, and seemed ever to be parted amiably, was a tongue given to much lying. Let us add, too, the fact that that brain was capable of inventing acts which would have shamed an Englishman, and of producing orders even more dastardly than that which had already been given. Indeed, there was no limit to the crimes which von Hildemaller could perpetrate, more particularly if they were for the ultimate benefit of his own country. With the smooth, smiling, genial face almost of a child, he was at heart a wretch, a cruel, scheming, cunning creature, an unscrupulous agent, capable of planning any atrocity. When that was said, we have von Hildemaller's full character, and we have merely to add that, like many of his kidney, when the planning was done, when the schemes for assassination and murder were arranged, the power for evil of this German suddenly subsided. He could scheme, but he lacked the courage to carry out his enterprise. His was the crafty brain which arranged the deed but contrived to get another to carry it out for him. Thanks to a Government which supplied him with ample funds, he could command in this country a host of ruffians. Pooh! The assassination of a British officer was quite a small matter, to be arranged on the spur of the moment, and to cost not so much as a second thought, and no great sum of gold when all was considered.

Von Hildemaller snapped his fingers and mopped his face again as the Turk sped away from him; then, lighting a German cigar, and puffing at it till he got it going to his satisfaction, he strolled — waddled rather — through the Bazaar, and on to his own quarters.

"Quite a nice sort of fellow, that Douglas Pasha!" he was telling himself as he went. "For a Briton, quite a respectable individual! Conceited? Yes! But then, that's a fault of the nation; but honest, clear-headed, I think, friendly and—yes—certainly—simple!"

"Simple!" did he say? If the worthy German, waddling through the Bazaar, could have seen Major Douglas at that moment, he might have had cause to reflect a little, and to change his opinion. For, though the gallant Major may have made pretence at simplicity when meeting the German, though he may have given the impression of being shallow, of being thoughtless, and of possessing not so much as an atom of cunning, yet Douglas Pasha had not travelled through Mesopotamia, had not met hosts of Germans, had not studied the history of Germany and her people, without learning many lessons. It was a habit of this gallant officer to study unconsciously the character of every individual with whom he came in contact, and thus it happened that the worthy von Hildemaller had, as it were, come under the microscopic examination of this British officer.

"Very charming, ahem! I am sure. A most excellent fellow to meet in a café, say on the Grand Boulevard in Paris, or in the Unter den Linden in Berlin. A generous host, a loud-speaking, merry fellow, but insincere, unscrupulous—like his people—out for something big, something to benefit his own country; to be carefully watched, and distrusted, and yet to be met in the most friendly manner possible."

That was the Major's summing-up of the excellent and cunning von Hildemaller; and now, as he took the nearest cut back to his own apartments in the city of Bagdad, apartments which he had occupied on more than one occasion, there was something in his face which, if the German could have seen it, would have warned him that Douglas Pasha was hardly so simple as he anticipated.

"Unfortunate meeting that German," Joe Douglas was telling himself as he hurried along. "Of course he knows just as well as I do that war has been declared between Great Britain and Germany, and that Turkey is likely to come into the conflict. That being the case, he and I are hardly likely to remain on speaking terms after this; indeed, he'll look upon me as a dangerous enemy, just as I look upon him. Shouldn't wonder if his hirelings are already watching me, and — yes — there are tales of the worthy Herr von Hildemaller which aren't too pleasant."

Rapping sharply on the door of his lodgings, he was admitted by an Armenian servant, and at once strode into his sitting-room. Throwing himself into a cane-seated chair and lighting a cigarette, he then rapped sharply on the table.

"Pack up," he ordered; "we leave in five minutes. Wait! What's that?"

Someone was rapping on the floor below them, someone who called in low tones for admission. Instantly Joe Douglas sprang to his feet, and, pulling the chair away, and the table, dragged a piece of Turkish carpet on one side, disclosing a narrow trap-door.

"Enter!" he called, and helped the person below who had demanded admission to raise the opening.

And slowly, as he did so, there emerged from a dark hole below, by means of a roughly-made ladder, the big, bony, angular form of that same hook-nosed Jew with whom he had haggled in the Bazaar not half an hour before.

"H-h-'sh! Listen, Excellency!" The man stood half in and half out of the opening, one warning talon held upward, his beady eyes fixed on Douglas Pasha, his lips trembling. "That man! That German hound! That scoundrel!"

The gallant Major was the very last individual to show alarm. In fact, fuss and worry were things he hated intensely, and his nonchalance on all occasions was something which long ago had attracted the admiration of his comrades. He still smoked on, and, throwing himself into his chair, and flinging his legs on the table, he smiled at the Jew and bade him proceed with the story.

"Yes, the German, von Hildemaller!" he said. "A most excellent gentleman! And you said beware, my friend, did you not? But surely — — "

He gave vent to a laugh, an ironical laugh, which grated on the ears of those listening, and which warned them that, though the German may have considered this British officer to be childishly simple, he was yet well aware of the danger which surrounded him.

"Listen, Excellency!" said the Jew, emerging now completely from the chamber beneath the room in which Joe Douglas was seated. "I watched the scene from my stall. Long ago I warned Your Excellency that this German had no love for you, that his hirelings were watching you and dogging your steps, and that some day he would do you a mischief. Now the day has arrived! Even as you hurried away from that accidental meeting with him, I saw him call to one whom I know to be nothing but an assassin — a wretch — whose knife is at the bidding of anyone who can pay him money — one who should long ago have been hanged in the market-place. Leaving my stall, I followed this rascal, and saw him call to others. Even now they are arming, and, as dusk falls — which will be within an hour perhaps — they will break a way into this dwelling and carry out the purpose of this German."

Joe Douglas whistled, a merry whistle, and smiled in the most friendly fashion at the Jew. He even got up from his chair, still smoking, and patted him reassuringly on the shoulder.

"My friend," he said, "I thank you from the bottom of my heart for this warning; not this time alone, but on many occasions, have you proved a real friend to me, and may it be many a day before I forget your loyalty. But, as it happened, I guessed the intentions of our worthy friend von Hildemaller. Already I have given orders to pack up all my belongings, and soon, in a little while indeed, we shall be out of this place, leaving it to the hired assassins of the German."

There was bustle in that little house in the ten minutes which followed, all hands being engaged in packing the Major's belongings. Then, having completed the work to his satisfaction, the Jew and the Armenian servant of Douglas Pasha dragged his trunks through the opening down into the cellar beneath. Long before that, Joe Douglas had transformed himself into an absolute replica of the Jew who had come to warn him, and, indeed, looked the part to perfection. Then, casting a hurried glance round, and throwing the light from an electric torch into every corner—for already the dusk was falling, and the house opposite darkened that in which he had been living—he slid through the opening in the floor, and gently lowered the trap-door after him, having just before that dragged the table across it. Then the three made their way to the far edge of the cellar, and, ascending some steps, entered a narrow alley. There, at the bidding of the Major, his two companions went off to their left, while Joe Douglas made ready to venture into the open.

"You will go to the old quarters," he told them in a whisper, "while I see what is happening in the street yonder. To-night, as the moon rises, you will have a conveyance ready for me, and to-morrow we shall be well out in the desert."

But a minute before, Douglas Pasha, in spite of the rags with which he was now covered, was without doubt the tall British officer who had made his way into the heart of the city of Bagdad; but now, as the need to act up to his disguise arrived, he became transformed in a manner which was really remarkable. Leaning on a long, stout stick, his head and shoulders bent, and his legs tottering, he stumbled from the alley into the open street, and shuffled and clattered his way along past the door of his own dwelling. It was there that he almost collided, in the dusk, with three Turkish rascals, one of whom was preparing to break the door in with a crowbar. Yet the Jew took no notice of them, but stumbled past, muttering into the cloak which covered his head, talking to himself, and pulling his rags round him. A little farther on, less than a hundred yards, perhaps, he caught sight of a rotund and perspiring figure in a sunken doorway—a figure which was faintly illuminated by an oil lamp hanging in a passage opposite. It was the figure of von Hildemaller, who had crept to this spot to watch the doings of his hired assassins. Again it was characteristic of the Major that he halted in front of the man, careless of the consequences.

"Money! Money to buy food and lodging," he whined, holding out a shuddering, shaking hand, while his whole frame swayed and tottered. "Money, Excellency, to keep body and soul within me!"

"Money! Bah!" The German struck at him with the light cane he was carrying, and threw a glance of hatred and contempt after the tottering figure of the Jew as he retreated.

Then with wide-open ears he listened as the door of the house along the street was burst open, and waited breathlessly for news from his assassin. It was with a storm of rage and disappointment that he learned that the place was empty, that Douglas Pasha was gone, and that the scheme for ending his energies in Mesopotamia had been defeated.

Yet the cunning of this German was not always to meet with such ill success, for though Douglas Pasha contrived to escape from Bagdad that night, and made his way into the desert, there came a day when von Hildemaller traced him. Also there came a day when Douglas Pasha — a prisoner then, and none too well treated — contrived to get a message out of the Turkish fortress in which he was incarcerated. Even as Geoff Keith, and Philip, and Commander Houston braced themselves for a stiff engagement with the Turks aboard the steam-launch which had been pursuing them, that message was speeding down the Tigris towards the British forces. It was a request for help, but with no definite statement of the position where Douglas Pasha was imprisoned. And there were miles of desert country to traverse, and hundreds of enemies to pass, ere the messenger could bear his missive to our Head-quarters. It was a toss-up, indeed, as to whether the news of the Major's plight would ever reach his own people; just as it was a toss-up whether Geoff and his comrades would ever contrive to beat off the Turks who were about to assail them.

CHAPTER VIII

The Motor-boat in Action

There was a deathly silence about the reed-clad island which separated the motor-boat, with its British crew, which was stealing along one side of it, and the wide-stretching marshes on the farther side, where the Turkish launch forged her way slowly, steering for the far end of the island. There was just the gentle purr of the petrol motor aboard the British boat as it slowly turned over — that and the occasional click of a rifle-lock, as one of the men saw to his weapon. From the far side, however, there came voices on occasion, smothered every now and again by the burr and hiss of steam as it escaped from the safety-valve above the boiler. Geoff looked over the side and peered into the water; then he took a boathook and thrust it downward till it struck the bottom of the swamp close beside them. An instant later he had plucked the Commander by the sleeve, and was whispering to him.

"Look, sir," he said; "not much more than two-feet-six of water; you can see the mark on this boathook; and it's hard ground down below — listen!" He sent the boathook down through the water again till the end struck heavily on the bottom, and sent forth a dull, ringing sound.

As for the Commander, he drew the inevitable pipe from between his lips and looked inquisitively at Geoff and then at the boathook.

"Yes?" he asked. "What then?"

"Might be useful," Geoff ventured. "A couple of men dropped overboard could take cover at the edge of the island in amongst the reeds, and might help us immensely."

Commander Houston smiled an indulgent smile at him, and gripped him by the shoulder.

"Well done, Keith!" he said in that sharp, commanding tone of his. "Take a man with you, and get a rifle. Quick with it! for those Turks will be clear of the island within a few minutes. Here, Smith! You're one of my best shots. Overboard with you!"

There were spare rifles lying in the open cabin of the motor-boat, and beside them clips of cartridges. Geoff instantly seized one of the weapons, and filled a pocket with ammunition; then he dropped overboard, while the man who had been called joined him within half a minute with a grin of expectation, while on the faces of his comrades there was a look almost of envy.

"Come!" said Geoff, wading through the water and finding the ground at the bottom as he had expected — hard, and giving firm foothold.

Indeed, it would appear that the wide swamps they were now traversing, and which seemed to be composed of practically stagnant water, were stirred and swept now and again by eddies from the main stream. Perhaps in those violent gales, which every now and again sweep across Mesopotamia, the waters from the Euphrates are driven into the marsh lands, and, instead of flowing slowly and almost imperceptibly across them, filtering through them, as it were, they rush and sweep through every channel, heaping islands of mud here and there where there happen to be eddies, and carrying on vast accumulations of ooze and slime to other quarters. No doubt, too, in dry seasons, when the Shatt-el-Arab has fallen considerably, and the depth of the water in the main stream is much reduced, the waste of water lying at such a time across these marsh lands drains away, leaving a glistening, sandy desert. In any case, there was good going at this spot, and Geoff and his comrade made the most of it.

Wading up beside the island, they advanced, within a couple of minutes, some yards towards the upper end, to which the Turkish launch was fast approaching.

"In here," said Geoff, seeing an opening between some reeds where the bank jutted out a little and formed an angle or depression. "Now cut some of the reeds away with your knife, so as to give you a good field of fire and clear vision."

"Make ready!" they heard the Commander call to them gently, just after they had got into position, and, turning to look at the motor-boat, they saw that she had moved farther out from the island, and was now lying end-on, her bows presented to the spot where the enemy was to be expected.

Almost at the same instant, the shriek of a steam siren came from the far distance—from that big Turkish steamer which had so unexpectedly opposed the advance of this British party on the River Euphrates, and, following it, an answering shriek, more piercing in its intensity, from the steam-launch drifting but a few yards away from them. Then her bows appeared, to be followed in a little while by her funnel, and then by the whole length of her. There was foam at her stern, while smoke was blowing out from the top of her funnel, for she was under way again, and, indeed, was steering a course towards another island which dotted the marshes in the distance. Perched on a raised portion of the deck, just in front of her funnel, was a Turkish officer, shouting loud commands; while on the deck for'ard of him were gathered some twenty or more soldiers, all eager and expectant; yet, as it happened, their gaze was fixed on the distant island, and not upon the water beyond that from behind which they were just emerging. Thus it followed that more than a minute passed before one of them noticed the motor-boat stealing gently, bow on, towards them. The man started and shouted, lifting his rifle high over his head.

"Look!" he shouted, so suddenly, and in such a voice of alarm, that the officer was startled. Swinging round, he too saw the motor-boat, and himself took up the shout with a vengeance.

"The enemy! Swing the ship round! Fire into them!" he bellowed.

"Steady lads!" cried Commander Houston, standing erect in his cabin. "Marsden, stop her! Now, boys, let 'em have it!"

A volley burst from the weapons of the sailors in the motor-boat, and several of the Turks fell from the steam-launch and splashed into the water. By that time bullets were sweeping about the head of the Commander, while not a few struck the sides of the motor-boat or the surface of the water near at hand, throwing up spray which swept over the heads of those who manned her. But not a man flinched; while Commander Houston, snatching his pipe from between his teeth, roared encouragement at the sailors.

"Let 'em have it!" he cried. "Now, Keith," he bellowed, swinging round to our hero, "put in your bullets as fast as you are able. Ah! That has dropped their officer. Just keep your eye on the man at the wheel, and the man who's running the engine, for we can't afford to allow that boat to get away from us."

His teeth had gritted on the stem of his pipe a few seconds earlier, and, unseen by his men, the Commander clapped a hand to one shoulder. Perhaps it was a minute later that he wiped blood from his lips with his handkerchief, and then, like the old "sea-dog" he was, thrust his pipe back into his mouth and went on smoking, still careless of the bullets humming about him, his eyes fixed all the while upon the enemy.

As for Geoff and the man with him, they were able to make excellent shooting from the point of advantage where they had taken cover. Seeing the Turkish officer level his revolver at the Commander, and pull his trigger—a shot which caused the Commander to act as already narrated—Geoff levelled his own piece on him, and gently pressed the trigger, sending the Turkish officer in amongst his soldiers. Then Smith, the watchful sailor beside him, grim and silent and stern now, picked off the man at the wheel of the steam-launch, while Geoff transferred his attention to the Turk whose head bobbed up and down above the engine.

Perhaps two minutes had passed since the first exchange of shots, two busy minutes, during which more than half of the crew of the Turkish launch had been killed or wounded, while as yet, but for a slight wound here and there, not one of the British sailors had been damaged. And now a figure suddenly took the place of the Turkish officer.

"An under officer," shouted the Commander, "look out for him!"

"He is giving orders for the steam-launch to get under way again," cried Geoff—for at the first discharge the engine aboard the enemy vessel had been stopped. "Come along, Smith, we'll wade out to her and stop any sort of movement."

Floundering out from behind the cover he had selected, and with his rifle held well above the water, Geoff led the way direct to the enemy vessel, while a well-timed shot from the motor-boat sent the under-officer in amongst his fallen comrades. Then the engine aboard Commander Houston's little vessel began to thud, while the water behind her was churned, and as the screw got into operation she darted forward towards the steam-launch, the rifles of her crew spitting bullets still at the Turks who remained in evidence. Then, at a shout from the Commander, the fusillade ceased absolutely, though the motor-boat still pushed on towards the enemy.

"Cease fire!" bellowed the Commander; "they have surrendered; see that man holding his hands up towards us."

Taken by surprise as the Turks were, and broken indeed by the first volley, it was not extraordinary that this little British force had at the very commencement the best of the argument. The raking volley which they had poured into the enemy had thrown them into instant confusion, while the shots which Geoff and the man Smith, who went with him, had fired, had contributed not a little to the success of the operation; and now, with her deck covered with wounded or dead, the launch surrendered; a soldier, a huge, well-grown Turk, standing there amongst his comrades, with both arms held over head, and calling to the British to spare them. By then Geoff was within a few yards of the launch, and, staggering on, clambered aboard her. A glance into the open engine-room showed him a man cowering there, the one whose head he had seen bobbing above the side of the vessel a few moments earlier.

"Come out!" he commanded briskly. "No, you won't be shot, and don't fear it, for you've been captured by British sailors. Smith, get hold of that wheel.

Now let every man who has escaped injury 'fall in' on the deck, so that you may be counted."

A hail reached him a moment later from the motor-boat, and, turning for a second, and so taking his eyes from the Turks now mustering on the deck quite close to him, he saw Philip waving frantically to him; but of the Commander there was not a sign, for indeed that gallant individual was reclining in the depths of his cabin.

"Geoff, ahoy!" he heard. "I'm coming up close to you. Commander Houston's wounded."

"Stop!" Geoff shouted back at him. "Back your boat in behind the island, where I'll join you. Smith, can you see any sign of that Turkish boat we met in the river?"

There was half a minute's pause before he received an answer, and then the fine fellow he had posted at the wheel called gently to him.

"Not a sign, sir," he said; "those islands yonder, through which we came on our way here, hide the channel of the river. She's out of sight, and can't see us either, though there's no doubt that she's within fairly close distance."

"Which means that she will have heard the firing. Hum!" thought Geoff, as he swept his eyes round the waste of waters and wondered what would happen. Then he called to the Turk who had been manning the launch engine.

"Get down to your engine again," he commanded, "and give her a little steam. Smith, swing her round behind the island. We'll lie up there with the motor-boat for a while, and see to the Commander, and repair damages."

The minutes which followed were busy ones indeed, for, as may be imagined, there was much to be done after such a brisk little encounter. Swinging the launch round, while the Turk gave the engine steam, Smith steered her in till she was quite close to the island; then the motor-boat came alongside her, and the two vessels were moored there, the crew of the British vessel taking ropes ashore, and their own and the launch's anchor.

"I'm not a sailor," Geoff told the men aboard the motor-boat, when at last they were secured to the island, "so I'll leave it to the senior amongst you to look to your damages. You've got some shot-holes about your hull, I'm sure, for I heard the bullets strike, and I can see water spurting in in more than one direction. Just post four men up on to the deck of the launch to look after our prisoners, and let one man make his way through the reeds of the island to the far side to keep watch for the arrival of more enemies. Now, Philip, give a hand and let us look to the Commander."

Leaping down into the cabin, they found Commander Houston lying full length upon the floor, his face wonderfully changed from that to which they had become accustomed. Instead of displaying a ruddy countenance, and cheeks which glowed with health and vigour, there was now a deathly pallor upon the merry face of their friend, which seemed to have shrunken and grown smaller. But if the gallant sailor had suffered an injury, as indeed he had without a doubt, and if he were placed hors de combat by it, there was yet no loss of spirit, no lack of joviality; indeed the same happy smile wreathed the pallid face of this most gallant fellow, while he was still actually making a pretence of smoking.

"A nice brisk little affair; eh, boys?" he said weakly, in tones which evidently astonished and disgusted himself, for he apologized for them. "Don't take any notice of my voice," he told them; "it's nothing, believe me; merely a shot through my chest, for which I have to thank that Turkish Commander. A mere trifle, I assure you," he went on, and then coughed violently, while blood dribbled from the corner of his mouth.

He shut his eyes, and, in the midst of calling to them again, fell backwards heavily, leaving both Geoff and Philip dismayed at his appearance. Springing forward, Phil lifted his head and supported the Commander against his knee, while Geoff rapidly undid his tunic, and, seeing clearly from the stain upon it where the wound must be, tore the shirt open. But what to do further was the question with him, for, though our hero may have had some experience already of travelling, and had undoubtedly seen rather more of foreign places than is the lot of most young fellows, yet he was singularly ignorant of wounds, had seen few indeed, and had practically no training in minor surgery. But amongst the crew there was one who was quite an experienced old sailor, who, had he cared to tell his tale, no doubt could have yarned to them of many a naval scrap in out-of-the-way places. It was the Cox who joined them now—a short, broad-shouldered, rather wizened fellow, with a cheerful smile always on his face, and with that brisk, respectful, helpful way about him so common to his counterpart, the non-commissioned officer, in the army.

"You just hold on to him like that," he told Philip, who was supporting the Commander's head and shoulders. "No," he added in a warning voice, "no, I wouldn't let him lie down flat, sir, if I was you, 'cause, you see, sir, he's hit through the lung, and he's bleeding internally. If you just think for a moment, sir, you'll see that that sort of thing is likely to drown a man, to swamp his lungs, as it were, and the more you can sit him up for a while the better. Hi, Marsden," he called, "let's have that surgical pannier!"

If Geoff and his chum were entirely ignorant of wounds beyond what knowledge was required to place a first field dressing in position—and that was a task which every officer and man learned as a matter of course—the Cox was, on the other hand, quite a respectable surgeon. While Philip held the Commander's heavy frame up, the broad-shouldered little sailor cut away his tunic and shirt, and, having exposed the wound both at the front and at the back—for the bullet had passed right through the body—he swiftly dabbed each wound with his brush loaded with iodine, and then clapped on a dressing.

"Next thing is to bandage him up so as to leave the other side of his chest free to move, and keep this side just as still as possible," he told Geoff, "that will give the damaged arteries and veins a chance to heal and stop bleeding. Beg pardon, sir, but if you'd hold the box of dressings I can help myself easier."

With dexterous hands—hands which were as gentle as might be, in spite of this sailor's rough calling—the Cox rapidly secured the dressings with a roller bandage. Meanwhile, at a call from Geoff, the cabin cushions had been laid on the boards at the bottom of the cabin, and on this improvised bed the Commander was now laid, his head well propped up with cushions.

"And we'll just roll him over on to his damaged side, like that," the Cox told them. "That means that, as he breathes, that side won't move, and can't move overmuch, while the other one will be doing all the work for him. He is opening his eyes, I do declare! Why!——"

Two penetrating and rather fierce optics were fixed on the trio in the cabin at that moment, while the Commander struggled to move. Then the eyes opened quite widely, the lips curved, and in a second or two he was smiling serenely.

"So the Cox is practising on me all that I've taught him, eh?" he asked, and Geoff noted with relief that the voice was stronger and steadier. "I knew it would come to that some day; I kind of guessed it. Well, Cox, what's the verdict? What's the diagnosis? Is it a cure this time, or has that Turkish officer put in a shot likely to deprive His Britannic Majesty of a somewhat valuable officer? Ahem!"

The gentle cough he gave brought another driblet of blood to the corner of his lips, and caused Geoff to kneel down beside the Commander and expostulate with him.

"Really, sir," he said, "you must keep quiet and stop talking. You——"

The eyes of the old sea-dog who had seized so greatly upon the fancy of Geoff and his chum, opened widely again, and that same expansive, warm-hearted grin was turned upon them.

"Oh! oh!" he exclaimed; and, there was no doubt about it now, his voice was growing steadily stronger. "So our young officers wait until their senior is knocked out, and then start bullying and ordering! Oh! So that's the game, is it, Keith? You are beginning to show up in your true colours! Believe me, my lads, I'm not nearly so bad as you imagine, and, 'pon my word, in a little while I shall be fit to get up and start smoking."

Then he laughed, or, to speak the truth, cackled, for the effort of real laughter was beyond him, while he glanced quizzically at Geoff as that young officer coloured furiously. Yet, though he knew that the Commander was making fun of him, he was delighted at his progress, and a moment later was joining in the merriment.

"Come now," said the Commander, a little later, "tell me all about the thing. You had just knocked that Turkish officer out, and a huge Turk was lifting his hands in token of surrender. I don't seem to remember anything after that; I must have tumbled backwards into this cabin. And now that you have laid me on the floor, there's no seeing anything but the sky above me. Where are we? Where's the Turkish launch? What happened? And, of course, we captured the beggars!"

Very quickly Geoff told him precisely what had resulted from their attack upon the Turkish launch, and how they had captured the vessel, and what remained of her crew.

"We are lying to, behind the island, at this moment, sir," he added, "for by doing so we are hidden from the enemy. I thought it best to repair damages."

"Yes, yes! Human and material," smiled the Commander, who was ever on the look-out for some little joke. "But wait! I may not be the only one wounded. What's the report from my fellows?"

Philip had already obtained it, and at once communicated the facts to Commander Houston.

"One man hit through the fleshy part of his arm, and only slightly incapacitated; another has lost the tip of one finger. That's all the human part about it, sir," he said, with a grin. "As for the material: there are half a dozen holes bored through your motor-launch, and I believe the Cox has already made a cure by means of filching material from the box containing surgical dressings."

"Good! We have come through that little business splendidly," said the Commander. "And now, what next?" he asked, fixing his eyes on Geoff and then swinging them round to Philip. "What next? You have captured the launch — —"

"We!" expostulated Geoff. "You were in command, sir, don't forget that! And by the time you fell their resistance was almost finished."

"Then 'we' — we have captured the launch, and that, you will remember, was a point I laid stress on. Then?" asked Commander Houston, peering into Geoff's face. "Did it occur to you, young Keith, that— —"

Geoff smiled at the wounded Commander, and seated himself opposite to him.

"I think the same idea occurred to me, sir," he said, "and perhaps somewhere about the same moment. You see, the Turks aboard that steamer, the fellows who fired that gun at us, know now well enough that the British have sent a motor-boat up the River Euphrates, and a motor-boat is a thing they will be hunting for. But a steam-launch, one of their very own, manned by a Turkish officer and Turkish soldiers, would have a chance to pass up the river right under their noses. In command of a boat like that, a fellow might find out a great deal more than if still aboard this motor-boat. So I thought that if we were lucky enough to capture the launch we might send off a party on her."

"Showing that wise heads think in the same direction," the Commander laughed a second later, though his eyes were twinkling with excitement. "Confound this wound! But for that, I can tell you, I should have commanded this second expedition. The scheme is just one that is likely to succeed, and, as you say, Keith, has better chances than we should have, now that the Turks have dropped upon us. Being wounded myself, of course, I shall have to give way to another, and it looks to me as though our friend the Cox would have to command this little expedition."

You could have knocked Philip and Geoff down with the proverbial feather. Their faces, which had been smiling before and lit up with enthusiasm, suddenly lengthened, while they regarded the Commander with something akin to horror, if not positive anger.

"But," exploded Philip, "I—you—we——"

Commander Houston laughed again, laughed till he choked and coughed, and until Geoff begged of him to take things quietly.

"I—you—we——" he said at last, mimicking Philip. "Well, well! I'll tease you no further. Of course, Keith will take charge of this little affair; and seeing that you, Denman, are, as it were, under his direct command, why, of course, he'll take you with him. For me, though I like to take things in the right way, and not make a fuss, I realize well enough that that Turkish officer has knocked me out completely. Don't worry!" he went on. "I'm hit hard, I know, but it takes a precious deal to kill a man of my stamina; and, to tell you the truth, though I feel weak and rather knocked out for the moment, I'm very far from dying. But marsh lands and swamps, such as we lie in, are not good for wounds; and that being the case, and since I should be a hindrance to the whole party, I shall 'bout ship and steam down to the Shatt-el-Arab. We know the route now, we shall have little to fear once we are away from this neighbourhood, and we can travel with a diminished crew. Keith, my boy, set about investigating the contents of our capture."

Leaving the Commander in the cabin, and taking the precaution to haul a piece of sailcloth over the opening above so as to shelter him from the direct rays of the sun—which were now pouring down upon the marshes—Geoff and Philip stepped aboard the captured launch, and made a thorough survey of her, discovering a quantity of rifles and ammunition, besides a supply of dates and coffee. In a cabin aft of the engine-room there were some tinned provisions, which no doubt had belonged to the officer. For the rest, there was sufficient fuel aboard to take the vessel a considerable distance, and, in fact, little was required to make her fit for service.

"We could go off on her right away," Geoff told his chum, his voice exultant, "for there is food enough on board to feed you, and me, and the crew we shall require to man her. As to water, we can get that from the boiler at any time, and so need have little fear of fever. I vote we ask the Commander to allow us a certain supply of provisions and ammunition for the men we take with us. As to the number of the latter, of course, he will decide upon it; but the sooner we select our men the better, for they must discard their present clothing and dress up in the uniforms of the Turkish soldiers."

When they came to the point of selecting the half-dozen men that the Commander decided to allot them, Geoff found that he was face to face with an unexpected difficulty. For, calling the sailors about him on the deck of the Turkish launch—as he wished to leave the Commander quietly resting—he had barely opened his mouth sufficiently to explain what was about to happen, and to call for volunteers, when every man of the party stepped forward. More than that, there was an insinuating smile on the faces of all, without exception, the sort of smile a man indulges in when he wishes to ask a favour. It was a kind of dilemma which an older man than Geoff, and one far more experienced, would have dealt with at once, though not without difficulty; but Geoff, we admit the fact, was utterly confounded.

"But," he stuttered, "I—don't you know—I—well, that is, I only want six of you, so what's the good of all of you volunteering?"

"That's just it, sir," the Cox explained. "There's not a single man jack here who don't want to be one of the party. Beg pardon, sir," he added, a moment later, seeing that Geoff was puzzled and perplexed, "if you was to leave it to us we'd soon fix the business. We'd draw lots, and then not a single one of the men could feel that he was out of favour. The lucky ones would be envied, that's all, and the rest of 'em would go back with the Commander as pleasant as possible."

Within a few minutes, as a matter of fact, the whole matter had been amicably settled; and thereafter Geoff and Philip were busily engaged in dressing the men they were to take with them, securing for that purpose the clothing of Turks who had fallen during the conflict. Then, about an hour before dusk fell, they set off from the place where they had been lying behind the island, the Turkish engineer still manning his engine, while one of their own men was at the wheel. Philip was right for'ard, quite a fierce-looking Turk in his dirty khaki uniform and fez head-covering. As for Geoff, he sat on the little platform just in front of the funnel, and no one taking even the closest look at him would have suspected him of being a British officer. A moment before, he had gripped the Commander's hand and had received a cheery send-off from him. Then smoke gushed from the funnel, the Turkish engineer pulled gently at his throttle, and the screw of the steam-launch began to churn the water. Signals were exchanged between those seeming Turkish soldiers on the deck of the launch and the British sailors still remaining on board the motor-vessel. Then the launch gained the far end of the island, and, swinging round it, disappeared, the last glance which Geoff cast over his shoulder showing him a number of disconsolate individuals watching their departure, while, seated aft on the motor-vessel, were the nine or ten prisoners whom they had captured. Stealing silently across a wide stretch of swamp, and answering cheerily a signal flung out from the bigger Turkish steamer somewhere away on the river, the launch was headed to the left until she gained a group of islands.

"In here, Excellency," said the native, who, naturally enough, formed one of the party. "There's a channel amongst those islands which I have followed, and which will take us up within half a mile of the river stream, yet hidden from it. Let the man drive the boat faster while there is nothing here to impede us."

As darkness fell that night, the launch was tearing along through the stagnant water, flinging a bow wave on to the islands which cropped up, now to the right and now to the left of her. Sometimes her steersman was forced to make her swerve somewhat violently, to avoid an obstruction consisting of ooze and mud and covered with thick-growing reeds, but for the most part her course was directly forward, and parallel to the river. At length, as darkness fell, the engines were stopped, and the boat was brought to a halt between two islands. There the anchor was dropped, and the little force made ready to spend the night and to prepare for an eventful to-morrow.

CHAPTER IX

A Cutting-out Expedition

"What's that? Listen! I heard something!"

Geoff cocked his head up over the side of the cabin in which he and Philip had been partaking of their evening meal, and turned his face towards the River Euphrates, across the waste of ooze and mud and water which separated their captured launch from it—a waste hidden by the darkness, and yet illuminated ever so faintly by a crescent of the moon, which was already floating above them, while stars peppered the sky in every direction, and helped to make things visible. Across the waste of water, dulled by the whisper of the evening breeze as it rustled through the reeds and osiers, a sound had come to Geoff's ears, a sound which caused him to enjoin silence upon all aboard the steam-launch. Then, as he listened, there came to his ears, at first faintly only, but growing steadily yet gradually louder, the plug, plug of the paddles of a river steamer.

"The Turk who had the cheek to fire that shot at us!" exclaimed Philip. "Listen to him! He's going up the river, and I dare say he's wondering what's happened to his launch, and whether he'll find that rather nice and comfortable little vessel waiting for him up-stream. Eh, Geoff?"

"Listen! The paddles are going slower, and it sounds to me as if the steamer was going to pull up for the night. You must remember that the Euphrates isn't the sort of river that one cares to steam up at any kind of pace during the hours of darkness, for by all accounts it's stuffed full of sand-banks and muddy islands, which are always changing, 'specially after rains and storms. There's a voice," Geoff went on; "that's someone giving an order! And now the paddles have ceased altogether."

"Plunk! There goes her anchor. She's come to a roost without a doubt!" ejaculated Philip. "That's rummy, ain't it? Our Turkish friends will be settling down for their evening meal—or whatever sort of thing they have—within sound of us, and, I'll lay my hat, without suspecting that their precious steam-launch is within easy reach of them."

Geoff stretched out a hand in the semi-darkness and gripped his chum by the shoulder.

"Splendid!" he said.

"Eh?" asked the other, a little bewildered. "What's splendid? Having the Turks so close to us? 'Not 'arf', as 'Tommy' is fond of saying. Why, we shall have to lie as quiet as mice here, and the next thing you'll be doing will be to order us to cease smoking, for fear the light of our pipes should be seen aboard the steamer. Most inconsiderate of that Turk, I call it! For he might at least have stopped down the river, or gone a little higher, so that we might have passed a peaceful night, and made ready for all sorts of things to-morrow. 'Splendid!' Hum! Sorry I can't agree with you, my dear fellow."

If he could only have guessed what was in Geoff's mind at the moment, and could have seen that young fellow quite clearly, Philip might easily have given expression to quite different opinions. For, to be precise, our young hero, dressed in the uniform of a Turkish officer, and with a Turkish fez perched on his head, was as near the actual thing as could well be imagined. In daylight, in the city of Bagdad, and, for that matter, in any other city, he might very well have passed muster; while the fact that he was able to speak the language fluently—as fluently as any native—made his disguise all the better; and now, with some idea in his head to which Philip was a stranger, there occurred to Geoff the thought that the coming of this steamer to such close quarters presented a splendid opportunity. He shook his chum savagely, so as to silence him.

"You don't let a fellow finish!" he exclaimed. "But it's splendid, really splendid, that that steamer should have dropped her anchor within easy reach of us."

"And why, pray?" asked Philip, rather inclined to banter with his senior officer.

"Why, being so near makes it all the easier for a fellow to get aboard her."

"A — bo — ard her!"

Philip opened his mouth wide, and his eyes too, though that didn't help him to see his chum any the better.

"Well — but — surely — you don't mean to — — Well, I'm hanged!" he exclaimed. "And — of course — of course it's splendid, as you say — a splendid opportunity. But you'll never think of going alone, eh, Geoff?" he asked, with a pleading note in his voice. "Supposing a Turkish sentry caught hold of you? Supposing you got 'lagged' immediately you were on board, what then? I — —"

"You would be required aboard this launch to take command of the expedition," Geoff told him curtly. "But let's be serious, Phil. We're out to learn all we can of the Turks, and, as you know, it's been reported that the enemy are gathering somewhere up the River Euphrates, behind or in this long stretch of marsh land. We might push up the river in the early morning and discover them. We might barge into the very midst of them, and find ourselves surrounded, with no chance of getting away and carrying our information to Head-quarters. But what we want to know is known aboard that steamer. The officer in command is nearly sure to be of superior rank, and in any case he must know where the Turks are assembling."

"And so," argued Phil, as he bit at a cigarette, "and so, my boy, you've designs on the steamer. 'Pon my word! I wish I was able to speak the lingo. Languages are things I've always hated; but I can see what advantages they give to a fellow, what fun they bring him, and — ahem! — what chances of promotion. So you'll go aboard? Wish the dickens I could come with you."

"I shall go aboard and find out the whereabouts of this officer."

"And then you'll listen to his conversation through the keyhole if need be," said Philip, whose buoyant spirits always made him seize upon the smallest opportunity of being facetious. "Keyhole, eh? Wonder if Turks have 'em? Anyway, you'll contrive to find a spot from which you can hear the old bounder; and then, of course, the business will be to make him converse upon the subject upon which you are most interested. That's a teaser, eh? How will you do it? Supposing he's immersed in an argument about the war, and about the rights and wrongs of the Turks and the Germans; or supposing he's only telling his under-officer—for I suppose there is such an individual—all about his home life, his wife and his children, his house and his garden. Supposing, in fact, he won't get on to your line of argument, and won't babble about the Turks and their concentration in the marshes."

Hum! It certainly was a teaser, and the situation as Philip drew it had not occurred to Geoff before. That it was possible to reach the steamer in the tiny dinghy carried aboard the launch, and to clamber unseen aboard her, he did not doubt; that he might, by skill and cheek, contrive thereafter to get within sight and sound of the Commander, he thought was within the bounds of possibility; but to make that Commander talk, to make him give the information which Geoff sought, was an entirely different matter altogether.

"By George!" he exclaimed; "that would be awkward."

"It would," Philip told him in tones of irony. "You're aboard the steamer, you've—not actually, but let us say metaphorically—sat down in the cabin occupied by this old bounder, and then he won't talk, you can't make him talk; he's glum, we'll say; he's agitated about the loss of the steam-launch; he can't make up his mind what all that firing meant, and where his twenty-odd soldiers and the two officers who commanded them have got to. In fact, he's in the dickens of a stew, in a beastly temper, smoking a cigar, and won't say 'nothink'."

"Oh, shut up!" Geoff told him angrily.

"Like the Turkish captain, in fact," Philip laughed. "But, seriously, just as you said a moment ago, seriously, what's to be done? You know the old adage: 'You can take a horse to the water, but no amount of kicks or coaxing will make him drink'; well, this old Turk may be just like that obstinate old horse. He's there, aboard his steamer, and nothing will make him talk, not even——"

"Stop!" commanded Geoff abruptly. "'Nothing will make him talk,' you say? Won't it? I mean to get information out of the old beggar—for I presume he is old—but don't forget that neither of us have seen him yet, so he may be young and active. All the same, I am going aboard now, and, of course, if I don't come back within reasonable time you will have cause to believe that I have been captured. Then the command of the expedition devolves upon you, and it is for you to carry out the work entrusted to us. Just launch that dinghy, quietly, my lads," he called over the front of the cabin, "and see that there's a paddle in her."

Geoff began to grope in the cabin of the steam-launch, till his hand presently lit upon the pannier containing dressings, which had been handed over to them by the gallant Commander, whom they had left wounded aboard the motor-boat.

"You may want it, lads," he had told them. "There is never any saying when you may come up against the Turks, and, having had one brisk little engagement with them, you may have another, and, of course, may very well have some of the crew wounded. Of course, I hope that that won't be the case, but you never know your luck. For that reason we'll divide up the dressings, I taking sufficient for my own purposes while you take enough for yours."

"Got it!" exclaimed Geoff, as his hand lit upon the pannier. "Now for a pad of cotton-wool and a couple of bandages."

"Eh!" asked Philip curiously; "'Couple of bandages,' 'cotton-wool'—you're going aboard a steamer, now what in the name of the dickens is that for?"

Geoff didn't tell him to mind his own business, for he was far too polite a young fellow to give such an answer, neither did he speak to his inquisitive chum gruffly even; instead, he maintained silence, whilst he carefully

122

picked out the bandages and the pad of cotton-wool. Then Phil suddenly gripped him by the shoulder.

"I've got it!" he exclaimed.

"Got what?" asked Geoff curtly.

"Got it, of course," came the answer; "the bandages and the pad of cotton-wool; the idea, my dear boy, the very smart and brilliant brain-wave that's come to you. You're going to— —"

"What?"

"What! Why of course the brain wave," Philip told him hotly. "I've guessed your idea; you're going to get aboard that steamer, and just because that old bounder of a Turk— —"

"What old bounder of a Turk? The Captain?" asked Geoff. "He isn't old. At least, how do we know that he's old? He may be young, middle-aged, bald-headed and toothless."

The two of them were getting quite angry, and for a moment or two it looked as though the wordy warfare in which they were beginning to be engaged would develop into quite a battle. Then Geoff giggled—an excited little giggle—while Phil joined his chum heartily, and brought one hand down with a thump on the broad of his back.

"Jingo!" he exclaimed. "You're right, of course we don't know whether the old bounder is young or old, or even toothless; but we do know that there's a captain or an officer in charge of that steamer, and, what's more, we know, what you want and didn't tell me, that we're going to capture him."

"We're going to!" exclaimed Geoff. "I thought I'd already said, as the officer commanding this expedition— —"

"Ahem!" coughed Philip. "Certainly, sir, you did say that," he said in his most demure manner. "But the job, if you'll allow me to say so, is rather a big one—in short, and in fact, it's a 'tough nut' you propose to crack, and in cracking it you're just as likely to come to grief yourself, and possibly to have your head cracked. Indeed, as your immediate junior, as one anxious for the success of this most important expedition, it becomes my duty to point out that failure on your part, failure because you have gone into the matter without sufficient forces at your command, will lead inevitably to the ghastly failure of the whole expedition. Once the alarm is given, once there is no longer the chance of a surprise, in fact, once the Turks are on the qui vive, and know what we are up to, the game's up, and we've lost! Nice to have to return to the camp on the Shatt-el-Arab, and tell 'em that we've been a hideous failure!"

He was piling it on with a vengeance, was Philip, but then he was an artful, if light-hearted and jovial fellow, and here he had a most distinct object in view. He plucked Geoff eagerly by the sleeve.

"Rotten, that!" he told him. "Just fancy what the fellows would say! They'd not forget to tell us all about it, and make nasty remarks about chaps with swollen heads who'd gone up the river on their own, thinking to do a heap, and returning without carrying out their object, or even nearly completing it. See?" he asked Geoff, with decided emphasis, and repeated his demand as a movement of his chum seemed to denote some signs of giving way. "Just think it over, Geoff! You go aboard the steamer and creep along the deck till you come to the Captain's cabin. Don't forget that you want the bounder to talk about the Turks and their position, and just remember what I said when I suggested that he'd talk on any and every subject rather than that. Well, aboard the steamer you can't make him answer your questions, or launch out into an explanation of the Turkish plans of campaign; so you decide to kidnap him, and have the idea of plugging his mouth with that cotton-wool, and winding a bandage about his head. Very pretty! Awfully nice if the thing works! But will it? Supposing he shouts before you plug his toothless mouth — he was toothless I think we agreed — supposing he's not alone, what then? You're done! Your plan's defeated. You might just as well have stayed aboard this launch and rested. But — —"

"But if Phil — the eager Phil — happened to be close at hand, ready to brain the other fellow. Ah!" exclaimed Geoff, and for the life of him he couldn't help laughing at the excitement and the eager pleading of his chum.

It made him laugh when he remembered how adroitly and how expertly Philip had worked round the question, had pointed out so very clearly the chances of failure, and then had come in at the end with the greatest arguments for his own inclusion in the adventure. Arguments which Geoff himself could not deny; for a friend at hand, a stanch friend, might very well turn the scales in his favour, and, after all, what a prize the Captain of that steamer would be, if they could only lay their hands on him.

"Better far than the chief I bagged at the very beginning of the campaign," he told himself, though he spoke aloud.

"Agreed!" said Philip. "I don't, of course, want to say that that wasn't quite a nice little business, but then, this is really 'It', or will be if we bring it off. So I come, don't I?"

"You do. Your revolver's loaded, eh?"

"And ready," Phil said, "and the dinghy is alongside."

"Then come on."

Leaving the oldest sailor in charge of the launch, with instructions to lie in that position till morning came, and then to look about for them, and to return down the Euphrates in the event of not discovering their officers, Geoff and Philip crept gingerly into the dinghy, which had been brought close alongside, having been launched from the deck of the little steamer where it was usually carried.

"Push off," said Geoff, "and keep your ear open for a hail, for it'll be no easy job to find you in the darkness."

"Aye, aye, sir," replied the man, "good luck to you."

Geoff dipped his paddle in the water, and thrust hard with it, while Philip, seated in the stern, used a paddle as a rudder. Stealing along the narrow channel in which the steam launch lay, they soon rounded the end of one of the islands which formed it, and halted there for a while to allow their eyes to grow accustomed to the darkness. Then they turned sharp left, facing the direction in which the River Euphrates lay, and stole onward across the waste of waters, threading their way between muddy banks where the slime and ooze clung, and often diving under perfect archways of reeds, where the islands were close together. Once or twice they had to return on their tracks, finding their way obstructed, and on one occasion they bumped gently into an island, and stuck fast for a while, till Geoff came aft—thus tipping the bows of the dinghy upward and so loosening her. It was perhaps half an hour later that they felt, rather than saw, that they had gained the main stream, the wide expanse of smooth, almost motionless water, where eddies from the river sometimes stirred the surface, and where the flow, moderately rapid in the centre, was so retarded as to be almost imperceptible.

"Straight across," whispered Geoff, "there are the lights of the steamer just up-river of us, so we'll cut across to the centre, where I reckon her to be lying, and then steal up behind her. Gently with your paddle, Phil, for a splash might attract the attention of a sentry and bring rifle-fire upon us."

Another ten minutes passed, during which they plunged their paddles gently though firmly into the stream, and forced the little boat steadily upward, and during that time the dull, dimly visible hull of the vessel lying out in mid-stream gradually grew bigger and bigger. At length they were right under her stern, and found that, though low-built in the centre, and indeed generally, she was yet well above their heads, so much so that the dinghy lay close to the rudder and practically under the stern of the vessel. It was just then that the end of a trailing rope struck Phil gently across the face, and, groping for it, he had soon seized upon it firmly.

"Half a mo'!" he told Geoff. "What's this? A rope, a rope to make our boat fast to. Now I call that particularly accommodating of this old party we've come to visit."

"What, eh?"

Geoff chuckled. It did him good to hear Philip's innocent banter, and showed him also at the same time what an excellent fellow he had to assist him.

"Make fast," he whispered. "Give a good haul on it first, though, and if it's stout enough I'll make use of it to get aboard, though I imagine by getting on your back I could easily reach the rail, and so the deck of the steamer."

A minute later they had secured the dinghy to the rope, and the wise Philip made fast the other end of it to a bolt-hole in the rudder, thus keeping their little boat right under the stern of the steamer, where she would remain unseen. Then Geoff gripped the rope which had been dangling over the rail, and, putting all his weight on it to test it, swung himself out of the dinghy and clambered up till he could grasp the rail above. One strong heave and his face was above its level, and he was able to look along the deck of the steamer. Then very slowly he clambered upward, and slid on to the deck, where he crouched under the rail to watch and listen.

Hark! There were voices somewhere. There was a light shining on the deck on either side, through what appeared to be the skylight of a cabin, while the voices, no doubt, came from that direction. But it was not that alone which Geoff had heard, it was something else — the gentle slap, slap of feet on the deck, the soft footfall of a man shod with sandals perhaps, or more likely entirely unshod, perhaps a barefooted sentry pacing the deck to and fro, turning when he had accomplished a dozen paces. Geoff peered into the darkness, hoping to see the man, but failed, though the sounds were still quite audible. Then he stole forward till quite close to the cabin's skylight, where he hid behind a mast in a dark corner between it and the bulkhead of the cabin. Yes, the sounds made by that sentry — for if not a sentry what else could he be? — were clearly audible, while the figure now came into view, feebly outlined it is true yet quite sufficient for Geoff's purpose. There was a Turk, perhaps a Turkish sailor, striding to and fro some twenty yards farther forward, turning about each time he reached the rail, striding this way and that like an automaton — as if indeed he were a clockwork figure.

"Rather too near to be pleasant," thought Geoff, "and the bother of it is that he makes it difficult for a fellow to peer into the cabin. Ah! one of these sky-lights is lifted. It's been a hot day, and I've no doubt it's stuffy down in the cabin. That's really very considerate of our friend, the Captain, as Phil would say. Yes, voices — Turkish voices — let's see what's happening."

He went on all fours, and stole along beside the cabin's skylight till he came to the panel which was lifted. There was an opening, perhaps some six inches in width, through which the light was streaming, and also the voices of two men, at least, down in the cabin. But six inches is hardly sufficient space to admit a head, and Geoff at once increased the size of the opening by lifting the panel.

"Stop, there! Enough! It's cool enough below!" he heard someone exclaim an instant later. "Idiot, leave the thing as it is now, and wait next time till you are told to make an alteration."

By then Geoff was flat on the deck, listening to the voice so near to him, and watching that sentry, that automaton, as he moved to and fro; watching him and hoping that he would take no notice. Indeed, he need hardly have worried himself, for the man did not even deign to turn his head, but strolled on across his beat, his rifle now visible as it thrust upward above his shoulder. For the life of him Geoff could not help chuckling again, and repeating the words which Philip had used but a few minutes earlier.

"A most accommodating sentry," he said. "If only he'll continue to march to and fro without looking this way it'll give me a chance of peeping into the cabin. Here goes! Oh! Three of 'em, eh! All officers, and, by George, the chief of 'em is bald-headed, or I'm a Dutchman!"

How Philip would have laughed had he been beside his chum and recollected their conversation aboard the steam-launch, for as Geoff peered down into the cabin, his head screened to a certain extent from the view of those below by the supports of the skylight, and by the swinging oil-lamp which illuminated the interior, his eyes fell upon three individuals — three Turkish officers — one of whom sat back in a chair in the most dilettante attitude, smoking a cigarette; a young man without doubt, handsome as the Turks go, but decidedly effeminate. Near him was another officer, rather older, with a handsomely curled moustache, who leaned both elbows on the cabin table and seemed to be already nodding. And opposite the two, lounging full length on a divan, was a stout broad-shouldered Pasha, a senior Turkish officer, whose fez now reposed on the floor, exposing a head which shone and glistened in the rays of the lamp-light. As to his being toothless, that was another matter, though the memory of what had passed between himself and Philip, once again caused Geoff to give vent to a silent chuckle.

"And so you think, my dear comrade, that this firing on the part of the crew of the steam-launch resulted in the annihilation of a party of the British, eh?" the elderly Turkish officer was asking, whilst he waved a big, fat hand, upon which glistened many rings, in the direction of the young officer at the head of the table.

"I do. To-morrow they will return with a fine tale of their doings. You will discover, my chief, that you have been the means of stopping a reconnoitring-force of the enemy ascending the Euphrates. It will be good for you, good for me, good for us all."

They lapsed into silence for a while and then started on some other topic. Indeed, though Geoff listened for the better part of quarter of an hour, not once did they broach the subject of Turkish troops, nor that of their position in these marsh lands about the Euphrates. It was clear, in fact, that to stay where he was, risking discovery at any moment, on the chance of such a question rising between the Turkish officers below him, was madness, and that some other scheme must be adopted to get at the information which he and Philip coveted. Lowering his head, therefore, and making sure that the sentry had not discerned him, Geoff crept on all fours across the deck, and, clambering over the rail, dropped gently into the boat. And there for a while he and his chum discussed the matter in low tones, making their plans so as to accomplish their purpose.

It was half an hour later when Geoff led the way up over the rail again, followed by Philip, and the two crept for'ard along the deck of the steamer.

"There's the cabin," whispered Geoff, pointing to the skylight, "and down below is the old boy we're bent on capturing. Just creep along and look in, then come back at once, for we've no time to waste, and must complete the business."

CHAPTER X

Geoff and Philip manœuvre

"Lor', Geoff, you didn't tell me, you didn't say a word about it!" gasped, rather than whispered, the excited Philip, as he crawled back to our hero's side, having sprawled along the deck of the steamer and peeped into the cabin wherein were those three Turkish officers, the possession of one of whom the two young British officers so eagerly coveted. "What d'you mean by it?"

"Mean by it! By what? Shut up, you idiot, or that sentry will hear us!"

"Hang the sentry!" came the whispered answer, as Philip lay down beside his chum and close under the rail of the vessel. "But, I say, what a joke! Just fancy our guessing so exactly. He's as old as they make 'em, the chap who commands this ship—an old, fat, and bloated bounder—and, Christopher! he's bald and as toothless as a baby."

The fellow actually cackled, till Geoff pounced upon him and closed his mouth with his hand.

"Shut up, you fool!" he exclaimed, in a fierce whisper. "You'll have every man aboard the ship upon us and will wreck our chances. I begin to wish that I hadn't brought you with me; but I thought that at least you had some sort of sense."

Philip sniggered. He knew that Geoff didn't really mean to be so fierce as he made out, or even so vindictive, and, after all, there seemed little chance of the sentry suspecting their presence or overhearing them. For, in the first place, though farther away amidst the marshes, an almost complete silence covered the waste of waters—broken only by the faint whisper of the evening breeze as it rustled amongst the reeds of the thousands of muddy islands—out here, in the centre of the stream, there was the swish and swirl of water as it flowed past the steel sides of the vessel, the lap of the current, and the whistle of the breeze as it swayed the cordage to and fro and hummed a gentle tune round the funnel, the steam whistle, and the other contrivances hampering the deck of the steamer. And, secondly, there was the sentry himself, a mere doll he seemed, an automaton—as Geoff had thought—a man who marched barefooted, to and fro, to and fro, backwards and forwards from one rail of the vessel to the other, never appearing to turn his head, never shifting the rifle which rested across one shoulder, apparently deaf to sounds, and oblivious to all that was taking place about him. Not that much could be said to be within his vision, for, be it remembered, darkness lay over the Euphrates and the adjacent marshes—darkness made a little less intense by that crescent of the moon which floated in the heavens, by the million brilliant stars with which they were peppered, and, to a lesser degree, in one particular part, by the feeble rays which struggled through the skylight of the cabin and fell gently on the deck of the vessel.

Still, too much cackling on the part of the jovial Philip might easily have been fatal; and, besides, it was not a time for expressing one's feelings, for ribald laughter, or even for jests, and certainly one would have thought that even the recklessness of a junior British officer would have been suppressed by the occasion. Philip checked himself with a gulp. He was thinking of that bald head down below, and of the extraordinarily good guess which he and his chum had made as to the appearance of the Commander of this boat long before they had set eyes on him. Then, suddenly, the question of his capture filled his mind, to the obliteration of everything else.

"A big bounder!" he told Geoff. "It'll want some doing. How?"

Geoff gave vent to a subdued whistle, a mere puff of air from his lips, and then he nudged his comrade.

"See that sentry over there?" he asked abruptly.

"Faintly. Not having quite the eyes of a cat, I can't say that I see him distinctly. What of him?"

"Of him? Nothing. But you'll take his place within a minute."

"Oh!" Philip exclaimed, and stared through the darkness at his chum. "Take his place in a minute? Certainly!" he said. "But—er—supposing he objects?"

"That's his business," said Geoff, "and ours too, of course. I shall ask him in the politest way possible to step below; or, to be more precise, I propose now to march up to him as if I were one of those three officers down below in the cabin. If he doesn't obey the order I give him——"

"That's our business," said Phil, and he chuckled again. "I've got the whole scheme, Geoff, and you can fire ahead at once. I shall come along quite close behind you, and if the fellow wants to kick up a row, or doesn't like taking orders from a superior officer, I'll knock him overboard. You can leave that part of the business to me. I'm just itching to tackle a Turk, and to start the campaign in real earnest."

"Then come along!" Geoff told him. "We'll creep along as far as the cabin, and peep in to make sure that those fellows below are not likely to be moving, and then I'll go for'ard and accost the sentry. Come along!"

The two of them were already on their knees, crouching below the rail of the vessel, and at once crept forward till they were level with the cabin; then, peering in, Geoff made out the figures of the three officers below, still in the same positions they had occupied before—the fat, bald-headed man, undoubtedly the senior of the party, nodding on the divan, while the officer at the head of the table still smoked and still prattled to his neighbour. Then he nudged Philip, and, passing behind the skylight, stood at his full height, and stepped quickly along the deck towards the sentry, who still marched to and fro, to and fro, apparently without hearing his approach, as he paid no attention to it. Indeed, Geoff was within five yards of him before the man suddenly turned his head and noticed his coming, and just as suddenly came to a halt and grounded his weapon.

"Who goes there?" he challenged, in quite low tones, and it was evident that he was not in the least concerned by Geoff's appearance.

Indeed, he had been anticipating the exit of one officer, at least, from the cabin, where he knew that his betters were smoking and chatting, and no doubt the figure now coming towards him was one of them. Nor was Geoff in the least disconcerted; for, thanks to the dress he wore, to the fez which was perched on his head, and to his command of the language, he felt no doubt of being able to deceive the fellow.

"Officer, going rounds," he answered to the challenge. "Dismiss, my man, and go to your quarters; the Commander feels that there is no need of a sentry while we lie right out here in the river, and, that being the case, there is no need for you to spoil a night's rest. Get down with you!"

The man shouldered his rifle at once and turned as if to obey the order, and then, of a sudden, he swung round again, as if an idea had struck him, or as if he were suspicious. Indeed, there was something which had attracted his attention, a dark, shadowy something which his eyes, hitherto seemingly so useless to him, had discovered following the officer who had just given him the order. It was the dark shadow of a man, creeping along close to the rail of the ship, as if prepared to spring upon the back of the officer.

"Beware!" he cried. "There is a man behind you, one who sneaks along in the shadows."

That shadow launched itself from beside the rail while the man was shifting his rifle from his left to his right hand, and something flew through the air and hit the sentry so heavily in the face that he stumbled backwards. Then the officer who had given him the order was on the unfortunate man like a whirlwind, and the shadow beside him.

"I've got my hand over his mouth," gasped Philip. "To the side with him; now heave!"

Geoff backed his chum up with a vengeance, gripping the man's hands and tearing his rifle from him. Then, seizing him by the legs, while Philip managed to grip the man's shoulder, still holding his mouth firmly closed, the two rushed him to the side and flung him over into the river, Geoff tossing his rifle into the water after him.

"Now back," he whispered to Philip, taking him by the sleeve of his coat, "the chap is sure to shout and alarm the others. Let's get back and down to our dinghy till things quiet down again. Of course, if he doesn't shout, all the better, for then we shall be able to tackle the other business."

Even before they could turn to run along the deck, the splash which the man's body had made as it fell into the water was followed by a shriek, and then by a hoarse shout as he sang out loudly for help, by a shout which stirred the silence hanging over the river, and brought the men bobbing up from their quarters for'ard, and those three officers stumbling up the steps of their cabin and out on to the deck. And in that short space of time Philip and Geoff had stolen aft, and, slipping over the rail, had slid down into the dinghy.

"Quite a little commotion!" laughed Geoff as he listened to the shouts above him. "Of course I'm sorry for the sentry."

"Rather a dirty game, eh?" said Philip. "But I suppose all's fair in war, eh, Geoff? And besides, supposing I had been the sentry, and you'd come along and chucked me overboard, I should naturally enough howl out so as to give the alarm and to ask for assistance; but I shouldn't be dead, not by a long chalk, and, seeing that I can swim, I should do my best to keep myself afloat till the river twisted and deposited me on one of the banks. If that sentry's sensible, that's what he'll do; on the other hand, if he can't swim—which is hard lines, of course, but not our fault, and a matter we can't deal with—of course, there it is, he'll drown, and neither of us can help it. The best we can do is to wish him luck, for he's now out of the way and not likely to harm us."

Meanwhile there was pandemonium on the deck of the vessel, shouts and cries coming to the two young officers in the dinghy, shouts and cries which were drowned by the stentorian voice of one of the officers, undoubtedly the bald-headed individual who was senior of the party.

"What's that? What's happened?" he bellowed. "Someone shouted, and I'm sure I heard a splash in the river. Where's the sentry? Pass him aft here so that he can report on the incident."

But of the sentry there was not a sign, though a faint shout coming from farther down the river, whither the unfortunate fellow had now floated, was sufficient evidence of the cause of that splash which the Commander had heard, and explanation of the absence of the sentry.

"Deserter!" cried one of the officers, seizing upon the first idea which came to him.

"Who dives into the river and risks drowning? A wise suggestion indeed!" the irate voice of the Commander answered. "But if not, how comes he to have fallen into the river. Foul play, eh? One of his comrades with a grudge against him, a sneaking hound who has crept up from the quarters for'ard and has suddenly pounced upon him?"

"More than likely!" came the answer. "More than likely!"

There was silence for a while, and then the tread of boots on the deck just above the stern beneath which the dinghy was lying.

"It's a strange thing this disappearance of the sentry," Geoff heard a voice saying—the voice of the Commander. "But there it is, and one man more or less makes no difference."

There followed a loud guffaw which made Geoff wince, so heartless did it sound, and in a moment he recognized the voice of that young and elegant Turkish officer who had sat at the end of the cabin table, smoking lazily and curling his dark moustache.

"The sort of sentiments he would give utterance to," he told himself. "It's the kind of thing a fellow hates to hear, and though I was instrumental in pushing that poor beggar overboard, yet I am at least sorry for him, and hope that he will have escaped drowning, and will have landed safely on the bank of the river. And here's one of his own officers laughing as though it didn't matter how many men were lost. Beastly!"

"Eh?" asked Philip in a whisper. "What's that? Listen to those fellows up there!"

For a few moments there had been silence above their heads, where they knew now that at least two of the three officers were standing, and the breeze wafted down to them the smell of tobacco smoke. They heard the boots of the Turkish officers scraping on the deck, and a louder sound as one of them rested his foot on the rail of the vessel. Then the voice of the elder man came to their ears again.

"Yes, there are plenty of them, and one more or less makes no difference," he told his comrade carelessly, and then puffed heavily at the cigar he was smoking—so heavily, indeed, that Geoff could hear him. "Well, well!" he continued; "it's a peaceful night for drowning, my comrade, a peaceful night! See, there's the moon above us, and stars, while the water trickles away below our keel in the most delicious and refreshing manner. A cool night after a hot day, and a sweet breeze to blow away the smell of the marshes. But there, it is nearly time to turn in; go to your bunk, my friend, for I have a mind to sit here and finish my cigar in peace and quietness."

He interrupted the younger officer in the midst of a loud and noisy yawn, and there came the heavy fall of a foot upon the deck, which made it appear that it was the younger man who had placed his foot upon the rail of the vessel. Then something fell beside the dinghy, and hissed for a moment as it struck the water—the stump end of the cigar which this young elegant had been smoking.

"A fine night, and a cool one, as you say, Commander," he said languidly, stifling another yawn, "and time for all of us to be in bed. But I know your ways; you are one of those who burn the candle at both ends, who sit up till the dawn is breaking, and tumble into your bunk only to appear again as the sun is rising. Good-night, Commander!"

From the sharp sounds above, it appeared that he must have drawn himself up at attention and clicked his heels. Then there was a short pause, and immediately afterwards the sound of his retreating feet as he went along the deck towards his cabin, and Geoff and Philip, listening down below, heard him descend the companion-way, somewhere farther forward, and later the sharp crash of a cabin-door being closed. Then there came to their ears the softer patter of feet just above their heads, as the stout Commander of this Turkish steamer strolled to and fro on the stern of the vessel; and again also the aroma from his cigar was wafted down to them on the midnight breeze. Philip gripped Geoff's shoulder and shook his chum.

"Hist!" he said; "you hear the old bounder?"

"Of course. All alone! Smoking a reflective cigar. Now, if——"

"Just if," Philip told him. "If—of course we could, only it'll want some careful doing."

"What will?" demanded Geoff, though the same thought had struck them both, and was passing through their minds.

"Why, if we managed to shy that sentry overboard, and so got rid of him, why not do the same for the old buffer up above us; he'd be over the rail in next to no time, and would be only too glad to find a boat near at hand to rescue him. Look here, Geoff! I've a little plan that's worth considering."

"H—h—sh! He's stopped!" declared Geoff, his voice sunk to a whisper, and his lips close to Philip's ear: "Wonder whether he suspects our presence?"

The steps above them had indeed stopped suddenly, though the aroma of the cigar the Turkish officer was smoking was still wafted down to that space beneath the stern where Geoff and Philip were hiding. They heard a cough, a gentle cough, as the Turk cleared his throat, and later the sound of whistling, while within a minute the man began to pace to and fro again, very slowly, very languidly, as if there was no haste and no hurry, and the Commander was enjoying his little solitary tramp and the peace and quietness of his surroundings.

"Go on," said Geoff; "what's the plan? We kidnap the beggar, of course— that's the plan we set out with this evening. I can see farther than that naturally enough; for, as you've hinted already, we shy him overboard, and then come to his rescue. Now?"

"There'll be a tremendous row and ruction," Philip told him. "The new sentry that they've posted for'ard will give the alarm, and, once it's found out that the Commander's disappeared, every man aboard will be turned out, and if they've got boats, as is most likely the case, for we saw a number trailing behind this steamer, they'll man them and row about in order to try to find the beggar. Now suppose we counter that move?"

"Yes?" asked Geoff eagerly, for he realized the truth of Philip's statement, and could see that, whereas the loss of a humble sentry had caused no great commotion, that of the Commander of the vessel might very well lead to a general alarm, to the disturbance of the whole ship's company, and to a frantic search in which they might easily be discovered. "Yes?" he asked again impatiently.

"That's where my extra little plan comes in," said Philip, and the young fellow chuckled, whereat Geoff gripped his wrist savagely, and shook it.

"Shut up!" he said; "the fellow's only just above our heads, and might easily hear you. Idiot!"

"Thanks!" giggled Philip. "But really, if it comes off, it will be tremendously funny. Now here's the plan: I hop into the water just here, and swim up alongside the steamer, and when I get to her bows, I clamber aboard somehow. We all know that she's anchored in mid-stream, and I'm pretty well sure, from the sounds which came when she dropped her anchor, that she's moored by a hawser. A chain would have clanked out over the side, and we should have heard it, whereas there was a sharp splash and nothing followed. See the point, eh?" he asked eagerly. "She's moored by a rope, and I have a knife here that would cut through a ship's cable."

It was Geoff's turn to exclaim, a smothered exclamation, while he gripped Philip's arm again with fingers which were like a vice.

"Fine!" he told him in a whisper. "And then? You've cut the cable, you've set the ship free, and of course she floats down the stream without any of them being the wiser. The chances are she'll be washed about three or four or more hundred yards before the crew know what's happened, and then it'll only be because she strikes ground, and comes to a stop on a sand-bank farther down the stream. But—but, won't it rather throw us out of our bearings. Just remember that it's pitch-dark in the marshes, and that we've got to find our way back to the steam-launch. It'll want some doing in any case, I can tell you, and if we once get off our bearings it'll be almost an impossibility. But what follows when you've cut the cable?"

"What you'd expect," Philip told him with glee. "I'm on the ship, and I've set her loose, and for the matter of that I should saw through the hawser till it's not quite parted, and leave the stream and the weight of the vessel to do the rest; then I slip aft, and if I find that it's out of the question to pass the sentry, I drop overboard again, and float down beside her till I am nearer the stern; then I clamber to her deck again, crawl right aft, and give that old chap above us a punch that will topple him right over."

It was Geoff's turn to giggle. For the life of him he could not help smiling and chuckling, and indeed found it hard to prevent himself from laughing outright. The gusto with which Philip outlined his plan, his tremendous eagerness and enthusiasm, and the glee in his tone—whispered though it was—were simply infectious. It was only by clapping a hand over his mouth, and gripping Philip's wrist so firmly that that young fellow expostulated by shaking the grip off violently, that Geoff could master his feelings.

"Tremendous!" he told his chum. "And if it doesn't succeed, well it—er—ought to."

"Then, right oh! I'll leave my tunic and revolver here, and go in my shirt and breeches. Boots ain't wanted for swimming either, so I'll take these off. Listen to the old beggar whistling!"

As the young British officer rapidly divested himself of his coat, and of his boots and puttees, he could hear the Turkish Commander still sauntering to and fro on the deck above, every now and again whistling gently and cheerfully. That he was still smoking also there was no doubt, for occasionally the whiff of his cigar was swept down towards the dinghy.

"And a ripping good cigar, believe me," whispered Philip, "and an awful shame to deprive him of its enjoyment, and to waste it before it's quite finished. But war, don't you know, Geoff, is no respecter of things and circumstances and people. The old bounder above will suffer for the cause — our cause, I mean — for we jolly well mean to have him."

What a thing it was to have as a companion in such a critical adventure a young fellow gifted with such splendid spirits, with so light a heart that all thought of danger slipped from his shoulders. Not that Geoff himself was the one to consider risks in the midst of such an undertaking, or even before setting out for the venture; though, to be sure, like every other young officer, he had his serious times, and, as they had paddled their way towards the steamer, had wondered what would happen, whether they would meet with success or dismal failure, and whether capture or death would be the result of their visit. But long ago he had thrown off all doubts, and was ready and eager to face anything — a readiness made all the more pronounced by the encouragement he received from Philip.

"You are simply splendid, Phil, old boy," he told him enthusiastically, and still in the lowest of low whispers. "Of course I'll back you up through thick and thin. I'll wait till I hear the old boy plump overboard, and have the dinghy already cast loose, and ready to push off into the river. Hauling him aboard will be no easy matter, but it's got to be done, and without capsizing the dinghy. Then you'll have to join us, though the combined weight of the three will almost sink this cockle-shell. Still, it's the smallest of our adventures, and once we are all aboard we'll have got through with the greater part of the business. Ready?" he asked.

"Aye! Ready!" said Philip in the most careless manner possible.

Stretching his hand overhead, he caught the rope to which the dinghy was made fast and put his full weight on it. Then he lifted himself out of the dinghy, and very slowly and gingerly lowered himself into the water, making not so much as a splash in doing so. A vigorous stroke with his legs took him as far as the rudder of the steamer, and for a moment his fingers played about it; then, gripping the bilge keel which ran round the side of the steamer, and against which the water lapped continually, he pulled himself forward up-stream, finding but little difficulty in carrying out his purpose. It took him perhaps five minutes to reach the bows of the vessel—five solid minutes, during which he had to stop on two occasions, the first to allow the Commander of the vessel to tramp to the opposite side, and the second for the same reason when he came opposite the beat of the sentry. Then his fingers lit upon the stem-post, and, pulling himself up out of the water, he reached for the rail, only to find that it was a foot or more above him, and quite out of his reach, in spite of all his efforts. But Phil was not the sort of British officer to give way easily, or to allow himself to be lightly beaten. Indeed, there are few of them of whom this cannot be said; for a more resourceful, more gallant, and a more dashing set of young men no country has ever possessed, and no finer set of young fellows have ever obeyed the national call to duty.

"Beastly high up—rather a bother!" was all he told himself while he clung to the stem-post and considered. Then, placing his stockinged feet against the post, and heading up-stream, he shot himself forward through the water with a violent kick, and, groping about, soon gripped the cable to which the steamer was moored.

"Cable all right! Good, sound, honest rope," he chuckled. "And there's that sentry to be considered. It seems to me that I might easily cut through the rope just here on the water-level and leave it hanging by a thread; then, by the time it has parted, the stream will have washed me down to the after end of the steamer, and I shall be ready for the last act in this drama. That's it! That's the ticket! And here goes for the cable!"

He hooked one arm over the rope, while he extricated — not without difficulty — the jack-knife which he had in his trouser-pocket. Opening the big blade with his teeth, he then gripped the cable and commenced to saw through it till it was almost two-thirds severed. At that point he desisted suddenly, for there came an ominous crack from the rope he had been cutting, while he could feel with his fingers that the severed strands were separating widely.

"It will be through in a minute," he told himself; "for, though I had no idea of it, the stream here is running fairly fast, and the weight of the vessel with the stream on it must be giving a strong pull on the rope. There it goes, cracking again, and I can feel the strands pulling themselves asunder. It's time to be off."

He wasted no valuable moments in closing his knife and pocketing it again, for, owing to his drenched clothing it had been a difficult enough task to extricate it from his trousers; he dropped it, therefore, and let it sink to the bottom of the river, while he himself let go of the parting cable and struck down the stream till his fingers touched the side of the vessel and he was washed down along it. Then the fingers of both hands gripped the bilge keel, and he listened for the tramp of the sentry, only to find that he was past him and well on towards the stern of the vessel; in fact, he reached the spot where he might safely hope to clamber aboard without observation. And now, with the help of the bilge keel, which gave him a leverage, Philip raised his body from the water, and, throwing one hand above his head, just managed to reach the rail and grip it. The rest was an easy matter for a young and active fellow such as he was, and within a few seconds he was on the deck, gasping after his exertions, and dropping pools of water which ran away from his feet into the scuppers.

"What's that? Someone on the deck!" he heard the Commander exclaim, though Philip did not know the meaning of the words uttered.

This, however, he knew perfectly well — that his presence was suspected, and that the sauntering steps of the Turkish officer had suddenly come to a rest, while without doubt the man was staring in his direction; the dull glow of the end of his cigar was sufficient indication of that fact, while the voice supported the suggestion. Then from right for'ard there came a dull, sharp snap, while a subdued shudder ran down the deck of the vessel and communicated itself to Philip.

"Cable's gone!" he told himself. "Time I was moving."

With a bound he went along the deck till he was within a yard of the glowing end of that cigar and within striking distance of the Commander. Throwing himself upon the astonished Turk, he gripped him with both arms, and then hurled himself and his captive over the rail of the vessel. At the same moment Geoff pushed his dinghy from under the stern, and, taking his paddle up, waited for the appearance of the two who had so suddenly been immersed in the water. It was perhaps five seconds later when two heads bobbed up quite close to him, and he heard one of the two gasp and splutter. Giving a swift stroke with his paddle, he dropped it in the bottom of the dinghy, and, stretching out a hand, gripped the hair of one of the figures.

"Let go; it's me! Get hold of the old beggar!"

Philip was quite indignant, and, to tell the truth, the grip which Geoff had inadvertently fastened upon his chum's head of hair had been excessively painful; but in a moment he had transferred it to the shoulder of the Turk, and had drawn him close to the side of the dinghy. The stout and somewhat elderly commander was puffing like a grampus, and spurting water out of his mouth, while he wriggled and struggled to free himself from the one who had thrown his arms round him. Thoroughly scared by the unexpected assault which had been made upon him, and deprived utterly of speech by his sudden immersion in the river, he yet managed to get rid of the water which filled his mouth, and to give vent to a shout, a subdued shout, it is true, but one which easily reached the ears of the sentry aboard the steamer. Indeed, that individual had already halted on his beat, and was staring over the side into the Euphrates. He had felt the sudden tremor which had gone down the decks of the steamer as the cable parted, and there was now a curious movement, a strange bobbing of the ship, which was so different from her placid stillness of a moment or so earlier that he became suspicious, almost alarmed, and it required only the call of his Commander to cause him to shout at the top of his voice, to run to the companion-way which led to the quarters of the crew, and to beat upon it with the butt of his rifle. In fact, long before Geoff and Philip had accomplished their purpose and completed the capture of the Commander, men were pouring up on to the deck of the steamer, shouts were startling the air, while two or three of the men fired their rifles and thus increased the confusion.

Geoff leaned over the side of the dinghy, threatening to capsize it, and, placing his lips to the ear of the thoroughly startled Turk, spoke to him sternly.

"You are a captive—a prisoner," he told him. "Shout again, make the smallest show of resistance, and we shall push you under the water; but if you are quiet, and come aboard this boat readily, your life will be saved on certain conditions. You agree?"

The big bald head of the Turk nodded energetically, while the moonbeams were reflected from the wet and polished spot which a few moments before had been covered by his fez.

"You agree?" asked Geoff again. "We will save you on condition that you tell us all you know of your people. You refuse, eh?"

The hand which a moment before had gripped the shoulder of the Turk, in lieu of the missing hair, closed even more firmly, while the relentless Geoff pressed the unfortunate Turk lower in the water, till it looked as though he would send him right under.

"Stop!" gasped the Commander. "Save me! I agree!"

"Then come aboard! Give him a hoist, Phil, and gently with it!"

It was no easy matter to get that big Turk into the tiny little dinghy; and yet, with his willing assistance now—for to tell the truth the unfortunate Commander was innocent of the art of swimming, and had a horror of the water—Geoff and his chum contrived to roll him over the side, and deposit him on the bottom. Then Philip went right aft, and, with Geoff's help, came aboard in that direction, the three of them causing the dinghy to sink so low in the water that now and again the stream lapping against the sides splashed over.

"Sit dead in the centre and don't move for your life," Geoff told the Turk. "Now, Philip, paddle."

Dipping their paddles into the water they struck off to the left, and didn't slacken their exertions till they had emerged from the river and were in the streamless waste of waters from which they had stolen that evening. Now and again they had cast their eyes over their shoulders to see what was happening on the steamer, and, thanks to the lights aboard her which now flared up from many of the cabins, and thanks also to the shouts of her crew, to the hoarse and furious commands of the officers left aboard her, they had no difficulty in learning what happened.

"She's gone right down stream and round the bend," chuckled Philip.

"So we needn't bother any further about her—at least not for the present," said Geoff. "Let's sing out for our fellows."

Guiding the boat in beside an island, he stood up, and, placing his hands to his mouth, hallooed. Then he waited a moment and repeated the shout.

"Listen! That's an answer, and from a point not so very far away," said Philip. "Shout again! Yes, within easy distance, I should say, for after getting this old gentleman aboard we struck up-stream so as to make allowance for the drift after I had cut the cable. Christopher, Geoff, what a jolly good business!"

For a hail persuaded them that they were indeed quite near to the steam-launch; and within the five minutes which followed, by dint of repeating their calls and listening to the answers, they were able to find their way back to the narrow channel in which their comrades lay waiting.

"Pull that dinghy aboard at once," commanded Geoff; "and one of you can take charge of this prisoner. I don't think you'll find he'll be a nuisance, for I've told him to expect a shot if he tries any nonsense. Now then, get up steam as fast as you can, for, at the first streak of dawn, I mean to get away and make a rush for the river."

Long before the sun was up, and whilst a thick mist still hung over the marshes, the launch was poled out of the channel in which she had been hidden, and was gently forced towards the Euphrates. Once arrived in the centre of the stream she was allowed to drift, power now and again being applied to her propeller so as to keep her under control and allow the steersmen to direct her. Half an hour later she slowly drifted by the hull of the steamer aboard which Geoff and Phil had made such an adventurous visit on the previous evening, now stranded high and dry on a sand-bank. Unobserved, the launch swept onward, and very soon, when the first rays of the sun had sucked up the mist, and made the course of the stream easily visible, the engine was set to work, and they shot down-stream at a rate which rapidly brought them to the Shatt-el-Arab.

By then the Turk had recovered his composure, and, thanks to the blanket with which he was provided, had been able to get rid of his wet clothing. Indeed, he became quite communicative, and long before the launch had reached the opposite side of the Shatt-el-Arab he had told Geoff all he knew of the disposition of the Turkish forces.

Thus the two young officers who had been sent into the marshes to gather news of the enemy returned, having brilliantly achieved their object.

"The information will be of the greatest service," they were told. "We are making dispositions to meet this Turkish force of whom you have gained tidings, and then the expedition will fight its way up the Shatt-el-Arab and into the heart of Mesopotamia."

Fighting, indeed, was before the British Expedition, for though their goal was the city of Bagdad — a jewel in the eyes of the Turks and the Arabs of this region — there were leagues of sands and marshes between them and it, and thousands of the enemy.

CHAPTER XI

A Soldiers' Battle

Bugles were resounding throughout the expeditionary camp, stationed close to the bank of the Shatt-el-Arab, within two mornings of the return of Geoff and his chum from their adventurous journey into the wastes and marshes of the Euphrates. There was, perhaps, a sharper, more jubilant ring about the notes of those instruments on this particular morning, notes which brought men hurrying to join the ranks, which set troopers saddling their horses with an energy and rapidity which perhaps had been lacking on the previous day, and which caused radiant smiles and a glow of enthusiasm to spread throughout the ranks of the force.

"It's a general move, eh?" Philip asked his chum, meeting him as he crossed from his bivouac of the night before to fall in with his regiment. "Please note that I am appealing to you, Geoff, as a man who ought to know everything that's happening; if not, what's the good of a fellow being on the Head-quarters Staff. What's up?"

"I know as little as you do," came the laughing rejoinder; "but I can guess, and my guess is that we are on the way up the river to take Kurna. It's somewhere about there that the Rivers Tigris and Euphrates come together, and I suppose it's a point of some strategical importance."

"Strategical! Ahem!" coughed Philip. "Ain't we going it! From talking Turkish we're now getting to use quite military sort of language!"

It was just one of his little pleasantries, and, indeed, Geoff was the sort of young fellow who never resented being twitted, and, moreover, he was rather given to being facetious himself, especially when with Philip. However, he was too busy on this eventful morning to spend time in bantering, for indeed much was about to happen.

We have mentioned already that the head of the Persian Gulf is of no little importance to Great Britain, and that for many reasons, one of which, no doubt of somewhat recent origin, has to do with the supply of oil for our battleships—a supply which is piped from the oil-fields in Persia, under the control of Britain. The pipe-line itself passes down in the neighbourhood of Ahwaz, towards which place a portion of the Expeditionary Force was at that moment proceeding, with a view to seizing it and holding it against the enemy. But the safe possession and protection of that oil-line was not the only reason for sending an Expeditionary Force to Mesopotamia.

There were other, and perhaps somewhat complex reasons, which can only be broadly dealt with in this cover. International questions are involved, the discussion of which would take up an abundance of space, and might well prove not altogether interesting. But it becomes necessary at this stage to give some idea, even if it be only a meagre description, of other reasons which induced the British Government to dispatch a force to the valley of the Euphrates.

The Persian Gulf and the coast which borders it may be said to be the eastern end of the Turkish possessions, while Turkey in Asia is bounded to the north and east by the difficult country of Persia. Already we have sketched in the position of Russia and of the Caucasus frontier, and have stated that the coming of Turkey into this gigantic conflict on the side of Germany and Austria—the Central Powers—had a distinct and direct effect on the fighting in Europe, seeing that the Turks were able to dispose of some excellent troops, and were able to dispatch them promptly to the Caucasus area, where, fearing the invasion of southern Russia, the Tsar was forced to march and post an adequate army—an army which, but for the Turks, might have been merely a frontier guard, allowing of the bulk of the troops being dispatched to Poland, there to meet Germany and Austria. Thus the entry of Turkey into the war affected Great Britain and her allies, but yet cannot be said to have called for an expedition on our part to the eastern end of the Turkish Empire. Distances are huge in the country governed in name by the Sultan of Turkey, and in actual fact by the Young Turk party, who, let us explain, are themselves swayed, if not actually governed, by the emissaries of the Kaiser in Constantinople. From Constantinople itself to Bagdad, or to the Caucasus front, is roughly a thousand miles, and from Bagdad to the head of the Gulf of Persia is perhaps some five or six hundred more. But, as we have shown, a blow dealt at a distance may, in the war which is now raging, affect the course of that war at some far-off point—as the amassing of Turkish troops on the Caucasian frontier had already undoubtedly affected the fortunes of the Russians in Poland. Thus our Expeditionary Force sent to the valley of the Euphrates and of the Tigris might very well, though that point is at such a great distance from the Russo-Turkish frontier, affect the fortunes of the Turkish troops fighting the Russians in the Caucasian Mountains; for undoubtedly the enemy would need to send troops against us. But, and this is a matter of considerable importance, the valley of the Euphrates is notoriously unhealthy and is an extremely difficult country to negotiate. Practically roadless, and without a railway, it is not a country easy of invasion, and at the best no rapid advance was to be expected. Thus the force which Britain could afford to send to this somewhat out-of-the-way part of the world, though it might affect the Turks to some degree, could not be expected to make a very serious difference to them. It would seem, therefore, that there was another reason, and a better one, for our sending troops to Mesopotamia.

Indeed, a consideration of facts well known to the British Government makes it clear that fear for the safety of India had something to do with the matter. It was known, and had been known for a long time, that German emissaries had been exceedingly busy, not only in Turkey in Asia but also in Persia. Persia itself is inhabited by a decadent nation, unable to keep order, disturbed by bands of outlaws. The country lies, as a glance at the map shows, squeezed in between Russia, Afghanistan, and Turkey; and passage through it, though difficult, gives access to our possessions in India. There are not wanting signs that Germany would, if she could master her Turkish friends, quickly accomplish the subjection of Persia, and from thence make her blow against India. For recollect, though the seas give a clear passage to our Indian Dominions, there is a British fleet to be reckoned with, and the first day of the war saw that fleet paramount, sweeping the seas, making the invasion of our Eastern possessions on the part of Germany hopeless by the sea route. Thus, Germany had need to look for another way, and for long her thoughts had been at work, scheming and conspiring to obtain the assistance of Turks and Persians.

No doubt it was for this reason, amongst others, that an Expeditionary Force left India for Mesopotamia; for, with Russian troops able to invade Turkey from the north, and to keep a watchful eye on Persia, and with British troops advancing up the Tigris River to the very boundaries of that country, there was every prospect of being able to counter the moves of the Kaiser's agents, and to ruin their fortunes. Actual opposition from the subjects of the Shah of Persia was hardly to be expected or feared, for, if anything, the ruling powers in Persia were likely to be friendly; and then again the condition of the country has now for some considerable while been in a chaotic state, almost devoid of a standing army, and so feebly governed that anarchy and outlawry had at one period been rampant. Indeed, the unsettled condition of Persia, its contiguity to Russia, and the danger of outlaws invading that country, had led, some while before the outbreak of this huge war, to a penetration of the Shah's dominions by the soldiers of the Tsar, which had at once created international jealousies. No doubt Germany, scheming at that time, as she undoubtedly was, to obtain a hold over the Shah of Persia and over the country, was furiously jealous of the coming of the Russians, and as furiously antagonistic to British influence in southern Persia. It may be said that the three nations, and others who may have been interested, watched the position in Persia with no little misgiving; and, seeing that outlawry was rife, and that some means must be obtained for bringing peace to the inhabitants, an amicable agreement was arrived at, after a while, which resulted in a system of policing — the officers of the force employed being brought from Sweden.

Thus, at the moment when Russia was facing the Turkish armies along the Caucasus frontier, and when the British Expeditionary Force was marching up the Shatt-el-Arab towards Kurna, Persia, seemingly quiescent and under the nominal governorship of its Shah, was controlled in some considerable measure by a police force commanded by Swedish officers, and no doubt the integrity of those officers was not all that it should be. That an attempt would be made to tamper with them, to suborn their allegiance to the Shah, to bribe them from the carrying out of their duties, was nearly certain. Germans were already in the country — those peaceful penetrators sent by the ambitious Kaiser — and might be trusted to make the utmost of the opportunity. For see what an opportunity lay before them! Here was a police force controlled by officers of a nation which was not a party to the war now raging, officers whose goodwill might perhaps be obtained by the offer of the Kaiser's money. There was a police force there, too, ready organized, and practically no army raised from the people of Persia to oppose it. Even had the Shah any considerable number of soldiers to boast of, there were yet in the country scores of outlaws who could be bought with the same gold which purchased the allegiance of those Swedish officers. The moment was almost ripe to strike a blow for the country, to seize it while Russia and France and Britain were busy elsewhere, and to lay the foundation in Persia for the march through Constantinople of Turks and Germans, and for the campaign destined to strike a blow at India.

Such a state of affairs would, if allowed to proceed unchecked, present a danger of no small degree to Great Britain and her Indian dependencies. The condition of Persia in fact, the known activity of German agents there, and probably the doubtful position of the Swedish police were factors in the decision to send a force to Mesopotamia. We shall see later how Russia, furiously engaged as she was in Poland and Galicia, and heavily attacked in the Caucasus, still found troops to march into northern Persia; and how, when the conspiracies hatched by German agents came to a head, and the police force we have already mentioned seized certain of the Persian towns and some British subjects, those Russian troops intervened in the most summary and drastic manner.

If one seeks for other reasons for the dispatch of a British force to the notoriously unhealthy valley of the Tigris, one may suggest that, in addition to combating German influence in Turkey, it was equally important to attempt to overthrow the hold which the Kaiser and his emissaries had obtained over the Young Turk Party, and through them of the Turkish nation. We may go further, seeing that the course of events proved this latter to be the case, and add that the progress of the war, and the peculiar geographical situation attached to our Russian ally, made it of paramount importance that Great Britain should engage the Turks and endeavour to break their opposition. For Russia, with its teeming millions of men, is yet not a manufacturing country, and warfare nowadays has become more or less a matter of mechanics. To raise an army, where men alone are required, is not a difficult matter where men are to be found in abundance; but, in these modern days, when arms of precision are of paramount importance in the waging of war, and when, as in the case of Russia, a country is unable herself to provide her thousands of soldiers with those weapons, it behoves her allies to send them to her. It is here that the peculiar geographical situation of the Tsar's dominions provided another serious difficulty. Southern Russia — the ports of the Crimea — is easily get-at-able at all seasons by way of the Mediterranean and the Black Sea; but close the Dardanelles — as the Turks had now done — and Russia is only approachable by way of the White Sea, or through her possessions in Asia — for the closing of the Baltic Sea may be taken as effected the moment war was declared between Germany and Russia. The result of such a closure can be easily realized if one looks at the map; for in the winter months at the opening of the campaign Russia was entirely cut off from her European allies, and could only be reached from the direction of Asia; while in the open months of the year Archangel could not be described as a port either convenient in position or of vast dimensions. Thus we arrive at another reason for attacking Turkey.

The opening of the Dardanelles, the capture of Constantinople, and the domination of the Black Sea were of vital importance to Russia, and of just as vital importance to Britain, seeing that Russia was our ally. We know, too, that, as the months rolled on, and failure to burst a road through the narrow Dardanelles by means of our battle fleet became certain, an expedition was organized to seize the Isthmus of Gallipoli, to dominate the land forts, and so clear the road to the Sea of Marmora and Russia – an expedition which, in the course of the few months it fought on the isthmus, put up a glorious record for Great Britain and her colonies, and which, if it were unfortunately wanting in success, at least proved to the world at large that the youths of our nation are not wanting in prowess.

No doubt one might suggest even further reasons for the sending of an expedition to the valley of the Tigris and Euphrates, but, as we have said already, the question is a large one, and hardly fitted for our discussion. We turn, therefore, once more, to Geoff and Philip, the two young subalterns who had already seen much adventure on the Euphrates.

"Hi! Stop! I want to talk to you," Philip sang out, as Geoff went swinging by on Sultan when the troops had covered a few miles from Basra. "What's up?"

It took Geoff quite a few minutes to pacify his fiery steed, and to quiet him down sufficiently to allow of an answer to his chum's question. For, if Geoff himself were full of energy and enthusiasm, Sultan was overflowing with spirits, the sort of spirits which caused him to rear up time and again, which sent him bounding and curvetting from side to side till the sweat dropped from his narrow shoulders; while often he would have been off at a mad gallop, perhaps right through the marching division, had it not been for the strong restraining hand which held him. In short, and in fact, Sultan had taken most kindly to the valley of the Tigris, and if his master was pleased at being one of the expedition, Sultan, had he been able to give an opinion, would have voted Mesopotamia the place above all others for himself and his master.

"What's up! Oh, well!" began Geoff, patting the neck of his charger.

"Well you needn't say it like that," Philip answered hotly. "I'm not asking for any secrets, and, besides, it would be swank on your part to try to make out that you possessed 'em. Anyone can see that something's going to happen."

"And that 'something' is a good brush with the enemy," Geoff told him. "We've had information that the Turks have come down the river and propose to attack us, and I hear that they are within only a short distance. What will it be like with shells bursting?"

Neither of the two had, so far, been actually under shell-fire, though they had watched the British ships shelling the Turkish forts at the mouth of the Shatt-el-Arab before the landing of the expedition. But the day was not to be very much older before both of them were considerably wiser, and, may we say, considerably startled. It was, indeed, but a couple of hours later that the deep note of a gun reached their ears, followed by two others, and then by the shriek of shells coming towards them. There followed a commotion within a hundred feet of the point where the two young officers were standing, a commotion which sent Sultan rearing into the air till he nearly tore away the reins which Geoff, now dismounted, had swung over his shoulder. And then a column of sand and dust was blown high, while bits of metal and gravel swept like locusts round the heads of the soldiers. Philip turned his back, and coughed, and rubbed his eyes to get rid of the grit, while Geoff fought for his breath for quite a few moments.

"Like it?" asked Philip, with a mischievous grin, proceeding to mop his face with a handkerchief which had once been white, but which was now a beautiful desert colour. "There they go again; heavy metal, eh?"

"Four-inch, I should say," Geoff answered; "bigger perhaps. You'd better make sure of it, Philip. Why not catch one of the shells and let me know the measurements when you've finished — that is to say, if there's anything of you left after the skirmish? But there go our guns, and it sounds as though the advance-guard had already got into action. Ta-ta, old boy! I must get off, for I was returning to Head-quarters after delivering a message."

As he swung himself across the back of the restive Sultan, and galloped towards Head-quarters, he heard the guns aboard the sloops which were accompanying the force up the Shatt-el-Arab open on the enemy. Bang! Bang! Bang! Quite sharp, sailor-like reports; while, in the far distance, through his glasses, he observed splotches of sand and dust springing up between himself and the flat horizon.

"Take this 'chit' along to your old Commanding Officer," he was ordered the moment he reached Head-quarters. "Be good enough to ask him to act on the order immediately. You know the position of the regiment, and therefore need not delay to ask questions."

Geoff saluted briskly, and tucked the note between his belt and his body; then, swinging Sultan round, he set him off at a pace which sent sand and gravel flying out behind them, and sent him across a wide open space — already passed by the troops — to that point where he knew the Mahrattas were marching. By now, the division had stretched itself out on the left bank of the river, its right flank protected by the water, and supported by the guns and rifles aboard the British sloops already mentioned. To the left it had deployed till the ranks were opened out considerably, while behind those ranks, now stationary, were the hundred-and-one followers always attached to an Indian army — bearers of ammunition for guns and rifles, water-carriers, stretcher-bearers, and other useful, if not ornamental, individuals. Here and there tall brown figures lay inertly on the smooth expanse of desert, while already stretcher-bearers were crossing the open space, bearing human bundles enclosed in stained khaki clothing towards the dressing-station opened for the reception and treatment of the wounded.

It was a battle-scene in fact, the view one obtains behind the fighting front of an army — a view, up to this day, foreign to Geoff's eyes, save for what he had seen in the course of peace manœuvres. But this was the real thing.

For from the British front, and on beyond it, there came the rattle of rifles, punctuated every now and again by the sharp rat-a-tat-tat, rat-a-tat-tat of machine-guns, and drowned every few seconds by the deeper, hoarser, more venomous bellow of cannon. A shell plumped into the ground almost under Sultan, though the leap that animal gave carried him clear before the resulting explosion. As it was, he and his master were stung by the gravel flung out by the explosive, while a splinter of shell, singing past Geoff's leg, crossed the open space and found a billet in the body of a stretcher-bearer carrying one of the wounded. Crash! Down the man went, and with him his burden, and for a moment or so Geoff watched as a comrade bent over him and examined the wound he had suffered. He saw the tall native lay his brother soldier out straight and stark on the desert, and then, helped by another, seize the stretcher and march on towards the rear of the army. It was just an incident. Those men carrying their stretcher, and assisting their damaged brothers, were doing their duty just as well as, just as unflinchingly as, and in circumstances of equal danger with those armed with rifles in the forefront of the battle.

And what a sight it was when Geoff reached the Mahrattas, and came upon the officer he sought, occupying a shallow trench scooped in the sand behind his battalion.

"A message, sir," he said, pulling the note out from his belt and presenting it, and then watching the officer as he opened it and read the contents.

Then he swung his eyes over the backs of the men of the Mahrattas, who were now lying flat on the ground, digging their way into the soft gravel, seeking shelter from the Turkish enemy. Across the plain stretching before him, perhaps six hundred yards distant, were deeply dug trenches, parapeted, and manned by soldiers of the Sultan, and no doubt commanded in many cases by German officers. Farther back, and almost out of view, and dug in just as deeply and as securely as were the infantry, were guns — invisible almost, yet showing their positions every now and again by the dull-red flash which shot up above them. Geoff watched an instant, and listened to the rattle of musketry from the men stretching along the British line who were not engaged in digging but in holding down the fire of the enemy—watched those sharper red flashes in the distance, listened to the roar of British batteries, and saw a sudden blinding flash above one of those dug-in Turkish guns, and heard the splitting, thunderous report of a British shell as it got home on an enemy cannon; and then, though he watched for some few minutes, no sharp red point of light appeared above the spot, no answering report came from the gun dug into its hollow, for no doubt the British shell had put gun and crew out of action. As for bullets, they swept through the air like bees, humming and droning, splashing the sand and gravel here and there, throwing dust and stones over the soldiers lying full length and eagerly digging for shelter. They screamed and hissed past Sultan and past our hero, and between him and the officer to whom he had brought a message. They fascinated Geoff, and certainly did not frighten him in the slightest. So interested was he, in fact, with his view of the Turks—an excellent view considering he was mounted—and so taken up was he with watching those Turkish batteries and looking for the result of British shells amongst them, that he did not heed the voice of the officer he had accosted.

Then a shout attracted his attention.

"That will do," he heard sharply; "you are bringing fire on us with that white mount of yours, and it would be a pity to see him damaged. Get off back out of rifle-fire, or I shall have you on my hands wounded."

Phit! Phit! A couple of bullets whizzed past Sultan's nose at that precise instant, and in a moment he was dancing on his hind legs, thrashing the air with those handsome fore legs of his, shaking his head, and neighing, while foam flecked his lips and soiled his beautiful arched neck.

"D'you hear? Confound you, young Keith!" shouted the officer. "You'll get me shot next. Clear off, for you're drawing fire from the whole of the enemy front upon us."

Crouching in his little hollow, the officer watched as the punctilious Geoff pulled Sultan to his feet again with a steady hand, and, sitting very upright—bolt upright—in fact, the position adapted for formal parades, saluted his senior.

"Hang it," he shouted; "go off!" and then smiled—an indulgent smile—as Sultan broke into a furious gallop and went off at mad speed across the open. "Fine boy! Nice boy!" that officer said as he glanced backward from his "funk hole". "Knew his father—and that's the sort of thing he would have done; and how proud he would have been of the boy if only he'd lived to see him."

Plunk! A bullet struck the lip of the parapet which one of his men had hurriedly thrown up before the officer, and sent a shower of sand and gravel all over him. Indeed, it drew his attention once more to the battle now proceeding and to the position of his own men. With glasses fixed to his eyes, and himself kneeling in his little shelter, the officer scanned the Turkish lines with the eye of an expert and a critic. Undoubtedly the enemy had taken up a strong position, and, moreover, were in strong force and were well supported by guns of large calibre. There was, in fact, no question of the British Expeditionary Force coming in contact with an enemy indifferently organized, badly armed, and meagrely supplied. No! Those Turkish troops sent to meet the British, and those others then fighting in the Caucasus Mountains, were the product of German energy and German money. They were part of that vast organization built up during some forty years past, which aimed at making the Kaiser the Emperor of the World, and not merely of humble Europe. If there had been any doubt about the question of the arming of this force which barred the progress of our soldiers, the shells flung at the latter were sufficient indication, while the rattle of rifles and the sharper staccato tack-tack of machine-guns proved the case without room for doubt or argument. Looking at those positions, those prepared trenches of the enemy, and guessing at their number of troops, which was considerable, it seemed almost hopeless for the Expeditionary Force to expect to be able to advance farther. And yet, as the dusk of evening came on, and the fighting died down, there was no sign of a British retirement.

"We're going to hang on to our trenches all night," Geoff told his friend Philip when he hunted him out, after snatching a meal at Head-quarters. "You mark my words! To-morrow will see something that'll startle the Turks and send 'em flying."

CHAPTER XII

Esbul, the Armenian

A grilling sun poured its rays down on to the desert and on to the heads and backs and shoulders of the Turks and British and Indians alike. Its glancing rays shone and flashed with startling brilliance from the broad sheet of water flowing so smoothly along beside the right flank of the British, making the naval sloops, which had come up the Shatt-el-Arab, stand out more prominently, more vindictively, as it were, than usual. The scene of this conflict might, but a day or two before, have been described by a visitor to this portion of Mesopotamia as entirely and absolutely uninteresting; for where could there be interest in a wide, almost flat stretch of sandy-gravel desert, bordered in the far south-west by a stretch of noisome green-clad marshes, and on the right by a river some seven hundred yards in breadth perhaps, almost innocent of vessels, and whose banks showed scarce a habitation.

But see it now on this day of battle. As deserted it seemed as ever, as flat and devoid of landmarks as possible; and yet, when one looked closely at it, when—supposing one had clambered to the top of the tallest palm-tree—one peered at the desert and searched its every yard through a pair of glasses; see those lines of trenches—trenches which the British Expeditionary Force had delved at furious speed during the hours of darkness—stretching away at right angles to the river. See those British guns dug in behind the trenches, well behind, and those others craftily hidden amongst the palm-trees, close to the Shatt-el-Arab; and cast a glance to the far left of the lines of trenches, and note those horsemen well away in the desert, waiting for an opportunity to outflank and round up the enemy. Yes, and beyond, in parallel lines, were the Turkish trenches, just as Geoff had seen them on the previous day. Deep lines cut in the soil like those of the British, seemingly unpeopled, and yet swarming with soldiers ready to do battle.

But as yet the time had not arrived, and those swarming soldiers sat in their trenches invisible, save for a busy sentry here and there who peeped warily over the parapet and looked towards the enemy. But tiny columns of smoke hung above the troops, and doubtless many a meal was being cooked over many a brazier. Perhaps it was five in the morning, for men must fight early where the sun is hottest. A gun sounded from the river, while a puff of smoke belched from the bows of one of the sloops anchored in the fairway. It was answered almost immediately by a trumpet-call in the far distance, and that imaginary person watching from the top of a palm-tree would have observed that the British cavalry were in motion.

"It's coming off!" Geoff told Phil enthusiastically, as he cantered up to the position held by the reserves of the Mahrattas. "We ain't going back, not a foot, and before nightfall we ought to have cleared them out of their trenches. A frontal attack, my boy, and not sufficient time nor sufficient guns to blow a way through them."

Phil grinned up at his chum, a rather nervous little grin, for that was this gallant young fellow's way when he was excited and there were things doing.

"Cold steel, eh?" he said. "Then the Mahrattas are the boys to do it."

And yet the hours wore away with little else but gun-fire and rifle-volleys, while the men sweltered and sweated in their trenches. Imagine the heat in those narrow dug-outs, with a tropical sun pouring right down into them, and men congregated closely.

"A charge ain't nuffin' to it," one of the men told a comrade, as he wiped the sweat from his forehead with a grimy, desert-stained hand. "Swelp me! I wish I was in at 'em. What's a-keepin' of us?"

The comrade addressed stared back at him blankly, for indeed the question was entirely beyond him. Mechanically, abstractedly, he pulled a little cloth bag from his tunic pocket, and from another a clay of venerable appearance, and somewhat attenuated it is true, seeing that the stem had broken off midway, and slowly stuffed the bowl with the weed he favoured. Just as slowly, just as abstractedly, he applied a lighted match to the bowl, and began to smoke almost sadly, growling into the stem, puffing huge columns of smoke against the parapet of the trench, and giving vent to low, angry growls, as though he were a dog in a very bad temper. Then, of a sudden, he delivered himself of well-considered opinions.

"Whoi ain't we a-doin' nuffink?" he asked in the most excellent cockney. "Whoi nah, if Oi was the G.O.C. — and Oi tells yer there's more things than that what's more unlikely — if Oi was the G.O.C. Oi'd just be up and doin'. See 'ere, Bill, Oi 'aint got nuffink up against 'im — that's the G.O.C. — for every chap along of us knows that 'e's a good 'un, but you just moind me, if that there G.O.C. was along 'ere in the trenches, a-swelterin' and a-sweatin', whoi, 'e'd know what it was, and 'e'd be for gettin' along with the business. 'E ain't afraid, not 'arf! But well, what's 'e after?"

His comrade coughed, a satirical, nasty, impatient sort of cough, and again dashed the sweat from his forehead.

"That's just what I was askin' you," he said, contempt in his voice, deep displeasure, disgust if you will, for indeed these two gallant fellows were eager to be up and doing, while inertia told upon their nerves and their tempers. "That's the very question. What is he doin' this 'ere G.O.C., a-keepin' us sweltering away in these 'ere trenches. Now you've wondered what you'd do if you was 'im. I'll tell yer what I'd do if I wore 'is shoes, and 'ad control of the troops what's with us. I'd — —"

A Turkish shell plumping into the sand just a yard in front of that parapet somewhat disturbed the deliberations of these two arm-chair (that is, arm-chair for the moment) soldiers, for it burst with a splitting, thundering, shaking report, and promptly blew in the face of the trench on them. It was a couple of very angry, somewhat startled, and very disgusted individuals who finally scooped their way out of the mass which had almost buried them, and again sat down on the firestep of the trench to compare notes on the occurrence. But they had little time to continue, for that shell seemed to have been the signal for more active operations. Turkish guns belched missiles at the British, while British guns answered them with a vengeance. Then those horsemen careering out on the left flank of the Expeditionary Force were seen to be making off at an angle which would carry them beyond the flank of the Turks, and threaten to surround them. A movement, too, was seen amongst the men in the British trenches. Officers' whistles sounded shrilly, while hoarse commands were shouted.

"Make ready to leave trenches! Fix bayonets!"

From the far end of the line numbers of figures suddenly clambered over the parapet of the trench and darted forward, only to throw themselves on the ground when they had covered perhaps a hundred yards, and before the Turkish rifles or machine-guns could get at them. Then the same movement was repeated farther down, in another spot, and in another, and another. In an incredibly short space of time rifle-firing had become furious and unceasing, and had been transferred from the line of British trenches to those figures lying out in the open. Nor were they left there for long unsupported, for once more the movement commenced, and other groups dashed out to join them, while British guns thundered on unceasingly. In this way, little by little, by short rushes, the infantry advanced towards the enemy trenches, while the cavalry and the naval sloops had also come into action. Turks could be seen moving to their right flank to oppose the former, while the sloops steamed higher up the river till they outflanked the Turks, and could enfilade their position.

It was at this stage that Geoff was again sent out with a message, and, taking the precaution to leave Sultan well in the rear — for to have ridden him forward would have been to court disaster — he made a dash for the trenches, and from there to the line of the swarthy Mahrattas stretched out in the open. On the way he had delivered his message, and the temptation to join his old regiment and to hunt up his chum Philip was too strong for him. Creeping and rolling he finally came upon that young hopeful beside his platoon, and lay down near him.

"How d'you like it?" Philip shouted at him, for the rattle of rifles drowned the ordinary voice. "I hope they won't keep us out here very long, for those Turkish soldiers are fairly good marksmen, and it is hard luck for men to be shot whilst lying here and doing nothing. Looks as though we were going to charge the trenches."

"That's the order," Geoff told him. "We're near enough already, and if you look towards the enemy's position you'll see that some of them are already retiring."

A glance over the figures of his men showed Phil indeed numbers of Turks crawling from their trenches and fleeing across country. Farther back a team of battery horses swung in behind a gun position, and, raising his glasses, Geoff watched as the gunners endeavoured to hitch the team to their weapon and pull it out of its dug-out. But it was an operation they never accomplished, for a shell sailing over the position spluttered shrapnel in all directions, putting the better part of the team out of action and scattering the gunners.

"Charge!"

Whistles shrieked down the line. Officers sprang to the front of their companies, while British and Indians, helmeted and turbaned figures, leapt to their feet, and, with bayonets advanced, dashed across the space which intervened between themselves and the enemy positions. Hoarse guttural shouts left the throats of those British warriors who had come to Mesopotamia, while the higher-pitched cheers of the Indians mingled with them; and then, reserving their breath for the assault, heedless of the bullets which picked out numbers of them, and caused men to roll and bowl over, and which laid them out stark and stiff on the desert, the men went on in silence—that British silence, that dour, cold, remorseless calm which before now on many a field has scared the enemies of Great Britain. But it only lasted a few moments, until, in fact, the Turkish trenches were reached, and the men were in amongst the enemy. Yes, in amongst the enemy, for the Turks, to do them justice, had not all of them deserted their position. Many clung to their trenches with reckless bravery, and now crossed bayonets with men of the Expeditionary Force, with reeling, shouting men from the good County of Dorset, with tall, lithe, dusky sons of the race of Mahrattas, with sweltering, cursing white men, with dusky subjects of the King-Emperor who leapt at their enemies with the swift bound of a tiger. There was the crash of steel, the rattle and thud of rifle-butt coming against rifle-butt; there were yells and screams; there was the dull ugly sound of the bayonet-point as it struck some metal object — perhaps a button — and, sheering from it, went silently through its victim. There were the groans of bayoneted Turks; there was the cough of men whose chests had been transfixed, and whose lungs were flooded with blood.

It was a charge, a charge home, a charge which swept the British force into and over the enemy trenches, which hurled the Turks from their line, and which won a position for our men which, earlier in the day, the German officers had considered impregnable. Yes, German officers, white-faced sons of the Teutonic Empire, officers of the Kaiser, sent to carry his mission of world-wide conquest into Turkey in Asia, lay still and cold and white, their sightless eyes staring up at the burning sun which hung like a blazing orb above them.

It was war, this scene; and what was left when the howls and shouts of the soldiers had died down was the result of war, as it has been from earliest times, with just a few little changes and alterations which the growth of knowledge, the advance of science, and, in these latter days, the enormous increase in mechanical inventions have brought to it. Men die much in the same way, whether they be transfixed by the short stabbing sword of one of the old Roman Legionaries or by the bayonet of a British soldier; an arrow sent by a cross-bow, or by one of the old bows of England, has, or let us say had in the old days, much the same effect upon the man it struck as have bullets discharged from these-day weapons. A vital part is struck, and the man dies, and lies there, looking much the same to-day as when Roman Legions traversed this very spot in Mesopotamia.

"An ugly sight," you will say, "the horrible result of men's passions."

War? Yes, the result of war! But war not sought by King George or his people. That somewhat ghastly scene which Geoff looked upon, once the Turkish trenches had been captured, was not the doing of Great Britain, of France, of Russia, or of any of the Allies. It was the direct result of an ambitious policy fostered in Germany, a policy which had thriven and grown during forty years or more of ceaseless activity, which aimed at world dominance, and which, here in Mesopotamia, in France, in Poland, in a thousand places, was to produce the same and worse scenes — scenes of slaughter; scenes where men were robbed of their lives — young men who might have lived on and been of vast use to their own country, and would have done so, no doubt, had the Kaiser and his war lords not hatched that conspiracy to seize the whole world and bring it into subjection of the Hohenzollerns.

Philip plumped himself down beside Geoff, and, pulling his water-bottle to the front, presented a cup of water to him. There was sweat on his brow; his face, his hands, his tunic, every part of him, was stained with sandy dust, which had been washed into little furrows on his face by the perspiration which had streamed from his forehead. He was gasping still, as was Geoff; his eyes were shining, while a glance at the young fellow showed that he was still filled with excitement.

"We got home," he told his chum, "and the Mahrattas went in like lions."

Geoff nodded, and, tossing his head back, drained the cup of water.

"Like lions!" he agreed enthusiastically. "And the Dorsets, my boy! Did you hear them? Did you hear those boys go in at the Turks? It was ter — r — if — ic! Hallo, what's that? Look over there!"

Away on the left they could see British horsemen galloping in wide circles to round up fugitives from the lines so recently vacated by the enemy, and here and there parties of troopers were cutting across the desert so as to encircle men who were striking towards their left and looked like escaping. And amongst the fleeing Turks were some who were mounted, and amongst them, no doubt, more than one German officer. Geoff had been watching them for a moment, and now had his attention attracted to a little group clear of the British horsemen just then, and appearing to have every chance of getting away safely. Of a sudden he saw a horseman burst from the group, while shots were fired as he spurred away from the others; then a couple from the group swung their horses round and set off in pursuit, careless of the fact that the fugitive was turning his mount in the direction of the British. It was an amazing sight, and drew exclamations from many.

"What's it mean?" demanded Philip, still puffing and blowing after his exertions.

"Don't know, but I'm going to see."

Geoff leapt across the trench, at the bottom of which lay many wounded and dead Turks, and sped across the open over which our troops had so recently and so gallantly advanced. In the distance he caught sight of his own fine Arab, of Sultan, and, signalling wildly with his hands, managed to attract the attention of the syce in charge of him. The man leapt into the saddle in an instant, and before many minutes had passed, Sultan, blowing and stamping and fidgeting, was pulled up within a few feet of our hero. To change places with the syce was the work of only a few moments, and in a trice Geoff was off again, and leaping his mount over the trenches sped on towards that horseman who had so strangely and so inexplicably burst his way from the group escaping from the British. He had a mile or more to cover, but Sultan made nothing of it. Indeed, in a little while Geoff had drawn quite close to the man, and, swinging Sultan round, was soon riding beside him. At the same time he turned, and drawing his revolver emptied it at the two men still pursuing. Whether his bullets went wide of their mark or narrowly escaped meeting a billet he never knew, but their effect was excellent, for the men pulled in their horses, and, having fired in return without result, swung their mounts round and galloped off to join their companions.

"Who are you?" demanded Geoff, pulling in Sultan.

"An Armenian, Excellency."

"And why with the Turks? You are not a soldier," said Geoff, noticing that the man was in civilian costume.

"A soldier? No, Excellency. A messenger merely, one who bears a missive to the British."

"Then a friend of the British, eh?" asked Geoff.

"A friend? Yes, always. In the service of a British Pasha these many years. A friend, at heart, of England."

Geoff stared at the man, and then, setting Sultan in motion, rode along, the man trotting his horse beside him.

"A message, eh?" asked Geoff after a while, having pondered deeply. "For the British, you say?"

"For the British, Excellency, for any whom it may concern. News of an English pasha who came but lately to this country."

"Oh, whom? The name? For whom is the message intended?"

"Excellency, I was to find the British force invading Mesopotamia. I was to hand my missive over to an officer of distinction, and I was to search amongst the officers who came from India for one, a youth, who might be with them."

"His name?" asked Geoff, now beginning to tremble with excitement, for who could this white man be who had sent a message? Who could the pasha be to whom this Armenian referred? Could it be Joe Douglas, his guardian, that excellent fellow who had befriended him these many years, and who had so recently gone on an expedition to Asiatic Turkey, and who, after his custom—a custom that Geoff knew so well—had disappeared entirely? There was no news from Joe Douglas these many weeks past, not a line, not a chirrup from him. But could this be his messenger? If so, Geoff should know him. Swinging round in his saddle he gripped the man's arm and stared into his face. A moment later he uttered a shout—a shout of happiness.

"You are Esbul, eh?" he asked.

"And you, Excellency, you are Keith Pasha."

"The message; give it to me," demanded Geoff fiercely, worked up by the occasion. "Yes, I am Keith Pasha, and your message comes from Douglas Pasha, my dear guardian."

It was with a shout of joy that he recognized the handwriting of that gallant soldier who had been as a father to him, and tearing the missive open he read it with an eagerness which was plainly apparent to the man who had brought it.

"If this reaches the hand of my ward, Geoff Keith, or of any British officer, let him give information of my position to the Commanding Officer of any expedition which may come from India to Mesopotamia. I have little time or space or means whereby to write a long message, and therefore must compress my information. I am a prisoner lying in a cell within a Turkish fort to the north and west of Bagdad, but where precisely I cannot say, nor do I know the name of this fortress. I was captured by a German named von Hildemaller. His agents trapped me at a place I sought outside Bagdad, and seized me. But for a friendly Turk they would have murdered me on the spot, and, as it is, they handed me over a prisoner. I make no complaint, but if the expedition advances towards Bagdad, let it make an effort to relieve me."

Geoff gasped, and re-read the message—devoured it in fact—for it was good to hear that Joe Douglas was alive, even though he were a prisoner.

"Tell me, Esbul," he said at last, while they continued to ride on slowly side by side, "this message—you received it from Douglas Pasha himself? You know where he is imprisoned?"

"Not so, Excellency, not so, Keith Pasha! This man—this devil, I call him—this German, the smiling, sweet-faced von Hildemaller. Ah! how I know the man, how I hate, detest, and fear him—he is too strong, too cunning, too artful to allow your servant or any other friend of Douglas Pasha to know of his whereabouts. Only von Hildemaller and Turks in high places can tell of the prison in which my master is shut up."

"But then," said Geoff quickly, "how—how came you to get the message?"

"It is shortly told, Excellency. There is a Jew, an Armenian Jew, in the city of Bagdad, a great admirer of my master, an old and trusted friend of his, who has been ever loyal to him."

"I know the man," said Geoff; "tall, angular, and bony; a man who sits in the market-place and sells embroidery."

"The same," said Esbul; "a wonderful man, who knows secrets that are hidden from many of us. He it was who brought the message to me in Bagdad, and bade me bear it in this direction. Yet, clever as this old Armenian Jew is, he too is ignorant of the place in which Douglas Pasha is imprisoned."

"But could help one to discover it," cried Geoff, still holding the message in his hand.

"Who knows, Excellency? This Jew, this Benshi, as they call him, is a man of parts, and, seeing that he is a friend of the pasha, he will surely help. But remember, Excellency, Turkey is now at war with your people; even I, riding towards your camp, and coming upon the Turks in this position, was seized upon. There was no time in which to cross-examine me, to find out why I came and whither, and for that reason, when the retreat began, they—the Turkish officers, and with them some Germans—were carrying me off with them. But you, Keith Pasha, they would know at once as an enemy, while I might pass, as indeed I have, through the country."

Geoff smiled at him, a smile of assurance.

"You forget, Esbul," he said, "you forget that I too have been in Mesopotamia with Douglas Pasha, that I speak your tongue and Turkish like a native, and that a fez or Arab clothing can make a wonderful difference. Why indeed should I not make this attempt to relieve my guardian? Tell me, Esbul, if in your case your father were imprisoned by some enemy, and there lay danger and difficulty between you and him and his prison, would you then count the danger and the difficulty and allow them to deter you from an attempt at his rescue?"

The tall, lithe young Armenian brought his hand with a sounding flap against the neck of his horse, while he gave vent to a sharp exclamation.

"Master," he said emphatically, "I would not! There are many who count the Armenian people as a shameless, effeminate race, who look upon the denizens of Erzerum and the surrounding country in which our race dwells as beneath contempt, unfit for this world, who hate us — and who thereby show some jealousy of us. But yet, peace-loving as we are, there lies deep down in the hearts of my brothers a source of courage — courage which, should the opportunity present itself, will spur them to fight the Turk and attempt to throw off his governance. Yet the hour might never come; and, while we wait, massacres take place, and indeed, even now, my people are being slaughtered. Yes, my master, if there be danger and difficulty in a task such as the one you mention, it should not perturb you. For listen, have I, the humble servant of Douglas Pasha, not braved many dangers in my journey hither? And he, though a good and liberal master to me, is yet not my father."

Geoff brought his hand down on the Armenian's back with a smack, and smiled encouragingly at him.

"You've done splendidly, Esbul," he told him, "and you shall see that I will make the most of this message. Now let us make our way to Head-quarters."

Still riding slowly side by side, so as to give their horses an opportunity of cooling, they crossed the desert over which the Turks had retired, in many cases so precipitately, passing many dead and wounded. Then they rode their horses over the vacated trenches—that is, vacated by living men, and now tenanted only by the dead who had so bravely held them. Beyond, there was the space across which those British and Indian troops had come hurtling in their mad charge, as they threw themselves toward the enemy trenches. A little while ago the desert here had been dotted with figures, some lying prone and stiff and stark, while others were sitting up and looking about them, and others, yet again, crawling towards the position now captured by their comrades. A little farther and Geoff and his companion reached the broad belt of palms which clung to either side of the broad stretch of the Shatt-el-Arab, to find horses picketed in the shade, munching contentedly at their daily rations, to see carts of every description parked beneath the trees, while, in the open, motor ambulance-wagons purred their way to and fro, as they brought in the wounded or went off across the hard, sandy desert in search of others. And in a retired part, just beyond the wagon-park, they came upon and halted beside a huge tent, over which flew the flag of the Red Cross. British and Indian orderlies were moving briskly about, while through the open sides of the tent Geoff caught a glimpse of stretchers laid in rows, and upon them bandaged soldiers lying very contentedly, out of the heat of the sun and with the cool breeze playing in upon them. And out in front of the tent, with the shadows of the trees cast across it, stood a table whereon lay a wounded man in the hands of the surgeon. Geoff shuddered, and then looked again; looked and admired the calmness and unconcern of the officers attending to that wounded man, their dexterity, the swiftness and silence of the orderlies who assisted; and then, catching the eye of the wounded man himself—one of the Dorsets—he returned with a grin the wink with which that incorrigible individual greeted him.

Geoff turned away, and, dropping from his saddle, hunted up his friend of the Head-quarters Staff, to whom he presented his message.

"Hum! Douglas Pasha! Glad to know that he is alive. But in prison; eh, Keith! And he's your guardian!"

For a while the officer looked at the message, and from the message to Keith, studying his every expression, and then back again to the message, pursing up his lips and wrinkling his brows thoughtfully.

"Of course," he said, "if this expedition fights its way to the neighbourhood of Bagdad it might give us an opportunity of relieving the Major; but then Bagdad happens to be far away."

"Yes, sir," agreed Geoff, vainly attempting to make his voice sound jubilant and hopeful.

"A long way," repeated the officer, "and we may never cover the distance; in that case— —But of course," he added thoughtfully, looking again at Geoff, "of course, seeing that you know the country and can speak the language, you might—eh?—you might make the attempt yourself, if you could get permission. But such permission is out of the question now, and you must leave it to the future."

And leave it to the future Geoff had to be content to do, though by night and by day he still remembered that message, and indeed discussed it and a prospective journey to Bagdad threadbare with his chum, Philip, and with Esbul.

"Of course I shall go the first moment I get the opportunity," he told them both.

"And, with you, Esbul," the Armenian answered him immediately.

"And what about me?" asked Philip. "Ain't I good enough for such a job? Don't I begin to know Mesopotamia by heart by this time?"

"We'll see," rejoined Geoff enigmatically. "If there's a chance though—well, you may be sure that I'll go, and take anyone I can with me."

CHAPTER XIII

An Amphibious Expedition

"Garden of Eden, indeed!" growled Philip, some few weeks after that fine combat in which the Indian Expeditionary Force had proved so successful, and had cleared the road to Kurnah. "Where's the garden?"

The disdainful Mahratta subaltern looked round him from the doorstep of the house in which he and a few of his brother officers had taken up their quarters, and to which at that moment his chum Geoff had paid a visit. And well might the youthful and disgusted Phil have turned up his nose, have scoffed, and have shown the most infinite displeasure, for rains had set in since the occupation of Kurnah, and the whole country-side was soaked. That smooth, sandy, and gravelly desert was covered a foot deep in sticky, sandy mud, different from any mud encountered elsewhere; mud which clung to the boots, which piled up on the feet of those who trudged about the camp, and who must needs therefore carry about with them so much extra weight.

A hot, stifling mist hung over the country and blotted out the River Tigris. For, bear in mind, the Expedition had now advanced beyond the junction of the Euphrates and the Tigris Rivers, and had camped on the banks of the latter. Time was, centuries before, when these two historic rivers had come together in the neighbourhood of Kurnah — the little town now captured — where the country-side was drained, and fertile, and productive, and where, no doubt, date-palms had offered grateful shade, and patches of green had relieved the dull, dirty yellow of the desert. But that was in days gone by. Now, a change in the course of the River Euphrates — a river which, like many a one in China, changes its course in the most fickle and unforeseen manner — had cut a channel for itself farther to the south, where it now met the Tigris. "Garden indeed!" The place was a muddy swamp, set amidst the most depressing surroundings.

"Not so very cheerful," Geoff had to agree, as he puffed at a cigarette and smiled at the indignant Philip; "but then we're campaigning, my dear

176

fellow, and soldiers should take things as they come, and not grouse and grumble."

"Shut up!" Philip told him. "None of your Head-quarters airs for me! What's doing?"

It was always the way with Philip to demand of his chum what movements might be expected, as if indeed, though attached to the Head-quarters, Geoff was likely to be in the confidence of his seniors. Yet he knew something of their intentions at times, and knew well enough that further movement was anticipated.

"You see, it's like this," he told Philip, there being no one else about. "The party we sent off along the Karun River and the pipe-line into Persia have seized Ahwaz, and have secured the oil-supply for our battleships. Just look at this map I am making in the mud! Rather a good place for drawing one, ain't it? Now, here's the Tigris and Kurnah, and there are the swamps that we went into with Commander Houston. By the way, glad to hear that he's doing well. He's on his way to India now, and good reports have been received about him. Well, there are the marshes."

"Where our good friend the Turk did us the honour of joining us, eh!" grinned Philip. "What an adventure that was, Geoff! Wish we could have more of 'em!"

It was Geoff's turn to tell his friend to "Shut up!"

"Don't interrupt!" he said irritably, thrusting the point of his stick deep into the mud, and pointing impatiently to the map which he had been outlining. "Let a fellow get on with his description. There's the Tigris."

"You've said that already," grumbled Philip.

"Well, I say it again! There it is!"

"Yes, the Tigris, we all know that! Put a T against it!"

That made Geoff laugh, and obediently he sketched a huge T in the sand and mud before him.

"Right oh!" he said. "Tigris."

"Get on," growled Philip. "Here are the marshes," and bending swiftly he scraped a row of lines in the mud. "Marshes — M — there we are, and just about here, I suppose, will be the spot where our dear friend the Turk joined us."

He dug a finger deep into the mud in the midst of the patch which he had designated "marshes", and then, standing up, grinned irritatingly at Geoff.

"We know all about that," he went on. "T for Tigris, M for marshes! What next? K for Kurnah, I suppose."

"It's there — K!" said Geoff, laughing, for who could allow himself to be irritated with Philip? "K for Kurnah, and B for Basra. There's the head of the Persian Gulf, and there's Ahwaz. Now let's move up this line we call the Tigris. Perhaps a hundred miles up there is a place called Amara, from which the enemy can easily reinforce the troops they have in front of Ahwaz; there's nothing to prevent them but marshes and desert, and seeing that they've lived all their lives in such surroundings they know all about them. So the next move is there, to seize Amara, and make doubly secure that our pipe-line cannot be cut or damaged."

As a matter of fact, the sketch-map which Geoff had drawn in the mud for the edification of his chum, was not entirely complete or informative, and we hasten at this point to supplement the information he had given. Had he prolonged the line which represented the Tigris River farther to the north and west, as it bent in that direction, he would, when he had covered sufficient space to indicate perhaps another hundred miles of desert country, have come to a place called Kut-el-Amara, where at that very moment Turks were in force; and, arrived at Kut, he would no doubt have carried on the line, making it twirl and twist in many directions — for above Kut-el-Amara the Tigris winds considerably and is most difficult of navigation — to Bagdad, that city where Major Joseph Douglas had taken up his quarters, and where the onset of this huge world war had found him an alien in a nest of enemies.

Going farther, Geoff's stick would have scratched the line in an almost due southerly direction till it struck that broad patch which Philip had contemptuously designated marshes. Unknown then to the leaders of the Indian Expeditionary Force, a channel runs from Kut-el-Amara down to the head of those marshes into the midst of which Geoff and his chum had so recently ventured, and ends at a spot on the River Euphrates where that broad, sluggish, and ever-changing stream plunges into the mass of sandy and reed-covered islets which form the marshes at Nasiriyeh, where at that very moment Turks were collecting. Not, let us add, that the Indian Expeditionary Force was entirely ignorant of their situation, for, indeed, the Intelligence Branch, thanks to the capture of that fat Turkish officer, had considerable news of a force of Turks collecting at Nasiriyeh. Yet they did not know of the Kut-el-Hai, connecting Nasiriyeh and Kut-el-Amara, and therefore were not aware that the Turks could reinforce the garrison already collected at the head of the marshes, and were at that moment hastily doing so. This force, joined by numbers of Arabs and tribesmen, was even then moving down beside the marshes, following their edge, and taking advantage of the drier parts where the desert was not submerged, their objective being Shaiba, hardly ten miles to the south-west of Basra.

Information of their coming reached the Head-quarters of the division within a few hours, in fact, at the moment when Geoff and Philip were so eagerly discussing the situation, and the blare of bugles, and the stir in the camp, immediately gave occasion to Philip to demand once more of his friend: "What's up?"

"Remember that old Turk?" asked Geoff.

"Not 'arf!" grinned Philip.

"And the tale he gave us of the Turks at the head of the marshes?"

"Get along with it!" Philip told him.

"Well, the enemy are said to be now at Shaiba, within striking distance of Basra, and we are sending back to reinforce our troops there."

"Mahrattas?" asked Philip eagerly.

"Can't say," came the short answer. "You'll know precious soon. So long, Philip! I'm busy."

Geoff was, as a matter of fact, frantically busy; so busy, and so engaged in carrying messages, that he might, had he been inclined to arrogance, have suddenly formed the idea that he was the most important individual with the division. Dashing backwards and forwards on Sultan's back, he had hardly time to think of the Mahrattas, of Philip, or of anything else but his present duties; and it was not until some days later that the two met in the neighbourhood of Shaiba.

"Somewhere about twenty thousand Turks opposite us," Geoff was able to tell his friend, "and plenty of guns. We're moving out to attack them. The beggars are entrenched at the foot of a slope along a line about two miles in length, and their supports occupy the high ground behind them. Of course there are German officers with them."

That early morning, was repeated in the neighbourhood of Shaiba the action which the Indian Expeditionary Force had fought on its way to Kurnah; for the troops advanced over the open, there being not a vestige of cover, while the cavalry manœuvred towards the flank of the enemy; a guard of Arab horsemen, and amongst them the chief whose acquaintance we have already made, supporting the regular cavalry and making ready for a dash upon the enemy.

To hardened campaigners, as Geoff and Philip had now become, the roar of guns, the splash of shells, and the detonations about them made hardly any difference; they were as cool as cucumbers, and went on with their work as though nothing were happening. And gradually, as the hours flew on, Indian and British—those gallant troops who had invaded Mesopotamia— advanced upon the Turks by little rushes, advanced, and then lay down, throwing up a parapet of sand in front of them to give them some protection, while British guns thundered in the rear and plumped shells into the Turkish trenches. And then that long blast was repeated, that shout down the line of attacking troops, the shrill shriek of officers' whistles, and the charge which was to carry our men into the enemy's position had begun. With those shouts there mingled the shrieks of hundreds of Arab horsemen — those excited individuals manœuvring at that moment towards the flank of the Turkish trenches. Their shrill cries could be heard right across the field of battle, while their robed figures, their waving arms, and their gesticulations could be observed from the far distance. Waiting till the British troops had plunged into the Turkish trenches, and until the enemy were broken and were fleeing, the Arabs burst like a bolt towards the open, and, swinging in behind those trenches, went charging amongst the enemy, cutting them down, shouting as they rode, riding over the unfortunate subjects of the Sultan and those scheming German officers who had come to train the enemy. One moment there was Bedlam — shouts and shrieks, the rattle of rifles, the sharp splutter of machine-guns and the deeper roar of cannon — and the next there was almost complete silence, save for the distant calls of those fierce Arab horsemen wreaking vengeance upon the Turks.

"And now commences the march on Amara," Geoff was able to tell his friend a few days later. "We've got the Turks running, and I expect the G.O.C. will make the most of it. A sharp and rapid advance might allow us to capture Amara with little opposition, and then we should be firmly posted on the river and able to take up a defensive position."

As a matter of fact, the capture of Amara was, in its way, a startling and most dramatic affair, and proved, if proof were necessary, that the nerves of the Turks had been considerably shaken. For though the advance-guard of the Expeditionary Force advancing towards Amara was of but slender proportions, it met detachments of Turkish troops coming towards it, troops anxious to surrender, so that the town of Amara was seized without so much as a shot being fired, and was promptly occupied by the British.

But the task of the Expeditionary Force to Mesopotamia was not yet completed, not by a great deal, for now there came news of that channel, the Kut-el-Hai, leading from Kut-el-Amara to Nasiriyeh, and it became necessary to seize both points before our troops could have any security. Preparations were therefore made to attack both places, and, to the delight of Geoff and Philip, they were both detailed to accompany an expedition, designed to strike at Nasiriyeh, through those marshes which they had already penetrated.

Meanwhile, to bring our tale up to date, one needs to mention that, as the months had gone by, as that trench line had been dug firmly across Belgium and France, and had held up the advance of the Germans on Calais and Paris, the Russian line too had checked the enemy, had advanced across Poland and into Galicia, and was within an ace of invading Austria-Hungary. In the Caucasus, a Turkish army corps had been severely dealt with by the Tsar's forces called to that inhospitable region; while an ambitious if reckless attempt on the Suez Canal, on the part of Turkey, had met with dismal failure.

The taking of Amara, in fact, coincides with the period when Britain had recovered from the first shock of this sudden and unexpected conflict, when she was training those hundreds of thousands of volunteers who had answered the call of their country, and when, while fighting beside the French in France, she still had troops sufficient to attack the enemy elsewhere. Even as those gallant Indian and British troops with the Mesopotamia Force charged down upon the trenches at Shaiba, other British troops—men from England, from Australia, and New Zealand— were gathering in the neighbourhood of Egypt. Indeed, within a few days there occurred a landing on the Peninsula of Gallipoli, a most desperate and gallant undertaking, which launched Great Britain and France into a conflict the difficulty of which was stupendous, and the result of which cannot be said to have been altogether a failure, though it failed to gain for us the capture of those forts which line the approach to Constantinople. A conflict, in fact, abortive, as it proved, yet one which struck the Turks an exceedingly heavy blow, and set up a record of bravery and determination on the part of British and French which will never be exceeded.

Was there ever such an expedition as that which set out for Nasiriyeh?

"Queer, ain't it?" remarked Philip, on the point of embarking with his chum Geoff on board the steam-launch which they had captured from the enemy in the midst of the same marshes whither they were now bound. "Did you ever see such a collection of boats and fellows? and the navy look as though they meant to make a race of the business."

There was a string of bellums—the shallow light craft common to that part of Mesopotamia, and used by the natives for progress through the marshes—towing at the tail end of the steam-launch—bellums crammed with British soldiers and with Indians. There were motor-boats near at hand, pushing their busy way across the Shatt-el-Arab; there were shallow-draft steamers brought from India, cranky, dilapidated, rusty vessels, which looked as though they had done long service, and had arrived at a time when they were fit for the scrap-heap only, or to be relegated to long and continuous rest. As a matter of fact, many of these curious craft—long since abandoned as useless by their owners—had been brought across from India, surviving in a most extraordinary manner a voyage which might have been expected to smash them to pieces, and to shake their already quivering sides so severely that if they had been swamped, if the ocean had poured through many a crevice, it would have been a wonder to no one. And there they were, at anchor in the river, their decks packed with men of the navy—men in duck white or in khaki, grinning fellows, who shouted to their comrades of the army.

"Cheer oh, navy'll be in first!" they bellowed. "We're in for the Turkish stakes, and back ourselves to beat the army."

What a scene it was when the expedition set off at length! The lighter craft finding their way through the marshes, and steering an irregular course amongst the muddy islets, whilst the vessels drawing deeper water ploughed their way along the uncertain course of the Euphrates, and stemmed the gentle flood down which Phil and Geoff had steamed with their Turkish prisoner. Little tails of open boats trailed at the stern of every steamer, while not a few, manned by natives, with soldiers aboard them, were paddled into the marshes farther afield on the outskirts of this huge inundation. There were other troops wading knee-deep, all with the one objective—Nasiriyeh and the Turkish camp. Perhaps never before had such an amazingly curious, amphibious expedition been undertaken, and it is quite certain that never before had British and Indian sailors and soldiers enjoyed a thing more hugely.

"A regular sort of mud lark," Phil called out as the launch ran on a submerged bank of mud, and came to an abrupt halt, causing the bellum towing nearest to her to collide violently with her stern and capsize promptly. There were roars of laughter as the men fell into the water and got to their feet again, dripping, and standing there with the water hardly higher than their knees, grimacing and shaking themselves like dogs.

"All overboard!" cried Geoff, who was in command of the launch. "There's no use in trying to pole her off, for she's hard and fast. Overboard with you!"

Pulling his long boots off and his breeches higher up his legs, he was over the side in a twinkling, while the crew, enjoying the experience amazingly, followed him, Phil helping to set an example.

"Now, all together, boys!" shouted Geoff. "Pull her off! Pull her back! That's done it; she's moving!"

Not once, but half a dozen times, in the next two or three days, were they forced to extricate themselves from a similar sort of situation by similar methods. For, let us explain, there was no opportunity to take careful account of the obstacles before them, to steer a slow and cautious course, and to make a complete reconnaissance of the route they were to follow. Under ordinary conditions, with time at their disposal, Geoff would have steered his launch at a placid pace, and would have avoided enclosed waters where islands of mud abounded; but now, with this expedition, it was a case of each man for himself, of push ahead all the time. It was a race, in fact, a friendly race, between the army and the navy, each service vying with the other in its efforts to push onward, and each secretly determined to get to the goal before the other.

"If we don't look out we shall be running our heads into a hornets' nest," Geoff cried irritably, when, for the fifth time at least, he and his crew had had to leap into the shallow water and pull their vessel free of a mud-bank. "This sort of headlong course will not help us to beat the enemy, but will give them an enormous opportunity."

Whereat Phil grinned. He was one of those incautious, careless, happy-go-lucky sort of subalterns who never think of consequences, and who, perhaps for that very reason, so seldom come to grief. Perhaps it was a lucky star which always watched over Phil's progress, for, in any case, happy-go-lucky though he was, careless to an irritating degree, he yet had so far come through many a little adventure unscathed.

"Tremendous opportunity—yes!" he told Geoff. "But—but will they take it? Bet you they're already thinking of bolting; for don't forget, my boy, we've given them a pretty hard hammering. Besides, an expedition such as this is, spread out through the marshes, ain't so jolly easy to tackle. You could stop a portion, perhaps—say one flank, or the portion in the centre of the ground, or rather the water. What do you Head-quarters chaps call it? It would be called terrain if it was a question of land operations, and I don't happen to know the term under these conditions. But that's what might happen; one portion of our spread-out front might get stopped, but the others would push on like blazes! Cheer up, Geoff! It'll all come right, and you'll earn promotion yet."

It always ended like that with such a fellow as Phil, and Geoff, cautious and earnest young officer though he was, was forced to laugh uproariously, and join in Phil's merriment. And, after all, if caution had been thrown to the winds by all of them—which was far from being the case—caution on his part would hardly remedy the situation. Pushing on, therefore, and taking the most out of his steam-launch, thrashing her across every open strip of water till her bow waves washed almost aboard, and until the rope to which the bellums were attached was drawn like a bow-string, and the unfortunate individuals aboard those craft drenched with spray, he wriggled his way forward with other boats of the expedition, determined to be well in the van at the coming conflict. Then, as the dusk fell, and the boats tied up or anchored for the night, he selected a likely spot towards the edge of the marshes, and dropped anchor. Entering a bellum, he went off towards one of the bigger craft, aboard which the Staff conducting this extraordinary expedition were quartered.

"What's up?" asked Philip on his return, the inevitable question that young officer fired at his comrade. "Of course, everyone knows that we're jolly near this Nasiriyeh, so to-morrow there'll be something doing, eh?"

"Come over here," Geoff said, nodding towards the stern of the vessel.

"Secrets, eh?" grinned Philip, yet wonderfully eager to hear what Geoff had to say. "Now then, what's the business?"

"A forward move to-morrow, as you might expect, but before that a reconnaissance."

"A re—con—nais—sance! Jingo! Ain't that a mouthful? Put in simpler language, a sort of scouting expedition," smiled Philip, sucking furiously at a cigarette.

"Just that; an expedition by a small party to discover the actual site of the Turkish camp and to hear what they are saying."

"Oh! And—but you don't mean——George! That would be ripping!"

Geoff cooled his ardour most brutally. "What would be?" he asked curtly enough—coldly, in fact, knowing full well what would be the result of such action.

And, indeed, in a moment the hitherto eager and impulsive Phil was reduced to a condition almost of despair, was grumbling, was far less elated; and then, in the dim light which still existed, he caught just a glimpse of Geoff's bantering smile, and gripped him by the shoulder.

"So you're pulling my leg, eh? It—it——There's a job for us to do? Something special?"

"There is for me. I have orders to make my way forward as quickly as possible, and learn all that I can of the enemy. Of course, if you cared——"

"Cared!" Phil almost shouted, though Geoff warned him instantly to subdue his tone. For let us explain that if, during the first stage of this expedition, the rush and hurry and scurry of the navy and army had been accompanied by cheery calls, by shouts and laughter, by whistling and singing for some hours, now, at least, silence had been enjoined upon every man in the marshes. Orders were given by signs, men whispered to one another, while not an unnecessary shout came from the vessels of the expedition.

"You'll call the enemy down on us," said Geoff severely. "Of course you'll come. Everyone knows that, I more than anyone. We'll take Esbul with us to paddle the bellum, and with a little luck and a little care I think we shall be able to discover something. You see, Phil, we have, as it were, a better chance than the other fellows, for we've been in these marshes before, and know quite a heap about them."

Standing aboard the steam-launch, now that darkness had settled down over the River Euphrates and the stagnant marshes stretched out to the south of it, one would have found it difficult indeed, on this particular night, to imagine that there were other inhabitants of this inundated area. Broken up as the surface of the water was, by innumerable muddy islands, by heaped-up patches of sand, and by banks of reeds, it was difficult enough even in the daytime to catch a full view of any other vessel, and now that the night had fallen and hidden the ships entirely not one was to be seen, though here and there, in fifty odd places, perhaps, the ruddy glow of pipes could be seen as the men smoked tranquilly. A gentle hum rose, too, above the water and the islets—the hum of voices of men of the expedition, men who talked in undertones, who giggled and laughed and joked only just above a whisper, and who, eager for the success of the morrow and for the defeat of the enemy, implicitly obeyed the orders which had been issued.

Geoff stripped off his service-coat and put his belt round his shoulder, thus raising his revolver well above the water. Pulling off his long boots, he donned a pair of tennis shoes – the only change he had from the heavy pair he wore during the daytime – then, followed by Phil, he stepped into a bellum, which had been drawn alongside the steam-launch, and, pushing away from her, at once felt the thrust of Esbul's paddle.

"Directly ahead!" he told the Armenian; "and don't stop unless we are brought up by a mud-bank, or unless I snap my fingers."

It was uncannily still all round them, once they had got some two hundred yards from the somewhat irregular position taken up by the expeditionary vessels, and banks of reeds and columns of mist seemed to spring up out of the darkness at them, to hover round them, and to settle right over them in the most ghostly and inexplicable manner. Once Geoff snapped his fingers with unexpected suddenness, and gripped Phil by the wrist to enjoin silence upon him.

"Eh?" asked that young officer rather breathlessly a few moments later.

"Thought I saw something," said Geoff.

"So did I. I thought I saw somebody or something half an hour ago. I've thought it every moment since we left the steam-launch. Bogies, Geoff?"

"Not nerves, I hope!" came the cheerful answer. "But it's rather uncanny work, ain't it? I could have sworn just now that a fellow stood on the edge of an island into which we were running, and I snapped my fingers; but the way of the boat carried us right on to the very point where he was standing, and right over it. He had gone though."

"Like a nasty nightmare!" said Phil. "Let's go ahead; it's cold and chilly here, and takes the courage out of a fellow."

It was perhaps an hour later, when they had slowly crept forward towards the Turkish position, and when they had caught sight of a glow in the distance—the glow of camp-fires—over the position occupied by the enemy, that the bellum suddenly came to an abrupt halt, grinding noisily upon the edge of the desert.

"Hard ground," said Geoff. "Looks as though we'd come to the edge of the marsh land, and—and—I've thought it for some while, the sky over there shows the reflection from camp-fires. We're near them, Phil."

"Then let's get nearer. But how are we to find this bellum again, supposing we leave it?"

That set them cogitating for a few moments while they stepped ashore, followed by Esbul, and, lifting the bellum clear of the water, carried her into a bank of reeds which could be heard rustling beside them.

"How to find her, that's it!" said Geoff, while the respectful Esbul listened.

"My master," he said of a sudden, for thanks to Major Douglas's tuition the man could speak English tolerably well. "My master, perhaps were we to return from the Turkish camp before the dawn breaks these reeds would aid us. There may be other banks; but, on the other hand, there may be no more, and thus we should be aided."

"In any case we've got to chance it," said Geoff lightly. "Now, come along, and let's make direct for the glow of those camp-fires."

Stealing away from the place where they had hidden their boat, the three crept cautiously but swiftly towards the enemy's position, and, ascending slowly as they went, soon gained a ridge, from which they were able to look right down into the camp where the Turkish soldiers were concentrated. Lying flat on their faces, they were busily engaged in taking full stock of what they saw, when a sudden exclamation came from Esbul.

"Excellency, something behind us!" he whispered.

"Stop! There's someone coming up from the Turkish camp," muttered Philip, making a dive for his revolver.

Glancing swiftly in both directions, Geoff was on the point of leading his comrades to one side, so as to escape the danger of discovery which seemed to threaten them, when shouts resounded all about them, and in a trice figures dashed up from every direction, surrounding the three, and throwing themselves upon Geoff and his friends with a swiftness that was dramatic.

CHAPTER XIV

Captured by the Enemy

It was with a shout of astonishment that Geoff realized that he and Philip and Esbul were discovered. Giving a loud shout of warning, he flung himself against a figure bounding towards him, and, having no time to seize his revolver, struck out wildly in the darkness, and the blow he gave, delivered with all the force of which he was capable, meeting with no greater resistance than the air, for it shot past the ear of the individual at whom it was aimed, caused him to lose his balance and to topple over.

"Ha! Infidel dog!"

The man was down upon him in a moment, and, seizing Geoff's throat, pinned him to the ground, while, within an instant almost, our hero felt the prick of the sharp-pointed dagger with which the man threatened to transfix him. The sudden pain it caused sent a sickly chill all over his body, and then stimulated him to action.

"Get off!" he roared, and, jerking himself over, swiftly had the man beneath him. Then, holding the arm which wielded the weapon, he dealt the man a furious blow between the eyes, and, shaking himself free, leapt to the assistance of Philip.

"Coming!" he shouted, hearing his chum gasp and seeing his figure indistinctly in the darkness. And then he went down again, for one of the band of Turks who had crept so silently towards the three figures watching their camp, leapt upon his shoulders and bore him, nose down, to the sand.

"Infidel dog!" he heard again hissed into his ear. "Move, and I strike life out of you. Move, utter a word, and I slit your throat from ear to ear."

It was not very pleasant; indeed, a sharp stab of pain in the region of his shoulder-blade sent another chill down Geoff's spine, and, together with the increased weight which now held him so firmly to the sand, helped to discourage further efforts. He was cornered, he knew; common sense told him that there were many of the enemy about, that quite half a dozen of them were already seated upon his body, his legs, and his arms, that further resistance was useless, was madness in fact, and could end in only one way—in sudden death for himself and Philip and Esbul.

"Right!" he gasped, spluttering and blowing the sand out of his mouth. "We surrender!"

"Ah! the dog speaks Turkish, eh! Pull him to his feet; let us see him."

It was another voice that spoke, the voice of a Turkish officer, and at once those six lusty individuals who had thrown themselves on Geoff, and who had almost squeezed the life out of him, jerked him to his feet and held him in an erect position. Had they not done so, indeed, he would have stumbled and fallen, for, though the contest had been but a short one, the struggle, whilst it lasted, had been terrific: the efforts he had made to throw off those men, his kicks and plunges, and the blows he had endeavoured to aim had taken it out of Geoff in the most startling manner. He was gasping for breath now, sweat was pouring from his face, whilst his knees shook and refused to support him.

"So, infidel dog, you are one of the British who have dared to invade our country!"

A dusky figure seemed to rise up in front of Geoff, and, approaching quite close to him, thrust a heavily-moustached face close to his and peered at him in the darkness. So close indeed was the man that his breath blew on Geoff's face, and, acting as a tonic as it were, almost stimulated him to further action. But again discretion, common sense, told him that to renew the struggle would be futile. "Better wait till another time," he told himself, gasping in the face of the Turkish officer—spluttering, indeed, for still sand remained in his mouth, whilst his nostrils were tickled with the same material. "Better wait for a while and try our chances in a different manner. There's Philip!"

Men were approaching from a point but a few feet away, their figures standing out against the reflection of the camp-fires dotting the Turkish position, and in amongst them was Geoff's chum, held firmly by the arms, his head pushed forward by a brawny individual who gripped the nape of his neck, and his legs already encumbered by a rope which had been passed loosely round them.

"So, a British officer. Ah!"

"A British officer. Yes!" Geoff admitted between his gasps.

"And one who speaks Turkish, eh?" the man who accosted him demanded.

"That is so."

"Then how?" asked the Turkish officer. "Where did you learn to speak our tongue? You are British, you say, and few there are of that nation who speak our language. Then how? Where? When did you learn it?"

"One moment; let me sit down for a while," said Geoff, panting so heavily that he could hardly make the request. "In a little while I will answer any reasonable question that you may put before me, and in the meantime you need have little fear; for see, there are perhaps twenty or thirty men here to support you."

A grim, harsh chuckle came from the Turkish officer, and yet a laugh which was not altogether disagreeable. If he had been a German officer, no doubt he would have stormed and raved, and might even have suggested shooting his prisoners on the spot, so as to get rid of them; but, being a Turk — and Turkish soldiers, whether they be officers or fighting-men, have ever proved themselves to be possessed of gentlemanly feelings — and being moreover satisfied that the three prisoners he had captured were completely in his hands, this Turk was by no means ill-pleased, was, in fact, in quite a genial humour, and, if the truth be told, rather curious as to the prisoner who spoke his language.

"Sit down," he said. "Now give me your word that you will not attempt to escape, and I'll tell my men to stand away and to give you breathing-space."

Seating himself upon the sand, in fact helped in the movement by the man who had been holding him, Geoff remained for a while panting heavily, while his guard, at a sharp order from the Turkish officer, stepped aside and remained at some distance. Then Philip and Esbul were brought along by the men who had captured them, and were allowed to seat themselves beside him.

"Now," said the Turkish officer, after a while, when he was satisfied that his prisoners were rested, "your promise. Say that you will make no attempt at escape, and you shall march back to camp at my side as friends, as you will, not as prisoners; only, when you arrive there, it will be my duty to hand you over to the guard, and you must take the consequences of your visit here this evening."

"We promise!" Geoff told him promptly.

"Then that is sufficient. Listen, my friend! Though I command a detachment of Turkish troops down in this part of the world—this terrible quarter, where there is nothing but sand and marsh and water—yet I am from Constantinople, and, unlike many other Turks, I have travelled somewhat. Thus it happens to have been my fortune to have met many peoples, and amongst them men of your country. Always I have heard that an Englishman's word is his bond. My friend, you have given your word, and that is quite sufficient."

He showed his friendly spirit within a moment, for, diving a hand into a pocket of his tunic, the officer produced a cigarette-case, and handed it in turn to each of his prisoners; and then, as they sat on there, on the sandy ridge above the twinkling camp-fires dotting the hollow below them, this Turk became quite communicative, as friendly as one could wish, chatted with Geoff as if he were an old friend, one with whom he was well acquainted.

"Come!" he said encouragingly. "Be not so close, be as frank and as friendly as I am, for let me tell you that I am more than interested in you, for, as I said before, how many of your nation are there who can speak our language? And you, you speak it as a native almost—fluently, glibly, with the tone and accent of an educated gentleman. That you are an officer I know, indeed I knew it from the moment of your capture. Now tell me how it came about that you learnt our tongue."

There was no doubt about his earnestness, nor about the fact that his curiosity was purely friendly; quite frankly, therefore, withholding nothing, Geoff told him how he had once, not so very long ago, visited Mesopotamia, and how his travels had taken him as far as Constantinople.

"I have a guardian," he told the Turkish officer, "a British officer, one who for many years has taken the place of my dead father. He it was who brought me to this country, who led me by the Tigris to Bagdad, and with whom I sat in many an Arab camp making friends with the natives."

"Wait! A British officer who led you to Bagdad! Who lived as a friend with Arabs! But surely," said the Turk, "there is but one British officer who could have done that, one with whom I am well acquainted. Had it been a German now, there would be a host of them, though it is little friends they are of the Arabs inhabiting these deserts; but this man, listen my friend, I will give you his name—Douglas Pasha, eh?"

"The same," Geoff admitted.

There was a long pause after that while the Turk slowly puffed at his cigarette, the glowing end showing his features for a few brief seconds, and then dying down between the puffs till it was only possible to make out the dull outline of his figure. No doubt he was thinking hard, thinking furiously, for a Turk, while he puffed clouds of smoke into the dusk around him.

"So," he said at last, giving vent to a low-pitched whistle, "you are Douglas Pasha's ward—and Douglas Pasha is an old friend of mine, one to whom I am much beholden. Well, it is the fortune of war, my friend. The fortune, or shall we say for a moment, while there are none to overhear us, yes, the misfortune? For see the dilemma in which I am placed. As a loyal Turk I have taken steps to make you a captive, you, who were discovered in the act of watching our camp and making a reconnaissance. As a loyal Turk I have made captive the ward of one whom I admit my friend, one whom I would go far to help, and whose esteem is of value to me. Yet, see the dilemma in which I am placed. This I have done as a loyal man, and one who does his utmost for his country; though all the while I know that it is not my country for which I fight, but that Young Turk Party which, alas! controls its destiny. Listen! There are none to hear us, and therefore I can speak the words. Had the Sultan been able to control the affairs of our nation, there would have been no war with Russia, no war with our ancient friends the British, no alliance with these hated Germans. There! I have said enough. Let us walk as friends as far as our Head-quarters, and after that, well after that you pass out of my hands, though Tewfic Pasha will think of you kindly, and maybe might help you on some occasion."

Truly the adventure which had befallen Geoff and Philip and Esbul was turning out to be as strange as it had been sudden and unexpected; for here, captives in the hands of the enemy, they were yet friends already with at least one of them, while Geoff had discovered in this Turkish officer one who in other times would have gone out of his way to be helpful, considerate, and friendly. But Turkey was at war with Britain, and whatever Tewfic Pasha's private feelings may have been towards our country he had a duty to perform, like every other loyal man; and Geoff, realizing that fact, honoured him the more when at length he gave a sharp order and called his men about them.

"You'll fall in round the prisoners, allowing them to march freely," he said. "When we reach the centre of the camp two of you will attach yourselves to each of these three men, and will escort them to Head-quarters. But listen, ye dogs! No violence, no brutal treatment, for these young men have behaved most gallantly, have fought for their freedom, and now, having lost to us, who are the more numerous, are content with their lot, are cheerful, and are facing the future with courage."

"After all, things might have been worse," chirped Philip, as the trio marched along in the centre of their escort, the officer now at the head of his men. "Quarter of an hour ago I thought my last moment had come, particularly when one of these fellows round us indicated to me in the most unpleasant manner that he was armed with a knife, and was longing to push it through me. Ugh!"

He gave vent to an exaggerated grunt of horror, which set Geoff giggling, for it reminded him of his own feelings, of that cold shiver which had gone down his spine, of the extraordinary indescribable shudder which had shaken him from head to foot, and which, courageous though he hoped he had been, had set his limbs trembling.

"Jolly nasty!" he said, sympathizing with his chum immediately. "I had the same sort of experience, and it isn't nice, particularly on a dark night, and when it comes so unexpectedly. But we've been wonderfully lucky when you come to think of it—though it's awfully unfortunate that we should have been captured—for this officer in charge of the party actually knows Major Douglas, and if it weren't war-time I believe he would himself see us to a place of safety."

"And might even now look the other way if there was a chance of our escaping," suggested Phil.

"No, decidedly no!" Geoff answered. "He's loyal to the core, this Turkish officer, unlike so many of them."

"Then what's to be done?" asked Phil. "You don't mean to tell me that you are going to allow yourself to be taken as a prisoner, say, into the interior of the country, and give up all hope of joining the other fellows?"

Geoff laughed, a gruff, determined sort of laugh, which sounded rather impressive in the darkness. There was a note of satire in it too, a note seldom indulged in by our hero.

"Sorry that's the impression you've got of me after all these months," he told Philip curtly. "Sorry you think I'm so soft, so lacking in spirit, as to

197

give up just because I am captured. What about that trip we proposed which was to carry us to Bagdad, and was to allow us to make a search for Major Douglas?"

A sudden exclamation escaped from Philip's lips, and, diving at Geoff's arm, he gripped the wrist with a suddenness which was almost disconcerting:

"And—and, why not?" he said in a hoarse whisper, "why not? Aren't we now away from the expedition, aren't we more in the heart of Mesopotamia than ever we were before? Just think for a moment, and suppose you had gone off on that expedition that you've been planning, that you've been dreaming about every day and night since that letter came from your guardian. Supposing you'd slipped away from the British camp and had got behind the enemy's lines: where's the difference?"

Geoff brought his eloquence and enthusiasm to a somewhat sudden end by giving him a disagreeable reminder.

"Difference! Difference!" he remarked caustically. "Only this, that whereas, in that case, we should be behind their lines, but free; in this, we are in the midst of their lines, not free, but captives."

But you could not damp Phil's ardour or his spirits however much cold water you threw upon them. He gurgled for a while, gasped rather loudly, and took to whistling. Then, when they had covered perhaps a hundred yards, he again opened the subject; indeed, he proceeded with the discussion as though it had never been broken off, as if there had been no such thing as an interruption.

"Well," he said testily. "Well, who wants to be told that sort of thing? Don't I know just as well as you do that the case ain't quite the same, that we are prisoners and in the enemy's lines, instead of being free and behind them? But it's near enough, surely. A chap has only got to escape from these fellows who have bagged us, and—and—and there you are!"

198

"And—and—there you are!" laughed Geoff, catching his enthusiasm instantly; indeed, our hero had already been thinking furiously as to how he and his friends were to circumvent this difficult position in which they found themselves, and to shake off the hold which the Turks had cast upon them. And why, as Philip said, if only they could make their escape, seeing that they would then presumably be behind the lines of the enemy, why should they not turn their faces towards Bagdad, and go on with the rescue of Douglas Pasha.

"Jingo! We'll do it," he told his friend.

"You—you—you consent? You think it's possible?" asked Phil, his voice eager, his face lit up—though, to be sure, it could not be seen because of the darkness.

"Hush! We're in the centre of the camp, and the guard is closing in on us," Geoff warned him. "But, just a last word in case we are separated, I am going to do my best to escape, and if I succeed, and can get you and Esbul free also, I am off for Bagdad."

"Done, with you! Shake hands on it!" cried Phil, gripping his chum's palm and shaking it warmly. "Ripping! The thought of such an expedition makes up for this ghastly business; perhaps to-night we'll do it, perhaps to-morrow, and—and—well, you can rely on me standing by you, old fellow. If they separate us, and the chance comes to me to slip my cable, you know, don't you, Geoff, that I'll stand by until I get you and Esbul out, so as to complete the party?"

There was no time for Geoff to make a reply, no time to thank his chum for an expression of loyalty which was just like him, for the guard had already closed in, men were gripping their arms on either side, while, despite the caution of Tewfic Pasha, one at least of the men showed little love for the captives.

"Dog," he whispered in Geoff's ear, "you infidel who speak our language, be silent, or I will screw the head from your body."

"Unpleasant fellow," muttered Geoff, yet smiling serenely, for he knew well enough that a call to Tewfic Pasha would relieve him of this threatening fellow's attentions. "Ah! That appears to be the Turkish Head-quarters."

It was lighter now that they had arrived at what appeared to be the centre of the Turkish concentration; for numerous camp-fires were dotted about the place, lighting up the surroundings with their reflection, and indeed making the outer darkness even denser, even more impenetrable. There loomed up now in front of them a row of tents, one larger than the others, over which a flag could be heard fluttering in the breeze, though its folds could not be seen so easily. There were lamps burning in the tent, and towards it the guard escorted their prisoners.

"Halt!" commanded Tewfic Pasha, and then entered the tent.

"Master," whispered Esbul at that moment, taking advantage of the fact that the guard had released their grip of their prisoners, and were now standing at attention dressed in two lines, one in front and one behind their captives. "Master, let me say a word in your ear while there is time. Listen! I am an Armenian."

It was a fact of which Geoff was thoroughly well aware, and yet a fact the seriousness of which had not struck him till that moment.

"An Armenian! An Armenian, yes!" he said, speaking his thoughts in a whisper; "and the Turks have no love for that nation."

"Love, Excellency!" exclaimed Esbul, with a bitterness which was strange to him. "Love, my master! Of a truth, where the Armenian race is concerned, the Turk has nothing but bitterness and hatred to show. You have heard maybe of their doings in past years?"

"I have," Geoff said consolingly.

"How these Turkish fiends massacred our people, how they hate us perhaps because we are Christians, and how they have done their utmost to exterminate us, to grind us under their heel, to rid this land of Turkey of us."

"I have heard the tale," Geoff told him sadly enough, for for many years the massacre of unfortunate and helpless Armenians in Turkey had been carried out by the Sultan's people, and had more than once roused the bitter anger of peoples in Europe. Yet who could control the Turk in the centre of his own country? What nation could prevent the Sultan from wreaking his fiendish hate upon these people? And now that this gigantic war had broken out, and Turkey had declared herself in favour of the Germans, who could prevent the agents of the Kaiser, those sinister individuals, from persuading the Young Turk Party once more to commence their hideous work in the neighbourhood of Erzerum and the Caucasus Mountains? Already, urged on by those satellites of the Kaiser — those ruthless individuals, possessed of as little mercy as their fellows in Europe — massacres of the Armenians had once again begun, and ere they were finished were to account for almost a million of these miserable, unfortunate individuals. No wonder Esbul was trembling — Esbul, the Armenian, the faithful servant who had followed Douglas Pasha into the heart of Mesopotamia, and who had borne that message to our hero.

"Master," he said again, making violent efforts to control his words, "for you, who are a prisoner, and for your comrade, things may be well enough, for at heart the Turk is kindly disposed, and thinks well of the British, but for me, an Armenian, what is there to hope for?"

"What indeed?" Geoff sighed, when he grasped the full import of what Esbul had been saying. For he knew well enough the hardships of the Armenian race, and was well acquainted with the fact that the Turks hated, despised, and tortured them. Were, then, these captors of theirs likely to treat Esbul leniently once they discovered that one of the trio they had laid their hands on was an Armenian? Would they treat him as an honoured captive? — as Geoff hoped would be the case with Philip and himself. Or would they drag him aside, stand him out in the open, and shoot him like a dog? — the treatment they were meting out to his brothers.

"Listen!" he told him. "Listen, Esbul; you must go, you must go now; you must slip away; you must never let them see you! Wait! I will fall to the ground and feign illness, which will create a disturbance. Go then, take advantage of the opportunity; and, later, when you are free, and perhaps have reached Bagdad, look out for me and my comrade, and search for the whereabouts of Douglas Pasha."

He pressed the hand of the faithful fellow, and then, coughing violently, suddenly fell to the ground and writhed there, rolling from side to side, groaning and creating as much noise and fuss as was possible. At once Philip leapt to his side, kneeling on the ground and bending over him.

"What's the matter?" he asked distractedly, for he was thoroughly startled by this strange occurrence.

"Shut up!" Geoff told him. "I'm shamming. I'll tell you why later."

"What ails the dog? Come, what has happened to him?"

Turks in the rear rank, drawn up behind the captives and nearest to them, had darted forward almost at once as Geoff fell to the ground, and now one of them bent over him and gripped him by the shoulder, while he bawled into his ear. A second later a figure darted from the tent — the figure of Tewfic Pasha — and, pushing men of the front rank aside unceremoniously, came upon the scene.

"Hold your tongue!" he commanded the man shouting at Geoff. "What has happened? Ah! This officer is ill. Carry him into the tent, two of you idle fellows."

Picking their burden up, the men bore him into the tent, illuminated by swinging oil-lamps, while Philip followed unbidden.

"And the third?" asked Tewfic Pasha, casting his eyes upon Geoff and Philip, and seeing them clearly for the first time since he and his men had laid hold of them. "The third, that other fellow; where is he?"

Yes, where? There was a hue and cry outside: men were rushing to and fro, shouting and bellowing at one another, while a couple of the guard were speeding across the camp calling a warning to the sentries. For Esbul had disappeared. He had been at Geoff's side just a second before he tumbled, and those men in the rear rank of the Turkish guard could have sworn that he had knelt beside his comrade and had bent over him; and yet—and yet the darkness had swallowed him up; he had gone, slipped away like a will-o'-the-wisp, and no one had caught sight of him. Meanwhile Geoff had made a reasonably rapid recovery, and stood now beside Philip, swaying just a little—for he had to act the part—his face flushed just a trifle after his exertions, his breath coming in panting grunts.

"I'm sorry," he told Tewfic Pasha; "but the thing is over now; merely a spasm, a sudden dizziness, perhaps produced by those lusty fellows of yours who sat so heavily on me."

"And the promise you made has been kept," Tewfic smiled back at him, indeed his eyes twinkled—twinkled knowingly. "You gave me your word that you and your comrades would march towards this spot without attempting an escape, and when my guards laid their hands on you, within sight of this tent, and marched you forward, you were absolved of your promise. Listen!" he whispered in Geoff's ear a moment or so later, when he had an opportunity. "It is as well, my friend; it is just as well, for that other man was not of your country. Maybe he was of ours, maybe he was an Armenian."

The bright friendly eyes of the Turkish officer twinkled again, and a smile lit up his face, then, turning away, he accosted a Turk who approached at that moment from an ante-room erected behind this tent, which served as the Head-quarters of the Turkish Concentration.

"Prisoners, Excellency!" he said. "We captured three of them on the ridge, and doubtless they are scouts of an enemy party coming in this direction. They are British officers, Excellency, and once they were captured have behaved well and quietly. I have given them your word—the word of a man of honour—that they shall be well and kindly treated."

As a matter of fact, Geoff and Phil had no cause to complain of the treatment meted out to them, for, as we have said before, the Turks had already given many an illustration of the fact that they were both good and stanch soldiers and most excellent fellows. Once the fighting was done, once they had made captives or been captured, they forgot their enmity, and in the case of those they had made prisoners, treated them like human beings.

"You are to be sent up the Kut-el-Hai to the Tigris," said Tewfic Pasha, when the General in Command of the Turkish Concentration had inspected the prisoners and had cross-examined them. "I am commanded to see that quarters are found for you, and that you are given food and clothing. You will start on your journey to-morrow."

The following morning, in fact, at an early hour, found the two young officers aboard a small steam-launch, which at once set out for Kut-el-Amara. Arriving at that place on the River Tigris some three days later, they transhipped to a larger vessel, a paddle-steamer—as rusty and dilapidated as any of those which had come to the Shatt-el-Arab from India for service with the British. Then they were carried up the winding Tigris, and in due course, after days of twisting and turning along the numerous bends of the river, after running aground on sand-banks on many occasions, they reached at last the city of Bagdad—the Mecca of the Turks of Eastern Turkey and of the Arabs of Mesopotamia—and there, having been interrogated again by a Turkish officer, they were sent to a prison—a fort outside the city—the clanging gates of which shut on them with a force and a jar which, in spite of their buoyant spirits, sent a chill of despair through them.

"Nasty strong sort of a place," Philip whispered to his chum, as they passed under a low flat roof and along a stone passage. "No picking a hole through these walls with a penknife, my boy. It will have to be a case of strategy."

Geoff looked round him, for the bright sunlight outside sent slanting rays into the passage and lit up their surroundings.

"Beastly strong place," he agreed with Philip; "built of stone, and every piece set close to the other. But we'll see, Phil; the cage that's to hold the two of us will have to be a pretty strong one, for I'll tell you this, I've made up my mind that I'll break out of this place, and carry on that little business."

"Douglas Pasha, eh?" asked Phil.

"Of course. Ah! The fellow's opening a door, and in we go! A cell big enough for the two of us! My word! Breaking out will take a lot of doing."

CHAPTER XV

Von Hildemaller's Intervention

A silence settled down upon the prison and the cell in which Geoff and Philip had been thrust, once the clanging of the iron door which closed it had subsided — a silence which told rather on their nerves, and helped to rob them of their spirits. They sat just within the door, staring about them, noticing with concern, almost with dismay, the solid masonry built up above them, the two narrow windows which gave air and light, and the absence of any sort of opening which might give them a means of making their escape. Then Philip sat down on the edge of a low platform built against one of the walls and burst into loud whistling.

"No use being down-hearted! No use crying before we're hurt! In other words, it ain't no use giving up before we've tried, eh?" he blurted out when he had accomplished a few shrill bars of an air popular amongst his fellows.

"In fact, keep on hoping!" said Geoff, laughing now, though he had felt singularly depressed but a few moments earlier. "And, besides, Philip, I've an idea!"

"Let's hear it; something new, eh? An idea! Well, you astonish me!"

The incorrigible subaltern began whistling again, a shrill, exultant, happy whistle, and continued it though a moment later steps were heard in the corridor outside. There was a bang on the door, and the heavy iron concern was burst open. A smooth-faced, bald-headed, and raggedly dressed Turk thrust his head and shoulders in and grimaced at them. Then he opened his mouth, or rather let his lips fall apart, showing a set of gleaming white teeth which perhaps might have frightened younger people.

"Silence, dogs!" he shouted at them, and at the order Philip ceased whistling.

"Tell the old boy that we want food and water," he said to Geoff. "And, by the way, about that idea of yours, I suppose one can take it that this rascal can't speak English."

Geoff gave him a quick look, and, turning, to the jailer, demanded food and drink from him.

"As to calling us dogs," he said severely, realizing that to cringe to this ruffian would be to invite harsh treatment, and that sternness and unconcern on his part would be more likely to impress him — "as to calling us dogs, you rascal, bear in mind that we are not without friends in this country. Listen! You may know of one Tewfic Pasha? Ah! You know the man then! That is enough — bring food and water."

It was clear in a moment that if this jailer were inclined to be a somewhat rough and rude, if not a bullying, sort of individual, he yet had a certain fund of discretion, and, moreover, that even if he were the guardian of this cell, interned as it were, far away from active operations, he yet had knowledge of others outside the prison. He had heard of Tewfic Pasha, that was certain, for on the mention of the name his face had fallen, the grimace, the snarl, which he had turned upon the prisoners, was changed at once to a sly, fawning smile, while he even bowed in Geoff's direction.

"I was mistaken then, Excellency," he said at last, after some seconds had passed, during which he racked his brains for something to say. "Food and water? You shall have it, for I have orders to treat you with indulgence."

"Wait!" demanded Geoff, determined not to lose his hold over this fellow, and arresting him in the act of closing the door, "wait, my good fellow! Doubtless you will be caring for our comfort for some while to come, so that it may be as well at this moment to come to an understanding. Doubtless, too, money is of some value to you, and if that be so, and you treat my comrade and myself to favours, then, when we are released, you shall be rewarded. Say now, is that a bargain?"

The man's face lit up immediately, while he even smiled quite a pleasant smile upon them. Sour dispositioned, ill-grained, and surly — perhaps because of the work allotted to him — this man, at the bottom of his heart, was really not without his virtues. Cunning like many a Turk, avaricious, and apt to trade upon those at his mercy, he had — in spite of the order which he had just admitted he had received — namely, that he was to treat his prisoners with indulgence — in spite of that, he had looked upon them as helpless, as penniless, as likely to be only a nuisance and an encumbrance. But now Geoff's tones, the peremptory words he had uttered, and, more than all, that suggestion of a reward quite altered his intentions.

"A reward, Excellency! Then indeed I am fortunate," he told Geoff. "Let your Excellency declare what is wanted, and that which I am able to bring shall surely reach you."

"And a question," said Geoff, determined to make the most of his opportunity. "This prison, where is it situated? How far from Bagdad?"

"A day's march — not more, not less, Excellency!"

"And there are other prisoners? Others from Britain or Russia?"

The man shook his head and raised his eyes as if Geoff were encroaching upon a subject which was forbidden. Then, backing out of the door, he pulled it to after him with a clang, and went off along the passage in a different frame of mind from that in which he had entered it. As for Phil, he gave vent once more to a shrill whistle, which ended in a blast of air which came through his parted lips soundless.

"And that's the idea?" he asked slyly, pointing at the door, and jerking his thumb over his shoulder in the direction of the passage. "If you put a bird in a cage, and the doors are so strong that breaking through 'em is out of the question, that bird ain't necessarily deprived of a chance of getting his freedom. There's the door left, an iron affair on this occasion, and as strong as a rock from the look of it, and then there's the jailer!"

"But there's something more than the jailer no doubt!" Geoff warned him; "there'll be sentries perhaps, officials in charge of the prison, other doors, with doors beyond them."

"Which don't say that even then we shouldn't be successful," said Philip airily. "It's a chance, of course. What would they do if they caught us?"

"Depends. Perhaps shoot us, though I hardly think it's likely — your Turk doesn't indulge in frightfulness, like his German ally. It's worth the chance, Philip, and we'll risk it; but, like sensible individuals, we'll first of all find out as much as we can about local conditions. We'll rest content here for a while and plumb this jailer fellow as far as possible."

"And then we'll scrag him. Not that one wants to be violent with him," said Philip; "I'd like to treat the fellow as gently as possible. But where a man stands between you and a chance of getting freedom, well, it ain't your fault, is it? It's his, if he gets hammered."

The two were still discussing the matter earnestly, almost eagerly, when steps were heard again in the corridor outside, and the door was pushed open by the jailer, now smiling widely, and bearing a Turkish tray upon which were set coffee and food in abundance.

A week passed, during which Geoff and his chum did their best to while away the weary hours, and to ascertain something of the outside of their cell and the conditions existing in other parts of the prison. By dint of carefully probing the jailer, by flattering him and raising his hopes of a reward, they ascertained that the Governor was lying ill, and that his subordinate was often enough away from the building. There were troops there, they gathered, but how many, and where quartered, no amount of questioning would extract from the jailer; nor was it wise to ask him about the plan of the building, the position of the cell, the corridor outside, and the road which led to the gates giving access.

As to the cell itself, the first complete day had imprinted every feature of it upon their minds, till they knew every crevice, every flaw in the stone, every little hole and excrescence. They knew the exact height of those two windows which admitted air and light to their prison, and, by standing upon one another's shoulders, had contrived to look outside—only to find that both windows looked out upon a courtyard, surrounded by a wall the top of which would undoubtedly be well beyond their reach. As to the windows themselves, they were barred so heavily that to attempt to get through them was out of the question, and even were they provided with a saw or a chisel the job would still be beyond them.

"So it's got to be the jailer," grinned Philip, when the week had passed, "and, 'pon my word, I'm awfully sorry about it. Of course we must do the square thing by him; we've promised him a reward, and he must have it. Let's form our plans for gagging and tying him up safely."

There was more discussion after that, eager enough to be sure, while plans were made and unmade, every eventuality likely to occur foreseen and overcome as far as possible.

"Naturally enough, we shall not make the attempt until nightfall," said Geoff, "and, seeing that this fellow gives us a last call just about dusk, that will be the most convenient hour to nab him. Let's go over the scene for a moment. If we happen to be fairly close to the door when he enters, he won't be suspicious, for he's found us in every sort of position during the last week. A chap would get soft and out of condition if he stayed in one place in a cell like this, and it's only by walking up and down and running round that we have been able to get exercise. Exercise, by Jove! Why didn't we think of that before? We might have sent a message to the Governor of the prison asking him to allow us out of our cell for certain hours of the day, and that would have given us an idea of our surroundings."

It was strange indeed that they had not thought of that before, and, acting on the impulse of the moment, they called loudly for the jailer, and having attracted his attention sent him on a mission to the Governor.

"But no, Excellency!" he told Geoff on his return; "it is not permitted—not for the moment at any rate. You must wait. The Governor is in ill-health and out of temper, and he bade me return with a peremptory refusal. Have patience. Perhaps in a little while you will be liberated and allowed to walk on the roof, where you may enjoy the sunlight."

"Prophetic!" said Philip when the door had closed again. "In a little while we may be liberated—this evening, if possible, I think. What do you say, Geoff?"

"I'm with you," answered our hero; "let's get the gag ready for him, and arrange about his money. Funny, isn't it, that we've been able to keep what we had in our pockets? I imagine that if Germans had captured us they'd have rifled us of every coin, and we should have been paupers."

Yet, as it happened, despite their anxiety to break loose from the prison and find their way into the open, the evening passed without event, and was followed by days of waiting. Days which stretched into weeks— miserable, lonely weeks, the hours of which dragged by on leaden wheels, while the days themselves were often like a nightmare, so long did the minutes take in passing, so long were they drawn out, so utterly unending did they seem.

"But it's no use being despondent," said Geoff; "and just because the jailer seems to be on the qui vive all the time, and has not yet given us an opportunity, and, indeed, has been accompanied by another man on many occasions, we mustn't think that the plan is 'off', or even dream of giving up the undertaking. We're going to break out of this place, Philip."

"You've said that time and again," grinned the irrepressible and ever-jovial Philip, "and so have I; and, by Jingo! we will—only when? This waiting is getting a bit trying. I declare my joints are getting stiff, and if I had to run a hundred yards I'd lose the race."

Lack of exercise and of fresh air was indeed telling upon the two very greatly; for, be it remembered, they were young, enthusiastic, and open-air creatures, who, in months past, had spent the better part of their waking hours out in the free open air, under the blue sky of Mesopotamia; and when in India or in England, outside buildings whenever possible, enjoying the sunlight and the fresh breezes which played about them. And now, to be cooped up between four stone walls of this unpleasant prison, this stone vault, was depressing, to say the least of it; it was enervating, taking the colour out of their cheeks, and, in spite of their courage and their youthful enthusiasm, was tending rather to take the heart out of them.

"We shall rot if we go on like this," said Geoff desperately, when a few days had passed. "I quite believe you, Philip, for my joints, too, feel stiff and useless almost. Supposing we were to beguile the time by a little active exercise — sort of Swedish gymnastics. Eh? Why not?"

"Why not?" Philip said eagerly, grasping at the suggestion with the energy almost of a drowning man grasping at a straw. "You've taken squads in that before. Fire away, Geoff! Let's see what we make of it."

Thereafter the astonished jailer peeped in more than once on these curious white prisoners of his, to find them perhaps stretched on their backs on the stone floor of the cell, their hands clasped under their heads, and their legs, stretched stiffly in front of them, being slowly raised towards the ceiling. Or he came upon the two facing one another with absolutely solemn visages, on tiptoe, bobbing up and down in the most extraordinary fashion.

"Allah, but this is a strange sight!" he told himself on the first occasion, and looked suspiciously round the cell. "No, no! There is no sign of attempted escape — windows are barred as usual. Truly this is a strange experience. Surely these young men, no doubt nobles in their own country, have gone crazy."

He was more than dumbfounded, absolutely staggered, one day, when, entering the cell very quietly and very suddenly, he discovered Geoff standing behind his chum, gripping him firmly by the waist and slowly raising him upward, raising him till the lanky figure of Philip was lifted to a horizontal position above Geoff's head, and was slowly pushed upward to the full extent of his arms and then lowered again, only to be pushed once more into the old position; then, as the gaping jailer watched, the figure of the subaltern was brought to a vertical position and lowered ever so gently to the ground till his stockinged toes touched the stone floor of the prison. By then the man's eyes were starting out of his head, and he gripped the edge of the iron door as if to support himself.

"Allah is great!" he stuttered. "Surely Allah is great! And these white youths are the strangest of people. See now what they do! They are here in a prison cell, none too comfortable, perhaps, none too bright and cheery, yet with four peaceful walls about them, and a wooden divan on which they may without hindrance sit or lounge the day long, staring maybe at the wall, and dreaming of the past or of the future. And surely the future, in spite of such a prison, has much that is of rosy colour for such youths — youths who are but on the threshold of manhood. There is hope for them, a peaceful life to contemplate, and, within these four walls, no need to do aught else but dream, but let the hours slide away, but let others work for their existence."

That was the Turkish outlook on life — an outlook which permits a man to reach man's estate as he may do, and which enjoins on him the need thereafter to live as placid, as workless a life as he may find. Pass your Turkish bazaar, wend your way through some Turkish café, and see the individuals of that nationality seated there. Cross-legged, they rest in comfort where Britons would be seized with cramp within five minutes. Cross-legged, they rest placidly, their open eyes fixed on nothing, their thoughts barren, their minds perhaps a blank. Or they sit with one hand resting in their lap or toying with the tiny egg-shaped coffee-cup which brings them refreshment, the other hand gripping the long, braided stem of the narghile. Then puffs of white smoke escape slowly, reluctantly, as it were, from their lips, and are gently wafted above by the breeze circling round the stalls or the café into the open air. Who knows? It may be that in the midst of those clouds your Turk sees his future, and gathers inspiration for those dreams which keep him a placid occupier of his stall or his portion of the divan in the café, holding him enthralled in lazy, idle speculation, in gentle, easy wondering, in an aimless endeavour to burst the mists of the future and discover what may be his fortune in the years to come.

For a Turk that may be good enough, sufficient exercise both for mind and body; but the fresh blood, the keen intellect, the wonderful energy of Anglo-Saxons require more movement, require some better pabulum for their thoughts — something far more stimulating — and they find it in active, open-air exercise, in the seeing of interest in all things, and in the taking of energetic steps which may bring into motion every joint, every muscle, and every fibre of their bodies. Thus what appeared to be a form of increasing mania in Geoff and Philip in the eyes of their jailer and of the man who accompanied him on occasion, who both of them stared, amazed — though they had now seen those curious actions of their two prisoners on many occasions — was no more strange and astonishing to them than were the sloth, the ease, and the aimless existence of the Turks to our two heroes.

See the result of this extraordinary mania on the part of Geoff and Philip. The hours began to glide away. The days fled as if there was some driving force behind them, and slid by at such a rate that a week was gone before they could look round, while week piled on week in rapid succession. Nor was that the only advantage obtained by these two energetic and restless prisoners. Little by little their colour came back, till they were rosy in spite of those four blank walls about them; and little by little their muscles hardened, their joints became more flexible and elastic, and their strength increased to a point at which both of them, in spite of their moderately heavy build, threatened to become young Samsons. Little did the grinning jailer realize that, whereas he might have proved an easy victim of these two, attacking him together, at the commencement of their captivity, he would now be but as a child in the arms of one; for Geoff's fingers alone had become so powerful that he could have taken the Turk by the neck and shaken the life out of him single-handed.

"I think, old boy, that the jailer won't stand a dog's chance when we get busy," he told Philip.

"And I believe you, dear chap," grinned his chum, "only — —" And then Philip's face lengthened till it had attained the length of the proverbial fiddle, "only this waiting is all rot. I believe myself that that beggar of a jailer suspects us. He's been awfully decent, of course, in bringing us food and water, but, all the same, he's got it into his narrow head that we mean to tackle him on the first occasion."

It was Geoff's turn to grin — a happy grin — for the exercise had improved his digestion, and had brought him to a position where he might be said to be in the pink of health, and therefore looked on the bright side of everything.

"I believe you, dear boy," he said, repeating Philip's statement. "As to when the chance will come, well, who knows? Only we are ready."

They spent that afternoon in carefully devising a gag and ropes, which they obtained by tearing strips off the blankets which had been provided for their covering; and then counted out the sum of money which, though not very great, was likely to prove a small fortune to the jailer. In fact, they had not yet completed their preparations when steps were heard in the corridor outside and halted at the doorway.

"Ready?" asked Geoff.

Philip nodded, and, sauntering to the corner of the cell, placed himself in a position which would allow him to throw himself on the back of the jailer. Geoff crushed the gag into his trouser pocket, and stood, as he had often stood before, facing the door, waiting for it to open. The bolts were pulled back with a clang, and slowly the heavy iron frame-door was pushed open, disclosing the smiling, friendly face of the jailer at first, and then a second individual — a stout, fat, heavily-built man, dressed in the loosest of European clothing, who mopped his streaming forehead with a red silk handkerchief, who panted and grunted, who blew gusts of air out of a mouth which was out of all proportion, from between two irregular rows of yellow teeth, hidden almost entirely by a moustache, which flowed on either side of his fat cheeks, and which was stained by cigarette smoke in the middle. More than that, the man wore on his head a panama hat which shaded his features, the exact expression of which was made all the more indistinguishable by the dusk already settling in the corridor, but which could yet be seen to be more pallid, of a whiter hue, than was common to the Turkish nation. It was no Turk in fact; it was a European, and none other than a German. More than that, what German in the heart of Mesopotamia could have answered to such a description as that above delineated but von Hildemaller? Yes, it was that urbane and kindly fellow, that perspiring, panting individual, that emissary of the Kaiser who dealt ostensibly in dates, but clandestinely in political matters. It was the garrulous, the charming, and the most entertaining Herr von Hildemaller, that cunning, scheming, unscrupulous wretch who had been instrumental in obtaining the imprisonment of Joe Douglas.

No wonder that Geoff stared at this apparition as though it were a ghost, a well-grown, beefy, and extremely solid ghost to be sure, yet one which filled him with amazement. No wonder, too, that Philip, after his own particular custom and habit, pursed up his lips and allowed a low-pitched whistle of astonishment to escape him. And then it was von Hildemaller's turn. He grunted, he mopped his forehead and face more violently, and greeted the two, first with a penetrating, suspicious glance, and then with an expansive smile, which took them both in at the same moment as it were, as if he were inordinately proud to meet them.

"Ach! It is vat I haff heard—two Englishmen—hein?" he grunted, and then, turning on the jailer, exploded: "Begone, dog!" he shouted; "close der door and go to your quarters, and haff no fear dat deese prisoners will escape, for see, I am armed and prepared to hold dem."

He waited, mopping his forehead and standing just within the cell, till the jailer had departed—had crawled away in fact, showing terror of this

German—then, stepping well within the cell, von Hildemaller closed the door, and once more treated Geoff and his friend to an expansive grin, which was most friendly and most inviting.

"I haff heard dat you are here," he told them, casting a glance first at one and then at the other. "I haff remember dat you are white men like myself, and not dogs like deese Turkish; and although we are at war—we Germans and you British—yet it is far from here to Germany and England; and I haff said: 'Von Hildemaller, you are not such a craven fellow, so wrapped up in Germany, that you cannot befriend deese white men. Dey are nearer to you dan to deese Turkish dogs, deese heathen.' Mein friends, let me tell you something. I haff come to offer you friendshib and liberty."

They were sheep's eyes that he was casting at the astonished Geoff and Philip, little, swift, sidelong glances, which fastened upon their faces in turn—critical and almost anxious, penetrating glances, which, swift though the glimpse was of the faces of the British subalterns, marked every feature—their open guileless expressions, the look of astonishment, of relief, in their faces, the gleam of coming friendship in their eyes.

Von Hildemaller chuckled, and all the while turned on those unsuspicious and inexperienced subalterns his own peculiar and expansive smile—that smile which had deceived so many people, that smile the friendliness of which gave rise to no room for suspicion. He chortled, and mopped his streaming forehead again with his bright-red handkerchief. He was making progress he felt sure; these two stalwart young men were taking him to their hearts already—this big, fat, ungainly German. And why not? For see what an offer had been made them! And consider by whom! By none other than von Hildemaller, a person, it seemed, unknown to either of them, though let us not forget that Geoff already had some knowledge of this individual, and Philip also. Yet—yet could these tales that had come to them be true?

"Can the fellow be a rascal really?" Geoff was asking himself; while Philip stared at the huge perspiring German amazed, troubled for one of the few occasions in his life, disconcerted, his heart fluttering with hope at the opportunity of swift liberty, his better judgment, his common sense, overcome by his eagerness to be quit of this cell and prison.

And von Hildemaller, that scheming, cunning German, ogled the two with that pair of fat eyes of his; he curled his moustache, lifting it just for a second sufficiently high to allow them to catch a glimpse of that row of tobacco-stained teeth – that row of cruel teeth which gave perhaps a better inkling of this man's real nature than any other part of his anatomy. Von Hildemaller pushed the red handkerchief into one of his bulging pockets, and then threw out the two fat palms of his hands in a manner characteristic of him. He had made an impression, he felt; he must drive the thing home; now that the thin edge of the wedge had been introduced he must drive it in firmly, securely, till he had won by his very impulsiveness, by his open friendship, the goodwill and confidence of these young fellows.

"Mein friends, mein lieber friends," he said in his most unctuous and oily manner, that expansive smile now exaggerated, his broad face shining with indulgent friendship, "though I am a German, still I loff the English; yes, how I loff them! And, mein Gott, it is fortunate that I came upon a man who told me of you, a Turkish officer who indiscreetly whispered to me of two brave British officers who haff been made captiff. And den I say: 'Von Hildemaller, you are like deese young officers'."

He stopped and panted for a moment, and once more dived for his handkerchief with which to mop his face.

Like these two young officers! As if anyone in his common senses could have compared the huge, fat, ungainly German to either of these two spruce young officers, or could have seen the smallest likeness between the broad, smiling, yet cunning face of this Teuton and the open, frank, healthy expressions of our heroes.

"Ha!" von Hildemaller grunted, catching his breath and panting still more heavily, for speaking so rapidly was rather a tax on his energies. "And I say: 'Von Hildemaller, though you are a German, you loff deese English; dey are lost, forlorn captiffs in a strange country, a country of brutes and beasts not worthy to eat their food with Europeans', and den I make one big, noble resolve. I say: 'Von Hildemaller, mein brave, kind fellow, you will go to seek deese young men, you will rescue dem, you will take dem to a place where they can be on der parole — living like white men, treated with kindness and consideration'."

Out came the red handkerchief again, and the mopping process was repeated, while, as the folds of the red handkerchief swept across his forehead and cleared the vision first of one eye and then of the other, the Teuton's deeply sunk and penetrating optics lit upon the faces of Geoff and Phil, while his lips almost trembled with joy at the thought of coming triumph.

"Dey are fools, deese British pups," he was telling himself, chortling loudly, and chuckling at his obvious success. "First I haff the Major Pasha — that Douglas Pasha, and one day I will kill him — and now I haff deese odder, deese two more British officers. Himmel! How I hate der breed, deese British, who haff come so soon between der Kaiser and his object.

"Ach! If I could, I would screw the neck of every Englishman; yes, sweep them into the desert, bury them out of sight, clear them away from the steps of all Germans."

And yet all the time his perspiring face beamed upon our two heroes, beamed, whilst his words rang in their ears — those lying words which invited them to trust to this monster, which gave them hopes of liberty, which offered them a haven where they might rest in comfort and in safety, a haven which, for all they knew, might give them complete liberty to return to their own people. Indeed, though the German had not mentioned such a thing, had not even hinted at it, yet his openness of heart, the warm friendship he expressed for them, made such a possibility not entirely out of the question. It raised hopes, hopes which, in the case of Phil, had now almost undermined his judgment, had gone dangerously far towards winning his confidence, towards making him trust von Hildemaller absolutely. For—see the cunning of this German—he did not tell our heroes a fact unknown to them. He had met a Turkish officer who had let fall some indiscreet words with reference to British prisoners. The crafty German did not tell them that that was Tewfic Pasha, who, meeting the German, and, discovering that he already had news of such prisoners, had asked him to befriend them.

Tewfic Pasha himself was ignorant of the rascally work von Hildemaller had already perpetrated in the case of Douglas Pasha, otherwise he would have been on his guard. He distrusted Germans as a general rule, but yet, from force of circumstances, was compelled to trust von Hildemaller. He had taken a huge liking for Geoff and his chum, and wished to do them a real service, but found himself helpless. Here was an intermediary, for surely the German would help—this German with the smiling, friendly countenance—and von Hildemaller had pledged himself to do so, had eagerly assented to see to the welfare of Geoff and Philip, and had gone off chuckling, scheming—smiling no longer—with a set purpose—a purpose to wreak his hatred of all Englishmen upon these helpless subalterns.

And see him there, just within the door of the prison, perspiring horribly, mopping his face constantly, panting, chuckling, smiling—the smile of a tiger as he glanced at his two victims.

And Geoff, taken aback by his entry, by his unexpected coming, deceived for a moment by his demonstrative goodwill, by his words and his offer of help and liberty, almost fell into the net that was spread so cleverly for him, almost succumbed to the wiles of this Teuton. But his better senses, second thoughts if you will, came to the rescue. He remembered von Hildemaller's evil reputation, he knew well enough what part he had taken in the capture of Joe Douglas—for had not Esbul brought the story?—and now, as he stared unflinchingly, inquisitively, searching for the reason of this visit, into the eyes of the German, he saw, right behind them as it were, behind that broad smile, the cunning hatred and craft of the man, and delight at coming triumph. Then, shifting his gaze to Philip of a sudden, he winked, grimaced at him, and slowly pulled the gag which he had thrust into his pocket into the open.

Did he intend to take this German's offer? Or did he propose some other course? And if so, what course? What action would he take?

A second later what doubts there may have been were cleared up in a manner dramatic enough for the odious von Hildemaller—stunning in its unexpectedness by swift action which swept the blood from his face, and caused those ogling eyes of his almost to start from their sockets. For Geoff called in a low voice to Philip, and, leaping at the German, threw one arm round his neck, and clapped the other hand over that cunning mouth which had smiled so widely at him.

CHAPTER XVI

Breaking Out

What a picture a snapshot photographic artist could have made of that scene in the narrow cell occupied by Geoff and Philip for so many weary weeks, and into which the unctuous and scheming von Hildemaller had thrust himself so unexpectedly. A portrayal alone of the features of that huge and unwieldy German would by itself have provided a picture of consuming interest. That is to say, a portrayal of what features were left visible now that Geoff's strong muscular hand was tightly clasped across them. For above the hand there were left merely the closely-cropped head which gave the Teuton such an uncouth appearance, a forehead broad enough to give the impression of brain-power, a pair of eyes, deepset enough as a rule, and sparkling with suppressed humour if it happened to be a stranger who looked into them, with suppressed cunning if the observer knew the man, eyes now projecting in a hideous manner over the strong fingers which gripped below. And below those eyes a stubby nose, from which burst gusts of air as von Hildemaller grunted his astonishment. Underneath the hand, there was left just an edge of the somewhat square and determined chin possessed by this extraordinary individual. As for the rest of him — the huge body, the arms, the legs — all were in motion, writhing, kicking, plunging, striking out and tearing at the captor who gripped him so firmly.

"The gag!" Geoff called softly to Philip, who, appreciating the situation in an instant, had leapt from his position near the door to assist his comrade; "it's in my left hand. Jam it into his mouth as I force it open."

In a moment Philip had the gag, and, standing by, made ready to introduce it.

"Supposing he shouts though?" he asked.

"He won't," said Geoff abruptly. "When he opens his jaws it'll be with a jump, for I'll squeeze him. Ready?"

There was an emphatic nod from Philip, while the gay features of the young subaltern were again smiling jovially; he was grinning indeed, a grin of pure delight and triumph. Then those powerful fingers of our hero sought the interval on one cheek between the upper and the lower jaw, while his thumb sought the similar spot on the other cheek. A second later he pressed fingers and thumbs together and shot the German's mouth wide open, displaying a huge cavity out of which not a sound could come, for even if the grip on his jaw had not incapacitated von Hildemaller, the grip which Geoff's left arm now had round his bulky chest, the crushing power with which he compressed it, had driven all the breath out of the Teuton's body.

"In she goes, pop!" gurgled Philip, thrusting the gag in between that double row of yellow teeth. "Now we bind her!"

Quick as a flash he ran the strings from the edge of the gag out through the corners of the open mouth, and bound them tightly behind the German's neck. He needed no further instruction from his chum, seeing that the two had discussed the matter so very often, had discussed it, let us remember, not in connection with the tricing up of a visitor — a visitor so unexpected as von Hildemaller — but in connection with their Turkish jailer.

"Somehow I'd have been sorry for him," Philip murmured, as he seized the blanket-ropes already prepared, and tied von Hildemaller's wrists behind his back.

"What, this beggar?"

"No, no! I was thinking of the jailer. I'd have been somehow sorry for him, for he's been such a decent fellow, such a friendly beggar," corrected Philip. "But this chap! Jingo, ain't it jolly!"

He set about the completion of the job in a manner which showed his delight almost better than words could do, and in a trice had von Hildemaller's wrists most scientifically tied together, and his elbows pulled so close that movement of his upper limbs was out of the question. Then, at a nod from Geoff, these two powerful young fellows gripped the heavy German and lifted him, as if he were a babe, to the wooden divan. It took, perhaps, another two minutes to secure his legs and ankles, and to leave him like a helpless bundle.

"And now?" asked Philip, mopping his forehead, for the work had been furious while it lasted.

"We move!" declared Geoff promptly. "It's getting dusk already, and it's quite dark in this cell. Though, 'pon my word, von Hildemaller's eyes pierce the dusk like gimlets. My word! If only he were free and could do his worst for us! Now let's put the money we promised the Turk on this table, and then go. No time like the present."

They were indeed in the position of being unable to choose the time for the attempt to regain their liberty. In any case they were bound to seize the first opportunity that came, to seize it whenever it came, regardless of the hour or of the circumstances. But the coming of von Hildemaller had forced their hand in a manner neither had anticipated. He had, as it were, complicated their difficulties; for, now that he was secured, trussed like a bird, and laid out helpless, there was still the Turkish jailer to be considered — the man they had proposed to capture, the man who, once shut up in the cell, gagged and triced just as was von Hildemaller, would be out of the way, unlikely to run up against them in the corridor outside, unable to give the alarm and let others know that they were escaping.

"Can't be helped, the change in our plans," said Geoff, as he took another look at the German; "just squint outside, Phil, and tell me whether there's anyone in the corridor. If not, we'll pull off our boots and make our way along it in stockinged feet. Of course, if the jailer turns up, well, we'll have to be guided by circumstances."

In any case there was no time for discussion, no opportunity for making further or other plans, nothing to do but seize the opportunity, strike while the iron was hot, and free themselves from this prison. To strip off their boots and tuck them into their belts was the work of a moment, and then, unarmed but strong as lions—thanks to their own forethought and energy—they tiptoed into the corridor outside and stole rapidly along it, having gently pulled the iron door of their cell to upon the German. Some twenty paces along they found themselves at the head of a short flight of stone steps, and were quickly at the bottom. A turn to the left took them along another corridor, and then both suddenly halted.

"Voices—men talking—the jailer."

Philip nodded.

"The jailer and that fellow who often visited us with him. They're in that room to the left, the door of which is ajar, and the sooner we pass it the better."

Stealing forward again they were soon opposite a massive iron door, similar to the one which had closed their cell, and, halting for a moment, listened to the conversation of the two men within it. Listened long enough to assure themselves that they were right, and that within the cell their jailer and his friend were certainly seated. Then they moved on again, and, traversing a long corridor and turning to their right, found themselves in a different part of the prison. They had reached, in fact, an entrance-hall, as it were, out of which a heavy, barred door led, probably to the open.

"Locked and barred," said Geoff, inspecting it rapidly and as well as the dusk would allow; "no way out for us there, I think. Now, what happens?"

"S—sh! Someone coming," whispered Phil, "someone coming down the stairs, I think. From the sounds he is making he is coming towards us."

For a moment or two they stared in the direction from which the noise of feet descending the stairway had come to them, and then looked desperately about them, for not even the dusk in that big entrance-hall would prevent them from being discovered once an individual was within some yards of them. What were they to do? Bolt back towards the cell they had so recently vacated? Stand still and chance discovery and recognition? Or advance and throw themselves upon the individual who was approaching? Geoff threw out a hand and caught Philip by the sleeve, pulling him towards his left, towards the door which he had been so recently examining, pulled him in fact into the angle the door made with the heavy stone pillar which supported it. No one in his wildest thoughts could have described it as a safe hiding-place, no one in fact in similar circumstances would have willingly entrusted his chances of liberty to it, or would have leapt at the scanty security it barely offered. Yet it was a chance, a chance in a hundred, the only chance the occasion could produce, the only spot possible for Geoff and Philip. And there together they crouched against the stone pillar, wishing that the dusk might grow rapidly deeper, and that some friendly shadow would cast itself about them and hide them from the eyes of the intruder.

Those seconds which followed were long-drawn-out, agonizing seconds, seconds during which the slow, plodding, heavy footsteps which they had heard descending the stairway drew nearer, and nearer, and nearer. Then a figure came into view, a figure but dimly illuminated, which, reaching the centre of the hall, came to a halt, while the man — for undoubtedly it was a man — peered about him inquisitively, as if seeking for something, as if he too had heard sounds, sounds which had roused his curiosity and perhaps his suspicion. It gave the two young subalterns hiding in that shady corner quite an unpleasant start, sent quite a chill through their frames when they first cast their eyes on that figure.

"Von Hildemaller!" said Geoff under his breath, speaking to himself in fact. "Now, how — —?"

Philip moved and nudged his comrade.

"That beast," Geoff heard him whisper; "he's got out somehow! But how? I — —"

"S — sh! It's not. It's a Turk, awfully like him," Geoff whispered back, putting his lips close to Philip's ear. "Not a word more or he may hear us."

True enough, the figure dallying in the centre of the hall was indeed almost a facsimile of that of the ponderous von Hildemaller. Of moderate height and thickset, his feet encased in Turkish slippers, the man's general appearance was alarmingly like that of the German, while, dimly to be seen through the dusk now settling deeper about the hall, were the ends of a pair of moustaches quite as fierce and flowing as those proudly flaunted by the German. Only the head was different, for it was bald, and perched on the back of it was a fez. Evidently, too, if this new-comer had had his suspicions roused, if he had actually heard sounds as he descended the stairs, he had now brushed the matter aside and was prepared to treat it as a delusion, as something easily explainable; for he moved on again, crossing the stone-flagged hall with heavy steps, and passing out into the dusk beyond, in the direction from which Geoff and Philip were escaping. It was then that Geoff mopped his forehead with what was left of a somewhat dilapidated and dirty handkerchief, while Philip allowed a breath of astonishment to escape his lips in a subdued whistle.

"Jingo!" he exclaimed; "that's a near one!"

"The Governor!" Geoff said. "The Governor, I'm sure. Ponderous and filled with dignity, a regular second von Hildemaller. But come along, we've no time to wait. Let's move on up the stairs and see what sort of a place the fellow came from."

Still in their stockinged feet, with their boots tucked in between their belts and their bodies, the two crossed the hall and ran lightly up a stone staircase. Turning abruptly as the stairs twisted upward, they presently reached a doorway where their further progress was barred by a door, framed in iron like that which had shut the opening from their cell, every feature of which they had studied so completely.

"Bah!" exclaimed Philip in disgust. "Trapped inside the place."

"Don't let's shout till we're hurt," said Geoff resolutely. "Perhaps it isn't locked; we'll try it; here's the latch. Hallo! It opens!"

"And we go through, as a matter of course. Wonder what the Governor'd say if he knew that his two prisoners were about to investigate his quarters?"

More stairs faced them, but a short flight, the top of which they reached in a few moments, to find themselves in a wider corridor from which three or four doors gave access to rooms, the first of which was spacious and airy, and lit by windows which looked down into a central courtyard. The second was airy, like the first—even larger—with divans spread here and there, and a carpeted floor, while its windows, like those of the other room, had a similar outlook. A hasty inspection of the third showed it to be a sleeping apartment, while the fourth provided, without doubt, the quarters for the Governor's servant.

"And the windows? Let's take a squint out of them," said Geoff as he crossed the room rapidly towards them. "Beast of a drop, eh?"

"But possible if one had a rope," said Philip, pushing his head out of the open window and imbibing the first breath of fresh air for some weeks past. "Bedding's what we want, and food. There was some in that big room with the divans."

For a while they stood peering out of the window and measuring the distance between it and the ground below—a drop of quite fifty feet, but a drop the bottom of which provided open country, a drop which, if it could be accomplished, would give them liberty and would set them outside the prison.

"Stop a minute!" said Geoff suddenly, as a thought struck him. "There doesn't seem to be another entrance to these quarters, and, seeing that we are in occupation for the moment, and can't afford to be disturbed, why, we'll lock the Governor out. Let's get back to the door at once and see if it's possible."

The very suggestion set the amiable Philip grinning; the cheek of such an action delighted him intensely, and was just the sort of thing that jovial subaltern could appreciate fully. He was out in the corridor in a moment, and, running along it in his stockinged feet, soon reached the door beyond. Then Geoff heard him shoot a couple of bolts, and watched as he came smiling back towards him.

"Case reversed," grinned Philip, as if he were making an official report. "Prisoners, a little while before, locked into a cell, are now prisoners no longer, but have locked their jailers out. And next, sir? What about that food?"

It was Geoff's turn to smile, for he too had caught sight of a dish of fruit in the Governor's sitting-room, of some Turkish sweet-cakes, and of a carafe, probably containing water. Better still, the aroma of coffee tickled his nostrils as he entered the room occupied by the Governor's servants, at the door of which he was now standing. A swift glance showed him a Turkish brazier, a kettle of Turkish design above it, from the opening of which steam issued. He dived into the room again and sniffed at that steam, sniffed and smacked his lips with appreciation.

"Coffee, my boy! All ready!" he said. "But don't let's do things in too great a hurry; let's look round first for something with which to make a rope. We shall be sorry, of course, to inconvenience the Governor, or to damage his property, but the cushions over those divans, if cut into strips and twisted, would do the trick splendidly; while, if they ain't strong enough, there are carpets and rugs which must be sacrificed for the purpose."

"And cushions enough to drop from the window and break a fall in case we have to jump for it," laughed Philip. "Let's bring the grub along here, and the cushions and what not, then we shall be ready in case the alarm is raised; for, once there is a hue and cry, sentries, no doubt, will be posted outside the building, and long before that we ought to be away from it."

It was tantalizing to have to leave that steaming odoriferous coffee, but undoubtedly the question of safety came first, now that liberty lay within their grasp. The two resolutely put all other thoughts aside, and rapidly made their preparations to accomplish their object. Magnificently embroidered cushions decked the divans in the Governor's sitting-room. There were rugs, too, which were perhaps of priceless value—Turkish rugs which, it may be, had been manufactured years before, and would have commanded in London or any European city a fabulous sum, far beyond the somewhat shallow depths of a subaltern's pocket.

"Sorry! Frightfully!" Philip grinned, as he deliberately slit one of the cushion-covers—a cushion, by the way, not of ordinary dimensions, but some seven feet in length and as many broad; a regular mattress, indeed, upon which, no doubt, the bulky Governor was wont to recline during his moments of leisure. It may have been the act of a vandal to destroy such a handsome covering, and at any other time, no doubt, Philip would have hesitated, for he was not such a scamp that he would deliberately destroy goods of such value and elegance.

"But it's our liberty or the Governor's goods," he grinned a little sheepishly at Geoff, as he dug the blade of his knife in again and sent the stuff ripping.

Nor was his comrade behindhand in the work, and already had stripped another of the enormous cushions. Perhaps it took them ten minutes, perhaps even longer, to construct from the strips of strong material a twisted rope made up of a number of lengths firmly knotted together, knots which they tested by a form of tug-of-war, dragging at opposite ends of their rope to be sure that it would provide a safe means of descent to the bottom of their prison. Then, lashing one end fast to the stone window-post, and coiling the other end in preparation, they went once more to the Governor's room, and staggered back again carrying a number of those huge cushions.

"And now for coffee and something to eat!" said Geoff. "What we can't finish now of the fruit and cakes we'll carry with us. Better still, as we're not particularly hungry at the moment, supposing we drink the coffee, which will take only a few moments, and finish the other when we have secured our liberty."

They had poured out two steaming cups of coffee, and were sniffing the contents with delight, when a sudden shout, a clamour in some portion of the prison, caused them to arrest the progress of the cups to their lips and listen. There were more shouts, a howl from some distant quarter, and then a loud hammering. As if determined not to be upset by any sort of commotion, and not to be robbed of a golden opportunity — for such coffee as this now underneath their noses had not been tasted by our two heroes during the long weeks of their captivity — Geoff resolutely raised his cup to his lips and drained the contents, smacking his lips afterwards in a manner not perhaps too polite, but very indicative of his feelings. Philip followed suit, and, gripping the kettle, replenished both cups, as if determined that he too would not be hurried. Then, setting the empty cups down beside the stove, they left the room, and, darting along the passage, peered out of the windows which gave access to the courtyard.

There were men down below — Turkish soldiers — some fully dressed and some in their shirt-sleeves. They were running hither and thither as though confused, and as though ignorant of the cause of the alarm which had just been given. Then, as Geoff and Philip looked, a door to their right at the foot of the courtyard was suddenly torn open, and a figure rolled rather than ran out, a man who tripped on the lowest step and fell face downward, only to bound to his feet again and rush off till he was in amongst the soldiers. Undoubtedly there was something behind him which was accelerating his progress, and which had made his entrance into the courtyard anything but dignified, abrupt, in fact, startlingly sudden and unexpected. It was something which appeared within a moment, someone who dashed after the unfortunate jailer, a fat man, wearing a fez at the back of his head — undoubtedly the Turkish governor — followed by another of similar proportions, broad and stout and beefy, with closely cropped head, a man who shouted and hurled threats through the doorway.

"Von Hildemaller!" gasped Geoff. "Someone's discovered him, someone's set him free! Perhaps it was the jailer."

"Or perhaps the Governor," Philip added. "He must have known that von Hildemaller was coming to see us; he must have given him permission. That's it, and when he came down the steps to the hall he was on the way to see what had happened. Lor'! what a shock he must have had when he discovered our German friend tied up like a bundle, and the two prisoners usually in that cell disappeared, gone entirely."

For a few moments the two watched the Governor and the German as they raged amongst the soldiers in the courtyard. Catching the unfortunate jailer, they beat him with their fists unmercifully, and no doubt, had one of them possessed a weapon, or had they thought to borrow a rifle from one of the soldiers, they would have shot him. Instead, they vented their fury on the man by beating him, and when he fell to the ground, so as to escape their blows, they kicked him in the most furious manner. As one can imagine, too, their anger, the shouts to which they gave vent, the sudden apparition of the jailer and his two tormentors, did not tend to lessen the agitation and perplexity of the Turkish soldiers. Even now, nothing had been said by which they could gather precisely what had happened, for there had been no mention of the two British prisoners, of their escape, and of the curious position in which von Hildemaller had been discovered. Breathless, and not a little fearful, they watched the scene going on in their midst, waiting for some word which would clear up the situation; and suddenly it came, when von Hildemaller and the Governor were breathless after their exertions, were satisfied with the blows and kicks they had rained on the jailer. It was the Governor, in fact, who suddenly recollected that his first business should have been to seek for the prisoners, for the jailer was always there, and could be punished on some future occasion. He suddenly swung round upon the startled soldiers and bawled orders at them.

"The prisoners," he bellowed, "the two British prisoners; they have escaped, I tell you! You numskulls, why have you not guessed it? Ah, but perhaps you are in collusion with this wretched jailer! Search the prison! Search every part of it! Be off with you! Give me a rifle, so that I may go to my quarters and there watch for these young ruffians. Come, von Hildemaller," he said, gripping the sleeve of the perspiring German, "to my quarters. From there every part of this courtyard and of the ground outside is visible. If we clamber to the roof there is none who may leave the place without our seeing him. Snatch a rifle from one of these fools and come with me. Then, should the prisoners elect to leave whilst we are watching, you will be able to put in a shot which will punish them for what has happened."

"Time to be going," Geoff told Phil, and his chum agreed with an emphatic nod which showed his willingness.

"Then out with the rope. It's lighter here than it seemed to be in the courtyard; but no matter, we've got to make the best of it, and, I can tell you, it will want quite a lot to stop us."

"It will!" the enthusiastic Phil admitted, with one of his happy, encouraging smiles. "You may take it from me, my boy, it ain't going to be von Hildemaller—or whatever's his name—or any Turk that's going to lag me this time if I can help it. There goes the rope and another cushion. Jingo! They've landed splendidly, and I believe if this old rope lets us down, and breaks of a sudden, we should land quite comfortably at the bottom. Who goes first—you?"

"Either. I don't mind. Out you go—you're nearest."

Phil made no bones about the matter, and wasted no time and no breath in attempting to argue the question. He was on the window-sill in a moment, and, swinging himself out, gripped the rope, and with splendid youthful assurance at once trusted his life to it. Geoff watched him slithering down, stopping every few feet as his hands and feet came into contact with the knots they had made, till at last he was at the bottom.

Meanwhile the shouts and noise about the prison had increased in proportion if anything, while sounds, echoed by the stone, vault-like walls of the place and the large corridors, came even to the Governor's quarters. Steps could be heard on the stairs which led to the door—now firmly bolted—and the panting of at least two individuals. Then blows were rained upon it, and voices shouted to those within to open. The Turkish governor—for undoubtedly it was he, with von Hildemaller at his elbow— jerked angry threats through the keyhole, and bellowed loud orders to his servants to admit him. And had Geoff been able to watch the scene he would have observed the worthy von Hildemaller leaning against the stone door-post, his face a purplish colour, his nose shining, his eyes, still prominent, flashing angrily and indicating the temper and hatred which consumed him, while his wide lips were set apart, the moustache—that moustache so disagreeably stained with the smoke of cigarettes—was distinctly bristling, and the teeth were set in a snarl which, had the Turkish governor had time to take note of it, would perhaps have scared him considerably. For the rest, the German was out of breath, utterly unnerved by what had happened, positively shaking in every limb, perspiring more heavily than he had ever done before, and spasmodically dabbing at his face with his red handkerchief.

"Open, fools, dolts, wretches!" shouted the Governor, and then turned despairingly to the German.

"What—what next?" demanded von Hildemaller fiercely, panting half-way through the sentence.

"There's something wrong. I cannot make these dolts of servants of mine hear me. The place is locked, and yet I left the door unlatched when I came down to visit you but a few moments ago. The thing is inexplicable."

If the Turkish governor found the matter hard of understanding and difficult to explain, the wily, cunning von Hildemaller rapidly saw to the bottom of it. A man such as he, gifted with a scheming brain, was just the one to realize that prisoners interned in such a place and escaped from their cell were yet not at large nor at liberty. This was just the reckless sort of thing that those British subalterns would do. It was like their effrontery to usurp the place of the Governor himself and secrete themselves in his quarters.

"Bah!" he yelped in the face of the Turk. "Then your servants are not the only dolts and fools that I know of. Can you not see that the door has been locked from within—or rather bolted? You are shut out of your own quarters, and by whom? By whom, tell me? By none other than those two whom we are seeking. Break the door open! Beat it in! Call for men to bring hammers!"

It was indeed time for Geoff to be moving, for if the Governor and his companion were making a considerable din outside that door, shouts were coming from other parts of the prison. Those of the soldiers who had not entirely lost their heads, or who had not absolutely been bereft of their better senses by the violence of the Governor and the German, were now making a complete search of the place, while some of them were at that moment dragging the outside door of the prison open. Geoff clambered through the window, gripped the knotted rope, and began to slide rapidly downwards. Yet he was not to reach the ground without a further, if only a small, adventure; for that improvised rope, strained as it had been by supporting Philip's weight, succumbed to that of our hero. It parted at one of the knots a foot above his head and some thirty from the ground, and a moment later Geoff found himself plunging on to one of those cushions which they had so thoughtfully dropped to provide against such an occasion. There Philip gripped him and steadied him, helping him to his feet.

"What now?" he asked.

"Round to the back of the prison. I heard some of the beggars pulling the front door open. Thank goodness, it's getting darker every second, and if we can only hide for some five or ten minutes we shall be safe for to-night at least. Lor'! Look at the fruit I had in my pocket—smashed to a pulp."

Philip shook him, and then the two turned away from the scene of their escape and ran softly along beside the wall of the prison. Gaining the farther end, they turned a corner, and then, at a suggestion from Geoff, Philip ran on to the opposite corner. Thus they were able to watch two sides of the prison, and could warn one another if an enemy were approaching. Fortune favoured them, favoured those two young fellows who had so cleverly achieved their escape, and the darkness, settling down over the country, safely hid them from view, while the noise of the searchers within and without the prison subsided.

"And now?" asked Philip, when it was quite certain that they were not likely to be apprehended.

"Oh — —! 'Now,' well, that wants some deciding."

Geoff scratched his dishevelled head of hair and pondered, for indeed the matter was one which would have taxed the wisdom of an older man — even the cunning of von Hildemaller. For they were out in the open, free of their cell it was true, but yet in an enemy country, surrounded by Turks, without a friend to appeal to. Yet what they had done so far gave them encouragement for the future.

"We'll have to be like that Mr. Micawber of Dickens," said Phil, as they crouched beside the wall, "we'll just have to wait for something to turn up, and you bet your boots something's bound to."

CHAPTER XVII

The Road to Bagdad

Free from prison, after an adventure the success of which might well stimulate them to greater effort, to greater daring, and give them hopes beyond any they had possessed during the weary weeks of waiting which had passed, it was yet not by any means certain that Geoff Keith and his chum Philip would ever win their way back to that Expeditionary Force with which they had landed in Mesopotamia. It was weeks and weeks, and it seemed to them years, since they had been captured with Esbul at Nasiriyeh; and though their jailer had not been entirely uncommunicative—for at heart he was quite a genial fellow, and the thought of reward warmed his heart wonderfully—yet they had failed to hear of the easy, bloodless capture of Amara. Indeed, all tidings of the Mesopotamian invading force had ceased; and whether it had retired, whether it still hung on to the banks of the River Tigris, what its fortunes were now, were withheld from them.

"If we don't get out soon there won't be an Englishman left in the whole of Mesopotamia," Philip grumbled one day during their long and tedious imprisonment, when he was perhaps a trifle bilious, and feeling out of sorts and out of temper. "Everything's wrong".

And Geoff had grinned at him, an irritating grin, which had roused the irate Philip to a state of anger which set him stuttering, and which caused him to clench those powerful fists of his—made powerful by the exercises he and Geoff practised. But just as suddenly as his cheeks had flamed with anger, just as quickly as he had allowed natural vexation and irritation to get the better of him, Philip's better sense, his honest heart, his real affection for his chum, caused him suddenly to beam upon him.

"I'm in a rotten humour," he told him, "just the sort of humour in which a fellow grumbles, asks 'What's the good of anything?' and grouses 'Nuffin'."

"I've felt the same often enough," Geoff told him, "and I dare say you've known it, and have seen what a nasty sulky beast I could be. You see, fellows chained up like this, close together in a cell, get to know all there is that's worth knowing about a chap—all the good side, you know."

"And a precious deal of the bad side too," grinned Philip. "Trust a campaign to show up a man from every point of view. People say that aboard-ship life is the most trying of existences; but I imagine that one of those Arctic Expeditions of ours, when a hundred men, perhaps, are bottled up in winter quarters for months together, must try officers and men to the last extremity, must prove their good feelings and temper, and must bring them back to safety comrades for life—friends who will never be forgotten."

Doubtless the fact of hearing nothing of the Expeditionary Force did try the nerves and the temper of the two prisoners in their cell extremely. Yet what mattered such a trial now? Now that they were out of their prison; now that they had dropped from the window of the Governor's quarters; now that they had worsted that odious fellow, von Hildemaller—that mass of perspiring flesh and fat, that ogling, cunning, scheming German?

"Jingo!" Philip kept on repeating, as he and Geoff crouched by the wall, and then let go a chuckle. "To think that we've done that von what's his name—Hilde something—"

"Maller," grunted Geoff, sniffing his contempt of the fellow. "And now?"

"That's what I keep asking, now?"

"Well, we've the whole of Mesopotamia," Geoff told him a little politely, a little icily in fact.

"Right oh! Then all we've got to do is to choose some spot in it. Of course one naturally selects a part now occupied by our fellows."

Naturally enough that was the choice which any British officer or man would have made under similar circumstances. But where was the Expeditionary Force which had sailed from India, and which had fought its way by now into the heart of Mesopotamia? Unbeknown to these two young subalterns, it had driven a path up the banks of the River Tigris towards Kut-el-Amara—some hundred and fifty miles above Amara itself—and well on the road to Bagdad—the Mesopotamian Mecca, a city, almost a holy city in the eyes of the Arabs of that part, to which their eyes were attracted far more than to Constantinople. Driven from Nasiriyeh, from Basra, from every place down-stream on the banks of the Shatt-el-Arab, of the Tigris and of the Euphrates, the Turks, nevertheless, had not abandoned Mesopotamia. They were in strong-force at Kut, in prepared positions, engineered, sketched, and arranged by German instructors. And there, to be precise, some seven miles to the east of Kut, the enemy took up his position astride the River Tigris, extending his trenches to some six miles from the left bank of the river. Yet, in spite of those deep-dug trenches which gave such security from shell-fire, in spite of wired entanglements which might have aroused the envy of Germans in Flanders and Poland, notwithstanding preparations made without haste and hurry, and over a country which gave wonderful assistance, the enemy was defeated.

The same dash, the same almost reckless bravery of the British and Indians, the same natural, friendly rivalry between those two races of soldiers, sent them forward against the Turkish trenches like an avalanche, caused them to turn the position, and rapidly effected the capture of Kut-el-Amara. Not only that, it effected at the same moment the capture of the northern end of the Kut-el-Hai, that watercourse running roughly north and south between the Tigris and the Euphrates Rivers, and which, unknown to the British, had permitted the Turks to reinforce their post at Nasiriyeh, and collect that army at Shaiba, which had threatened the rear of the Expeditionary Force when in the neighbourhood of Kurnah. It may be said, indeed, that the Expeditionary Force had now captured a solid wedge of Mesopotamia, a wedge of land with its base pointing towards Bagdad, its lines of communication open—for the Tigris allowed of shipping reaching the British force at Kut as easily and almost as safely as that shipping had been able to reach Kurnah. For the Tigris was still deep and wide, though not entirely free of sand-banks. As to the size of this wedge—Nasiriyeh was secured, Ahwaz, the head of the Persian pipe-line, was in our hands, and there remained Bagdad alone—a jewel which must have strongly tempted the British Commanders. An expedition to that city, its capture in fact, would no doubt result in the crash of Turkish influence in Mesopotamia, would win over thousands of Arabs now wavering and prepared to join the side which looked like winning, and would inevitably destroy all German influence.

For many reasons then Bagdad was a magnet, a magnet which drew the Expeditionary Force onward. And in the heat of summer, even as Geoff and Philip were making that adventurous escape, British and Indians were once more on the move from Kut en route for Bagdad, hoping to capture the city. Whether such an expedition were justified, whether the risks of an advance along the River Tigris to the city of Bagdad were out of proportion to the advantages to be gained, and whether those in command were fully informed as to the strength of Turkish troops before them, one cannot venture an opinion, seeing that at this date little information has been published, little indeed more than the fact that such an advance took place, and its sequel.

If, however, actual news of our troops in Mesopotamia at this time is meagre, and if a cloud covers their operations and leaves us in doubt as to what has actually happened, we have yet left to us news of Geoff and Philip, and of others who participate in this story. There is, for instance, the stout, perspiring, and odious von Hildemaller. Boiling with rage, perspiring indescribably, he leant against that door outside the quarters of the Turkish governor, mopping his face perpetually with that red handkerchief, while he gripped the rifle he had seized from one of the Turkish soldiers, and glared from it towards the Governor.

"And—and—you are fooling me," he shouted at last, when he had got his breath; for that dash into the courtyard, the blows he had levelled at the unfortunate jailer, and his race from thence to the hall of the prison and up those stairs had left him gasping. "What means this?" he demanded. "You give me free entry into a cell in which these brutes are imprisoned; you — you — allow them to set upon me, to tie me hand and foot, to gag me, and now — now — you bring me here to be faced with a door that is barred and bolted, when you should have taken me to some other place from which I could have shot down those ruffians."

Of a truth, the Teuton was positively boiling over with wrath, indignation, and disappointment. Never before, in a somewhat long life, devoted in these latter years to crafty plotting, had von Hildemaller been so worsted. Like every other man, he had had his ups and downs to be sure, his failures and his successes; but of late, since the "All Highest", since the Kaiser had set his ambitious eye on Turkey, had ogled the Sultan, brow-beaten his particular adherents, and had gained the ear of the Young Turk Party, since, in fact, the influence of the Germans and of Germany had risen to such heights in Turkey, von Hildemaller had become quite an important person, one to be considered, an agent of the Kaiser to whom no doors were shut, who claimed entry anywhere and on any occasion. Yet here, when he had thought to succeed so easily, when he had planned to add these two British subalterns to that Douglas Pasha — then in prison — why, see here, the door was banged in his face, the tables had been turned most distinctly upon him, and all his plans had been shattered.

"I — it is monstrous!" he shouted, using the native tongue but indifferently, his words bearing a strong Teutonic accent. "Are you, too, in the plot? Did you then plan for them to seize me? I — I — — "

The poor fellow was stuttering more than ever, his flabby cheeks were positively shaking, while his whole person was quivering. It looked almost as if he would have thrown himself upon the Governor, that other stout man staring back at him now in frightened manner. No doubt, too, had von Hildemaller had breath sufficient for the task, he would have vented his wrath upon the Turk promptly. But, as it was, he cast the rifle on the stone steps and sent it clattering down into the hall below. Then, wobbling badly, his knees shaking after such unusual exertion, perspiring still in horrible fashion, and displaying that particularly close-cropped pate, he went off after the rifle, stumbling down the steps and into the hall, and from there out into the open. It was almost dark then, and for a while he stood still, blowing heavily, and enjoying the evening breeze as it played about his heated features. Then he gave vent to a faint and somewhat subdued whistle, and repeated it a moment later. A figure slid up from some dark corner and stood beside him.

"Master," he said, "you whistled."

"Whistled? Yes, twice, and you were not there at the first summons," snarled von Hildemaller, delighted to have someone else upon whom he could turn his wrath and vexation. "How now? Where are these prisoners? You saw them escape from the place? You followed them, eh?"

"Prisoners?" said the man, startled, stepping back a pace or two, so that a gleam of light, flashing through the open door of the prison from a lantern which had now been lighted, fell upon him. "Prisoners? But— —"

"But—prisoners, fool!" the German retorted, eyeing the man severely as he stood in the lamp-light. "You did not follow them then; you allowed them to escape without troubling?"

His tones were even more angry as he watched the man; while those beams of light, as they fell upon the German's companion, showed the features of that same rascal who had answered his signal in the Bazaar at Bagdad at that time when Major Joe Douglas had accosted von Hildemaller. Without a shade of doubt, indeed, this Turk was the ruffian who was in the hire of the German, who was ready to carry out any piece of villainy for him. Esbul knew it; that old Jew whom Douglas Pasha had questioned in the Bazaar at Bagdad knew it too; while the cautious yet seemingly unsuspicious Douglas Pasha knew it better, knew it so well that he had made that hurried departure from Bagdad, knew it better still now, seeing that it was thanks to this rascal, and the German, that he lay in prison.

No doubt, had the man not been of such great use to von Hildemaller, the latter would then and there have vented all his wrath and vexation on him; but if the German were angry he was still not so furious that he was altogether bereft of common sense and caution. Caution, indeed, was something which had helped the Teuton to be successful; it was his hard-headed common sense and cunning which had made of him such a plotter, and now that same common sense caused his anger to evaporate. In any case he became calm, and stood for a moment or so considering deeply.

"Listen, my friend!" he said at last, his tone completely changed. "You did well. You sat here, you tell me, and heard nothing. Then I will tell you what has happened. The two prisoners we sought are gone—escaped within a few minutes of my gaining the prison; they are nowhere to be found, and we must seek them. Tell me now, you who are clever in such matters, supposing you to be in their place, and to have shaken yourself free of the prison, whither would you turn? What quarter?"

The man answered him promptly, without a thought it seemed.

"Bagdad, Master."

"And nowhere else?"

"And nowhere else," the man repeated.

"Then in Bagdad you believe that we shall trace them?"

"I do, Master, and the sooner we can make our way there the better."

Early on the following morning, in fact, von Hildemaller could have been discovered in a shaky old country vehicle, drawn by a dilapidated pony, being rattled over an incredibly rough road close to that city. Perched on the driving-seat was the rascal whom he had encountered outside the prison on the previous evening. A picturesque rascal to be sure, for there was nothing about this man which denoted his calling. Very soon they entered the gates, and were swallowed up amidst the narrow, tortuous streets of the city, and finally gained the quarters habitually occupied by the German. Yet we have to recount the fact that, quietly as these two had entered Bagdad, unostentatiously as they had made their way through the streets, much as they had sought to escape observation, yet one at least had watched their coming. It was that tall, skinny, bony Jew, who sat, as ever, it seemed, cross-legged on his stall, perched like a bird of evil omen above those embroidered goods, the sale of which appeared to trouble him so little. His beady eyes marked the passing of that clattering vehicle and recognized, while they appeared to be looking at nothing, the picturesque rascal who drove it, and took in in a single fleeting glance the fat features of the German.

"So, that man—the one who tracked Douglas Pasha——" he muttered, appearing to address the words rather to the embroidered goods he had for disposal than to any particular person. "Coffee, boy!" he called, clapping his hands. "Coffee, that I may sip it and think."

Almost motionless, merely his eyelids blinking, while occasionally his long fingers played over the wares on his stall, the Jew waited for the coffee, and then, taking the cup with a deliberation peculiar to him, lifted it slowly to his lips and sipped it thoughtfully. It was at such times, too, that this curious old man, who had such a strong liking for Douglas Pasha, looked above the rim of the egg-shaped cup and cast his glance over the Bazaar. It masked his movements, as it were, and that cup disguised the fact, from any who might be looking, that he was interested in his immediate surroundings. Not that the man saw anything in particular, merely walls, merely long shadows cast by a brilliant sun, and stalls upon which other figures rested much as he did—motionless figures, men apparently indifferent to their success in business, for not an effort did they make to attract the attention of would-be purchasers and extract money from them.

"So!" he muttered again into the coffee-cup. "That man is back, and I have heard tales of a journey to another prison. Perhaps Esbul may give information; perhaps he followed. Who knows? We will wait till the evening."

And wait the old man did, placidly, with not the smallest show of impatience, till the shadows lengthened, till dusk fell over the Bazaar, and until other merchants were closing their places of business. Then, having seen his stall shut by the boy who did jobs small and large for him, the Jew tottered away from the place, dived into a narrow alley, and wriggled his way to a house at some distance. Entering this from a courtyard at the back, he rapped twice with his stick on the floor, and waited for an answer.

"What then?" a voice asked cautiously from the top of a flight of stairs, "Who is that?"

"A friend!" the Jew replied, and ascended promptly. Gaining a room at the top of the flight of stairs he sat down on a divan, and then turned to the man who stood before him.

"So they have come—that German and the ruffian," he said. "You saw them, Esbul?"

Esbul nodded.

"I saw them; they passed to their old quarters."

"And maybe you know from whence?" the Jew asked.

"Not so," Esbul told him. "They slipped from the city unbeknown to me, and were gone while I was sleeping. But—but—I have a feeling that they were bent on business which concerned my master, or which concerned those two who were captured with me at Nasiriyeh."

There was silence for some long while in that room, for the Jew was not given to much talking. Instead, he ate his humble evening meal slowly and thoughtfully, gazing at the opposite wall as if he could read there the mystery of Douglas Pasha's whereabouts, of the prison in fact where von Hildemaller had caused him to be sent. Let it be remembered, too, that though this Jew had means of learning much of what was happening, had learned, indeed, that Geoff and Phil had been incarcerated somewhere outside the city, yet he had no knowledge of the German's movements, did not dream, in fact, that von Hildemaller had so recently visited the place where they were held, and did not suspect his mission. But he guessed that the Teuton's exit from the city and return had something to do with Douglas Pasha, though it might not be directly. He hated this German — hated all Germans in fact — for, Armenian Jew though he was, Turkey was his country, and, as a wise man, he realized that Germany's interest in it was not disinterested. But the subject of Douglas Pasha touched him even more deeply, for he was devoted to the Englishman, had received much kindness from him, had, in days past, to thank him for an act which saved his life — a deed of bravery which might have cost Douglas Pasha his own quite easily. That was the secret of the Jew's attachment to this British officer, the secret of his solicitude for his safety, and part of the reason for his detestation of von Hildemaller. He turned after a while, solemnly and slowly, upon Esbul, who meantime had waited for him to speak, with too great a respect for the aged Jew to disturb him.

"My son," he said, and the beady old eyes flickered wisely at Esbul, "there has been a deep plot hatching in these parts, and the German has been weaving a web to cast about these British people. As I, a good Armenian Jew and subject of the Sultan — though he has sorely ill-treated us Armenians — as I hate this German, so he loathes all those British. He fears the influence of Douglas Pasha amongst the Turks; when there was no war he feared him, for even against their will our Turkish pashas could not help having a liking for the Briton, while for this Teuton they had nothing but contempt. Thus von Hildemaller was jealous of Douglas Pasha, feared his strength, and made plans to rid Bagdad and Mesopotamia of him. The chance came when war burst over the land, and the German seized it. Yet, surrounded by enemies as he was, Douglas Pasha evaded the danger for a while, evaded it till the hirelings of von Hildemaller tracked him down and cast their net about him. Then, but for those Turkish friends of our master, but for the news of Douglas Pasha's capture which I sent swiftly to them, the German would have killed him. Against the wishes of the Turks he could do no such thing, and therefore had to be content with his imprisonment. Now see what follows: the ward of Douglas Pasha is captured also, and with him a companion. The news comes to the ears of this scheming German. He can do no worse, for the time being at any rate, to Douglas Pasha himself, but he can hurt him through this young soldier — this young officer who is dear to him. Who knows? It may be that his journey outside the city was to secure the person of young Geoffrey Keith. Who knows? But it is likely."

"More than likely," Esbul told him respectfully.

"That we shall learn in time," the Jew answered. "I have ways of gathering news unknown to you — unknown to anyone, in fact. We shall learn. But you, Esbul, in the meantime you will set a watch upon these people, will disguise yourself and hover about the streets of the city, and perchance it may be that information will come to you sooner than to me, in which case you will be lucky."

Esbul, indeed, might consider himself an extremely well-favoured individual if it turned out that he was more successful in unearthing the secret doings of von Hildemaller than was Benshi, this aged Jew, this extraordinarily silent man who hovered the day long over his embroidered wares, and seemed to take no interest in things outside his narrow stall, and to possess no energy for doing so; for, indeed, Benshi was a deep, discreet, and clever individual — one to whom tales came in the most uncanny manner, to whom reports of doings outside the city of Bagdad were sent almost before they reached the Governor's palace. And yet the exact whereabouts of Douglas Pasha was hidden from him; while beyond the fact that Geoff and Philip had been imprisoned — a fact communicated by Esbul — he had no knowledge of them.

Donning a garb which was calculated to deceive easily any who might meet him, Esbul slipped out of the house that evening and plunged into the intricacies of the thoroughfares of the city. No need for him to seek for the quarters of von Hildemaller, for they were already known to him, and no need, therefore, to ask questions. But arrived at the house — one detached from its fellows, standing aloof and alone in a compound — there was little to encourage him to wait, nothing to prove that the German and the arch-scoundrel he employed were in residence. Not a light flickered from the windows, not a gleam came through a crack in the shutters; the place was clad in darkness, while not a sound came from it.

"But yet it may be that they are there, these crafty fellows," thought Esbul; "we'll see, we'll investigate the premises carefully."

To clamber over the containing wall was an easy matter, while the drop on the far side was nothing. With stealthy steps the Armenian passed round the house, squinting in through keyholes, staring at the shutters, seeking for something which might prove of interest. Yet, though he spent a good half-hour in the compound, not a sound reached his ears, and nothing rewarded his efforts.

Meanwhile, one may wonder what had happened to Geoff and Philip after their adventurous escape from the Governor's quarters of the prison.

"Where now, then?" asked Philip, darkness having fallen completely. "I say, Geoff, I'm sorry about that fall of yours and the fruit, for the supply I've brought is precious scanty; let's finish it now, and then consider matters."

It was, indeed, rather an unfortunate thing that the breaking of the rope and Geoff's fall upon the cushions — which they had had forethought enough to drop out of the Governor's window — had resulted in the pulping of the supply of fruit he was carrying on his person. Yet, if they were deprived of that, they had gained something immeasurably greater, for they had gained their liberty.

"And mean to keep it now," Geoff was whispering to himself, as they crouched beside the wall of the prison. "But what to do, where to go, and how to fare now that we are free?"

It was, indeed, rather a problem, and yet not so difficult after all; for, consider, Bagdad, they knew — they had learned from their jailer — was within a day's march of them, and Bagdad was just as much a magnet to these two young subalterns as it was to any Arab or any Turk in

Mesopotamia—just as much a magnet, indeed, as it was to the British Expeditionary Force then fighting its way towards the city from Kut-el-Amara.

"Of course it's got to be done; we've got to get to Bagdad," Geoff exclaimed, when they had finished their small supply of fruit. "Next question is—in what direction?"

Philip scratched his head; it was, indeed, a problem which floored him.

"Which direction, eh?" he muttered. "Yes, that does want deciding, for I've no notion."

"But here's an idea—a good idea, too," said Geoff. "Naturally enough the prison must be on some road, else how would one get to it? How could we have been driven here?"

"Brilliant! Of course, naturally enough—on a road. We look for it."

"Quite so; we look for it, and then——"

"Then we march along it, eh?" Philip told him cheerfully.

"Which direction?" asked Geoff satirically. "Supposing it runs west and east, do we turn west or east? And if north and south, which way, please, Philip?"

It was Philip's turn again to cogitate, to scratch his head even harder, and to wonder. It made him quite irritable and angry when he discovered how hopeless the situation really was; and then, seizing upon a brilliant idea, he almost gave vent to a shout of triumph.

"Of course; easy as smoking; we just get on to the road and wait for folks to come along it."

"Brilliant!" Geoff scoffed at him. "People don't travel so often during the night in these parts, but at any rate it's the only solution of our difficulties. We'll get on to the road and see what happens."

What actually happened was that, after a while, voices were heard in the neighbourhood of the prison; for by then Geoff and his friend had passed round the place, had found the road, and had sat down beside it. They heard the rattle of wheels somewhere on the road, and the ring of horses' hoofs. Creeping nearer, they heard those voices more distinctly, and after a little while, getting nearer still, Geoff was convinced that it was von Hildemaller himself who was talking.

"Go easy," he told Philip; "keep as far away as we can and listen to them. Von Hildemaller's in a nasty temper, I expect, and is quitting the prison. There! He's mounting into some sort of Turkish vehicle, and he's about to drive off. What's that he's saying? To Bagdad?"

"To Bagdad!" exclaimed Philip in an excited and eager whisper. "That's where we're going."

"I hope so, certainly," agreed Geoff.

"Then why not accompany our dear friend Hildemaller?" asked Philip, starting forward.

"Accompany him!" exclaimed Geoff; "you're fooling."

"Never hung on the back of a trap before?" said Philip immediately. "I have. Come along; let's get this German fellow to give us a lift to our destination."

The young subaltern had never given expression to a more brilliant proposal. Geoff seized upon it on the instant, and the two, running swiftly across the road in their stockinged feet—for they still kept their boots tucked close to their bodies—were within a few feet of the rickety chaise in which the German was riding. As it drove off, clattering heavily over the rough road, they raced up behind it, and, unknown to the German, clung on behind and accompanied him towards Bagdad.

CHAPTER XVIII

News of Douglas Pasha

"Bagdad! See it in the distance; watch the rising sun glint on the roofs and minarets!"

It was in a cautious whisper that Geoff drew the attention of his chum to a point some long distance in advance of the spot over which the rickety chaise in which von Hildemaller was riding bore them. Very craftily he had thrust his head out beyond the side of the vehicle, and though all was still dusk about them, though the night had not altogether faded, yet, happening to be on a considerable elevation, and looking down into the distant basin of the Tigris, he had caught just that faint gleam of the city for which they were making. Balancing unevenly, uncomfortably, and with many a suppressed groan, on the axle and spring of the other side, Phil shot his head out like a jack-in-the-box after Geoff had spoken, and stared ahead hard until he too saw flashes from the roofs of Bagdad. Then he gave vent to quite a loud "Jingo!" and instantly ducked his head low behind the back of the chaise, for von Hildemaller moved. Up to that moment, during weary hours, he had sat in his seat almost without movement, and undoubtedly had lapsed into sleep, for his snores, like his breathing, shook the air about him. Now he woke up with a start, stared about him in a frightened manner, and then called to the driver:

"Stop! I heard something. Someone speaking, and close at hand."

Obediently the driver pulled up his tired pony, and, looking back, stared sleepily at his master.

"A voice? Someone speaking? You heard something, master?" he grumbled. "No, no, surely; for we have been on the road alone, and not a soul has been near us — not a soul. You have been asleep, Master."

And yet von Hildemaller, the ever-suspicious von Hildemaller, was not satisfied. He stood up stiffly and with difficulty, gripping the rail behind the driver's seat to steady himself, and causing the light chaise to rock on its springs. He stared to either side of him, trying to penetrate the dusk of early morning; he even peered over the back of the carriage, whereat Geoff and Phil ducked even lower, while the former, gripping the axle with those strong fingers of his, made ready to reach up and grapple with the German. But the Teuton's eyes were still heavy with sleep, and, failing to see those two who had clung like limpets to his chaise throughout the night, he turned, setting the vehicle rocking again, and stared out before him. A guttural exclamation escaped from those broad lips of his:

"Ach! but Bagdad at last. And there, some comfort, some ease, after a terrible experience. But wait, wait! I have been thinking, I have been dreaming. Yes, he who strikes von Hildemaller strikes one who never forgets, never forgives; and who will repay, however long the interval, however long the debt may be owing."

He sighed deeply, yawned till his jaws threatened to crack, and until he displayed a cavity even bigger than that which Geoff had compelled and into which Philip had thrust the gag with such delight. Then the German sank back into his seat again, and bade the driver, peremptorily, to drive onwards. Soon, too, heavy breathing just in front of them told the two young subalterns that von Hildemaller was sleeping again.

"Rather a near thing that, eh?" grinned Philip, his head now close to his chum's, and displaying just a little more common sense and caution. "What would we have done if he had spotted us that time when he looked round?"

It was Geoff's turn to smile, a meaning smile, while he stretched out one hand, balancing himself in that uncomfortable position which he had maintained throughout the night, and slowly doubled up the fingers of the other hand—fingers bursting with muscle and with tendons as strong and as elastic as steel—doubled them up slowly, in a manner which seemed to emphasize the power within them, whereat Philip sniffed and sniggered. In a moment, in fact, he realized how much Geoff had longed for another tussle with the German, how he would have almost welcomed discovery at that moment.

"I know," he whispered. "I know what you'd have done, and the beggar deserves it. You'd have taken him by the neck, you'd have remembered Douglas Pasha, and you'd have squeezed the life out of his body."

Of a sudden he gripped the powerful hand held out before him, gripped it and shook it with energy, while he stared hard at his chum.

"Why not?" he asked. "Good idea! Why not? Why not squeeze the life out of him now that we've got him, that is, almost squeeze it out of him. There's nothing to fear, we ain't surrounded by a prison, and we'd soon clear that driver off, or, for the matter of that, force him to do our bidding. Why not grab this brutal German and squeeze him till his eyes bulge out of his head, till he's choking, till he'll be glad to give away that secret of his, till he'll beg and beg and whine to us that he'll release Douglas Pasha? Why not?"

He could feel Geoff's powerful hand suddenly compressed under his grip, could feel the fingers clench even tighter, while Geoff himself dropped from the axle to the road, as if the words had stung him to energy. It was what he had done, and Philip too, many a time throughout the night; on many an occasion, when meeting some long rise, they had been glad, in fact, to drop from the somewhat uncomfortable perches they had found, and to trudge along behind the carriage. Unbeknown to the German, unsuspected by the driver, yet doubtless to the knowledge of the animal which dragged it, they had even helped to propel the carriage up some of the risings, accelerating its progress to such an extent that the sleepy driver was amazed at the powers displayed by the animal he drove, and at length was so struck by its prowess that he wakened sufficiently to think the matter over and to weigh its value.

"Allah, but this is a strange thing!" he had said to himself more than once, at first very sleepily, and then with a little more spirit. "Allah, but the beast is possessed! For see, ever before when we have made this journey and have come to these hills I have had to use the whip with vigour, even I have had to dismount and walk beside the carriage. It is wonderful; for see how thin the beast is and old, and now he pulls like a giant, like a thoroughbred, like an Arab."

It entirely defeated him; the phenomenon was one he could not understand however much he puzzled; and puzzling and wondering made him even more sleepy. Thus the long hours of darkness had passed, if not comfortably for Geoff and his chum, yet cheerfully enough. Above all, their thoughts were filled with the engrossing subject of their liberty. They felt like birds entrapped who had broken from a cage after weeks and weeks of imprisonment. They were filled with a feeling of wonderful exhilaration, while the knowledge that, though free, they were in the midst of an enemy country, with enemies all about them, added rather a zest to the whole business.

And now Philip had made a proposition—a proposition of such importance and so momentous in its results—if the plan were carried out, that Geoff had felt compelled to leap to his feet and run along behind the carriage. It was perhaps five minutes later when he plumped himself down on the axle again, trailing his stockinged feet along the dusty surface of the road, while he stared out into the rising dusk behind them.

"Eh?" asked Philip, returning eagerly to the subject, knowing well from his experience of his chum that no decision was to be expected until sufficient time had elapsed for our hero to consider the proposition. Perhaps it was that Geoff was possessed of a certain sort of canny instinct, perhaps even it was those journeys with Douglas Pasha, those travels amongst Arabs and other peoples, which had taught him caution, which had in a certain measure taught him to smother his thoughts, and to hide his feelings from other people. Inscrutable his face never was, nor ever would be, for it shone with healthy, youthful frankness; but the eyes were thoughtful eyes, eyes which told those who looked into them that the owner was possessed of some degree of caution, while, as we have said, Philip, his best and most intimate chum, knew that Geoff was one not to be hurried.

"Eh?" he asked again impulsively. "You'd strangle the beast easily. I could with the fingers of one hand. Wait a moment. If we slip out here and hang on to these back springs we can pull up that old horse in a moment; then we tip the show over, and throw our German friend into the gutter. How's that? I'd love to see him roll."

And so would Geoff, very much indeed, and yet what would be the object?

"Let's just think the matter out, and chat it over quietly," he told the impulsive Phil, restraining him with a grip of his strong fingers. "Supposing we'd settled with the scoundrel—now I'd just love to."

"And I'd dote on it," Phil chimed in readily.

"We both would," said Geoff soberly; "and as to our being able to do so, pooh! there's no doubt about it. Single-handed I think we could easily handle both those beggars, so that we can put that question aside and take it for granted that we are easily the victors, but—and here comes the rub—supposing we've cornered the driver, and have squeezed this German's neck till his eyes are bulging, and until, in fact, he's whining and begging for his life, and ready to do anything for us—supposing we've got to that stage, eh?"

"Yes, supposing we have," Phil grinned, for the very mention of squeezing von Hildemaller till his eyes bulged reminded him of that scene in the cell, when Geoff had gripped the German across the mouth, while Philip stood in front of him. Those cunning eyes had bulged with a vengeance then, had bulged horribly, had bulged in a manner which showed the Teuton's terror. Oh yes, it would be pleasant enough to witness such a thing again, knowing well how much they owed to this treacherous German; but then—"Let's suppose he's collared then," agreed Phil at length. "Now then?"

"Well, he's collared, he's shouting for mercy, he's perspiring and blowing worse than ever," said Geoff. "He's ready to take us right off to this prison, and ready to hand over his captive. But where are we? We have got the German and his driver, and we have got this carriage and the sorry animal that pulls it, but please remember we are still in what remains of our khaki. We are obviously aliens and enemies, the first passer-by would recognize us and give an alarm, a crowd would collect in no time, even far out in the desert, and long before we could get to the place where my guardian is imprisoned we should be captured—possibly shot—at any rate foiled altogether."

It was with difficulty that Phil suppressed a whistle—a whistle of astonishment, of amazement, and of pride in his comrade. He had always known Geoff to be a strangely long-headed, logical sort of fellow, but now, hearing him talk so quietly and on such an occasion, he could not help but admire him.

"Spoken like a lawyer," he said at last, and quite seriously, "a fellow can see that there's nothing but solid reason behind what you're saying. We could, as you tell me, easily do for this German and make him howl—how I'd jolly well like to hear him—but where's the advantage gained, as you say? Lost altogether by premature action. Only, if we don't take advantage of the fellow now that he is, as you may say, in our power, what are we to do? for it's getting lighter every minute, and in a little while any passers-by there may be—and people will be beginning to move once daylight comes—will stop us, and will give the very warning of which you have spoken."

No doubt the problem was a knotty one, and one requiring a great deal of consideration. That Geoff and Philip could remain much longer on their unsteady and uncomfortable perches was out of the question, and yet, where were they to go? which way were they to turn? and, above all, where could they get refreshment? The sight of a collection of palms to the right of the road, and almost abreast of them, seemed to decide Geoff of a sudden, for he turned to Phil on the instant.

"Let's drop off here," he said; "those palms up there may give us some sort of shelter, and possibly we may discover food also. Later on we'll go on into Bagdad, and there I shall be able to find at least one friend who will give us assistance."

Dropping from the carriage at once, they stood in the centre of the road in a cloud of whirling dust, listening to the carriage as it rattled onward towards the city; and, as the dust subsided and allowed them to see farther, they caught once more those gleams of light from the roofs of Bagdad — flashes which seemed to signal them onward. For the rest, the country-side all about them was still half-hidden in mist, above which the tops of that grove of palm-trees which had attracted Geoff's attention could be seen. Turning towards them without a word, they scrambled their way uphill, till presently they had left the hard gravelly surface over which they had been travelling and entered upon an area clad in green, over which grass and bushes grew profusely; and, after a little while, found themselves in a thick grove of trees, which, if they promised nothing else, promised shelter once the sun had risen. There, standing beneath the palms, they waited until the morning mist had been dispersed by the rays of the rising sun, and until they could see far and wide over that portion of Mesopotamia, and even as far as the city of Bagdad. Then they turned, and, striding on amongst the palms, were soon far within them, and in little danger of being discovered by travellers on the high road.

"Hold on a moment," said Phil of a sudden; "I can smell something." He sniffed the air like a dog, turning in all directions.

"It's over here, behind us, deeper in the palms; there's a fire burning, I'm sure; and, Jingo! I'm positive there's meat cooking."

The aroma came to their nostrils more strongly as the minutes passed, and attracted them like a magnet. Slowly and cautiously they crept between the palms, until they gained the edge of a clearing in the midst of which stood a somewhat curious dwelling. It was neither tent nor house nor cottage, but a combination of all three, a domicile constructed partly of mud walls, partly of palm-leaves, and here and there finished off, as it were, with stretches of camel-hair material. In front of it a wood fire smouldered, while a thin wisp of smoke rose above it and was blown into the trees. A rough, iron tripod stood over it, and from it depended an iron pot, in which, doubtless, meat was stewing. The aroma made Philip's mouth water, and made Geoff quite irritable and impatient.

"Looks like the habitation of some nomad shepherd," he told Philip; "wonder who it can be, and how many there are in the family? In ordinary times I'd have gone straight up to the house and asked for food and shelter, but a fellow can't do that now, and it's more than likely that whoever owns the place carries arms with him always."

They stood under the shade of those palm-trees for perhaps half an hour, watching the hut, watching the smouldering fire, and sniffing enviously at the steam which blew over towards them. If they had never known before what it was to be really hungry, they knew it well that bright morning when so close to food, so eagerly desirous of it, and so far, it seemed, from the likelihood of being able to secure it. It made them almost desperate at last, till they were ready to risk anything; but then, again, common sense — that fund of caution possessed by both of them — held them back, kept them out of sight, and restrained their impatience. A man came out of the hut at last — a tall, bronzed Arab, over whose shoulders was slung an ancient rifle, and in whose hand was borne a long stick which he used to support himself whilst walking. Calling over his shoulder and whistling for a dog, which came bounding out of the hut, he set off along a path which led through the trees within some twenty yards of our heroes, so close, in fact, that it was a wonder that the dog did not discover them; and when he was gone, and they could no longer hear his steps, a woman emerged from the hut — an Arab like her lord and master. Throwing logs on the fire, and replenishing the contents of the iron pot with something she carried in a basket, she closed the door of the somewhat dilapidated house, and took the same path as the man.

"Better see where she goes," said Geoff. "We'll slink through the trees and make quite sure that they are both out of sight. Shouldn't wonder if he's a simple shepherd, and has gone to visit his flock somewhere about in this oasis; and it's more than likely that she has gone into Bagdad to buy things for the household. Sounds curious, doesn't it? But you've got to remember that people here are very much the same in many ways as people back in old England. Commodities of every kind don't grow in houses; they have to be bought. And stores and shops don't exist in the country, so Turkish and Arab women, like the folks at home, have to go off on shopping expeditions."

Whatever it was that had taken the woman off, it proved, indeed, to be a godsend to these two wandering and hungry subalterns, for the woman disappeared finally down the road leading towards Bagdad, while careful investigation proved that the man had gone off to the left, where he could be seen trudging over the grass-covered land quite a mile distant. As for the hut, it looked lonely enough when they went back, and uninhabited, though the fire still smouldered in front, and that delightful aroma still reached their nostrils.

"Well, do we stop here in the shade of the trees, and just satisfy ourselves with a sniff of that stew cooking in the pot we're looking at?" exclaimed Philip in somewhat injured, if not impatient, tones, as he looked out into the sunlit arena in which the dilapidated hut was situated. "Um!" he sighed; "it's mutton, or — or — or perhaps goat."

He snuffed at the air and projected his head beyond a leafy stem, his eyes attracted far more by the fire and the cooking-pot above it than by the hut, and his thoughts occupied with a possible chance of a meal rather than with the possibility of the hut harbouring further inhabitants. But the cautious Geoff, even then — his mouth watering at the appetizing odour of the cooking food, and his hunger made twofold by it — even then was not to be led into a position which might be harmful to them. Cautious by nature — as we have inferred already — possessed, that is to say, of a certain amount of discretion, which stood him and his subaltern chum in good stead on many an occasion, he was yet not altogether deficient in that dash and go which are so common in our subalterns, which, indeed, make all of them such a valuable asset to the British army.

"You hang on here," he told his chum. "I'll skirmish round a little and see what's doing. Perhaps there's someone else in the hut, and if so we should look silly, shouldn't we, if we tackled the food and had a fellow firing into us with a blunderbuss when least expected?"

Rapid strides took him along the edge of the palm-trees, the grass rustling at his feet as he trudged through it, and in a little while he was behind the hut, to find it rather less prepossessing in rear than it was in front, dilapidated, broken, and presenting many a ragged opening. Squinting through more than one of these, Geoff could see the interior quite plainly, for the sunlight was streaming in through the open door on the farther side. Then he boldly went round one end and entered, to find, as he had expected, that the place was entirely empty. Turning about, he and Philip met above the fire, their noses thrust over the cooking-pot, sniffing hungrily.

"Jingo! Mutton, I'll swear!"

"Goat'll taste just as good, just the same, no doubt," Geoff laughed heartily. "Hook it off, Phil, while I go and look for some sort of plates," he cried, "and let's be slippy, or else the owners will be coming back to dispute our right to make use of their property."

Hook it off Philip did, with a swish, and conveyed the steaming pot close to the door of the hut, into which Geoff had meanwhile plunged and luckily found a few articles of crockery. Not that the owners of the hut were possessed of a very elaborate suite of furniture, or a very complete equipment of other things usually found in houses in Europe and elsewhere; but the needs of your nomad shepherd in Asiatic Turkey are simple enough—humble enough if you will—and this man and his wife were no exceptions whatever. A couple of plates there were to be found, both scrupulously clean, so that in a matter of two minutes those two escaping subalterns might have been found, seated in the sunlight, careless of their surroundings, making use of their fingers as forks, and eating rapidly and heartily.

"Of course one's sorry to go and eat another fellow's dinner," grinned Philip in the midst of the meal, as though the thought had only just then struck him; "but, don't you know, dear boy, a fellow must eat, mustn't he?"

"Looks like it," grunted Geoff, helping himself a second time; "and mighty good this stuff is too. Let's get finished with it."

It took very little time indeed for these two hungry mortals to empty the steaming pot, whereat Geoff poured some water into it from an earthen vessel which stood outside the hut, and once more slung it over the fire. A deep draught from the same vessel refreshed them both wonderfully, when they were again able to look about them and take some interest in their immediate surroundings.

"'Pon my word, I was so hungry that I couldn't bother about caution any longer," said Geoff, "but now that that's been put all right I'm going to get moving—to do all that is possible so that we shall not again be captured."

"Hear, hear!" came from Philip.

"Then you get off into the trees again and watch for that shepherd returning. I'm going to look round the hut to see if I can discover something which will help us. For look at the two of us; we ain't exactly the sort of people who could march into Bagdad and escape notice now, are we?" asked Geoff, standing in front of Philip.

"Speaking for yourself, I presume?" came the merry answer. "Well, now, to be quite frank, you know, with you, and with every wish to avoid the suspicion of being personal, or rude, or what-not, don't you know, my dear Geoff, one couldn't describe your appearance as exactly attractive, hardly prepossessing; in fact, let's say, a trifle dishevelled, distinctly ragged, and frightfully dirty."

Philip wound up with a hearty roar of laughter which bent him double, and then stood up before his friend for examination, an examination which Geoff made with twinkling eyes and smiles which showed his amusement.

"Dirty has it first with you," he told Philip. "'Pon my word, after that drive last night at the back of the chaise, in clouds of dust all the time, you look rather more like a dust-heap than anything else. My word, wasn't I thirsty! That draught of water was a perfect godsend. But, to go back to what I was saying, we ain't, either of us, exactly the sort of people who could walk into Bagdad in broad daylight and escape the attention of the people. Now, are we? Not likely! They'd spot us at once; these ragged remnants of khaki uniform would tell against us promptly."

"It's a facer," said Phil; "we've either got to get a change of raiment or we shall have to sneak into Bagdad during the darkness."

"When we would probably knock up against sentries at the gates and be promptly captured," said Geoff. "You go and keep a bright look-out whilst I rummage round this place."

Humble though the occupants of that cottage may have been, and, indeed, undoubtedly were, the interior of the place was, like the crockery borrowed from it, kept scrupulously clean, and, wending his way from the main apartment into another, which did service as a sleeping-room, Geoff found it much the same—clean and tidy, with nothing distasteful about it. But, like the other contents of the place, which were few and far between, the store of clothing there was even scantier.

"Sort of shepherd's cloak and hat to match, with sandals for the feet," said Geoff, as he examined the articles hanging on a wooden peg. "They'd do for Philip; he'd look fine in 'em. What's this? Just the ordinary togs worn by a Turkish peasant—perhaps the very things our friend who owns the hut wears when he goes into Bagdad. Well, as Philip says, it's rather rough to deprive him of them; but then, what else is there to do? And are we to put his feelings and his losses before our own safety?"

Without more ado he brought the garments out of the house into the open, and whistled loudly to Philip. Then, for fear lest the owner of the place should return from a different direction and discover them, he crossed the open space, where the fire was still smouldering, and plunged into the trees beyond, where, later on, Philip, returning from the point he had reached, and from which he had been able to view the road beyond and the path taken by the shepherd, joined him.

"Put on those," Geoff told him, "and stick your boots into your belt. We'll sit down here and wait till the afternoon is passed, and then take the road for the city. Slip on the cloak and the hat over your ordinary clothes; I'll do the same with these things. They're scanty enough, so that we shan't be too warmly clad, and therefore there is no necessity to discard our own rags, and perhaps run the risk of having our tracks discovered by the shepherd or his dog coming across them."

Taking the opportunity of their enforced stay in the grove of palm-trees, and of the shade which it afforded them, they slept alternately, thus making up for their lost rest during the preceding night; and it was while Geoff was on watch, and Philip lay full length and sleeping heavily, that our hero saw the shepherd return by the same route that had taken him away and enter his cottage. Minutes passed, and though he came out and stretched himself in the sun, evidently awaiting his midday meal and the return of his wife, not once did he suspect that anyone had been there in the interval. Indeed, there was nothing to rouse his suspicions, for all was as he had left it, and the two subalterns had been careful enough to clean the plates they had used and return them to their respective positions. The dog, too, much to Geoff's delight, curled himself up at his master's feet, though at first he had sniffed round, and had shown some traces of curiosity, if not of momentary excitement.

As for the woman, there was not a sign of her as yet, though when the day had dragged on a little, and the afternoon had nearly waned, Geoff saw her coming along the road from Bagdad, and watched her as she turned off towards the grove of trees and finally entered the sunlit arena in which the hut was situated. It was as good as a play then, though he felt rather sorry for it, to watch the woman's amazement when she took the steaming pot from the fire, and, having brought two basins from the cottage and placed them upon a ledge just outside, poured some water into them from it. He watched as the dame dropped the pot and lifted her hands in amazement; and smiled grimly, too, as the man got languidly to his feet, not as yet understanding the situation, and then finally, when he realized that his midday meal was not forthcoming, clenched his fists and muttered, and showed his anger. Then bewilderment took possession of the two of them, and, having asked questions the one of the other, they stared at the pot as it lay on the sandy ground as if it were a thing possessed, and even edged away from it.

"But it's a strange thing this thing that has happened," the man muttered between his teeth. "By Allah, no such thing have I known in the course of all my journeyings! You say, wife, that you placed some flesh of a sheep within the pot?"

"Say it?" the woman replied in a shrill, angry, and rather frightened tone, glaring at her lord and master. "But, as Allah hears me, you yourself saw me add flesh to the pot ere you went, and after you had gone I added more. What then is this? Ah! A thief, eh?"

That idea had not occurred to either of them before; but now it seized upon their imagination instantly, and roused them to a pitch of anger and excitement.

"A thief! Yes, of course. Why did we not think of that before? Here, dog, find him."

Geoff bent down and shook the sleeping Philip heartily.

"Come along at once," he told him; "let us slip out into the open and run for the road. It will be dusk almost by the time we reach it, and if that dog doesn't trace us we ought to be able to get clear away. I ought to explain that the man and his wife returned while you were asleep, and now, having decided that probably someone has been there at the cottage in their absence, they are sending the dog to search round."

The yelps of the animal could be heard at that moment, as the two slid through the trees and out into the open. Then they took to their heels, and, following a hollow down which water no doubt poured in the rainy season, and which protected them from observation, they gained the high road within a little while—that rough high road, covered inches thick in sandy dust, along which the ruffianly von Hildemaller had passed in the hours of darkness.

"We'll walk along steadily, taking notice of no one," said Geoff. "If we pass people, and they address us, leave it to me to answer, and I'll find some excuse for you. In any case, if I have to stop for a moment, you walk on, for there's nothing else that you can do, and to stop might prove dangerous."

That evening, after dusk had fallen, and just before the gates of the city were closed, two rough shepherds from the desert passed into the city of Bagdad unnoticed, unchallenged, without raising the smallest suspicion. Passing along the main street which leads to the Bazaar, they turned off sharply into a narrow alley, which led them to an even narrower street, over which the rows of houses on either side met almost completely.

"And now?" whispered Philip. "Where to? Here's Bagdad all right, and a fellow begins to feel a little more free. But what's our next move? Besides, there's a meal to be considered."

"And a bed," Geoff told him. "This way. You'll find that we are not entirely without friends in this city. Follow straight up this street and turn off when I turn into another alley."

Proceeding along that other dark and somewhat noisome alley, Geoff suddenly ran into an obstacle—an obstacle which rebounded and which proved to be a man, who was not less startled than himself.

"Pardon!" the man cried, and would have hurried on.

"One moment; your name?" asked Geoff, using the Armenian tongue. "Your name, my friend, for there is something in your voice that reminds me of one I have known."

There was silence perhaps for a whole minute, while Philip slid up behind Geoff, ready to support him, and anticipating trouble. Then suddenly there came a glad cry of surprise from the individual who had cannoned into Geoff, and a hand gripped his arm firmly.

"My master, you are Keith Pasha. Yes?" asked the voice—the voice was Esbul's.

"I am," Geoff told him promptly in tones of relief, for indeed this was a most happy meeting.

"Then come, my master. I have a place of safety for you; there is one who will greet you warmly and find food, and space, and raiment for you. Come, my master, for I also have something which will delight your heart. Listen, Master! I have news of Douglas Pasha."

CHAPTER XIX

Tracking the German

"What luck! What splendid luck!" whispered Philip, as the trio—himself, Geoff, and Esbul—stumbled along the dark archways and across the rough courtyards of the city of Bagdad on their way to those hospitable quarters which the Armenian had mentioned; for Geoff had hurriedly told him who the man was against whom he had stumbled in the darkness, and had intimated to his chum that they were on their way to some haven.

"Spl—en—did!" emphasized Philip, muttering the word over and over again; "food, raiment, and a place in which to sleep safely. Well, it will be good to lie down and sleep soundly for one night, feeling that one isn't caged in like a bird, and isn't in immediate danger of arrest and further imprisonment."

"And better still to know that there is something before us," Geoff answered him as they reached a low doorway leading out of the courtyard, "better, far better, Philip, to hear that Esbul has news of my guardian—news of Douglas Pasha—news so valuable that he won't impart it to me out here, but is waiting until we get into this house and under shelter."

A sharp rap on the door was answered after a while by a gruff request to enter, and presently the three were stumbling up the flight of steps down which Esbul had gone when he left Benshi the Jew—that mysterious, silent, and thoughtful friend of Douglas Pasha. In a trice it seemed they were in the room he occupied, to find the Jew seated on a divan, his eyes fixed on the opposite wall, the same listless unfathomable expression about his haggard face. And yet that face could show animation when he wished, could show friendship and welcome.

"Be seated," he told the two subalterns. "Be seated, Keith Pasha, ward of that one who has been my friend for many years, of Douglas Pasha. So, Esbul, it came about that in passing on your way from the house where you were watching you hit upon these two, hit upon them by mere chance, by pure accident!"

"But how—how did you learn that then?" asked Geoff impulsively; for it was but a few minutes ago only that that unexpected meeting had taken place, and how could the Jew have gained tidings of it? Had he guessed it? Had he merely divined it because of their coming together? Or had this mysterious man obtained news of the event in the same mysterious manner in which other and more valuable information came to him?

"Be seated, my master," Benshi said, ignoring the question for the moment. "Let Esbul place food before you; and to-morrow he will lead you to that place where Douglas Pasha is imprisoned. Is it not so, Esbul? You who have watched over the German, were you not on your way hither to give me tidings of this von Hildemaller and of his movements on the morrow?"

A glance at the young Armenian proved indeed that that must be the case, though how Benshi had learned of that also was beyond him. Amazement was written on every feature; he gasped with astonishment, and then smiled at our hero.

"It is even so," he told him. "Men come and go, but Benshi sits here or in the Bazaar, seeing nothing it would seem, hearing no news, merely existing the day through, and yet—and yet, news reaches him."

"Aye! Reaches me, my friend, in a manner that I will not explain; news sometimes small and petty, sometimes of great doings, of great events. Listen now, whilst Esbul brings food before you. My master, you desire news of your friends, of your expedition which has come to Mesopotamia, which fought its way to Basra and Kurnah, and from thence advanced up the Tigris to Amara? You desire tidings of those friends whom you accompanied to Nasiriyeh, and of those others who struck to the north-east and seized Ahwaz? Then, I will tell you.

"Amara fell to them as easily as a ripe orange falls to the hands of the plucker. Then came an advance up the river to Kut-el-Amara, while Turks waited the coming of the British and the Indians in full force, in positions prepared most carefully for them under the leading of Germans — men of the same cunning and skill as this von Hildemaller. Yet they were defeated."

"Defeated!" exclaimed Geoff; "you mean that the Expeditionary Force has captured Kut, really?"

"They stormed those positions; they outflanked the Turks," the Jew told him, his listless eyes wandering for one moment from the wall opposite to our hero's face and to Philip's, and then back to the old position. "They captured the town of Kut-el-Amara and pursued the fleeing Turks. And then, my masters, they followed — —"

"Followed towards Bagdad?" asked Geoff, rising to his feet in his eagerness. "Followed in this direction? Then they are near already?"

Benshi waved him back to his seat with a listless movement of one hand, and went on with his story.

"Nay," he said, and sighed as if he were sorry that it was not so. "Nay, my master, the force of which we are speaking advanced in small numbers up the River Tigris towards Bagdad, till indeed but within a few leagues of it, till they reached the old tomb of the Caliph at Ctesiphon, where once more the Turks were awaiting them in prepared positions, where, indeed, they had amassed large numbers of soldiers — so much so that they outnumbered the British by at least three to one. There was a battle then in which the Turks suffered heavily and the British also, a battle which disclosed to your friends the strength of the enemy before them, and which made a retirement imperative. That was days ago — days ago; and now they are back, those British and Indian soldiers, back in Kut-el-Amara, having carried out an orderly and skilful retreat. Back in Kut, where my information tells me that they are surrounded."

He left Philip and Geoff with their mouths wide open with amazement at what they heard, their faces showing first delight at the prowess of their comrades, and then disappointment at their enforced retreat, and a greater disappointment that they too were not beside them to take their share in the fighting.

Yet Benshi did not tell all there was to be told about Asiatic Turkey, all that had to do with the British and other forces. We have intimated already in the course of this narrative how a force employed in one quarter of the world, if sufficiently powerful, may well affect the fortunes of other troops engaged in a different area altogether. We told of how the coming of Turkey into this world-conflict in partnership with Germany and Austria affected the fortunes of Russia on her European front, because of the need to hold her Caucasian frontier, and there is no need to enter into details of the fighting which took place in those mountains, almost in perpetual snow, where Turks and Russians faced one another. It will suffice if we say that, well-armed, well-equipped, and officered by Germans in numerous instances, the army corps which Turkey sent to the Caucasus at the commencement of hostilities, that is to say, during the first winter of this widespread warfare, suffered many a reverse at the hands of the Tsar's gallant soldiers. They failed to advance, failed to invade southern Russia, and indeed had their work cut out to prevent the Muscovite armies from invading Asiatic Turkey, and from pouring down into the land south of the Caucasus range — land itself some six thousand or more feet in elevation.

Indeed, the country south-west of the Caucasus range is broken up by innumerable ranges of hills and mountains, and presents large numbers of upland plateaus. It is the country in which the unfortunate race of Armenians were fostered, where they have dwelt for centuries, and on one of those upland plateaus, perched in a situation of natural strength, and defended by forts and gun emplacements, cunningly designed by German engineers, lies the city and fortress of Erzerum, the main base of those Turkish armies operating against the Russians — a fortress deemed impregnable, and one upon which the Turks and their German masters had placed the utmost importance. As that British force was fighting its way back to Kut-el-Amara, and was besieged in that little township on the River Tigris, the Grand Duke Nicholas of Russia, he who had led the Tsar's armies into Galicia a year previously, was mustering his forces and preparing his arrangements for a dash into Armenia—a dash made in the height of winter, through snow-drifts ten or more feet in depth, and in an atmosphere well below freezing. Such was the impetus of that dash, so good and careful were the preparations for it, and so great the courage and the élan of the armies of the Caucasus that, in spite of Turkish resistance, in spite of batteries cunningly placed, in spite of every obstacle, human and natural, the Russians poured down upon the fortress of Erzerum, and to the amazement of all—of the Turks and of the Germans, not less than of the others, captured it, its guns, and a goodly part of its garrison. Then, flooding over this upland plateau, carving their way westward and south-east, they rapidly forced their way in the direction of Trebizond—that port on the Black Sea by which Turkey had reinforced and revictualled her Caucasian army. To the south-east, Russian troops, in smaller numbers, pushed along the frontier of Persia, striking towards Mesopotamia, until patrols of horse and companies of foot were within measurable distance of Bagdad. Yet they were not near enough to seize the city, not in sufficient force at present to advance across the desert, not able, in fact, to lend assistance to the British force beleaguered in Kut-el-Amara, and to that other force, since organized, and sent up the River Tigris to relieve it—a force of British and Indians again, which, willing enough and eager to relieve their comrades, had, for weary weeks now, been held up by rains and floods in the country.

A narrative of the incidents of the Mesopotamian operations may be truthfully said to be one of brilliant actions, of most gallant fighting on the part of our soldiers, and of a display of soldierly virtues which equalled, if it did not surpass, those fine qualities shown by British troops in days gone by. This desert warfare was so different from that which had now fallen upon the armies battling in Flanders against the Germans. There, in the absence of forts constructed of masonry as formerly, there was nevertheless a species of fort running from Switzerland north to Verdun, and running in a north-westerly direction to the Belgian coast. A fort consisting of muddy trenches, delved deep in the soil, sheltering hosts of soldiers, and strengthened and supported in thousands of places by earthworks, by machine-gun redoubts, and supported in rear by an array of guns on either side, the number of which had never been seen before, had never even been nearly equalled in any warfare. But the desert of Mesopotamia gave opportunity for other fighting. Troops, both British and Turkish, were not sufficiently numerous to man a line running right across the country, and thus there was an opportunity to manœuvre, the chance of outflanking an enemy, and every now and again an opening for a charge, often enough brilliantly executed, by the British.

Yet the main line of advance must, because of that desert, of that arid country, follow the winding channel of the Tigris River, on which the troops were dependent for their water-supply. And that river itself was bounded in numerous places by marsh land, which often enough obstructed the march of troops, and which, in the neighbourhood of Kut, produced positions similar, on a very small scale — to those in Flanders and in France; that is to say, just as the sea bounds that line to the north in France, so marsh land in the neighbourhood of the Tigris River obstructed the advance of the British force marching to the relief of the beleaguered garrison at Kut-el-Amara. They could not easily get round those marshes, for the need of water held them to the river, and advancing along its banks they came upon a part where those marshes, coming close together, left but comparatively narrow space through which they could make progress, a space deeply trenched by the Turks, and fortified in similar manner to those trenches in France, held by a numerous and well-armed enemy, flanked by redoubts, and supported by machine-guns and artillery. A position, indeed, of formidable strength, more particularly as to outflank it was impossible, and a frontal attack must be undertaken. Add to those difficulties atrocious weather — rains which poured upon the British force, which drenched the men to the skin, bitterly cold rains, which, stopping at last, left the troops stewing in a watery atmosphere under a blazing sun, wading knee-deep in a muddy marsh which covered the country.

Having thus outlined to some small degree the enormous difficulties of the Mesopotamian force and its gallant conduct so far, we can now return to Geoff and Philip, and ascertain their fortunes after that momentous meeting with Esbul, the Armenian.

In the feeble rays cast by the guttering candle suspended above the old Jew's head there stood, on that memorable evening when Geoff and his chum reached the city of Bagdad, no more eager individuals, none more intensely interested in the tale of the prowess of the British forces, than they.

"And so our men have been quite close to this city, have fought their way nearly to Bagdad?" said Geoff, his face glowing with enthusiasm.

"That is so, Excellency," Benshi admitted, his lips hardly moving, his withered frame bent as he squatted, his eyes still wandering over the opposite wall as if seeking for something there; "a gallant force indeed, who struck boldly, and who struck heavily, against the troops of the Sultan. If their own losses were heavy, those of the Turks were treble perhaps; while the fact that they were forced to retire is not to be wondered at, does not take from them honour or credit; for those troops, handled by German officers, were three, even four, to one of your people, while the need for water, the lack of it, in fact, made a retreat—seeing that Bagdad could not be reached—a matter of urgency. But now, Excellency, you have heard of your people. They are back in Kut-el-Amara this many a day, besieged there, surrounded, they tell me, holding the enemy at bay, yet too weak to cut a road through them. Maybe you will join them there, maybe no; and meanwhile you are in this city, in Bagdad, wherein not so long ago I had speech with Douglas Pasha. Listen, then, to the tale Esbul has to tell us. Speak on!" he commanded, turning to the Armenian.

At once all eyes were cast upon the youthful figure of Esbul, now squatting on the floor, his face almost as impassive, almost as inscrutable, as that of

Benshi, yet his fingers working, his lips compressed, and sometimes twitching — indications of the excitement under which he was labouring.

"Then hear, Master," he began, "hear my tale. This von Hildemaller, this huge German with the pleasant countenance — — "

"Ah!"

Benshi gave vent to a grunt, a grunt which might have expressed disgust, appreciation, pleasure, anything, in fact, for his features did not relax, they displayed no sign of his feelings.

"With the pleasant countenance, my master; he who has deceived so many of us, who carries on the surface smiles which fascinate, which hide the crafty, cunning, cruel mind behind it. Early in the morning he came to this city, passing by silent ways to his quarters, endeavouring to evade notice. Yet Benshi saw him, while I have since been to those quarters, have clambered about them, have listened, and now know something of his movements."

"Ah!" it was Geoff's turn to give vent to a grunt of anticipation. "His movements! Yes," he said eagerly, "they are?"

"Indefinite!" Esbul replied. "Indefinite at present, my master; but so definite, so promising, that it may well be that you will think fit to take note of them. He is preparing for a journey outside the city. To-morrow, as the dusk comes, a conveyance will await him on the road beyond the gates west of Bagdad, and men also — but three of them — I gathered."

"Hold! Three men you said," Philip blurted out. "Turks, Armenians, or what? All cut-throats, I guess, in any case."

For a moment Esbul looked puzzled, for though he could speak English with some fluency the term "cut-throats" was a little foreign to him. But Geoff hurriedly explained, whereat the Armenian nodded his head emphatically.

"Murderers, yes!" he said. "One of them the same who drove him into this city, the one who was to have carried out the murder of Douglas Pasha."

"And they assemble, where?" asked Geoff, while the two subalterns exchanged swift glances, as though indeed the same thought had occurred to both of them.

"As I have said, my master, they assemble with this carriage outside the western gate of the city, where the German joins them as dusk is falling."

"And then?" asked Geoff.

"And then, who knows, my master?" said Esbul. "Those who follow the German and his escort may learn, for though I have striven to gather news of their destination I have failed completely. But this I know, it has to do with Douglas Pasha."

As a matter of fact, the crafty Esbul had been even more successful than he had anticipated, than he could have hoped, considering the difficulties of the situation. Having clambered over the walls of the compound which surrounded the quarters in which the German usually lived, and to which he had returned after that visit to the prison in which Geoff and Philip had been incarcerated, Esbul, as we have learned already, had found not a light, not an illuminated chink, not a sound, nothing to guide him as to whether von Hildemaller were there or not, or whether he had merely come back to go out again promptly. Yet Esbul was a knowing fellow, and gifted with an abundance of patience. Passing round the house, he reached a point where a wall enclosed a small yard within it, and, clambering on this, was able to reach the roof—a flat affair, on which the owner could rest and sleep, if need be, in the hot weather. Still, there was no sign of the German, not a sound to betray his presence. Esbul crept about the place, peeped over the parapet, laid his ear on the roof, and yet was baffled. Then, by a lucky chance, he went to the only chimney of which the place boasted, and, peering down it, saw a light far below, and heard voices. More than that, he found soon enough, or rather guessed, that this chimney was merely a ventilator for some chamber in which people were talking, in which von

Hildemaller, without doubt, was seated. More startling still was the discovery that sounds were accentuated by the chimney, were gathered together as it were, and were delivered to his ear louder, perhaps, than when uttered by those far below him. In that way, then, by a mere stroke of luck, by a fortunate chance, more fortunate perhaps than his accidental meeting with Geoff and Philip that night, the Armenian had unearthed the secrets of the German.

There was silence in the tiny room beneath the guttering candle for some few minutes, while two busy brains were hard at work piecing up the information given them, concocting plans, and seeking for measures to outwit von Hildemaller. Two busy brains, we have said, though no doubt Esbul's wits were sharpened. As for Benshi, he still sat on his divan, his eyes wandering over the opposite wall, his face—long, thin, ascetic, and angular—with not an expression on it. He might have been a wooden figure for all they knew, a silent, thoughtless figure. And yet the old man had already given indications of possessing unusual wisdom and acumen—of possessing, indeed, uncanny powers of looking into the future. It was he, in fact, who first broke that silence, and who, in the most amazing manner, seemed to have divined the very thoughts of Geoff and Philip.

He actually gave vent to a feeble chuckle, looked up suddenly at the spluttering candle, and then across at the two disguised subalterns. Indeed, he treated them to quite a long inspection—something strangely rare in the case of the Jew—an inspection which took in every feature, their dusty, dishevelled appearance, their borrowed clothes, and the transformation they had made with them.

"It is well, it is well, my masters!" he said at last, and his voice was positively cheerful. "It is well, this scheme of yours, this plan that you have been formulating. Listen, Esbul! To-morrow evening, as the dusk falls, a conveyance will be waiting outside the western gate of this city for the German known as von Hildemaller. This German hound will stride through the streets of the city, will push his way past the sentries, will browbeat any who may dare to stand before him, and will plump himself in this conveyance. Then he will be driven off, driven to a destination which I do not know, which I have sought for months past, driven, you tell us—and I can easily believe it—to the prison which holds my old friend Douglas Pasha. And then, my masters, let us take closer heed of the three who accompany this ruffian—of the one who drives the conveyance, and of those other two who, mounted on animals, ride beside it. Let me whisper a secret to you, a secret undreamt by the German, unsuspected by him, a secret which must be kept relentlessly from this German. That man who drives the vehicle is not the rascal ready to cut a throat for but a small reward, eager to slay even his best friend so that he may claim the gold of the German; no, my masters, it is Esbul, this Armenian youth who owes almost as much to Douglas Pasha as I do."

Geoff glanced swiftly across at the Armenian, and noticed, with something akin to amazement, that Esbul showed no sign of astonishment at the words he had heard, seemed, indeed, to have known the part he was to take even before Benshi had spoken, seemed to know it, in fact, just as well as he, Geoff, knew it, and doubtless as well as Philip also. The thing was positively uncanny, yet so simple, so calmly put before him, that he could hardly wonder—though when he pondered later it made him exclaim, as he realized how successful the Jew had been at divining his own thoughts and feelings.

"It is so, Benshi. I shall be on that conveyance," said Esbul, when a few moments had passed; "and beside me will be those two mounted men escorting the German."

"And they, Esbul, can you guess who they will be?" asked Philip, Geoff in the meanwhile having hurriedly interpreted Benshi's words to him.

"I can, my master. The one will be Keith Pasha, the other yourself. The thing must be done swiftly and quietly, done now, for here is an

277

opportunity to outwit the German, the only opportunity, perhaps, which will come our way."

That such a plan might easily undermine any which the German had made, and outwit him and utterly fog him, seemed possible enough, though there were other matters to be considered. Supposing Geoff and his friends were able to take the place of those three men, as seemed already to have been decided, there would be the journey with the German in their company to some destination unknown; then what then? Would there follow a meeting with Douglas Pasha? Or could it be that Esbul had been mistaken, and von Hildemaller about to journey on some other business altogether? Yet it was a chance worth taking, an opportunity in a thousand, one which demanded instant action.

Long into the night they sat in that room, with Benshi motionless before them, interjecting a word now and again, giving them advice, foretelling movements in the most uncanny and inscrutable manner. Then, wearied with their discussion, tired out after their long journey, Geoff and his friend lay down to sleep, and doubtless the Jew and Esbul retired also, though the two young subalterns were ignorant of the fact, for hardly had their heads touched the flooring when they were fast asleep and snoring.

The following day, however, found them alert and brisk and eager to be moving. Having eaten their full, and donned the clothing which Esbul brought for them—for a visit to the Bazaar had easily procured suitable raiment—the three young men passed out into the open street and wandered slowly in the direction of the house occupied by von Hildemaller. Stationing themselves at different points of vantage, they waited with what patience they could summon, and watched carefully for signs of the German and his followers. And when some hours had passed, and their patience was almost exhausted—when, indeed, in the case of Philip, that excellent young fellow was positively stamping with vexation—Geoff sent along a whistle—the signal agreed upon—and was observed a moment later to be following three men, who had appeared, it seemed, from nowhere, in the street, and were wending their way along it. In the wake of Geoff came another figure, slimmer than he – the figure of Esbul, dressed as a Bazaar porter, carrying a box on his head, slowly making his way over the cobbles, and behind him Philip fell in promptly, looking just as much a ruffian as Esbul, and as if he were following with a view of assisting him with his burden. In that order, showing no haste, keeping a considerable distance between themselves and the men who had issued from the German's house, Geoff and his comrade made their way through the heart of Bagdad, down cobbled, ragged streets, through narrow alleys, across courtyards littered with garbage, and so on till they approached the outskirts of the city, those walls which had been erected to keep out the barbarians.

It was at that point that the three men in advance halted and looked craftily about them; then they suddenly dived through an open archway and disappeared from view, leaving Geoff and his friends a little staggered.

"Come along," he cried, for Esbul and Philip had by now drawn quite close to him. "After them as quick as you can, or we may lose them. Keep close together, and carry the matter through as we promised."

Dashing along the street, they reached the archway within a few seconds, and, diving into the stone passage to which it gave access, raced through it and across a courtyard even dirtier than any they had passed before. There was not a soul in sight, not a voice to be heard, and it looked at first as if they had missed the men they were following. Then Geoff pointed to a doorway, held his hand up for silence for just half a minute, and later, without a word, turned and threw himself at the aperture.

CHAPTER XX

Success at Last

Dusk was falling over the city of Bagdad, that ancient city situated astride the River Tigris, which, if it could tell tales at all, could tell of ancient peoples, of past history of surpassing interest, of deeds and doings which would enthral all people. How many thousands of times must dusk have settled upon this ancient spot, and clad the gilded roofs of minarets and towers just as it was doing on this evening. How often, too, must figures precisely similar to those which now wended their way through its narrow and tortuous streets have passed over, perhaps, even the very same cobbles, hundreds of years before; maybe there was no difference even in their dress, in the raiment of those people of former days and in that donned now by the inhabitants of the city. Certainly no three less conspicuous people ever passed down the main street which runs towards the Western Gate than those three who emerged from the narrow courtyard into which Geoff and his comrades had dashed. One was mounted on the driving-seat of that same rickety chaise which had conveyed the cunning von Hildemaller to the city; while two others, ill-kempt yet well-set-up fellows, were astride stout Turkish ponies.

"Who goes?" the sentry at the gates challenged.

"A party, towards the west, in the service of one who is a friend of the Governor.

"One who is a friend of the Governor. Ho, ho!" the sergeant of the guard answered flippantly, as if he doubted the words. "Halt, there! Declare yourselves! Who is the high and mighty individual who is a friend of the one who commands our services?"

He stepped rapidly forward, while one of his men, at a signal from him, leapt into the centre of the road where it passed through the gates and barred the way with his bayonet.

"How now! By Allah; this is a strange saying that you have given us, 'a friend of the Governor?' One who walks in high places and yet employs such scarecrows? Who are you?"

The sergeant halted beside the driver of the carriage, and at the same time seized the reins of one of the ponies; then the driver of the rickety chaise bent over towards him, looked suspiciously at the sentry, and, bending lower, whispered in the sergeant's ear.

"Fool!" he said; "do you wish to harm even your own Governor? Must you then make a scene at the very gates of the city and so disclose his purposes? Listen a moment. Doubtless you have been on guard at this gate on many an occasion, and doubtless, too, you know of men of whom it may be said with justice that they walk in high places—even in the palace of the Governor. Then, if that is so, you will know of von Hildemaller."

Instantly the Turkish sergeant looked up at the driver with a startled, if not frightened, expression on his face.

"That man!" he exclaimed, "but surely——"

"S—s—h, no 'buts'," the driver of the chaise murmured in warning tones. "Pass us out without further ado, for it would be ill for you if I were to report to my master that I was delayed here at the gate, and that the Governor's purpose was defeated."

"Stand aside there! Pass without. Go on your way, friends, and may Allah bless you!"

In a moment the sergeant's purpose had been entirely altered, the mention of the Turkish governor, and of von Hildemaller's name, having acted like magic, and at once the driver, who had cautioned the man in stage whispers, so mysteriously in fact, sat upright, gripped his reins again, and whipped up his sorry pony; while those two who straddled their ponies beside him dug their heels into their mounts, the three clattering over the cobbles between the gates, and passing out into the gathering darkness. A quarter of an hour later they pulled up about half a mile beyond the gates and waited for their passenger.

"Phew!" exclaimed one of the trio, sliding from the rather uncomfortable saddle of the animal he was riding; "that was a near one as we were coming through the gates. Of course I couldn't understand a word of what was being said, but that sergeant fellow looked nasty. And, Geoff, what a scrimmage!"

"Scrimmage? Oh!"

"Yes, of course. In that yard and in that stable. Glad you downed that fellow who, Esbul tells us, was the leading ruffian hired by von Hildemaller."

Geoff dropped from his pony at that precise moment, slung the reins over his arm, and entered into conversation with his companions. He felt very gay-hearted and unusually cheerful, and, moreover, he had enjoyed every bit of that scrimmage to which Philip had referred, and even the scene at the gate, which at one moment had looked so threatening.

Let us explain that the coming of dusk had provided another adventure for our hero and his friends, an adventure filled with strenuous movement— an encounter, in fact, where the numbers were equally divided, and where victory, therefore, was all the more pleasing. Dashing in through that aperture which led from the yard into which they had traced those three in the pay of von Hildemaller, Geoff had found himself in a big tumble-down stable, in one corner of which a chaise stood, while three animals were haltered near it. The three men, who, unsuspicious of the fact that they were followed, had entered the place but a few minutes before, were at that very moment about to throw off the halters from these animals and prepare them for a journey. Then, hearing footsteps at the door, and seeing figures enter it, they turned, and, realizing at once that the intruders were likely to prove unfriendly, they dashed towards them, one of the men drawing a knife, while the taller ruffian—he who was von Hildemaller's right-hand man—snatched a revolver from his belt. It was at that precise moment that Geoff dealt the blow which had delighted Philip. Lunging forward, he struck the man with his clenched fist, knocking him backwards till the fellow's head came violently against a beam which supported the roof timbers. Nor was Philip behindhand in helping his comrades and in joining in the attack. He had no time in which to select his man or to make special preparations; but, leaning forward, he threw himself upon one of them, gripped him in his arms, and wrestled with him. As for Esbul, he was just in time to ward off a stroke launched at his heart by the man who had drawn the knife; quick as thought, he gripped the wrist and arrested the blow, and, with equal swiftness, clasped his other hand over the fist which gripped the weapon, and suddenly jerked the man's arm backward. Bump! The elbow struck the wall behind with a nasty jar, and forced the fellow's grip to loosen. What followed was done in a flash, was done with such swiftness that Geoff failed to observe what had happened, for Esbul had the knife in his own hand in a moment and had plunged it to the hilt in the body of the ruffian.

"Now, let's tie this other fellow up," Geoff had said, seeing that Philip had firm hold of the man he had tackled; "slip one of the ropes off this halter, and let's secure him to one of the mangers."

Wiping the blade of the knife he had secured upon the clothing of his victim, Esbul calmly stepped across the stable to where the animals were standing, and returned within two minutes with a length of rope which was amply sufficient for their purpose. Indeed, within five minutes, the third of the German's hirelings was bound hand and foot and tied securely to one of the mangers. Then Geoff bent over the man he had struck, and who, meanwhile, had made no movement.

"Dead, Master," Esbul told him, kneeling upon the floor. "The blow you struck was a strong one, and his head, coming with such violence against the wooden beam, was cracked. No longer will he do the bidding of von Hildemaller."

The end of those three whom the two subalterns and the Armenian had tracked so silently and so skilfully had indeed been as tragic as it was sudden, and the first part of the scheme to outwit the German had ended most successfully. No time was lost after that, and the animals were hurriedly harnessed and saddled and taken out into the yard.

"You'll drive the chaise," Geoff told Esbul, a note of authority in his voice; "and you'll just keep your mouth shut, Philip."

"Right oh!" came from that hopeful.

"Then march! We can leave this fellow who's tied up to the manger without much fear of his creating an alarm. Even if he shouts, I doubt if anyone will hear him; but no doubt he will have his own reasons for keeping quiet, and for trusting for release to some chance comer."

Then they had moved away from the yard, had passed down one of those narrow winding streets which intersect the city, and had finally gained the main street which led to the western gate.

"And now, all we want is our dear friend von Hildemaller," declared Philip. "He was to come at dusk, Esbul—that's what you said; you're sure?"

"Certain, Master. If you have any doubts, but think for a moment. The tale I told was that three hirelings were to await the German outside the western gate of the city, one driving a rickety chaise and two mounted. Then consider for an instant: we who went out to track these men, who watched outside von Hildemaller's quarters, saw three men emerge, followed three men, tracked them to the west of this city, tracked them, indeed, into a stable where a chaise was waiting and three horses. Is not that, then, proof sufficient of the truth of the tale I have told? Does it not lead one to feel sure that the rest of the plan will follow?"

"S—s—h, shut up! Get into your place, Esbul. Climb on to your pony, Philip; and don't forget—not a word. I can hear someone coming."

They had drawn up the chaise just beside the road, and were standing on the soft ground which bordered it. The road itself was so covered in dust that there, too, steps were hardly audible; yet the heavy tread of a man approaching now reached their ears, and a little later the deep breathing of one using much exertion. Then, when a few minutes had passed, a ponderous figure came into view through the gathering darkness — a figure which grunted and panted, which could have belonged to no other than the German.

"Ach, it is there!" they heard him say in his own language. "It is well, for I am tired, and this dust and the heat exhaust me."

Coming up to the chaise, he looked swiftly at the figures of the three men near it and clambered ponderously into it.

"You came direct here without attracting attention, eh?" he asked peremptorily of one of the figures mounted on a pony — of Philip, in fact, for the subaltern happened to be nearest. "Come, answer! You attracted no attention!"

He was speaking in Turkish now — execrable Turkish, with a strong flavour of German accent about it, and yet a language unknown to Philip. What was he to do? Attempt an answer or remain silent? Either might easily warn the German that all was not as it should be, and then a way out of the difficulty occurred to him. Philip opened his mouth as if to answer von Hildemaller, and immediately bent double over the neck of the animal he was riding and commenced to cough violently, as if he had caught his breath, or as if the cloud of dust which the German's heavy feet had stirred had almost choked him.

"Bah! Then you answer the question."

The words were shot at the other horseman, and received an instant answer.

"Master, all is well. We passed through the gate without creating suspicion. There is none who knows of our coming."

"Then drive on," commanded the German to the man seated on the box of the vehicle; "drive on at once."

"But where, where, Master?"

"Where? Ah, I had forgotten that you were ignorant of the place to which I am going. Straight on till I give you an order to turn; the place is some ten miles distant."

Never in all the course of their lives would Geoffrey, Keith, and Philip forget that journey — that journey, that slow, tedious journey over the rough road leading from the western gate of Bagdad, a journey occupying perhaps two hours and a half, a period which appeared to their eager, anxious minds like an eternity. They were tingling with excitement, with expectation, and with impatience. In spite of the many adventures through which they had passed, of the many tight places in which they had found themselves, this undoubtedly was the most trying of all their experiences; for at any moment the German might discover the ruse, might find out that the three who surrounded him were not his hirelings, and might defeat the efforts made to outwit him. Even his heavy breathing, his lolling head, and the fact that he was dozing, hardly helped to minimize the tension of the situation.

"Ah, a building ahead of us, I think!" Geoff whispered to himself, when, having traversed the main road for some eight miles, and turned to the left at von Hildemaller's bidding, they had made their way over a side-track which was indescribably rough and trying; "a building ahead of us. Looks like a big fortress; perhaps it's a prison."

He gave vent to a loud cough, so as to awaken the German, and then once more fixed his eyes on the dull shape he had seen in the distance. As for von Hildemaller, he awoke with a start, and, standing up with difficulty, and setting the rickety chaise swinging, he too peered ahead, and then, making out that distant shape, uttered a hoarse chuckle.

"The place! We are there, or almost so. Good!" Geoff heard him mutter. "Pull up at the main gate," von Hildemaller commanded Esbul. "Now, that will do! You will wait here till I come out again, and you will know what to do, for we have already discussed the matter. Wait, though, I will repeat my instructions: there will be a man with me, a man who will be tied hand and foot, a mere log, of no danger to any one of us. I shall join him in the chaise, and you will drive off immediately. A mile down the road which we have just covered you will halt, for that will be sufficiently far, and voices, even screams, will not be heard over such a distance. You will halt, and then — and then — — "

Esbul swung his head round and bent towards the German.

"And then, Master," he whispered, "the matter will be ended as you have already ordered."

"Good! You understand, then? There's no fear of an error being made, no fear of your becoming chicken-hearted, for we shall be alone — four of us — with this one man, and he tied hand and foot, remember, tied hand and foot," the German repeated, giving vent to a ghastly chuckle. "No fear of a blow, no fear of his struggling even, no chance of his breaking loose. If he screams — — Ah, well, you have heard screams before, and they will not unman you. You are ready?"

"Ready, Master," Esbul told him in that soft voice of his. "Ready, and willing."

Again the chaise rolled and rocked as the German stepped to the side of it and gained the ground. Waddling towards the prison, he ascended the stone steps which led to the doorway, and banged heavily upon the wall. Perhaps five minutes later, steps were heard within, the door was opened, and, having parleyed for a while, von Hildemaller entered, and the door closed instantly.

"Now, round with the chaise, and make ready. Good heavens!" exclaimed Geoff, only at this moment beginning to grasp the sinister designs of the German. "Did ever one listen to such a scoundrel? A bound man is to be brought out to us, we are to halt a mile down the road, a mile down it, Philip, at such a distance that screams may not be heard by the people in this prison, the bound man will be so securely fastened that he cannot even struggle for his life, and there, in cold blood, he is to be finished. You realize the plan? Its cold-blooded cruelty? You realize the frightful act that this von Hildemaller contemplates?"

For a few moments there was silence between them, and then a gasp almost of pain from Philip, a gasp of amazement, of horror, and of anger. Usually light-hearted, flippant in fact, his voice now, when he spoke, was grave, was trembling with passion.

"A fellow wouldn't kill a mad dog under such conditions," he said bitterly, "and yet this von Hildemaller chuckles. What'll you do?"

"Do!" There was an ominous ring about the answer. "Do!" repeated Geoff sternly; "can you ask that question, Philip? Now, listen: you'll cut this prisoner loose, you'll leave von Hildemaller to me. That's understood?"

"Distinctly."

"Then, silence; at any moment the door may open."

Yet minutes dragged along, slow, tense minutes, during which they waited for the reappearance of the German; waited, indeed, until they began to fear lest he would never return, lest he had avoided them; to fear that he had guessed what was happening, had suspected the three men who had accompanied him upon this journey, and was sheltering himself within the prison. So long did he remain, in fact, that Philip at length felt positive that the cunning Teuton had indeed outwitted them; while Geoff, a prey to all sorts of fears, was positively trembling with excitement. And then, of a sudden, when they had almost given up hope, when it seemed that all their plans had failed, and that their efforts had resulted in nothing, steps were heard within the prison—heavy steps—approaching the door, and at length the latter opened. A minute later more steps reached their ears, the heavy blowing of an individual, his panting in fact, followed by the appearance of von Hildemaller, his ponderous figure almost hidden in the darkness, yet sufficiently illuminated by the rays from some very distant lamp to leave no doubt of his coming.

Doubt indeed! No illumination was needed where this German was concerned, for even if his figure were invisible the man's heavy breathing, his ponderous footsteps were sufficient indication of his presence.

"Good—good—good!" Geoff heard him saying, chuckling in fact. "He is tied hand and foot, this fellow. What a thing it is to be a friend of the Governor of Bagdad. A friend indeed! He, he! One who can take him by the elbow, as it were, can whisper things into his ear, and can force him to do one's bidding. Bring the man along and throw him into the chaise.

"But—but—wait, go gently, for the vehicle is old and rickety enough. In with him."

Men were struggling down the steps of the prison, four men at least, who carried a bundle between them, which they bore towards the carriage. Lifting their burden with some difficulty, they pushed it on to the seat, thrust it well to one side, and then retreated hastily, as if they were ashamed of what they had been doing. A second later, indeed, the door of the prison was banged to, those distant rays of light were cut off, and the German and his three hirelings and the bundle in the carriage were left alone in the darkness, at liberty at last to depart on their journey.

"Good! Better than ever! Things could not have gone more smoothly," Geoff heard von Hildemaller chuckling again, as he waddled towards the chaise, and, mounting into it, depressed its springs considerably. He sat himself down with a bump beside the bundle resting there, and gave a peremptory order to the driver: "Move on," he panted; "drive fast, but pull up as we arranged when you have covered the distance. Bah! How that note from the Governor cowed the Turk in command of the prison. When this fellow beside me realized what was before him, I saw him squirm; he would have thrown himself upon me had he been able, and had his guards not surrounded him; but he's here—here—beside me, and as helpless as a log, as near his end as ever a man was."

The wretch gave vent to a hideous, wheezy chuckle, a chuckle which made Geoff's blood boil and his ears tingle as he listened; for by then he was riding quite close to the chaise, within two feet of that silent bundle, within easy hearing of the German, so near in fact was he that a moment later he heard, rather than saw, the bundle moving, wriggling upon the seat on which it had been deposited, and heard an instant growl escape the German.

"Ach! So you are alife, are you?" von Hildemaller hissed into the ear of his wretched prisoner. "So, Douglas Pasha, I haff you at last, securely, away from interference of the Turks, my prisoner, to do with as I will. Now, listen awhile, for I haff a few sweet words to say to you; and you, Douglas Pasha, haff little time on this earth in which to hear them."

The bundle stirred again, and, bending low, Geoff heard inarticulate sounds coming from it, sounds which suggested that the prisoner was securely gagged, and, indeed, was almost fighting for his breath. As he bent, too, he was so near to von Hildemaller that he could almost have touched the ruffian, and found it a hard task indeed to keep his hands off him; for by now every drop of blood in Geoff's manly body was boiling with rage, and he was trembling with eagerness for the moment to arrive when he might release his guardian. And then von Hildemaller's voice was heard again, subdued and venomous, his words coming in an angry hiss through those extensive lips of his, which had deceived so many people.

"Listen, Douglas Pasha," he began again; "you wonder why I, a German, should hate you so, should track you down, should haff you here beside me and be carrying you away from your prison for one purpose only, that purpose to rid the world of you! Well, I will explain. For you, personally, I haff no great objection, except that you are an Englishman. But you are an obstacle; for years you haff been an obstacle in my path—in the path of Germany. But for you the aims of my Emperor would haff been prosecuted with far greater success amongst these people, and Germany would haff obtained a greater hold over the Turks and their country. It was you who put a stop to that, who set our efforts at naught, who balked every move I made, and defeated us on every side. In those days before the war I did my best to get rid of you, and when the war came I again did my best to rid the country of a man who was in every sense an enemy to Germany. Yet again you outwitted me, till a day arrived when I was able to arrange for your capture. Even then you were too strong for me, you and your friends; they protected you, saved you, and kept you in security until this very moment. And meanwhile, having been beaten by you and your friends in every effort, I was beaten also by that ward of yours — one Geoffrey Keith — who came to this country."

The bundle moved again, the rickety, rattling chaise creaked and swayed as the prisoner struggled. A stifled growl came from the bundle, and then there was silence.

"Yes, Geoffrey Keith and another came to this country — your ward and a friend of his came — and were captured and thrown into prison. Now listen still further, Douglas Pasha. For the moment you were secure, and I, who had a grudge against you and aimed at your death, could find no other means of injuring you than through these two young fellows. I made plans to get them safely into my hands, when, seeing that they are enemies of Germany, I should have made an end of them; but they defeated me just as you had done, defeated me entirely. That left you alone to deal with, till the time arrives when those two are again captured. It is but a matter of two or three days since they broke loose from their prison, and surely within a little while the Turks will haff them, and I too shall be able to reward them for the trick they haff played upon me. Fear not, Douglas Pasha! For your ward shall come to the same end as you in a little time. Before the week is passed, perhaps, he may be riding in this chaise, tied into a helpless bundle just as you are, jogging on to his death. You understand? To his death, just as you are jogging now. You understand, Douglas Pasha?"

The voice was raised by then to a shrill shriek, while the German was trembling with passion — trembling with triumph and with anticipation of the moment so closely approaching. Little wonder that Geoff, riding so close, could hardly remain on his pony, that the perspiration was dropping from his forehead, and that his breath was coming in little gasps. Those minutes which passed, as they sauntered along the dusty road, were a purgatory, were almost insupportable, and were indescribably long. But at length, having by then driven perhaps a mile from the prison, Esbul suddenly pulled up his horse, and the whole party came to a halt at the side of the road, just as the German had commanded.

"And now," called von Hildemaller, struggling from the chaise to the road, "lift the ruffian out, pull the gag out of his mouth, and slit his throat."

Geoff slid from his pony almost before the chaise had come to a rest, and, dropping his reins, stepped swiftly up beside the German. Esbul clambered from the driving-seat of the carriage and leaned over the bundle which von Hildemaller had secured from the prison, while Philip, himself a prey to tremendous excitement, dismounted, and ran forward.

"Cut the Major loose," Geoff shouted; "you can leave this murdering rascal to me entirely."

There were sounds of scuffling in the darkness, clouds of choking dust arose and smothered every member of the party, while a scream escaped from the throat of one of them—a scream of terror. Then silence followed, and within a few seconds a sound of a man struggling, heavy breathing, and then a dull thud.

Geoff scrambled into the chaise and sat beside the bundle—now released—and, stretching out one of those strong hands of his, gripped the hand of Douglas Pasha. Esbul clambered into the driving-seat again, while Philip mounted his pony, and, taking the reins of the other, moved to the back of the carriage.

"Go on!" commanded Geoff huskily; "drive on to the main road, and then towards Bagdad."

A moment later he had turned towards the prisoner whom they had rescued, still gripping his hand, and hurriedly explained matters to him. The meeting in the carriage was indeed a most dramatic affair, so unexpected, indeed, that Douglas Pasha was at first almost speechless, and then almost hysterical after the trying experience he had passed through. As for Esbul, Geoff, and Philip, they were so elated, so excited, and so delighted at what had happened that they babbled like children, and could scarcely speak coherently. Indeed it was the Major who regained his self-possession first, and began to cross-examine his rescuers; and at last he asked a final question:

"This German—this von Hildemaller," he asked; "what happened to him?"

"Yes, what happened to him?" Philip chimed in eagerly, as he clattered along beside the carriage.

"Don't ask," replied Geoff, with a curtness which was unusual in him. "He's dead. I killed him."

And dead von Hildemaller was. Huddled in a heap in the dust, in the midst of the road behind, at the very spot where he had intended to murder Douglas Pasha. Retribution had indeed found this odious, scheming, cunning agent of the Kaiser, at the very moment when he imagined that triumph was coming, and who can doubt that that retribution was earned? For never before was there such a villain.

We have little else to relate with regard to the fortunes of Geoff and his friends and of Douglas Pasha. Reaching Bagdad at earliest dawn, and contriving to smuggle themselves into the city, they found safe quarters with Benshi. Later, they made their way from the city to a neighbouring tribe of Arabs whom the Major knew, and who at once befriended him. Then by easy stages they crossed the desert towards Kut-el-Amara, hoping there to join the British expedition.

As for the latter force, the remains of that gallant division under General Townshend, which had so boldly essayed to capture Bagdad, and which, having dealt most severely with a Turkish force vastly outnumbering it at Ctesiphon, was forced to retreat, it had conducted that retirement along the River Tigris in the most masterly manner possible, and, having gained a sharp bend in the river at the town of Kut, where the Tigris surrounds the town on three sides, it had there been forced to halt, and put itself on the defensive. Some sixty thousand Turks surrounded the place, and huge efforts were made to beat down the resistance of this gallant division; yet it held off all attacks, and forced the Turks finally to sit down and besiege it. It became a question now as to whether the relieving force, which had now advanced towards Kut, and which was already indeed within gun-sound of General Townshend's forces, could break through and bring relief before the supplies of the beleaguered army had dwindled. As a matter of fact, persistent rains, the most wretched weather, and the extension of those marshes created a position which helped the Turks, and frustrated every effort of the relieving force. It drew nearer, but could not come up to Kut. It struggled on against overwhelming difficulties, while the starving band of heroes at Kut still held off the enemy; and then, when more rain came, when the marshes swept farther afield and relief seemed farther off than ever, and food was gone entirely, surrender became inevitable, and General Townshend and his noble band fell prisoners to the Turkish enemy.

Yet, one may ask, was the loss of the remains of this gallant division all loss to the British and their Allies? and may reply with confidence that it was not so. For that hazardous approach to Bagdad had held a numerous force of Turkish soldiers, while the resistance of our men at Kut had kept the enemy troops from operating in other parts of Asiatic Turkey. Indeed the absence of those sixty thousand Turks round about Kut aided not a little in the operations of the Grand Duke Nicholas, who, having established himself firmly at Erzerum, now launched his armies into Northern Turkey, and, sweeping on, captured Trebizond and many another base of value to our enemies. Those parties of Russian horsemen who had been operating on the Persian frontier marched south and east almost without interruption, threatening Bagdad and the retreat of those sixty thousand Turks mustered in the neighbourhood of Kut-el-Amara. Indeed the noble resistance of General Townshend's forces may be said to have helped the

Russians wonderfully, and, seeing that Russia is our ally, that resistance helped Britain also.

Geoff and Philip and Douglas Pasha joined hands at length with that relief force which had unfortunately failed to relieve General Townshend and his band of heroes, and, as we write, our two heroes are in harness once more and are preparing to fight beside their new comrades right on towards the heart of Mesopotamia.

Milton Keynes UK
Ingram Content Group UK Ltd.
UKHW011016020923
427894UK00004B/160